Sonny Liston Was

a

Thom Jones is the author of *The Pugilist at Rest* and *Cold Snap*. He lives with his family in Ames, Washington. He is currently at work on his first novel.

Further acclaim for Thom Jones:

'A writer as brave as he is gifted.' Michael Herr

'Thom Jones has stormed the scene like an angry doberman at a garden party. He is shocking, he is gorgeous . . . A voice so relentless and felonious at once – that you ought to need a permit to carry it.' *Boston Globe*

'Thom Jones's stories are propelled by an amazing blend of knowledge and skill, terror and release.' Robert Stone

'Writers as good as Thom Jones appear but rarely. The original poetry of his fictional world is irresistible, and the sense that he knows this world absolutely has cleansed his prose and produced an affectless sheen . . . Thom Jones is a wonderful writer.' *New York Times*

'He is not only a quirkily gifted, exceptionally powerful writer but – and this is much rarer at a time when originality often has a derivative quality about it – a vital one too.' *Guardian*

Sonny Liston Was
a Friend of Mine

Thom Jones

faber and faber

First published in the USA in 1999
by Little Brown & Company
Published simultaneously by Faber and Faber Limited
3 Queen Square London WC1N 3AU
This paperback edition first published in 2000

Printed in England by Mackays of Chatham plc, Chatham, Kent

The following stories, in somewhat different form, have been previously
published: "Fields of Purple Forever" in *GQ;* "Tarantula" in *Zoetrope;*
"Mouses" and "Sonny Liston Was a Friend of Mine" in *The New Yorker;*
"A Midnight Clear" in *Playboy;* "Daddy's Girl" in *Harper's;* "My Heroic
Mythic Journey" in *Story;* "I Love You, Sophie Western" in *Nerve.*

© Thom Jones, 1999

Thom Jones is hereby identified as the author of this
work in accordance with Section 77 of the Copyright, Designs
and Patents Act 1988

A CIP record for this book
is available from the British Library

ISBN 0-571-20190-3

2 4 6 8 10 9 7 5 3 1

FOR MY MOTHER,

MARILYN

Contents

**Sonny Liston Was
a Friend of Mine**

Sonny Liston Was
a Friend of Mine

As soon as the turquoise blue Impala pulled in the driveway, Kid Dynamite was out of the backseat, across the lawn, into the house, and dancing out of his wool pants and tie as he vaulted up to his room. Sunday services at St. Mark's Lutheran, when communion was offered, were very long affairs. Sit down, get up, sit down again; up-and-down, down-and-up in a flesh-eating wool suit as voracious as a blanket of South American army ants. Out in the car, Cancer Frank had barely turned off the ignition switch. Kid Dynamite was already in his gray cotton sweatpants and boxing shoes. Church, man! If the boredom didn't kill you, the everlasting sermon could have you snoring in a bolt upright position. Add to that six or seven hymns where otherwise harmless old ladies howled like they were hell-bent on shattering more than nerves — they were out to break celestial crystal. So were the small babies who screamed protest against the stagnant oxygen-deficient air and the stupefaction of body heat. What a relief to be done with it. The only reason he consented to go at all was for the sake of his grandmother, Mag.

As Kid Dynamite carefully taped his hands in his bedroom, he heard Cancer Frank's heavy wing tips scraping up the front steps. There was the snap of his stepfather's Zippo and the clatter of an ashtray being placed on the piano. In his gray sharkskin and brown felt snap-brim, with a Pall Mall draped from his lips Cancer Frank was the Hoagy Carmichael of Aurora, Illinois. Kid Dynamite laughed to himself thinking that C.F. endured the services in nicotine withdrawal — served the chump right, too! As soon as his hands were wrapped, Kid Dynamite slipped a hooded sweatshirt over his head and was down the back stairs and out of the house. Out. Clean. Gone.

Kid Dynamite stepped through the wet grass in his boxing shoes, threw his shoulder into the side door of the garage, and stepped inside. It was cold and damp, smelling of musk. He snapped on his transistor radio. WLS was running a shitload of Sunday advertisements cheerfully promulgating the American life of living death. Kid Dynamite peered out the window where he spotted his mother, "the Driver," still sitting in the car preening in the rearview mirror. For the Driver (one trip to the Buy Right with her behind the wheel and you *would* get down on your knees and pray), church services were just another place, as all places were to her, where you went to show off your good looks and your latest outfit.

Kid Dynamite slipped on his bag gloves. It was early March and the wind was blowing hard. It had been raining off and on. Three of the garage windows were broken and the roof leaked, but the floor was made of smooth wooden planks. As Kid Dynamite did some side twists to limber up, he looked through the window again and saw his mother finally get out of the Chevy and walk into the house where there were bigger mirrors. He wondered what she had been thinking looking in that rearview. "How did I *go over* today?" No doubt.

Kid Dynamite spent a lot of time in front of a mirror himself, but only to examine his body alignment and his punching form. He was himself a good-looking young man but a realigned nose, a little scar tissue beneath the brows, and a cauliflower ear were beginning to make any comparisons with the Greek gods unlikely. Poker-faced, he threw a jab at the double-ended bolo bag and gave it a quick head slip when it bounced back. Slipping punches was the most accomplished means a boxer could employ to protect his face but also the riskiest. Kid Dynamite tattooed the bag and continued slipping punches until he began to sweat. Then he started moving in and out on the bag — started using his legs. In another few moments he was gliding around the greasy floor planks, the air so cold he could see his breath. Shadow boxing, he worked his legs, moving about the floor in a bob-and-weave style, watching himself in variously positioned mirrors. His Sunday afternoon workouts belonged to him alone and he used them to cover contingencies that had been skipped over in his regular gymnasium workouts. The old man once told him, "There are at least a thousand things that can go wrong in a fight, and how many of them can you think of — fifty?" As with most fighters, Kid Dynamite's *things going wrong* invariably involved the problem of fear. As the old man had said, "Control your fear and you are cooking with gas, baby."

At 147 pounds, Kid Dynamite fought as a welterweight. He had recently advanced through the semifinals in the open class of the Chicago Golden Gloves, but made the finals only just barely. Two of these victories were split decisions. In his last fight on Friday, he suffered a slight cut under the left eye. The opponent had pushed him to the limit and he knew that from here on in the competition would get much rougher. Four of the boxers from the Steelworkers' Hall had made it to the finals. They were all sky high that night, driving back to Aurora on the Eisenhower Freeway in Juan's junky-ass Cadillac. But after Juan dropped Kid Dynamite off and he came into the house with his gym bag, Cancer Frank was lying on the couch watching TV and didn't bother to even look up at his stepson. The Driver was already in bed and it was too late to call his girlfriend, Melanie. So he went upstairs and woke up the Driver. "I won. I got him good," he said.

The Driver's face was covered in a luminescent green mask. "Did you knock him out?" she said wearily. There was a bath towel on the Driver's pillow and flecks of cracked green paste dropped from her face as she spoke.

"Jesus. The creature from the Green Bog," Kid Dynamite said.

"It's a wrinkle mask. Did you knock him out or what?"

"My guy? No, I won on points. Chubby knocked his guy out. I won on points. Cuba and Eloise Greene won."

"What about your homework?" she said.

"What *about* it? It's Friday night. Man, I was feeling so right tonight. It was the best thing. I'm going to win the tournament," Kid Dynamite said.

"You're just like your father and where is *he* now? He's in the nuthouse. You've got to study. You've got geometry problems."

"I'm talking to a lima bean. Screw geometry. When was the last time you had to whip out a slide rule to solve one of life's problems?"

"You hang out with those lowlife boxers and you act crude. What will you do with your life? How can you hang out with such scrums?"

"They're my friends. Jesus! I come in here feeling great. Can't you just say, 'Good, I'm glad you won. You've made me a happy lima bean.' Is that too much to ask?"

The Driver stuck her hand out groping for the alarm clock. "I've got to get up at the crack of dawn, what time is it?" she said.

"Midnight. I'm going to take an aspirin. I've got a headache. Shit!"

As he left the bedroom his mother said, "I don't want to take the wind out of your sails, but you better pass or you'll end up in the gutter."

Kid Dynamite stepped into the bathroom and closed the door. She said, "I *am* glad you won. But don't stay up all night doing push-ups; I need quiet. My nerves are shot."

He didn't bother to reply. Instead he leaned against the sink and examined the cut under his eye in the medicine cabinet mirror. It wasn't that bad, but the tissue under his eye was swollen and tender. A couple of jabs, one good solid punch could easily burst it open. He went downstairs and got an ice cube, passing Cancer Frank on the stairs. Neither uttered a word in passing. Kid Dynamite wondered if C.F. even knew he was fighting. Suddenly the elation of reaching the finals returned to him full blown. His recent win was not merely a stay of execution. This time, one way or another, he would take it all the way. Back in bed he let the ice melt over his eye, feeling the water roll down his neck onto the pillow. He could hear Cancer Frank talking to the Driver. "He'll never get past the next round. He drew Louie Reine, the redhead that nailed him last year. It was three days soaking in Epsom salts after that —"

"Who knows," his mother said. "Maybe he's better now, he's bigger. He sure thinks he's going to win," the Driver said.

Cancer Frank said, "Not even if you tied one of Reine's hands behind his back does he win."

Kid Dynamite waited in the silence of the night for this defense attorney to speak up for him. For a long time there was nothing, then came the familiar animal sounds. Christ! The two of them were having sex in spite of her stiff green wrinkle mask. Kid Dynamite rolled over on his stomach, covering his head with a pillow, but it was useless. He felt *compelled* to listen. When it was over he heard light feet squeaking on the linoleum tile, followed by intensive Listerine gargling, a hard scouring toothbrush, then footsteps back to the bed. Next Cancer Frank's heavier feet could be heard padding into the bathroom. Kid Dynamite heard his stepfather take a long horse piss and do some Listerine gargling of his own. In a moment he was back in the master bedroom where body positions were assumed, covers were adjusted, and things finally became quiet. Then he heard the Driver say, "I don't know. He was in the paper again, fifteen in a row. Knocking them out left and right."

Cancer Frank spoke matter-of-factly, without rancor or malice. He said, "Those were prelims. Kids that don't know how to fight. This other fighter, Reine, has his number. The kid is scared. He isn't going to win. He'll blow it."

Kid Dynamite was suddenly up on the edge of the bed in a rage. He pounded his fists on the tops of his thighs. Through clenched teeth he said, "You don't know *shit!*"

Cancer Frank heard him and said, "Hey!" The voice that had so terrorized Kid Dynamite for so much of his life stabbed him now like a punch to the solar plexus. Stepfather or no, the man was supposed to guide and encourage him, not run him down and disparage his every move. Cancer Frank was the original and main source of his travail in the world thus far. Kid Dynamite imagined him poised up in bed next to his mother. C.F. said, "Watch your goddamn mouth or I'm coming in there!"

Kid Dynamite got up and crossed the hallway to the master bedroom saying, "Well, come on then, you son of a bitch. If you want some, come on!"

The Driver leaped out of bed, rushed to the door, and locked it with a skeleton key just before he got there. "God! I knew this was going to happen."

Kid Dynamite grabbed the door handle and shook it. Then he began pounding the door with the balls of his fists. His hands were already sore from the tournament. This only intensified his rage. He threw his hip and shoulder against the door. It was an old door. Solid oak. "I'll knock down the wall," he screamed. "I'll kill that cock*suck*er!"

The Driver's voice was a vicious rasp, "You get the hell out of this house!"

In the middle of a coughing spasm, Cancer Frank choked out the words, "Call the police!"

Kid Dynamite stood at the door and listened to his stepfather cough. From the sound of it, Kid Dynamite knew he was overdramatizing. He shouted, "Go ahead, call them, you car-selling motherfucker. I hope you *die!*"

He gave the door a last thump and went back to his bedroom where he dropped to the floor and pumped off two hundred push-ups. He knew the police would not be called. But someone would be brought in to straighten him out. Uncle Mikey, a seriously bad guy and a notorious overreactor. Since the onset of Frank's disease, Uncle Mikey had more than once dragged his nephew out of bed, kicking his ass all the way down to the basement. He came early, too, when the kid was most vulnerable. He was like some Eastern European goon squad in that regard. It would be better if the police were called — better they than Mikey.

Kid Dynamite lay awake all night in rage and anticipation. Mikey didn't show up until noon. He was wearing a suit and tie, an indication there would be no violence. At forty, the former heavyweight champion of the Seventh Army looked like he could still fight at the drop of a hat. Unlike his brother, Kid Dynamite's old man, Mikey did not become a professional fighter; he was too smart for that. Instead he went into sales and had become the most materially successful member of the family. As far back as Kid Dynamite could remember, Mikey had the best cars, houses, clothes — the best of everything. It was Mikey, however, who had introduced Cancer Frank to his mother, and the kid's admiration for him was severely mitigated by that factor. In his suit and tie, on an early Saturday afternoon, Mikey was very solemn. Kid Dynamite knew grave matters would be discussed and threats would be issued. Compromises and concessions would be few.

After shooting the bull with C.F. and the Driver, Mikey politely invited Kid Dynamite for a drive in his new Mercedes convertible. It was a nice car and Mikey was proud of it. He talked about the virtues of German engineering as he took the river road and drove south toward Oswego. Kid Dynamite fell into a pout and nothing was said for a few miles. Then Mikey looked over at him with mounting irritation and said, "What the fuck is the matter with you? Why are you giving Frank such a hard time? He has cancer, for Chrissakes. What are you busting his balls for?"

Kid Dynamite looked straight ahead and said nothing. His body was coiled to dodge a side-arm blow, but better that than surrender his pride.

Mikey looked over and said, "I know what it is. It's Mag — a goddamn grandmother. She's been poisoning your mind against him, hasn't she?"

Kid Dynamite kept his eyes straight ahead. "No. She doesn't poison anybody. In fact, she pays Frank's bills," he said.

"Don't get sarcastic with me!" Mikey said. "I'll pull over and give it to you right now, you stupid little fuck!"

Kid Dynamite removed the wise-ass from his voice and said, "It's true. She pays."

Mikey shook his head and sighed. He removed his Italian sunglasses and threw them on the dashboard so he could rub the bridge of his nose. "Okay, I'm thinking . . . let me think. You're in over your head in this boxing tournament. 'Hard' Reine is going to fall all over you, is that it? I saw a piece about this motherfucker in the *Sun Times*. The same guy that got you last year. He ran over you like a freight train."

Kid Dynamite was sullen. "I'm better now. But how would you know. I haven't seen you at any of the fights. Personally, I'd rather be me than him. In fact, I feel *sorry* for the guy. Frank was out of line badmouthing me. It wasn't called for. That's what the whole beef is about. I don't know what they told you, but I didn't do anything except raise my voice a little."

"Raise your voice a *little*?" Mikey said. He pulled the car over to a gravel culvert where two men in bib overalls were fishing with stink bait. Kid Dynamite braced himself as Mikey switched off the engine. The big man took a deep breath and exhaled. Nephew and uncle sat watching the river for a moment. Each of the fishermen had a can of Budweiser in hand. "The beer drinker's *stance*," Mikey said. "They always stand that way. Isn't that something?"

"Nothing in there but carp and bullheads. How can you call that fun?" Kid Dynamite said. "They ought to get off their asses and do something more active. You can *buy* fucking fish."

Mikey laughed, "The problem I'm having here is that I *like* you. You act like a spoiled little brat. No harm in that. I'm trying to get past *that* so I can help out. As troublemakers go, you're just a pissant. I was worse. Shit. There was a depression. It was different. It took the law of the fist to salvage me. Is it the same with you? I treat you decently, things are okay for a while and then you start in on him. Look," Mikey said, pointing his finger in the kid's face. "I'm on your side on this one. But you can't terrorize him in his own home. You scared the fucking shit out of him."

"I'm not a scary person," Kid Dynamite said. "I'm mild-mannered as all hell."

Mikey laughed again. He reached over and clapped his nephew on the shoulder. "Loosen up, kiddo. You're tighter than a drum."

Kid Dynamite shrugged. "I'll win the fight. I trained. I'm in shape. Once we start exchanging punches, I'll know what to do."

"Your dad had balls. He was half my size and would take on anyone. But the thing that makes you good in the ring is the very thing that makes life outside the gym impossible. I was hoping you would end up more like myself than your crazy father." The glare of the sun bounced off the river, and Kid Dynamite used his hands for an eyeshade. Mikey replaced his sunglasses and said, "You're *sure* Mag hasn't been ragging on Frank?"

"Yeah, I'm sure. She knows he's sick. She doesn't rag on him. In her way, she's trying to help him."

"He's *dying!* And he's cracking up a little bit, too. I mean, why else would he be going to church three times a week. Would you like to walk in those shoes?"

"Fuckin' wing tips, not me," Kid Dynamite said. "I don't think he's going to die, either. Two packs a day. The two of them are screwing night and day —"

Mikey spoke abruptly, "You call off the dogs, okay? I don't want to hear the piss and moan."

Kid Dynamite shrugged. "They fuck like animals; it's disgusting; I got to hear it —"

Mikey raised his hand like a stop sign. "I don't want the 'wah wah, boo hoo.' Confine your violence to the ring or you're going to end up in the bughouse, like your father, a paranoid freak. The world is not that bad a place."

Kid Dynamite turned his palms up in exasperation. "I'm

not a violent person. I'm a *shy* person. What do I *do*? I don't drink. I don't smoke. I *work*. I *help* around the house. You don't see my name on the arrest reports. I'm still a virgin. I don't even jack off. Fuck, I'm a super guy. The only black marks against me are that I flunked geometry three times in a row and I've got a filthy mouth. You gonna come and see the fight? I'm going to *pretend* this guy is Frank and I'm going to kick ass!"

Mikey patted his nephew on the cheek just a little too hard. He laughed and said, "All right, kiddo. In the meantime, stay out of his way for a while."

"Serious, Uncle Mikey! Are you coming to the fight?"

"I'll be at the fight. If you don't kick the guy's ass and make it worth my while, I'll be coming after you when it's over. Deal?"

"Hey! I'll kick his ass all right."

Mikey laughed at this and exchanged seats with his nephew. South of Oswego, Kid Dynamite found a straight-away and got the Mercedes up to 130 mph. It didn't seem as if the car was doing more than sixty. "German engineering," Uncle Mikey said. "Hard work, attention to detail, and a willpower that never quits." He gave his nephew a punch on the shoulder and said, "You're lucky to be a German. Who knows, someday you might conquer the world."

IN SPITE OF the cold garage, Kid Dynamite quickly broke into a full sweat. After the assault of advertisements, Dick Clark popped on the air with "Big Girls Don't Cry" by the Four Seasons and then Paul Revere and the Raiders. Kid Dynamite expected a full day of "suck" radio and he was getting it. Still, any music was better than nothing. The kid was working hard now, gliding around the floor with his hands carried high at the sides of his head and his chin tucked down. The plank floor creaked as he moved in and out on the bolo bag. It rebounded with such speed and velocity and from so many unexpected directions that he had to concentrate intently to avoid having it slap him in the face. He did flunk geometry and that was ironic. Boxing acumen involved calculating angles. The angles of the ring, Kid Dynamite understood perfectly. He would show Louis Reine angles aplenty.

Kid Dynamite had boxed him beautifully for two rounds the year before. He had fast hands and could hit Reine at will. Listening to Lolo was the mistake on that one. Reine was discouraged and out of gas after the second round. Lolo told Kid Dynamite to stay on the outside and box his opponent, "Take this one on points." So he followed the advice and boxed at long range. Then as Reine recovered his wind, Kid Dynamite got trapped on the ropes, where Reine went to work on his body. As soon as Kid Dynamite dropped his elbow to cover his liver, he got clocked along the jaw and after that it was essentially over.

This year Kid Dynamite was in shape, but he didn't actually have any better plan for Reine than before. He wasn't going to slug with him, he was going to give him angles and box. He was the superior boxer, and he was stronger than he had been the year before, if he saw a clear shot he would tee off, but he definitely wasn't going to go in trading. Although Kid Dynamite had garned a small notice on the *Beacon*'s sports page, as his Uncle Mikey had said, Louis Reine was touted in the *Chicago Sun Times* as the premier fighter of the tournament. At eighteen, he had won forty-two fights and lost none. He had been fighting stiffer competition from the South Side and the paper said he was likely to go all the way to the Nationals.

Kid Dynamite had more fights than Reine but had suffered, in all, seventeen losses in CYO, AAU, and Golden Gloves competition. He had also got his ass kicked in a half-dozen street fights. He had been knocked cold three times, hospitalized twice. His family doctor prevailed upon his mother to make him quit after the loss in the finals the year before. But Kid Dynamite had had the fight with Reine in the very palm of his hand and he knew it. Too often, after a fighter took a single solid beating, he did not come back to the gym. Or if he did, he wasn't the same. He was gun-shy. The test of mettle was to come back with burning desire, which Kid Dynamite had done. He had not lost a fight since. He tried to explain this to his girlfriend, Melanie, the first time he saw her after the initial loss to Reine. It was a conversation that happened a year before. A tall brunette with perfect posture, she stood waiting for him at their usual rendezvous point on the corner of North Avenue and Smith Street. Melanie's ankles were squeezed together and she held her schoolbooks clutched against her breast. She was a beautiful young girl and Kid Dynamite was still something of a mess. He had a sore neck, a broken cheekbone, a black eye, and swollen purple lips. He was somewhat mystified by her tears, since his appearance had improved considerably since the fight and he had prepared her to see black and blue. Still, there were tears. He tried to reassure her. "It's not as bad as it looks," he said. "I'm just sore is all."

Light snowflakes fell on her shiny hair. Melanie had high

cheekbones, a well-shaped nose to set them off, and a resolute but nice chin to better complement her heart-shaped face. She had a wide mouth and full lips, and she was quite beautiful. Her sparkling green eyes were the feature Kid Dynamite liked most. He learned to read her moods by watching her eyes. She had been the only girl he had ever cared about, and the two had been seeing one another since junior high school. Melanie was thin with frequent acne flare-ups but this bothered Kid Dynamite very little: she easily was one of the best-looking girls in the entire high school and one of the most loyal. Melanie was enough to make him believe that God was looking out for him. She approached him, reaching out to his cheek with a fuzzy woolen glove. Kid Dynamite gave her a gentle hug.

He stepped back and said, "You look so beautiful this morning. I never get tired of looking at you. It's so good to finally get out of the house and actually see you again."

"Oh, boy," she said cautiously, "are you okay? What happened?"

Kid Dynamite started to laugh but the pain of it stopped him. "He hit me so hard every tooth in my mouth rattled. But with you standing here in front of me, I'm an ace." Melanie wore a navy car coat with bone-colored toggles over her cheer-squad uniform. He said, "Why have you got the uniform on?"

"Basketball in Joliet tonight. We have a morning pep assembly. I don't want to go. I want to be with you."

They embraced again. Kid Dynamite kissed Melanie's slender neck. He could feel an erection coming on and tried to back away but she clutched him tighter. He gave in and let her hold him completely. Students were walking by, the late ones. He felt her tears rolling down his neck. "Baby, my ribs, careful!" he said.

She said, "I'm not going to the game tonight. I want to be with you."

Kid Dynamite felt hot tears of his own. He pulled his head back and kissed her. "You smell so good, you look so pretty. What you just said was the nicest thing anyone has ever said to me."

"Oh God," she said. "If it wasn't for the basketball team, I *would* have *been* there."

"You would have just seen me get creamed," he said. The procession of students hurrying to school began to thin out. Suddenly five black students came out of Fiddler's Grocery. Fid himself came out after them. He was a short heavyset man in a white apron. He stood on the wooden porch and took a final drag off his cigarette before flipping it out into the street and going back inside.

Kid Dynamite recognized the students, one of them was his friend, Eloise Greene, the club's middleweight. Jarvis Jackson packed a wet snowball and fired across Smith Street. It hit the top of the corner mailbox. Kid Dynamite tossed Jarvis the "bird" and Jarvis Jones cried, "Hey, motherfucker! You can suck my *motherfucking* dick, man!"

Kid Dynamite dropped his books and packed a snowball of his own. He aimed it at Jackson, but the snowball didn't even make it across the street. It felt like one of his ribs had broken loose and punctured a lung. He bent over, clutching his side, as the students who had stopped to light cigarettes laughed at his pathetic toss.

Kid Dynamite looked up at Melanie and said, "I'm okay!

I'm okay! Just sore and glad I missed. Jarvis a bad mo-tah scooter."

They watched the blacks proceed down Smith Street hill toward school. Kid Dynamite dried his hands by sticking them in his pockets. There was a brisk wind and he pulled his watch cap down over his ears. Both sides of North Avenue were lined with oak and maples, barren of leaves. It was a gray morning and the pristine snow was fouled by the black smoke of coal fires coming from the chimneys of the homes. Kid Dynamite stepped into a yard and snapped a small branch from a pussy willow, the first sign of spring. He traced a furry blossom around the edges of Melanie's mouth. He used his finger to trace the tears rolling down her cheeks. She wiped a wisp of tear-drenched hair from her face. She said, "My parents are at work. We can go back to my place."

Melanie's parents were both cops. Her stepfather, Vic, had been a boxer himself, a heavyweight from New Jersey who fought in club fights as a teenager. He still followed the sport and took an interest in Kid Dynamite's career. The summer after Kid Dynamite lost in the finals of the Golden Gloves tournament, Vic drove Melanie and the Kid out past the North Aurora Downs Race Track to watch Sonny Liston train for the first Patterson fight, which was set for September in Chicago's Comiskey Park. Kid Dynamite watched Vic shell out twelve bucks to get into the old Pavilion dance hall where a gym had been set up for Liston's camp. Kid Dynamite had never actually been inside before, but the Pavilion was the site of a number of his father's professional fights before the Second World War.

There were few spectators in the Pavilion. Vic led them to some front row padded loge seats. The world's number one heavyweight contender was in the ring working with a very fast light heavyweight. Although his size made him seem as ponderous as a water buffalo, Liston was in fact faster than the sparring partner. He worked on cutting off the ring, something he anticipated he would have to do with Patterson, who was lightning fast and a fine boxer as well. Time and again Liston trapped the light heavyweight along the ropes. Liston threw light punches and let him go, only to trap him again. After two rounds of this, a bigger man gloved up and got into the ring. A number of handlers in gray sweatshirts with "Sonny Liston" crudely stenciled on them bustled about. One of the men simply sat before a small phonograph and played "Nighttrain," over and over again. Kid Dynamite sported two fresh black eyes incurred when his doctor had to rebreak his nose to set it right, and because of this as many people were looking at him as were watching Liston.

At the first exchange, Liston knocked his new sparring partner down with a body shot. It didn't look like much of a punch but the pain was very real. The boxer writhed about the canvas in agony. In the end he could not continue. Disgusted, and out of sparring partners, Liston climbed out of the ring and began banging the heavy bag. This went on for three timed rounds.

As the workout ran down, Liston gave a rope-skipping exhibition on the solid maple floor of the depression-era dance hall. The record player continued to blare "Nighttrain" as Kid Dynamite looked about the sparse crowd. Most of them were reporters jotting notes on press pads. Kid Dy-

namite heard one of the trainers tell a *Life* magazine reporter that during training Liston ate nothing but rare
steak, carrot juice, goat's milk, and vegetables. He said
Sonny Liston was the only private citizen in America to own
a carrot juicer.

Kid Dynamite was amazed at Liston's speed and by the
compactness and economy of his movements. After watching so many amateur fighters, this look at a professional
heavyweight left him awestruck. Liston had a left jab that
would decapitate anyone with less than a seventeen-inch
neck. His display on the big bag was frightening, was light-
years beyond what Kid Dynamite imagined possible. Vic
gave him a nudge and said, "Bet the farm on this man. Patterson is dead."

Liston had surprisingly fast legs and was doing double
crossovers with the skip rope. Kid Dynamite looked at the
fighter's feet, and when he looked back at Liston's face,
he discovered Liston's baleful stare was locked in on him.
Charles "Sonny" Liston was the most frightening person Kid
Dynamite had ever seen, and at this moment Charles did
not seem very happy. He met Liston's gaze but found it almost impossible to sustain eye contact. Soon it became an
exercise in the control of fear. Sonny Liston gave Kid Dynamite the slightest hint of a smile and winked. Vic nudged
Kid Dynamite again, and leaned over, whispering, "Your
eyes. He's looking at your eyes."

Kid Dynamite had forgotten about his black eyes. Vic
laughed and said, "I almost shit in my pants before I figured
it out. That is one mean nigger."

As soon as the workout concluded, a handler tossed
Sonny Liston a towel. He mopped off his face, which was

glistening with Vaseline and crystal droplets of sweat. Another handler helped him into a terry cloth robe. The towel man cut off Liston's bandages. His hands were like hams. On his way to the shower, Liston stopped just short of Kid Dynamite to sign a few autographs. He paused briefly to talk with sports writers and then looked back at Kid Dynamite. He said, "What are you, kid, a lightweight?"

Kid Dynamite jumped back as if he had been shot with a forty-five. His voice squeaked. "No sir, I'm a welterweight."

In a sissy voice, Liston said, "No sir, I'm a welterweight."

The writers roared and Kid Dynamite's cheeks flushed. Sonny Liston motioned to one of the handlers who handed him an 8 × 10 black-and-white glossy. He said, "What's your name?"

Kid Dynamite seemed dumbstruck. Finally he said, "Make it out to Melanie."

"I thought you was going to hem and haw forever." Liston looked at Melanie. "Is that you?"

"Yes," she said.

"Looks like you thumped him pretty good," Liston said. There was another roar of laughter. A press photographer rushed over and staged a picture of Liston, Melanie, Vic, and Kid Dynamite. In the end, Liston had signed a picture for each of them. As soon as the fighter turned away and headed off to the shower, a man in a gray sweatshirt demanded two dollars each for the photographs. Vic paid gladly enough. "That was nice. He didn't have to do that."

Giddy with excitement, they compared inscriptions. Kid Dynamite's photo was signed, "To the Kid, from your friend, Sonny Liston."

Kid Dynamite beamed at the inscription like it was the writ of God. "Sonny Liston is a *friend* of mine," he said.

KID DYNAMITE applied himself to boxing with renewed vigor. In the summer as he recovered from his nose surgery, he worked as a lifeguard at the city park. He would come in an hour early each day to swim. This was after he did a full morning workout in the garage. He bought a set of Joe Wielder weights. In the garage he did extra neck bridges and he lifted weights, then he ran to work and swam. For the rest of the day he rotated along the pool stations with the other lifeguards. Sitting in the hot sun in a white pith helmet, with a whistle in his mouth, he felt completely at rest.

After work Kid Dynamite would meet Melanie at the Dairybar across the field from his house. Melanie served ice cream there in a blue-striped seersucker frock. One night after closing up, they sat outside under the blue bug zapper. Melanie was an only child and although, like Kid Dynamite, she was raised by a stepfather, she did not know her own father at all.

"Maybe it's just as well," Kid Dynamite said. "Vic is really nice. My real father was nice, but he just wasn't around much. He used to take me to the gym when I was a kid. He thought I was a sissy. Took me to Chicago where I met big-time fighters. Joe Louis, Ezzard Charles, Tony Zale, Ernie Terrell — guys who were his actual friends. I don't know what I'll do when it's all over. I'm not good at anything." Kid Dynamite poked a straw in a clump of ice cream at the bottom of his milk shake.

Mikey had somehow patched up the mess with Cancer

Frank. It seemed to Kid Dynamite that it was one of those
rarest of occasions where he had managed to skate on something. Frank did not speak to him but neither did he criti-
cize him. Kid Dynamite pretended that his stepfather was
invisible and vice versa. Fortunately, their schedules did not
converge that much. Kid Dynamite was up at four A.M. most
days to run. On Monday morning he awoke with a pleasur-
able sense of anticipation. It would be the last run before
the Reine fight. One more solid run and he would be ready.
He had omitted nothing; if he lost it would because Reine
was the better fighter. On the edge of his bed, he clocked
his resting pulse. Forty beats a minute.

This time around Kid Dynamite wasn't listening to any
more of Juan's bullshit advice. By now he felt he knew his
body better than anyone. And while he rested, the other
fighters would be playing catch-up. For them it would be
too little, too late. Kid Dynamite got into his sweats and
combat boots in the dark. He walked quietly downstairs and
out the door, falling into an easy jog across town to his
grandmother's store. Since North Avenue was lit with orange tungsten streetlights, this was the route of choice; this
was no time to sprain an ankle in a dark pothole.

Kid Dynamite picked up speed after the first mile. The
homes along the lower part of North Avenue were three-
story Victorians. Only in a few could he see the amber glow
of lightbulbs. It was early, but as he passed the Burlington
railroad station, he spotted commuters scouting parking
spots for the trip to Chicago. As he crossed the Fox River
bridge, a squad car passed and a cop waved at him. Kid Dynamite ran past the gas company and a number of factories,
most of which looked like chambers of Dickensian horror.

He used to like looking in the windows and seeing men at work on the graveyard shift. He had come to recognize many of them. How they could stand in front of a machine, a spot welder or a punch press, night after night was unfathomable to him. Did they suffer as he did in a high school classroom? Kid Dynamite knew that he might well end up in such a place himself. He did not deem himself college material, and he knew enough about boxing to know that his prospects as a professional were nil, just as they had been for his father. There was always someone bigger and better. Yet he was caught up into boxing and could think of little else. As he ran, the looks on the workers' faces were neutral, reflecting neither agony nor pleasure. By the time Kid Dynamite got to Lake Street he was in a residential area again. Here the houses were not so nice. He came down the hill, passed under the viaduct, and sprinted the last two blocks to his grandmother's store.

Mag was standing at the cash register going through bills. A bare sixty-watt bulb hung on a frayed wire above her. For the past few years, Kid Dynamite came in to do all of the heavy lifting for her — moving bulk cases from the basement up to the shelves. Shuffling milk and pop bottles, sacks of flour, bags of potatoes. He loaded the stove with coal and then joined Mag in the kitchen, bolting down a couple of egg sandwiches with black coffee. He opened the cupboard where Mag always had a homemade pumpkin pie. Kid Dynamite sliced a piece and shoveled it in his mouth. Mag asked him if he needed any money, and Kid Dynamite shook his head no.

The sun was coming up as he headed out, and as light flooded into the store, he saw that Mag had the "Kid Dyna-

mite" article posted on the cash register for all her cus-
tomers to see. On a shelf behind the counter she kept Kid
Dynamite's boxing pendants and trophies like a miniature
shrine. He waved good-bye and headed out the front door.
It was a four-mile run back to the house, most of it uphill.
He sprinted the entire way.

OF THE FOUR FIGHTERS the Steelworkers' Boxing Club
sent to the finals, Kid Dynamite was considered the most
likely to win. And as the lightest fighter from the club, he
was the first to go up. He hadn't slept the night before the
fight, but then he never did. As soon as Lolo taped his
hands, Kid Dynamite began to shadow box. After fifteen
minutes of this, Juan forced him to sit down on a folding
chair. The coach pulled a chair adjacent to him. "You know
the game plan?"

Kid Dynamite nodded. He was dripping with sweat.

Juan looked at him intently. "Louie Reine had trouble
making weight. Five hours in the steamroom, and three
trips to the scales. Don't make your move until the end of
the second round. If he's still strong then, wait until the
third. Are you listening to me?"

"The old man called me. He said I should jump all over
him."

Juan, normally implacable, registered disbelief, "Your
old man, who's in a mental hospital two thousand miles
away, told you this?"

"Yeah," Kid Dynamite said.

"Well, what do you think you should do?"

"It doesn't matter, Juan. I'm going to win tonight. I can
feel it. I don't care what he does; I'm going to kick his moth-

erfucking ass. I've been waiting a year to get this cock-sucker."

"So you're going to do a job on him? No plan, no nothing! Just kick ass!" Juan shook his head in dismay. "Well, I hope you do. Just remember, the crowd will be with him tonight. It won't be your crowd."

Kid Dynamite got up and started twisting his neck from side to side, bouncing up and down. Lolo ducked into the locker room. He grabbed the spit bucket and water bottle. "Let's go, Kid, you're up."

Kid Dynamite entered the arena and climbed up the portable wooden steps to the ring. Louis Reine was already in the opposite corner, his red hair shorn in a buzz cut. There wasn't a drop of sweat on him. He looked the same as he had the year before. Kid Dynamite turned away, bracing his gloves against the ropes as he rubbed his shoes in the resin box. He flexed his neck and bounced up and down in his corner trying to shake off the butterflies. The referee called both fighters to the center of the ring, reminded both fighters that they had received their instructions in the dressing room, and wished them both luck.

Kid Dynamite returned to his corner, where Lolo held out his mouthpiece. He set his teeth in it, clamping down hard as he slapped himself on the forehead a few times to make sure his headgear was tight. Then he turned and looked across the ring with a blank stare as he waited for the bell. As soon as it rang, Louie Reine came rushing across the ring to engage, and Kid Dynamite did the same. Just before contact Kid Dynamite spotted his grandmother, Mag, the Driver, Mikey, and Cancer Frank seated in the third row next to Melanie and Vic. The only time in his life that Kid

Dynamite could remember Mag leaving the store for more than an hour was the day she had her teeth pulled. The store was open seven days a week including Christmas Day. It had always been that way. He was so shocked to see her out of context he had to look twice to make sure he was see-ing things right.

Reine gave him a Walcott stepover to switch angles, and threw a left hook that just barely grazed the top of his head. Kid Dynamite heard it whistle as he ducked under it and watched Reine's elbow sail by. He came up off balance and started a left hook of his own, aimed over Reine's right hand. Reine's punch landed first, catching Kid Dynamite high on the forehead. Because his feet were too close to-gether, and because Reine was so strong, the force of the punch was sufficient to send Kid Dynamite reeling back-ward into the ropes. Reine then tagged him with a double jab and a straight right hand to the side of the jaw, and sud-denly Kid Dynamite was sprawled face down on the canvas. It seemed that the floor had flown up and hit him in the mouth. His whole body bounced hard. The canvas was as rough as concrete, and his face, elbows, and knees stung with abrasions. He had gone down like he was poleaxed, and the crowd went into a frenzy. Knockdowns, at least spec-tacular ones, were relatively rare in amateur boxing. The boxing reporter from the *Sun Times*, the prophet who picked Reine to go to the Nationals, was on his feet scrib-bling in his notebook. It was the first thing Kid Dynamite saw as he raised his head.

His face burned. Pinwheels spun behind his eyelids, and he shook his head hard. Looking over to his corner he saw Juan frantically motioning him to stay down and take the full eight count. Meanwhile, the referee was having a problem getting Reine to a neutral corner. Kid Dynamite distinctly saw a smile flash across Cancer Frank's face. Mag was on her feet screaming in German for him to get up. Never in his life had he heard her speak in her native tongue. Her face was red and she was pounding her cane on the floor like a savage. Kid Dynamite felt he was in a dream. Reine's corner was furiously shouting instructions, but Reine wasn't listening. His chest was puffed up and he looked supremely confident. Kid Dynamite shook his head again trying to clear out the cobwebs. The noise of the crowd seemed very far away. He managed to get his right glove up on the lower ring rope.

Off in the seventh row Kid Dynamite focused on a big man with a fleshy bulbous nose and frosty white hair. He watched him raise his hands to his mouth and shout encouragement to Reine. For such a big man, the sound Kid Dynamite heard was diminutive, but he could hear the man's harsh South Chicago accent. Kid Dynamite wondered if his eardrum had been broken. The man continued to scream. He was well built, and wearing a plaid flannel shirt. Kid Dynamite noticed that the threads on the man's second shirt button had unraveled into tan and brown sprouts, and he thought, "Mister, take that shirt off and put it on three more times, and the button is gone." Kid Dynamite wanted to go down into the crowd and warn him. For the man to lose his button seemed like a cosmic tragedy.

The referee picked up the count from the timekeeper. He was looking in Kid Dynamite's eyes. "Five . . . six," he cried. The smile on Cancer Frank's face widened. Melanie had her face buried in her hands. Vic was on his feet shak-

ing his fist in the air. Vic had a heavy beard and always
seemed in need of a shave. Kid Dynamite was certain he
could smell English Leather coming off of Vic. He could see
the fine black hairs on the backs of Vic's fingers. Next to Vic
he could see the redness in Mag's face. Her skin thinned to
parchment with age. She was dressed in a thick gray overcoat and pearl pop beads. Kid Dynamite had given them to
her because her arthritis made ordinary clasps impossible.
A six-dollar purchase. From directly behind, he heard a
fan's disembodied voice say, "Don't worry, this kid is tough.
He'll get up."

Time began to hurtle along again. He got up on one
knee and shook his head. Goddammit if something wasn't
wrong with his eardrum.

The referee cried, "Seven." Melanie lifted her head from
her lap. "Eight!" the referee cried. Kid Dynamite was standing. The referee looked in his eyes and rubbed Kid Dynamite's gloves clean. "You okay?" Kid Dynamite nodded. His
legs felt full of Novocain. The referee stepped back and sig-
naled for the fight to continue.

Reine marched across the ring in a straight line. He gave
the kid a real cool dip and roll, feigning a left as he fired his
best punch, the straight right. Kid Dynamite anticipated
this, and with the overconfident Reine walking in, he countered with a picture-perfect left hook to the point of Reine's
chin. It was the best punch Kid Dynamite had ever thrown,
but Reine did not go down. It was no reason for discourage-
ment. Reine had not gone down, Kid Dynamite knew, because Reine still had hope. His job now was to erase it. He
set about to do this, busily circling Reine, setting his body,
and throwing punches in combination. Reine wobbled but

didn't go down. The cheers of the crowd fueled Kid Dynamite's enthusiasm, but he kept his head and fought carefully. By the end of the round a frustrated Reine bulled
forward punching recklessly with both hands. Kid Dynamite
returned to his corner rubbing blood out of his left eye.
Juan didn't even bother with the mouthpiece, he was too
busy pressing adrenaline swabs in the cut.

During the next round Kid Dynamite withstood an onslaught of sharp combinations. He methodically outboxed
Reine, who began to tire and lose his composure. As Reine
started throwing desperate punches, Kid Dynamite found a
home for his right uppercut. By the end of the round,
Reine's fair skin was marked with red welts. In the corner
Juan encouraged him to go after Reine with both hands,
but Kid Dynamite was exhausted as well. His lungs felt
scalded by the smoke in the arena. His legs seemed as if they
had never recovered from the knockdown. Juan told him
Reine might have twenty seconds of gas left over after the
minute's rest, to lay back and let him throw his bolt. But
Reine had no gas at all. He came out arm weary and Kid
Dynamite was there to pepper him with left hands. Then
he moved inside, confident of his ability to slip Reine's
punches. He straightened Reine with the right-hand uppercut and then threw a left-right combination dishing out
all of his mustard. It turned Reine sideways, but it did not
knock him down. Reine pulled his gloves up and used his
huge forearms to ward off further punishment. It was tanta-
mount to giving up, since Reine did not mount another of-
fensive rally. Kid Dynamite moved in and out, working his
jab until the bell sounded ending the fight.

As he waited for the judges to compile their scores, Kid

Dynamite chided himself for not pushing it harder when in fact he had given his all. The referee announced a split decision in Kid Dynamite's favor. Juan barely had time to pick him up and swing him around before the ring doctor jumped into Kid Dynamite's corner and pressed a gauze bandage under his eye. In the excitement of the fight, Kid Dynamite hadn't felt the cut, hadn't been bothered by it after the first round. But now the doctor shook his head, and said, "You won the fight but your tournament is over. That's a seven-stitch cut." Louis Reine came over and slapped Kid Dynamite's glove. "Good fight. I'll see you next year."

Kid Dynamite felt an overwhelming affection for Reine. "Thanks," he said. Reine, who had turned away, looked back and said, "Next time I'll get you."

The only other fighter from the Steelworkers' Hall to win that night was Eloise Greene, the club's middleweight. Greene, the cigarette smoker, caught fire and waltzed through the finals, winning the open title. For this he received a trophy, a powder blue silk jacket, and his own headline on the *Beacon*'s sports page.

Kid Dynamite did not go in with the other fighters to watch the subsequent bouts. He did not even go back to the Steelworkers' Hall to clean out his gym locker. Boxing was finally over and the real world, which had seemed so very far away all these years, was upon him.

The Roadrunner

THE EAGLE FLIED on Friday and except for the assorted shitbirds, and certain vital N.C.O.s, Captain Barnes issued First Recon ninety-six hours of liberty. Until that it had been nothing but humping the boonies. All we knew was the field. Six months of that shit, and nerves were strung tight. Now we were awaiting orders to ship out for Da Nang. Since Captain Barnes didn't want us to start a brawl in Oceanside, he gave us ninety-six hours and told us to take all that tension south of the border. "Go fuck your brains out in T-Town, that is an order!"

No sooner than we collected our pay we were packed into L. D. Pfieffer's '51 Chevy, a car that needed three quarts of oil at every fill-up. We chain-smoked Camels and split a quart of gin on the trip down Highway 101.

We crossed the border and hit a strip club on Tijuana's main drag. A stripper with a gold tooth had just whipped off her g-string and shimmied her cooch into a sailor's face.

Half the crowd was cheering this swabbie on, like, "Go for it — eat her out." Others "pretended" they would never do such a thing but it was like, "So go to a Rotary Club Meeting, and get lost, motherfuckers!" First Recon wanted nothing short of Mexican Caligula.

Gerber sidled right up to the bar and said, "She's got a snatch on her like Bert Parks's toupee."

Sergeant Ondine said, "Either the bitch likes it or that sailor boy has got massive *salvation* glands."

L. D. Pfieffer, our machine-gunner, said, "Man, I'd like to stick my whole head up her pussy."

Felix Toliver, a radioman from Connecticut, eyeballed Pfieffer and said, "With a pinhead like yours it would fit like a glove." Toliver was 6′5″ tall and accordingly thought of himself as a badass, and well before the fun started these two marines locked eyeballs. Sergeant Ondine stepped in and told them to knock it off, but Toliver had this nasal Connecticut accent and said, "Stay out of this, Clarence."

There were two things you didn't do in First Recon — you didn't get on the wrong side of L.D. and you didn't call Ondine "Clarence." I figured Toliver must have a death wish, but just then a big whore came along, took L.D. by the hand, and turned him around. Pretty soon she's running her fingers up and down his thigh, squeezing his meat. Gerber handed me a beer and guided me to the back of the club where some of the classier whores sat. He was saying, "I'm in love, Hollywood. You should see this babe." But when we got to the back, Gerber's prostitute was nowhere to be seen. I suddenly found the love of my own life, negotiated a price, and went upstairs. A half hour later I was back.

The stage show was over and it was all jukebox. The Mar-Kees were cranking out "Last Night."

Ondine and Pfieffer were at the bar slamming down overpriced shots of tequila. Sergeant Ondine was a lifer. The Marine Corps was his career, but he was an all-right guy. With Vietnam on his mind, he was deep into his rap where the essential secret to being a good soldier was first of all to concede your own death. "If you do that, you can do anything. No one can outsoldier you. No one can take a run at you and live to tell about it. No one can take you out. You can do seven-mile forced marches in full field gear with a poncho over your head and call yourself a tough guy, but if you aren't ready to give it up, you're nothing."

I had heard all this before and didn't take it too seriously. I didn't want to concede my own death. I wanted to be a hedonist — drink, screw girls, and experience vast earthly pleasures. I didn't even want to talk about death; it was something that just wasn't going to happen for a very very long time. I ordered a beer and noticed that Pfieffer was really lit. He was a heavyset guy and heavy on his feet. Not coordinated. The bartender kept setting out shot glasses of tequila for him and he would migrate from the dance floor back to the bar, where he would down another shot and then go back to the dance floor, doing some kind of dipshit hula dance. He looked like a big, stupid, happy fat guy, but if anyone laughed or got into a critique about the finer points of dance, Pfieffer would flash them his goofy grin and then biff them on the nose with the meat of his fist. I watched him lay a few on a mouthy sailor. The man's head jerked back like he didn't know what to do.

Tears were running down the guy's face and L.D. stood in front of him with his goofus smile. The sailor got uppity and Pfieffer let him have another one, drawing blood this time. "There he goes again," Ondine said. Very soon a wild and woolly brawl rolled through the crowded joint in waves. I hadn't put a single beer in me before a bottle came sailing across the bar and struck me under the eye. The fight spread out into the street while the Mexican police forced their way into the front door.

All of First Recon managed to get out without getting arrested. We packed into the Chevy and spent the next hour trying to locate a whorehouse that Ondine favored. We ended up lost and stopped at a depressing little cantina to fuel up, drinking 150-proof rum. The bartender's "wife" and "sister" came downstairs and in no time we reconvened to the living quarters in the back of the building. One of the women filled a plastic bread bag with ice cubes for my swollen eye.

Waiting for your buddies to get laid is right up there with hanging out in a dentist's office. After Pfieffer got laid, I saw one of the prostitutes hanging back in the bedroom as she took a swath at her crotch with a sex towel. Then she dipped her fingers into a large tub of Vaseline containing pubic hairs of various colors and texture. This Vaseline jar brought home the true meaning of the term "sloppy seconds," but Felix didn't give a shit and he joined her in the room and soon a lot of bedboard-thumping sex was going on.

I said, "L.D., man, did you get a load of that Vaseline jar?" He was already three sheets to the wind and waved me off and said, "I'm so horny I could fuck a rattlesnake."

"You just did," Ondine said.

Pfieffer made like he was going to biff Ondine on the nose, but the Sergeant had his hands up and the two started grab-assing until the bartender came around back and threatened to throw us all out if we didn't promise to calm down. In the meantime, the bedbumping and loud groans in Felix's room were like the high drama of a full-fledged exorcism. Gerber was performing oral sex on the other prostitute on a cramped love seat in the little room without having "officially" negotiated a price. In addition to the black eye, I had that burning prostate sensation that some-times accompanies an orgasm that is followed by heavy alcohol consumption. Every three minutes I felt compelled to go to the bathroom, even though I wasn't putting out more than a few drops of urine per visit. It felt like blue flames were coming out my dick. Then I would walk back into a room that smelled so badly of funky pussy I could have done a back flip.

The rum after gin had hit me pretty hard, and although the night was fairly young, I was already seeing double. Afraid that I was going to puke, I went outside. I saw some lights about a half mile down the road and started off in that direction. A bunch of Mexicans were sitting along a curve in the road, and just before I reached them, I fell fully into a six-foot hole in the ground. The fall almost knocked me cold. I heard the Mexicans roar with laughter and I was so pissed I wanted to kill every one of them, but by the time I had managed to crawl out of the hole, I was muddy and cov-ered with sweat. When I got over to the tree where they sat, one of them passed me a bottle of wine and another passed a joint. I could see that I wasn't the only victim. Two of the men were grunts from the Seventh Marines and they had taken the fall together. "Some kind of road construction, man, and no warning signs either!"

Pretty soon we were all laughing when L.D. came strolling down the road. We hushed up and watched as L.D. took a dive. Then we roared. I was probably laughing harder than any of the rest until I could hear him curse me by name. With that I thought it would be a good idea to make myself scarce.

I teamed up with the two grunts and that was the last thing I remember until I came to in a Pasedena motel room, alone. I did not know how I got to Pasedena from Mexico. A motel manager with beefy forearms and a cigar clenched in his teeth pounded on the door and demanded money for another night. I didn't have a dime. Not only was I broke, I did not have my wallet nor my military I.D. What I had was a short afternoon to get back to Camp Pendleton. I took a quick shower, then guzzled cold water from the tap, and when I looked up in the mirror I saw a red and blue USMC bulldog tattooed on my left deltoid. Above the bulldog was the name "Shab." To this day I have no idea what it means. It's right up there with Stonehenge and Easter Island in the mystery department.

Acutely sick, I hitchhiked back to Pendleton. Two hours AWOL, I was greeted by a look of all-encompassing, universal disapproval. The First Sergeant could make you feel less popular than a burrito fart. For AWOL, I was put on report, had to undergo a series of punishments that were immediate and highly unpleasant, but in the end I suffered less, overall, than my drinking companions, most of whom acquired a case of the crabs or the clap or both. I had a black eye and the tattoo, but these guys were pulling giant red bugs from their drawers.

They were right on the cusp between being able to stand it and seeking medical aid. Gerber thought he could make it go away by taking aspirin, but just before we pulled liberty, he put a new combination lock on his footlocker and promptly lost the combination. He tried to pop the lock using an entrenching tool and after a couple of minutes of this everybody was taking turns. The lock was very durable but the footlocker was soon destroyed. Ondine told Gerber to diddybop up to supply to get a new footlocker before the First Sergeant got back. Supply was located on one of the low foothills just across from the company motor pool. When we got there Gerber gave the corporal in charge a fifth of whiskey for a new footlocker. It didn't take long before the bottle was getting passed around and I felt a wonderful sense of respite. The bunch of us had been counting the minutes until 1600 hours when we could go over to the enlisted men's club and get some hangover relief. It was a hot day at Pendleton and the sun was like a blast furnace. Felix rousted a roadrunner from a clump of brush and soon we were chasing the bird as it darted from spot to spot, zigzagging, impossible to catch. But Felix kept at it. I had never actually seen a roadrunner; it was a small drab-colored bird, and it didn't seem to have a great deal of stamina. Felix managed to ding it with a rock. He carried the bird back to the shady side of the supply shack and went to sip whiskey. The bird panted in exhaustion. Somebody said we should get a cup of water for it. The supply clerk filled an old coffee can with water and presented it to the bird, but the roadrunner wanted none of it.

Felix was itching so badly from the crabs the supply clerk made a joke about him playing with himself. Felix reached in his drawers and pulled out a crab to show to the corporal. It was a fearsome bug, out of all proportions as terrifying as the roadrunner had been unimpressive. The clerk was a southern boy and said, "You know what you do for crabs, don'cha? Just wait right here," he said. He took a coffee can and walked over to the motor pool where he had it filled with gasoline. In a moment he was back and handed the gas to Felix. "Here, pour some of this in your drawers. It will kill them right now," the clerk said. Felix did as he was told and in moments a look of relief washed over his face. About forty seconds later, he busted away from the supply shack like Superman heading for a costume change. Gerber followed him to the head and returned to tell us that Felix was sitting in a wash basin running cold water over his balls.

Gerber cracked up and did a little war dance, "Aiee aiee chi chi wawa!"

By the time Felix came back, the supply clerk was gone, and Felix was not one bit happy. He was a new guy, half bad — no one knew what he would do. Start a fight? Scream? We just didn't know. People in recon were capable of anything including mayhem and murder. Suddenly he picked up the gasoline and doused the ailing roadrunner. None of us said anything. I think we were too shocked to say anything. The bird hunkered down miserably as its eyes began to blink in rapid fashion. Next Felix pulled out a matchbook and started flicking lit matches at the bird.

Again, no one made a move to stop him. I'd like to report that we were about to do something, but the bird was pretty much written off as dead by that time. Finally Felix lit half the book and immolated the bird. His accent was pure Connecticut, completely new to me. He thumped his chest and said, "They-ya, you cocksuckah. Bo'ne to kill! Arroo-gah!" The bird hunkered down into the crouch of death. Sickened, Gerber hoisted his new footlocker on his shoulder and started down the hill back to the barracks. One by one, the rest of us followed him, each one of us alone with the guilt of our own complicity. It was exactly one week after that when we shipped out to Vietnam.

A Run through
the Jungle

WITH TWO Cobra gunships leading the way, Chief Warrant Officer Elroy rendezvoused with Second Recon at LZ Juliet Six. It was the alternative pickup zone and it was getting chewed to shit from NVA mortars until the Cobras began to lay down suppressor fire. Things on the ground had been hairy for the marines for some time. Three days previously they had blown cover and had since been experiencing something like an ongoing Chinese gangfuck thirty klicks into Cambodia. The NVA was on them like stink on shit, and if it hadn't been for the monsoons, they would have been dead on the first day. Charles had the team surrounded and was sweeping the area with tracking dogs. Fortunately the heavy rains that delayed the rescue effort also washed away the smell of the Americans. When the weather finally broke, Officer Elroy received last-minute orders to abort the mission. Headquarters maintained that radio contact had been lost and the marines were presumed dead. Elroy wasn't so sure. When the team first called for a dustoff chopper, he had been committed to go in; and no matter what the high command thought, there was no way the Americans could sneak out fast enough for Charles *not* to know that they had crossed the border in the first place. What pushed the flight commander forward was the fact that he knew he wouldn't be able to live with himself if he had left these grunts to hang out to dry. Yet he could only take this line of reasoning so far. I could see by the look on his face that Elroy was thanking his lucky stars that he was not a member of our insert team. We were packed in the back of the overloaded Huey like so many *killer* sardines with bad attitudes and a whole lot of personal firepower. Felix T., our own radio man and the tallest soldier in-country, pulled out his .45 as the orders to abort came through. Team Break on Thru was no more going to allow him to abandon Second Recon than Elroy would have done himself. It was a crass move; Elroy's courage was well known and Felix had been a cowboy from day one. His mind was locked and loaded in the gung-ho mode; jammed up on amphetamines and pulling out a side arm was a bad idea, but we all knew what he was thinking. While it was a mind fuck of an order, what we heard over the radio surprised no one. Unlike the grunts in the army, with superior logistical support and better equipment, marines were marines. We weren't used to hot meals, adequate gear, or being treated very well in the first place, but we were cranked up and ready to engage.

As soon as Elroy brought his bird down, Break on Thru hit the ground running. It was an exercise known as a "flip flop." Charles sure enough knew there was going to be an extraction, but he wasn't expecting an insertion on the same flight. Ondine and I helped the Second Recon corpsman load two wounded Montagnards onto the Huey while the rest of the Break on Thru laid out a quick perimeter. One of the 'Yards was squirting blood from his femoral artery while the other had a sucking chest wound. Both appeared to be in shock: their dark faces were ashen, and both seemed to be beyond the realm of pain. I knew they would both be dead before they got back to Da Nang and exchanged a look with their babyfaced corpsman, a kid who didn't look old enough to be in the war. Still, he looked a good deal older than the prisoner the team had grabbed on their "snatch" mission. The young NVA's hands were secured behind his back with wire, and whenever he looked up, a powerful marine poked him in the mouth with the flash supressor of his M-16. "Get used to it," the marine said. "It's called the Flavor of the Month, motherfucker."

I knew it was the first of many new exotic treats in store for the prisoner and was thinking that if it were me, I'd jump out of the bird as soon as they had some suicidal altitude. Over the wash of chopper blades, the corpsman was telling Ondine that the rest of the Second Recon ran for another LZ. "Make no mistake," the corpsman said, "Charlie has got spotters and fuckin' bloodhound dogs. You boys just bought the green wienie. Chuck is going to come looking presently."

"I can dig it," Ondine said.

"I'm glad you can," the corpsman said. "Because, *man*, I cannot. No shit, man! I'm getting too short for any more of this bullshit. I'm getting seriously flakey. I don't know if I can hack much more."

"Sounds like you got a personal problem," Ondine said.

As the chopper lifted off, Elroy gave Ondine the thumbs-up signal. The pilot banked the Huey sharply to the west and as soon as he started to gain altitude, small arms fire erupted from the treeline. The door gunner answered immediately with his .60. Break on Thru crashed through the narrow stand of elephant grass at a low crouch. As soon as we hit the treeline, we fanned out into the jungle, fading so effectively that when a company of NVA regulars diddy-moued over to the LZ sight, they ran right past us. I allowed myself a small smile of satisfaction. The flip flop had worked and getting into the bush was a whole lot like being back in the saddle again. I felt lucky. The team was luck all the way in recent weeks, and the sense of omnipotence was intoxicating. I was ready to infiltrate Hanoi, grab Uncle Ho by the goatee, pull off his face, and make a clean escape. Cambodia did not seem like a biggie in any way, shape, or form. The NVA didn't know we were there, didn't have a clue. In our tiger-striped fatigues and war paint, Break on Thru was invisible.

As soon as the enemy troopers rushed by, Ondine took the point until the team reached a fast-moving stream. He knelt down and shook a canister of CS powder along the banks to discourage dogs. As he did so, Dang Singh set an M-14 toe-popper under a pile of wet leaves and dropped a Baby Ruth bar next to it. It was pure meanness, what Singh liked to call "outchucking Charles," and across the Cambodian border where there was officially no war at all, it seemed like exactly the right thing to do.

At Ondine's signal, I picked up the point and continued moving north directly up the streambed. The team moved swiftly and silently. Eventually the stream dried out and its rocky bed converged near an NVA speed trail. I flashed an arm signal freezing the squad as three NVA soldiers toting howitzer rounds cruised past on Chinese bicycles. I could have sworn one of the slopes had eyeballed me and had been too cool to make a move. As I played with this in my head, Ondine moved forward and asked what was wrong. I told him, and Ondine resumed walking point while L. D. Pfieffer, who was covering the rear, sprinkled red pepper in our wake to foil the dogs Second Recon had been having such a shit fit over. The team picked up the pace, putting distance between ourselves and the speed trail. In another half hour we reached a bamboo thicket. There was no further hint of the enemy. Break on Thru was what you called down and happy. Ondine whispered something to the shooter, Pink, and smiled. Felix T. looked at Dang Singh. "What did the sergeant say?"

Singh looked at Felix and said, "Man say, 'Welcome to Cambodia.'" Singh removed a bottle of bug juice and squirted it on a thick leech that was attached to the side of Felix's neck. When he showed it to the tall marine, Felix recoiled in horror. Singh snapped the blood-engorged leech in half and grinned. Like Felix and the rest of the team, he was curious about the shooter, a small Chicano–Native American with an angular face and a pair of cheekbones sharper than razor blades. Pink showed up at Camp Clarke wearing Spec Five insignia and an Air Cav pink team badge just two nights before the patrol. Word circulated that Pink was a sniper from Special Operations. After Pink had lunch with the Colonel and Captain Barnes, he dumped his gear in Break on Thru's hootch, and broke out a manila envelope bearing grainy photographs of NVA Brigadier General Deng. Everyone knew about Deng — he was an unorthodox NVA strategist and major pain in the ass dating back to the battle of Dien Bien Phu. By all rights, Deng should have been in an old age home in Hanoi, not out in the field wreaking terror and mayhem. He had been *old* during the French occupation. There was no way he could still be in the field; it was supposed to be just another rumor. But then, too. You never knew. These motherfuckers didn't quit. Shit, they didn't know the meaning of the word.

Just before the mission got under way, I saw the shooter pass the pictures to Ondine. As soon as he handed them back, Pink pulled out his Zippo and torched them. Pink was giving Ondine some respect with this preview. A little r-e-s-p-e-c-t, so he doesn't come off like some FNG. I told this to Dang, who said that Captain Barnes had stonewalled Ondine, saying that the shooter had a target all right, and Ondine would be informed on a need-to-know basis. As far as Ondine was concerned, the team's main mission was cartography. Intelligence knew Charlie was running wild in Cambodia and they wanted B-52 targets. When I saw Pink burning the pictures and became part of the secret, Ondine told me to procure an M-14 from the armory. I was one of the better marksmen on the team, and if special ops thought they need to send us some lame-ass dogface for an assassination, Ondine was going to prove there was no need. Anyone on the team was up to it. Ondine was resentful that Captain Barnes had so little faith and to tell you the truth, Pink was not that impressive — he was a wiry little motherfucker, making the rest of the team look like Clydesdales in comparison. Actually, wiry wasn't such a bad condition. Ondine had been in a pisser of a mood — restless, edgy, and full of bitterness. I didn't think it mattered. I still believed that luck was with us. At least until I saw the dink on the bicycle. I was sure I locked eyeballs with the cocksucker and now felt like my luck was all used up. I was conflicted as all hell.

After we set up for the night, Ondine broke out a map and conferred with Pink in the fading light. Early the next afternoon we skirted the bunker where the snatch had been made. An hour later the team was poised on a hill overlooking a huge NVA base supply camp that was a beehive of transport and supply activity. Buried in a narrow valley, the camp was surrounded on three sides by mountains. A well-guarded single-lane road hidden by triple canopy jungle allowed truck traffic into the camp from the north, while narrow speed trails, too small for trucks or tanks, fed into I Corps to the south. Not only was the NVA able to move fresh troops and resupply into Vietnam, the base had a hospital complete with doctors, nurses, and sterile operating rooms. There were dozens of women, in fact. Undoubtedly the base served as a safe haven for the troops to R&R after excursions into I Corps. Judging by the look of relaxation on the faces of the NVA, it did not appear they had been receiving much in the way of harassment. Pink used his own binoculars to scout the surrounding valley. He marked possible target positions on Ondine's map with a red pencil. He was lining up shots at three, five, and seven hundred meters. The shot he liked best he penciled in last. It was a spot approximately one hundred meters behind the hospital. Ondine shook his head, like "no way!" Pink pointed to the heavy cloud cover and made hand signals to indicate rain and fog. We were far enough from the base to break out a high fi and have a party, but Pink was cautious to the point of paranoia. He was so quiet in fact that everyone on the team was beginning to get spooked. Not only had Ondine been acting strange, no one was overly thrilled with the fact that we were in Cambodia. Normally you could blame this sort of weirdness on the new guy, but while Pink may not have been an impressive physical specimen, he certainly had his shit together. While Ondine began to diagram a plan to provide Pink with diversionary fire, the rest of the team contented themselves passing the binoculars back and forth. We saw a pair of dog teams come into the compound followed by an NVA assault team. Felix T. nudged Ondine and said, "Look, Sergeant, those are *our* gooks!"

A few seconds later, General Deng stepped out of a fortified bunker, one that Ondine figured to be an ammo dump. "There he is," Felix said. "Goddammit, motherfucker!"

The General wore a tan uniform with no insignia but it was clearly Deng. He was a man in his early seventies. He had a full head of thinning gray hair that he wore in a sweptback fashion. His smile was warm and revealed a great deal of gold dental work. Deng walked with a limp. His left foot was shorter than his right by several inches. This was not from a war wound but rather a hereditary condition. With aides on either side of him, Deng leaned on his cane and spoke to the commander of the tracker platoon who pointed back at the jungle. L. D. Pfieffer mimicked the sort of lame excuse he imagined the platoon commander must have been reciting to General Deng, who had to be very concerned with the knowledge that the Americans were in Cambodia and had *made* their camp. You could barely see their lips moving but Pfieffer supplied the dialogue. "Oh yes man! We lit a fire under their ass, General. You betcha! Jarhead took a number one run through the jungle."

Pfieffer twisted his head to the side, screwed up his face, and took on the part of Deng. "What! You mean you let them escape! You *bungling* fools! B-52s come now. Boom Boom! Efferybody, get down and give me fifty. Very bad. Very bad."

Singh and I cracked up until Pink shot us a look and then Ondine raised his head and told Pfieffer to knock it the fuck off. Felix T. pointed his M-16 at the General and kept it trained on the officer as he moved back into the bunker. "He's a motherfuckin' ant." With a scope, the shot was doable from where we stood; it was just that we would have been pinned down on the same ridge where Second Recon had caught hell. We were out in the open.

Ondine was highly p.o.'d and said, "Put that weapon down and quit fucking around, Felix. That goes for everybody. Now listen up." He flattened out the map on a boulder. We gathered around Ondine's map. He said, "We recon the valley first, but I think we should place our shooters here and here," he said, pointing to the red Xs on the map with his forefinger. "Hollywood doesn't take his shot unless Pink is compromised. He's got the M-14, and if he shoots, he gives away his location. After Pink takes out the General, we detonate nightingales at the north end of the valley while the team runs south. That should give us time to boogaloo. Two escape routes," he said, pointing down to the valley. "Right there along the streambed or straight out of the valley on the high-speed trail. They won't be expecting it. Once we get clear, we fade into the bush, circumvent the bunker, and make our pickup. Felix calls in the coordinates on the camp and while we beat a retreat back to Camp Clarke, the carpet team comes in and levels our good buddies. They've got a lot of people down there, but we'll catch them with their pants down. It should be easy. Any questions? Sound like a plan?" Ondine said. "Okay. Break out your chow; we're going down into the valley in twenty minutes."

Dang Singh could second-guess Ondine better than anyone. "*That's* the plan?" he said.

Ondine said. "Shoot 'n' run."

"Keeping things simple," Singh said.

"I'm open to suggestions," Ondine said. "I'm always glad to hear a brighter idea. We can't make the shot from up here. We've got an ideal vantage but we're too far to make the fucking shot. I can't think of another way."

"Why don't we walk back, real careful like, and let the air force take care of General Deng?" Gerber said. "You got the coordinates. As soon as the shooting starts the gooks are going to hunker down. This is a job for the bomber pilots. Why can't the air force handle it?"

"Because that would be the smart thing to do," Ondine said. "Anybody else?"

We were quickly out of the rucks and tearing open C-rats. Everyone ate without saying much. Pink ate not at all. He took a swig from his canteen, swished it around in his mouth, and swallowed. While the marines carried three canteens each, the shooter carried only one. Also, while the marines carried the maximum amount of personal fire-power, Pink only had a single-shot bolt-action carbine. The end was tapped for a silencer and there was a scope mount on the rifle. He carried his ammunition in a single pouch on his cartridge belt. He wore a bush hat and no flak jacket. While the marines ate, he pulled a small copy of the New Testament from his pack and read a passage from the book of John. Then he spread a fresh application of greasepaint on his face. While Pink wore no dog tags, he carried eight morphine syrettes around his neck. I didn't really blame him. I had been captured once and it had been one time too many. Eight syrettes would certainly do the job.

As soon as it got dark, we slipped through the bush and infiltrated the valley with little trouble. A cold rain began to fall, and after we established a rendezvous point, Ondine went over the plan with everyone again. After Pink got his shot off, he would beat feet to the second shooter's position. That was me. I would be stationed south of the hospital where I had a clean shot at the General's quarters. Together Pink and I would double-time to the rendezvous point. The rest of the fire team would be planted back in the bushes waiting to lay down cover fire. If necessary they could run an IM drill, where each member of the team would jump out into the speed trail and fire his weapon at full automatic. As soon as a man shot off a magazine, he would run to the back of the formation, like a quarterback that had just passed off the ball to a running back. The next man would step onto the trail and shoot, followed by the next and so on. Within thirty seconds a squad could put out the concentrated firing pour of a fully armed infantry company. It invariably confused and frightened the enemy and gave the team our one chance to run. After running the drill ammunition would be essentially gone. The element of surprise would be gone, and if the rain were to stop, the dogs would be all over us.

The quickest way out of the valley was by using the same

speed trails the NVA were using to ferry supplies into Vietnam. The jungle leading out of the valley was thick, as we had already seen, and it was going to be quite a run to the LZ. If there was a major fuckup, we could take our chances in the bush. It was a bad option; it was the one Second Recon used. Ondine knew if we blew the pickup, we were in serious trouble. It wasn't like him to gamble in this fashion. There was an alternative LZ, but nobody even wanted to think about it. The Invisible Man couldn't make it to the alternative LZ.

Pink attached the sniper scope and silencer to his carbine. He removed two mesh screen devices known as nightingales from his ruck. These were simply screens wired to a web of firecrackers and cherry bombs and hooked to a detonator. Each would give off a five-minute explosion simulating the heavy weapons and M-16 fire of a full company. The rest of the team took positions along either side of the main trail and planted their claymores before huddling down in the bush establishing their fields of fire. The nightingales were covered with sheets of plastic to protect them from the rain. He gave one to me, along with a long coil of thin wire and a detonator. The rest of the team hunkered down and prepared themselves for the uncertainties of a long wait, while Pink and I slipped into the bushes, keeping away from the trails. It took several hours to get in position. I never saw a soldier more cautious than Pink. While my mind was jamming with amphetamine and the hot blood of fear, Pink was as cold as a snake.

We picked out positions and then moved north with the com wire, toward the feeder road. The trail coming down into the valley had a guard patrol and a pair of dogs, but the security was fairly lax. We set up the nightingales, camouflaging them with tent shelter halves, and then returned to our positions and spent the night in a bone-chilling rain. It was so cold I could see my own breath. My feet, ears, and fingers were numb. I wondered how a puny guy like Pink could take the cold since I had body fat and he did not. My teeth began to chatter and I was practically into hypothermic shock by dawn. I popped greenies and wolfed down Nestlé's chocolate bars. The mission was beginning to feel like some major suck. We didn't need to do this. We could walk out of the valley and let the B-52s take care of the situation. Headquarters, had they been there to see it, would have known for themselves. I guess they wanted Deng no matter what happened. He was a slippery guy, and people wanted confirmation.

A low fog clung to the camp and it didn't begin to lift until noon. I saw General Deng for a half a second, but suddenly he thought of something and returned to his bunker. I wondered what Pink was doing. There was no way of knowing if he had his shit together or not. I was determined to make the shot the next time I laid my eyes on Deng's skinny ass. I wanted to get out of that place before I froze to death.

At 1530 hours a truck carrying rockets rumbled into the camp and a number of people emerged from the bunker to inspect it. Finally, General Deng came hobbling out of the headquarters. The sight of the rockets seemed to give him a great deal of pleasure. As his face cracked into a wedge of a smile, a glimmer of sunlight reflected off of the General's gold bridgework. I drew a bead on his narrow chest and waited. Suddenly the General took a half-step back on his short leg and then dropped without a sound. The NVA aides standing with the General were busy inspecting the rockets. Deng collapsed of old age. One of the aides knelt down to lift the General's head when he saw that most of it was gone. The aides scurried, and in seconds a warning siren went off. I knew that in moments the woods would be crawling with NVA. But then came the sound of the nightingales exploding to the north of the transport truck. It sounded like a small war was coming down into the valley, and the NVA did just what anyone would reasonably do. They hunkered down before their guns and poured out a "mad moment" in the direction of the nightingales. By luck, a loose rpg round hit the truck, setting off an explosion that rocked the earth. By this time Pink and I were highballing down the speed trail. A two-man NVA security team stepped out of a small grass duty hut, but our machine gunner, Pfieffer, cut them both down with short bursts from his .60. I hated the fact that he was making noise, but it had to happen. More NVA began to appear, but the team was all up and moving now. In a moment a series of small explosions was heard as the claymores the team had planted were tripped. As we continued to run we heard the anguished squeals and high-pitched bellowing of dogs along with the more familiar cries of grievously wounded men.

Pink was ahead of me running alongside a pair of unarmed NVA who had just dropped a container of rice. Both of the men wore thick tortoiseshell spectacles and were clearly noncombatants. I watched the three run in unison for a second, then, in spite of my heavy gear, broke past them like a man hell-bent on the finish line. A few seconds later both of the dinks passed me with a look of terror on their faces. Motherfuckers looked like dinks with Down's syndrome. As they increased their lead, Pink raised his carbine and placed two rounds into the base of each man's skull. It was the best kind of one-handed "John Wayne" shooting I had yet to see.

Then Ondine was up running alongside me, laughing his ass off. "Man, what kind of stupid-ass shit was that?"

"They were unarmed," I said, panting for breath. "It didn't seem right."

"Tell me the last time Charles cut you a line of slack," Ondine said.

"Tell me the last time Captain Barnes cut us any," I said. "Everybody in the for-shit country is out to fuck us, Ondine. I mean fucking everyone."

"Tell me about it," Ondine said.

In moments the team gathered at the streambed that led back to our primary LZ. Everyone was accounted for except for Felix. The sound of small arms fire from behind began to pick up. Suddenly Felix T., with his long stride, came galloping down the rocky creekbed. In addition to his rifle and gear, he was packing a PRC-25 radio and two bandoliers of .60 ammo. As he passed by, Ondine began to laugh hysterically again. I said, "Christ, Ondine, what's so goddamn funny?"

Ondine was hysterical, which wasn't like him. I wondered if Ondine was going to maintain or not. He was pointing at Felix. "Yeah," I said, "the retard Olympics. It's a regular side-splitter."

Up ahead Felix slipped on a mossy rock and went sliding down the wet rocky bed. He looked like a man trying to make a hook slide into home plate. Suddenly there was a flat, muffled explosion and Felix T. gave out a sharp piercing scream. A white phosphorus grenade attached to his web gear had become unpinned as he fell. By the time Ondine and I reached him, he was holding on to his chest. Blood was spurting from his uniform. Ondine pulled his shirt back. "Lung," he said.

"I'm fuckin' burnin' up," Felix said through gritted teeth. The white phosphorus continued to burn within his flesh. Ondine looked him over, not knowing where to start. Felix was covered with holes. He cried, "Burnin' up, *do* something! Get me a fuckin' medic, Jesus!"

I pressed my field dressing against Felix's chest but all that did was send a gusher of blood from his nose and mouth. Felix's teeth began to chatter and in another moment he was dead. He was truly lucky. It was over in less than three minutes.

Ondine wasn't laughing anymore. He stripped the radio off Felix and handed it to me. "This is yours," he said as he hoisted Felix over his shoulders.

"You aren't going to try to carry him all by yourself?" I said.

Ondine said, "Greenie power," and his black eyes flashed amphetamine. He took a few steps down the creek before he stopped and dropped the body and frantically began brushing burning pieces of phosphorus from his shoulders. Singh and Gerber caught up and without saying a word helped carry Felix's large lanky body forward. Overhead we could hear the sound of Cobra gunships and in the clearing ahead I spotted smoke grenades in the LZ. Pink and L. D. Pfieffer came back to help with the body. We got into the slicks in a hurry remembering how Charles had locked in on Second Recon's pickup zone with mortars. Everyone braced to receive enemy fire but in moments the slicks were airborne and headed back to Camp Clarke. Singh turned to Pink and in a necessarily loud voice said, "Did you make the shot?"

Pink, the diminutive speaker, raised his voice in a shout

to be heard over the helicopter noise. "It was a perfect shot. One of the best I ever made."

"All right!" Singh said. Relief was written all over his face. His expression spoke volumes for the adrenaline euphoria of war. Once the perils of a situation have been escaped, the good times roll. It's a lot like hitting yourself over the head with a hammer. It really feels good when you stop, and beyond that there's no point or moral lesson to be learned whatever. Singh was Mr. Happyface. I suppose I was, too.

"Sorry about your man, Tall Paul. What happened?" Pink said.

"Felix liked to keep the pins on his grenades straight," Ondine said. "Like fuckin' John Wayne. Well, take heed. The cat rolled a willy peter."

"Jesus," Pink said.

"Uh huh!" Pfieffer said. "You remember that bird he torched back at Pendleton? That fucking roadrunner?"

"I *do*. That was some sick shit," Gerber said. "A low deed."

"Well, that's all I'm saying, man," Pfieffer said. "What goes around, comes around!"

"Man!" I said. "Don't start with that! One doesn't lead to another, like that. It just doesn't work that way."

Pfieffer looked back at me with a wide grin on his face. "I can't fucking hear you, man. What did you say?"

I didn't want L.D. inadvertently inflicting "boonie voodoo" upon the team by establishing prophecies, or a train of thought that made such prophecies seem logical. But I didn't have the strength to shout over all of the helicopter noise. I looked down at my hands, which were sticky with Felix's blood. My rough palms were blackened like charcoal from white phosphorus burns. They were little black bore holes,

the very opposite of white. Beyond those I had to thank God
that I made it through another mission without suffering
great physical harm. I cared not at all for Felix, never had —
and who could the stupid fuck blame except himself? Had
it been anyone else, it would have bothered me. I watched
smoke coming from the little bore holes in my hands. Adrenaline aside, they really did hurt, but it was the sort of hurt that
almost felt good. Christ! I was alive. Soon I would be guzzling
beer and smoking reefer. Maybe Barnes would give us five
days of out-of-country R&R. Bora Bora was supposed to be
very good. I could feel the smile muscles begin to activate but
couldn't help but wonder if Pfieffer wasn't right with his
boonie voodoo theory. Maybe Felix T. had hexed us when he
torched that fucking bird back at Pendleton. For all the
smiles, something felt wrong, and we all knew it and felt guilty
for not stopping him when he set the goddamn thing on fire.
I pulled a small jar of Vaseline from the medical ruck and
used it to cut off the oxygen supply to the white phosphorus
burns on my hands. As soon as the rest of the team saw the
Vaseline, they begged for me to pass the jar around. I wasn't
the only one suffering from internal combustion. Wisps of
rancid smoke were steaming from little pinpoint vent holes
off of just about everybody.

Fields of Purple
Forever

I LIKE TO RUB DOWN with some of Mother Wenzel's
Body Lanolin before my little forays into the deep
ocean seas. Slather it on extra in the armpits and the
crease of the neck — these being the stretches of skin which
can get raw on a long swim. Then lay on a top coat of
VapoRub just like you icing a devil's food cake (why, good-
ness me, how *apropos!*). Vicks is an ace of a shark repellent.
Makes ya feel tingly all over. Just like a big ol' sunflower is
gonna come popping straight outcha ass.

Ain't much of a thing with sharks in the Channel anymore, but the Vicks has come to be a habit. Sharks — they
fished them out. Probably ain't but four hundred great
whites of high caliber in all the Atlantic. Blame commerce.
Shark-fin soup is going for a hundred a bowl in Red China.
Things be changin' over there. They makin' money. I seen
how they do. Stroll along the Great Wall and some smiling
little zip will pop out of his Mercedes and sell ya Dixie cup

of shark fin — wants seventy-five in green. Soup more cost-lier than heroin. It ain't nothing for the Chinese merchant class to blow a hundred on a bowl of shark fin or lay out a grand for a scoff of rhino horn, then go home 'n' get laid. Can't figure their need for aphrodisiac. Already enough high-rises in East Asia to reach the moon, or sink them places in the ocean, wreaking vast devastation on a world-wide scale, knock out a monster-ass tidal wave an' convert Great Falls, Montana, into a seaport town. The whole world be doing the same thing. World got a serious case of fuck on the brain.

Your Chinese peasant class don't use a lot of electricity, gas, oil, or your basic services. Seen that in Vietnam. One Ray-O-Vac twelve-volt to power all of Ho Chi Minh City. I ap-preciate the fact they don't waste electricity. That's one good thing. But it's too late, the ecosystem is done for. Might as well take a flying fuck at the moon than straighten out that mess. If it just hang together until I die, then fine. What do Ondine care? He hates hisself. I ain't even going to blame my pessimism on the war. I tell it straight. Ain't no ra-tionalize.

Back in the Nam, Hollywood say, "'A rose is a rose is a rose,' but what's a *rhinocer-rose?*" He said that on his third day in-country and repeated it on a daily basis for two solid tours. Morning, noon, and night he say it, and the next day — repeat as above. Out on the line, you hear the grunts say, "I'm so fucking short I could parachute off a dime," or "I'm so short I got to stand on a chair to kick an ant's ass." Hear that shit a million times, or: "There it is." That one good for twenty million.

Newbie come along and say, "There *what* is?" By and by,

along about the third firefight, he be saying, "There it is . . . ," and he know what *it* is. Wished he *didn't* know, but he *know*.

That's what a ground-pounder would say out there on the line. Hollywood was a nervous individual, drank a lot of coffee and talk all kind of jive shit, mainly piss and moan. Complain about the rain in Spain and he ain't never been there. Bitch for days on end. "Hey, Ondine. Tell the CO to requisition a camel. I fucking *need* one! I'm sick of humping this goddamn radio, this goddamn flak jacket, fucking .60 ammunition, medic ruck — I'm sick of *all* this fucking bullshit. I got this sudden craving to hear string quartets and practice madrigal singing. The Marine Corps just isn't *me* anymore."

"I'll tell the Captain Barnes you said that."

Gerber get a smirk on his baby face and say, "What you gon' call this camel of yours, Hollywood?"

"Dave, fuck, I'm going to name him Dave."

"Good biblical name," Singh say, "David."

"Would Dave be a one-humper or a two?" Gerber say.

"A Bactrian camel habitates like, Mongolia. Like some kind of fuckin' yak, man. Dave gon' be a one-humper. A real mean, bad-breath Arabian sumbitch. Pack him up and ship him out. I am feelin' bad for Dave already. A camel can hack a dry heat, but he can't hack this humid, immersion-foot, gook-fuck, rot-you-pooty-ass heat. I mean why do you think they *haven't* got them here already?"

Dang Singh laugh and say, "You go too far, man! Sunny Vietnam. Great place."

"The only thing *great* about Vietnam is my suffering. I can't take *hot*. When I get out, I am going to go to fucking

Green*land.* I'm in the Green Motherfucker already. I guess that makes me a citizen."

Jack Jensen get serious. "Then why did you re-up, motherfucker? Just to get five days of pussy in Sin City? You love this place."

The pressure often too much for anyone to bear. Hollywood like run his mouth with this kind of shit. Jack his jaws, an' blow it out. I say, "You better lighten up. Square your shit away, man. You act like we in a *war zone* or something. Smell the rhinocer-roses, brother. Pacify."

Rhinocer-rose, he say it morning, noon, and night. It was far worse than some foolish song played on your radio: "Cherish," say, or "I Got You, Babe."

Shoulda seen the inspector at English customs on my last trip to G.B. When Ondine flipped open the Samsonite, he say, "Wot's this lot, then?"

"Ma deuxième peau, mon copain."

He look at my passport, then look at me like, can this be true? "It appears we have one very large jar of —"

"Ain't illegal to haul around a buncha grease, is it?"

He open up a jar of Vicks and take a whiff. "Well, then, too right. You must catch a lot of colds."

"Hardly ev'r do, su'h. On certain occasions, I just choose to inflect a little glide into my stride. I like feeling lubricious."

"Hmmm! Very well. What's the purpose of your visit to London, then, Mr. Ondine? Business, pleasure, or inpatient psychiatric treatment?"

I say, "Surf 'n' turf."

He check out my swimming mask like he's lookin' for a heroin compartment. "I see, vacation. Going to Brighton?"

"Belay that, I am going where many venture and but few return. I am your labor of Sisyphus, daddy. Carry the weight of the whole world. I hold it all together, me personally. Call me Atlas, if you will. When I drop the ball, it be over. You look like a perspicacious gentleman. Tell me this. If a rose is a rose is a rose, what's a rhinocer-rose?"

Inspector's eyes poppin' out now. I say it again, "What is a rhinocer-rose?"

"Hmmm. Well . . . hmmm."

Start workin' on his false teeth like he going into a trance. Forget he's on the case. Just stand there looking stupid.

I say, "Twenty-seven years it's been weighing on my brain and I could just about burst."

That customs agent snap out of his spell and says, "Slide the bloody heck out of here, mate? You are creating a queue."

I like to give my white brethren wide latitude, figure they needin' some, but even Ondine has limits. Ondine laugh. "You're a pretty cheeky fella, ain'cha? Wipe that sarcasm from your voice. A less secure individual than myself could take offense at your very tone and cause you grievous bodily harm."

The Channel crossing in August fantabulates. On 29 July 1978, Penny Dean made the fastest crossing on record. She swam from Shakespeare Beach, in Dover, to Cape Gris-Nez, France, in seven hours and forty minutes. Matthew Webb, a merchant navy captain, was the first to do it — 25 August 1875; it's twenty-one miles from Dover to Calais Sands, but due to the currents, Captain Webb swam thirty-eight miles with an elapsed time of twenty-one hours and forty-five minutes. He became a hero for all of that, and later, when his health was broke an' his fortunes spent, ol' Matthew drowned trying to swim the gorge under Niagara Falls. It was a last attempt to recapture his fading glory and win a $10,000 fee. Eighty'd ventured before Matthew and not one returned. Matthew was your eighty-one. I swam the gorge in the morning and found it so easy I did a repeat at noon, but I was in heyday condition.

Jean-Marie Saletti, a French prisoner, jumped off a British prison hulk at Dover and swam to freedom in Boulogne in August 1815. If the currents are predictable and nothing untoward happens, shore to shore go for eleven hours. The water is cold. When I was in prime form, I left Shakespeare Beach and made Cape Gris-Nez in just under ten hours — did the return trip in twelve, maybe thirteen.

Like the prisoner, Jean-Marie Saletti, I swim alone. The primordial condition. Before we was monkeys in a tree, we come from the sea, and all the seas are different. There are hot ones and cold. Some rock, and some do roll, each and everyone got their own share of soul. Unique characteristics and properties. The salt concentration in the Black Sea most closely matches up to the human body. To just dip into it makes you high, and it ain't really black. I'm the one's black — blacker than Alexander Graham Bell's first telephone. So black, I'm blue. Soul blue, like the deep sea. Ondine gots more *soul* than one mortal can con-*trol*.

The English Channel is the ocean swim by which all others are measured. Get that over with and Ondine will travel down to Spain and swim the Straits of Gibraltar, they being in the neighborhood. Lots of Gypsy camps along the coast of Spain and it's a good place to lay with women if your tastes run to the exotic.

Gibraltar is my most favorite swim and one of the few I do in the light of day. When the weather is clear, you can see the Mediterranean Sea meet with the Atlantic Ocean like two great souls coming together. A really grand liquefaction. Like yin merging with yang — in two very different shades of blue. Shimmers at you, like a living room picture of *Blue Boy*. They say Gainsborough's model was himself just a peasant. Ain't it grand the way he standing there, all regal and high on himself? He don't hate himself. Looks like he owns the whole damn world. In your life on the dry land, you do *this*, you do *that*, you read your lines, act out your part. You're walking around among people, intervolved, talking to them, go about business. You wonder what do they *want* from you? What do you *want* from them? Not just commerce. Not just food and shelter. Don't look like it when you talk with them but you know that they go home and make love, live their lives. They got their own private schemes. But what do they want? Why is it they falsify to you, and why is it you falsify back? You got to do it, I know it. One day they might whip out a guitar and sing, "We are children of the world," and then when they can't think of nothing better, they start fighting each other. Hard to sort things out. Peoples are half devil. Three-quarters. I live among them, but I don't have the first clue.

Gibraltar: At certain times, before they merge, the edges twixt your Atlantic and Mediterranean are so sharp and demarcated, Ondine can swim the very line half 'n' half. He can taste the differences in salt depending on which side he breathin' from. One side might even rise up three and four inches and measure an altogether different temperature than ta' other. From the ocean thermals, currents; I don't know why exactly. There's no need for a compass even. White clouds drift above you and the sun, all yellow, comes cutting down through them, pink turning to purple, and I remember the Nam and how I could see the Purple Fields when we had it all down. Thought and action one and the same. The universal energy exchange belonged to us. In fields of purple, there was no one and nothing that could stop fire team Break on Thru. It was my honor to serve.

Gibraltar: Beach anywhere near Tangiers harbor and your black ass going to jail. I got a Moroccan lawyer on retainer for that very eventuality. The man is a' ace. He say, "Hobba jigga bobba," and Ondine can go.

Last time I swam Gibraltar, I encountered a group of migrating tortoises and got to know them well. There was James Brown, the Godfather *Tortue*, Doctor John, Smokey Robinson Turtle. Jimi Turtle with his electric guitar singing, *I'm a voodoo chile* and more. Who was that Mafia cat, the Big Tuna? I believe I see him. The seas are spooky. The Dead Sea, she's a bad one. The San Francisco Bay is cold and turbulate, with wicked riptides, but the sharks there, they won't kill you. That's just another falsify. You drown and the shark might eat you. Or maybe a big one will blow in off course from somewhere and bite somebody by accident. But the homeboys, they're just scavengers. Warden told the convicts in Alcatraz otherwise. For them Jaws owned the Bay. Forget a' escape attempt, he say, they *will* get you, when they really *won't*, because it's all falsify. I know these things. I know lots of things. All alone in the sea: Ondine. Daryl Hannah in her mermaid costume, when I get tired enough and discouraged, I see her too. She's a product of my mind, like a mirage in the desert.

I see Hollywood running back to the crashed 'n' burn air force C-4 cargo plane, dragging me out of the wreckage and packing my black ass off and up a hill somewhere over yonder before the plane went up in flames.

That C-4 pilot had his fair share of nerve. It took nerve to fly into Khe Sanh during the siege. Since Break on Thru was purely recon and much in need elsewheres, we figured we was lucky to get orders out — but that was a bad day, and a bad plane ride. An NVA rocket tore off the right wing just after we cleared the airstrip. I heard the pilot call in his Mayday. He managed to land the plane on the side of a mountain no more than two miles from the base. Crashed so hard every tooth in my head rattled. By the time I worked my way up to the cockpit, the pilot had bled out from wounds sustained. The copilot got hit with a piece of shrapnel that lopped his head off like a cabbage. Everything was a mess up there. The air force crew chief was bleeding bad, too, but he and Jack Jensen managed to help Gerber and Dang Singh off the plane. Singh had a busted back, yet in a life-and-death affair like that, he was nimble out of the sheer force of will. Ondine too. He's walking through the plane on two busted feet by holding on to things. Hollywood grab his pack, rifle, and a couple of bandoliers of .60 ammo. He hoist Ondine on his back and run for the high ground. I can still hear his boots scraping through the red dirt, hear him breathe.

Hollywood went back and drug Gerber up the hill next. Slap his face a couple times for a wake-up call. Gerber clear his head, set up his machine gun, tripod, and then lock and load.

The air force crew chief was hanging back in the cockpit trying to make radio contact. When the fuel tanks in the remaining wing blew, he came runnin' out the cabin. A second later, he ignited into a greasy ball of black-and-red flame. The man's hair burn like straw and the fire pour out of his mouth like a flame swallower in a carnival. Ol' boy managed about fifteen steps before he pulled out a snub-nose .38, shoved it in his mouth, and said good-bye to Broadway, "It been a charmer, but I got to go."

While Gerber sat at the ready with the .60, Hollywood yanked my boots off — fractures in both ankles. Hollywood popped me with painkiller and I just kept thinking of what he said on his third day in-country, "What's a rhinocer-rose?"

We had gooks all over. It weren't the NVA coming after us, but villagers with single-shot Chinese rifles and pitch-forks. Like them highly pissed-off citizens in *Bride of Frank-enstein*. Give the poor monster a hard time. First he has women troubles — a harsh rejection she give him: "Even for a monster, you are *ugly!*" — they haul him off on a slab and chain his ass to the jailhouse wall. Burned him with torches. Monster pro'ly thinking, "When this evil day gonna end? Never. Pro'ly never. It just go on forever."

Them village people, Gerber cooled their action with his .60. We had the high ground but had to conserve ammunition. They was so many of 'em, an' they just kept on coming. All over gooks. When we seen they was circling around I ordered the team to fade into the jungle and leave me lay.

Catch ya later. No sense everybody gets dusted. But they don't want to leave me, so I stuck my .45 'longside of my head and said, "Make it. Move out, or I'll do the job right here!"

I LIKE TO TAKE IN the theater whenever I travel to London town. Place gets seedier by the year. Things be going down all over. But I'm your dandy boy in London town. A sportin' man. Already told you I'm a big black bastard. I got a shaved head, a gold tooth, and a black derby hat from Savile Row. I use my cane like a walking stick. Can't walk much with these ankles. Just enough to get around. I enjoy the theatrical performances and especially enjoy taking in a light opera. *The Threepenny Opera* is surefire pleasure — *The shark has pretty teeth, dear, an' he shows them pearly white.* Ondine a night swimmer and he *all over* the night. Captain of the night. I swim in the fields of purple. Nothing and no one can harm me, or take me out.

This one time a tiger shark bumped up under my leg — removed a stretch of hide like a power-belt sander. Left a wake like a ballistic submarine. Rubbed me the *wrong* way? You could say so, but he come back and say he's sorry. He know he better apologize. He know I had a pass and the Magic Universe will get him if he don't honor Ondine. That's how it is. That's some shit you just don't violate.

You see all kinds when the moon and stars are out. Once, about two in the morning, I seen a sorry pack of Cubans swimming to Key West. Least that's what *they* thought. *"Izquierda, hombres! Izquierda!* Hang a left if you know what's good for ya." Those boys didn't look too hot. I was gonna tell them to tighten up their formation, but I could see they weren't gonna make it, and I didn't want to discourage them any further.

Lord Byron, with his contracted Achilles, swimming the Hellespont? Much is made of this feat of which George was quite proud. I can only laugh. The strait between Sestos and Abydos is less than a mile wide. Currents ain't nothing special, either.

Beowulf took a five-day swim and some nasty sea monsters drug him down on the bottom. Took the cat deep down. But Beowulf kicked some ass and killed seven of them motherhumpers, trucks off to Lapland for a little R&R. After that caper, he gots to rest. Wait for the waters to clear.

The Spartans of ancient Greece used to chop holes in icy rivers and jump right on in to toughen up. Them Japanese samurai did much the same. Converted swimming from a leisure activity into a military art.

I swim the Yarra River in Australia. That's where Jack Johnson knocked out Tommy Burns and became the first black man to win the heavyweight title. Later Jack London got racial and wrote that Jim Jeffries would wipe that gold-tooth smile off Li'l Artha's face. A few days after Johnson knocked out ol' Jeff, Jeffries told it straight. Said he could not have beat Johnson on the best day of his life. Beginning of black pride was Li'l Artha. The public beginning.

I swim all the rivers. You ever hear of a brother swim the way I can do? I'm your Jack Johnson of the deep. The body is heavier in fresh water. You can train in a river and then when you plunge into the salty sea, you a lightweight. Edgar Allan Poe was a good river swimmer. After his swim up the James River, he said, it "outstrips the normal bounds of possibility." I swim a river to train, but I prefer the open ocean. The colder the better. Take your Bering Strait.

Forty-two degrees on a warm day. Ice floating all about you. Twenty-foot swells and winds blowing foam off the top of the breakers creating your Queen Anne's lace. It's all but impossible to see. I'm almost tempted to wear a wet suit and give it a try. Float on my back and navigate off Venus or find the North Star by lining up the last two stars on the Big Dipper. When you do that, you know precisely where you are in the universe. Swim to your heart's delight.

> *Ol' King Cole was a merry ol' soul,*
> *An' a merry ol' soul was he;*
> *He called for his pipe and called for his bowl*
> *And he called for his fiddlers three.*

Get the rhythm going. Establish your stroke. Even a swim of a hundred miles begin with the first stroke. Just like fucking. Precisely like fucking. Think about the Nam.

> *GI beans and GI gravy,*
> *Gee, I wish I joined the navy . . .*
> *Hup, two, three four . . . your left.*

Find the cosmic rhythm. Get a little high. Ain' this what motivates all human endeavor, the desire to get high? I find my cosmic rhythm in the Australian crawl. And I does get high. After the adrenaline of Vietnam, a six-pack and a night of TV viewing just don' cut it.

> *A rose is a rose is a rose, but*
> *what is a rhinocer-rose?*

BACK IN THE BUSHES, Gerber wasted a lot of ammunition layin' down cover fire trying to save my ass. Like he weren't worried about his own. I figured to be dead with them busted feet, but Gerber was my buddy. That's why he didn't care for hisself. Ondine is laying there. His *main* is down. He was gonna stand up for me, die if he had to. Do whatever it took to get the motherfucking job done, Jim. We was all that way.

When Charles got me, I was puking up from morphine. When you high, even to vomit can be fun. Because of my ankles, I could not walk, so the villagers forced me to crawl two kilometers on my hands an' knees through a monsoon rain to their nasty-ass village. For-shit village. Already they got Singh, who was hurting real bad with his back. Them gooks be smacking us around pretty good. Till they scuffed up their knuckles an' tired out. Two nights later a' NVA officer shows up at the tiger cage speakin' the King's English. He had his troops carry us north on stretchers. Saved us from the villagers. Them village folk was nothing but ruffians, doncha know. Their manners was bad.

Hollywood, Gerber, and Jack Jensen tracked us through the jungle. Called in our location. A deuce of USMC Phantoms buzzed the patrol to create fear and confusion on the ground. Gerber come out of the bushes, opens up with the .60 until the rest of Second Recon dropped in. Had a gunship along and put out some major firepower. I figured to be dead. I didn't think the shooting would ever stop. I figured we was just gone.

While the ground troops hacked out an LZ, I saw the educated NVA officer was bleeding from his legs. I sit next to him while Hollywood cranked tourniquets around the man's legs and look at me like, no way, they ain't no room on the birds for prisoners, 'specially dying ones. Hollywood slip me a .45 and I passed the man a cigarette. He weren't stupid. He is saying he is a human and I am a human. He said America was persecuting my race as we spoke. I said I ain't even getting into that. This was *it*, that's all. I told him that this here was *it*. Be a man. Go the way of the Tao, motherfucker. I believed him when he said he wouldn't hurt no living thing again, and I killed him anyhow. It made me feel good. I did it just for mean.

I was not alone in this. I believed I was the meanest motherhumper in all of Vietnam. I was not there to dispense mercy or cut nobody no slack. Swift, silent, deadly. But, that was then. Seemed to make sense at the time. I didn't wake up one day and say, "I want to go out and murder people. Rape people." What I done made me feel bad. I could tell you I was programmed by lies, but that isn't altogether true. Something evil was in me, and the devil was glad I did what I would do. He didn't even whisper encouragement. I thought it up on my own. How and when I went bad, I still haven't figured out. One day I didn't like to see people get hurt, and then one day I did. I done lots of bad things, real bad things. And I have got to live with myself. And that is now. Simple has turned into confused.

Dang Singh started a chain of convenience stores in the L.A. area. The man now has a Mercedes 450 SEL, a swimming pool, and a 5,000-square-foot house with central air. Got him a cleaning woman and a white woman cook. His kids go to fancy schools in the East, and he supporting eighty relatives in Calcutta. His sense of humor took a serious plunge. Can't even work it no more. Tries to. He tells me, "Ondine, you know, they say *'The best things in life is free. You can keep them for the birds and bees. Now give me money!'"*

You get just what you want in this life, and Singh got his money. What it don't *buy* Singh can't *use*. Can't say that I envy the man. Three operations and he still got the back trouble. Eats aspirin like candy then puts away a couple bottles of Pepto-Bismol a day to cover his ulcer. That's what he got to do to keep the show rollin'. Singh looks like Daffy Duck after a dynamite explosion. Smoke's coming out of his ears, eyes be twirling around like red and yellow pinwheels, the top of his skull is bulging, and he down to one black feather. One motherfucking feather.

These swims of mine keep getting more and more rambunctious. They are true adventures of a righteous man. Mark it down that a brother can do. Jack Johnson of the high sea.

Hamlet's dad, they killed him violent, and he went to ghost. *I am thy father's spirit; doom'd for a certain term to walk the night, and for the day confined to fast in fires, till the foul crimes done in my days of nature are burnt and purged away.* Belay that. *Swim* the night.

I wish Hollywood would have left me to die. Could have blowed with the plane or shot myself, but then I didn't — three hits of morphine gave me hope. A fourth pop might have given me the answer to this whole deal, why we just puppets in the big show with no idea of the whole picture; if there is one. I do believe there is. I am not the fool I sound. I read books. I know things I can't express. Serious things.

A U.S. Marine will save his brother whether he wanting saved or no. You want somebody to bring you out, dial Second Recon: "Swift, silent and deadly!"

Located in the Yellow Pages.

Start the big swims around midnight. I like getting down to the beach and have it all for my own. Take a minute to think things out, check out my gear. Strip off my clothes under a full moon, and be feeling so good I want to howl. Sometimes I do. I rub tobacco juice in my mask so she don't fog up. Go over the plan one last time and then I get right on it. Grease up and go. When you top off with a layer of Vicks VapoRub, you get to feeling tingly all over. Right dandy, doncha know? Just like a big ol' sunflower is gonna come popping straight outcha ass.

40,
Still at Home

THE GREEN ROOM would never make the pages of *Better Homes & Gardens*. The carpet was old pea green shag. Originally, it matched the green velvet cover of the springworn Slumber King, but somewhere during the Jimmy Carter administration the velvet dyes had broken down. Now, the bedcover, canopy, and the two sets of heavy green velvet drapes had lightened to a garish shade of lime. The room's textures and color schemes were a fright, like the marriage of Transylvania and Graceland. Margo Billis could no longer bear looking at it. The plan had been to renovate this atrocity as she had done with the rest of the house, but that had been B.C., before the cancer. The future seemed worthwhile. No longer was this so.

Yet it was Matthew, her son, who seemed to be the one dying. One Sunday evening after he had logged in twelve-plus hours of continuous sleep, anger forced her across the threshold into his hovel of a room. Matthew twisted his pale round face away from the blue light of the television, arched an eyebrow, and like a demented Charlie Brown, he said, "What are you doing?"

Margo jerked back. Her son's movement's, in the ghostly light of the TV, looked sickeningly macabre — the combination of a cartoon and a ventriloquist's dummy act; the Rod Serling version of "Peanuts."

She regained her composure and said, "What does it look like? What do I ever do, except pick up after you?" Her voice was hoarse and she had to sag to one knee as she hacked off a series of painful dry coughs. To Matthew's tender sensibilities it seemed that a crew of Northwest lumberjacks were ripping through California redwoods with seven-horsepower Husquauar chain saws. He knew that if she didn't leave soon, he would awaken fully, long before his body rhythm was prepared for anything so hideous as consciousness. His mother continued to cough with one hand poised on her very tender lower back. The last thing she needed to do was throw out her back.

Finally Matthew effected a sit-up and turned on her, "God*damm*it! Do you always, *without fail,* have to come crashing in here like some deranged fiend when I'm trying to sleep?"

A back spasm stabbed Mrs. Billis and she was seized by a cramp in her foot. She had to hobble upright so she could put bearing weight on the foot. The doctor told her the cramps had to do with a potassium imbalance or something. And the back pain! She thought that with all the morphine she was taking it was unfair that she would suffer back pain or any pain at all! The foot cramp eased but she took a few tentative steps to be sure. "*All* you do is sleep," she said.

Sensing weakness, Matthew boomed, "Baloney! I've been sending out résumés and you *know* it." His round cartoon mouth twisted into an "O" of hatred as he spit out these last words. Leonardo couldn't have drawn a more perfect circle than those formed by Matthew's pale lips.

Margo made three attempts to clear her throat before she said, "If you think sending out résumés is going to get you anywhere, *buster* — you're crazy. *No*body reads them. When are you going to get a job, dammit? I've totally had it with you." She brought her fist to her mouth and coughed.

Matthew's moon face sunk back on the pillow as he raised an arm and clawed at the air helplessly. "Oh, God! Stop with that coughing, will you, please? Use your inhaler or something." His anger quickly dissolved into a vapid puddle of self-pity and he spoke in a gasping whisper, "Just quit *torturing* me. I've got endogenous depression. If I don't sleep, I'll be dead by Friday."

Matthew's room was cold, and Mrs. Billis huddled in her red terry cloth robe, drawing it closed tightly against her neck. "Everybody's got depression," she said. "It's part and parcel of the human condition."

These words aroused Matthew's general sense of contempt for the world. He said, "No, they don't. Not like *mine*. People get a mild case of the blues and brag about taking Prozac or Saint-John's-Wort, but they're lightweights. They go to work, they do things. My case is worse than anything to precede it in the annals of recorded medicine." Prematurely awake, and wracked with exhaustion from head to heel, Matthew let his arm flop along the side of the Slumber King, producing a visible little puff of dust before the raybeam coming from his television. Matthew's speech had given his vocal cords too much of a workout and now his throat was raw. If he was in for another bout of strep, he decided he would just kill himself now and be done with it. He was utterly without codeine and couldn't face a sore throat without narcotics. A strep sore throat was akin to having your tonsils out by the Inquisition's ace torturing squad — red-hot irons and pincers and a holy relish for their gruesome duties.

Mrs. Billis said, "You *talk* depression, but it's just a game with you. People who are really depressed kill themselves. Suicide has never even crossed your mind; all you want is the life of Riley!"

Matthew rolled his head in his pillow and said, "I'm too depressed to kill myself. Jesus! Everybody knows that you can get too low to commit the deed! When I get better, I'm going to for sure," he said. "Mark my words! I'm getting off Zoloft and getting back on Nardil just to that end. I have to go two weeks cold turkey because you can't mix conventional antidepressants with MOA inhibitors. When I make some therapeutic progress, then I'll really be dangerous. In the meantime, if you have the least shred of feeling or compassion, leave me alone to lie here and wallow in my misery and self-loathing . . . please, oh God, make her go. If I'm getting strep again, just shoot me. Fuck!"

"Knock it off with that crap," Mrs. Billis said. "Get your ass out of bed, get a job, and go out and find yourself some cute girl! You are your own worst enemy, and mine, too! Lying in bed isn't going to solve anything. Look at me, I've got cancer and I'm not crying the blues. I'm seventy-three and I still get up and work like a dog!"

Matthew felt he might weep. Surely he was having a nervous breakdown. He said, "Why do you always have to come

busting in here with tough guy tactics when I'm ready for
shock treatments? Do you time my cycles and plan on coming at the worst possible moment? You don't know what *hell*
looking for work can be. Capitalism is the worst evil ever de-
vised by man. Hustle, hustle, hustle until you can't go on. I
can't do it anymore. I can't hack it out there in middle-
management hell. If you only knew how heartless those bastards are now. In your day people were still human. I'm
telling you, it's criminal and no one will stop them!"

Margo Billis barked off several shallow coughs. Her relationship with her son had come down to little more than
late-night arguments. Mornings, daylight hours weren't so
bad, but the nights were killers. When she could no longer
control the anxiety over her impending fate, she would
burst into his room on any pretext. "Be glad you aren't living in a car," she said. "Be glad you aren't trying to cut it in
North Korea with beriberi and a tablespoon of rice per day."

Matthew's throat was aflame. He pitched his voice higher
to work an unused portion of his larynx and Margo recoiled.
He sounded perversely like Mickey Mouse. Helium-voiced,
this cartoon son tossed out his hand and said, "Depression is
worst than any painful disease — cancer, starvation — whatever you got — *any*thing. I've seen more than a hundred
shrinks. I've taken every antidepressant under the sun. Engineering is all wrong for me. I need another *venue* to express
my peculiar point of view. I mean if I have a contribution to
make to the world, I need to go another road." Matthew was
proud of his vocabulary choice but when he saw that it failed
to impress his mother, his thin neck finally gave out and his
heavy round head fell back on the Slumber King. His voice
was piercing. "I can't take any further interrogation. What

you are doing to me is against Geneva Convention rules."
He folded a king-size pillow around his head and then
stretched into the full layout position and executed a body
roll-and-a-half toward the east wall. In one adroit, well-
polished move he not only escaped the sharp light from
the hallway, he also muffled the harsh gravel rasp of his
mother's incessant nagging.

By now, Mrs. Billis had worked herself into a state of
furious indignation. This unleashed a full convolution of
organic trauma, but her anger was greater than fear. She
swung Matthew's door shut with her lambskin slipper and
stalked into the kitchen with his breakfast tray. "Lazy ass son
of a bitch! He's *worth*less! Forty years old and useless! I've
had it. I'll kill him!"

She stabbed at the fried egg mess on her china plate with
a soap sponge. The eggs were harder than rocks. She wondered why she cared. Soon she would be six feet under.
Then what would he do? Then what "road" would he find?
She whirled around and in another moment she was back
wresting the blankets away from him. Matthew had already
dropped off to sleep again and clung to the blankets des-
perately. She backed away and turned to his closet. "I'm going to take all of this shit, throw it out on the lawn, and have
the locks changed! I can't take anymore. *I'm* the one who's
sick! You can just get the hell out!" She screamed as she began ripping Matthew's clothing out of the closet. Matthew
leaped from the Slumber King and forced her out into the
hallway. During the struggle he snagged his baby toenail on
the dresser, half ripping it off. "Goddamm it," he screamed.
"You're totally nuts! Just leave me the fuck alone. You're a
maniac!"

Mrs. Billis pushed at the door but Matthew had the full weight of his body pressed against it. "If you aren't out of here in one hour, I'm calling the police!" she screamed. "I am sick of waiting on you, picking up after you, and paying your bills. I want you out!" She sounded like Linda Blair in *The Exorcist*.

Although his mother weighed scarcely a hundred pounds and was dying of cancer, Matthew had to use every ounce of his strength to hold her off. It felt like Lucifer bucking the other side of the door. As soon as the pushing stopped, he clicked the lock shut and returned to bed. His pulse was racing and he felt short of breath.

Out in the kitchen she began to cough again. Little poppers. *Kaff kaff kaff!* He heard the hiss of her medicinal inhaler and seconds later the coughing stopped entirely. Why didn't she pick it up at the first tickle? *Why? Because she was a fiend and coughed simply to torment him with guilt! And Jesus Christ, did his toe ever hurt!* Matthew reached for the flashlight and sat on the edge of the bed examining his bloody nail. He needed to rip the thing off but lacked the courage to do so. Instead, he resumed the full layout position and began to practice hatha yoga breath control. He wasn't doing it right, just operating on the basis of some half-remembered instructions from a meditation book one of his many counselors had laid on him.

His toenail throbbed. He flipped on the flashlight again, gritted his teeth, and pulled the snagged edge of it loose and then flopped back in the position. Such a small few micrometers of tissue and such a great pain. A perfect metaphor for life! Fuck it, going to sleep now would be impossible!

On television he saw a report about twelve hundred people drowning in Bangladesh. He reached for the remote and turned up the volume. There were scrawny women in saris sitting in trees, shots of people on rooftops, and pictures of skinny white cows floating in the muddy floodwaters. When the camera panned through a major city, Matthew took great satisfaction in seeing that the floodwaters had submerged two-story buildings. That twelve hundred drowned in a far-off land somehow comforted him. Better they than he. In fact, when God reached out like that, *He* got something off His chest — some level of celestial wrath that just as well might have been directed at Matthew. It was like an Aztec sacrifice or something. A good way to blow off steam.

Oh, it was too true that *all* was *one*, and that if he personally knew any of the drowning victims, he would be heartbroken by their plight, but suddenly his mind had been delivered from his troubles and he could feel himself about to drift asleep again. A few more hours of sleep would complete his REM cycle, fostering revival. And he was close to snoozola. He was on the verge. He could *almost* get it. But then he had to piss with a vengeance, and to piss meant leaving the sanctuary of the Green Room. Go out; venture forth with the fiend of Fordham Avenue on the loose. Shit! Suddenly Matthew found that he had to squeeze his legs together to hold his urine. There was a nerve in the bladder, a kind of natural gas gauge like the one located on the dashboard of a car. Once it hit the danger mark, the signal became hard to ignore. But to go out there? She would be on him like a peregrine falcon. Suddenly Matthew spotted a discarded Burger King coffee cup in his wastebasket. It was a pretty seedy thing to do, but he retrieved the cup and let go. He had to piss so badly his eyes were watering.

"Take a memo," he reminded himself. "Empty cup at the first opportunity." Heh heh. Man, how low can you go? Well, lay around unemployed for two years and you could always *limbo a little lower, now — hey dere! Heh heh heh.* Suddenly the cup was filled to the brim and warm in his hands. He didn't know where to put it. Finally he set it along the wall next to his bed. With that done, he assumed *the position* and within moments was in deepest slumber.

MATTHEW AWOKE at seven the next morning clinging to fragments of a disturbing dream — a virtual night terror. Still, no matter how bad it had been it wasn't as bad as the scourge of raw dawn. He found himself in a tight fetal ball but rolled over. His stomach roiled with the corrosive acids and bile of inhuman stress. He might have to vomit. He had a nuclear meltdown of a hiatial hernia — either that or this was it. The big one. Heart attack at forty. The American Way. Goddamn them!

Matthew closed his eyes again and tried the deep-breathing exercise. No need to get in a shithouse panic. If he did that, he would start generating beta waves in his brain pan and once that happened the adrenaline would begin to flow. He'd wake up for sure. Peace, brother. *Just back off and try a little more of that free-floating action. Come on, man. Don't freak; just slide back into slumber. Breathe.*

Frightful thoughts raced through his brain. He was certain that the pain in his upper chest was heart pain, particularly when he recalled the shortness of breath he experienced after the struggle with his mother. His saliva tasted peculiar and he wondered if pus was festering in his throat or if he had brought about a bleed from so much screaming. He endured an age of agony and managed to fall asleep nonetheless.

Matthew awoke at four-thirty in the afternoon. He came to in the full layout position and stretched luxuriously, arching his feet as he scissored his limbs and made little snow angels under the covers of the Slumber King. Except for the interlude with his mother, Matthew had pretty much put together a near-twenty-two-hour package of sleep from the last twenty-four. A commendable feat! He continued to savor little dream fragments as he walked into the kitchen for coffee. His pride and self-satisfaction vanished when he saw that the carafe under the Mr. Coffee machine was completely empty — treason and high tyranny on her part. Shit! As Matthew fumbled through the cupboards looking for coffee filters, the memory of their argument last night came back in rich detail. It had been an ugly scene. Still, it wasn't like her to hold a grudge or not have some coffee going. When he finally found the filters and the package of ground Starbucks, he filled the machine and hit the switch. He put the biggest cup he could find under the fount since he didn't want to wait for an entire pot to fill before he got some caffeine in him. He could do a quick switch once his cup was loaded. Jesus, what a hassle! He wasn't the kind that could casually wait for coffee. When he had to have it, he had to have it. Furious over this inconvenience, he impatiently drummed his fingers as he waited for the coffee. Then Matthew spotted a full bottle of morphine tablets sitting across the room next to the Cuisinart — morphine tablets that his mother *always* kept locked up in the three-hundred-pound safe in her bedroom.

Matthew took a deep breath and listened for the least hush of sound. Suddenly thought and action were one. He closed the distance between himself and the drugs with the stealth and silence of a trained Mohican stalker. He quickly dumped a dozen of the tablets into his palm, shook the bottle to fluff it up, and then returned to his station next to the coffee machine. The entire action was completed faster than Superman making a phone booth costume change. He had been reckless with the morphine tabs on earlier occasions. The rustle of pills was a sound both mother and son were attuned to, and as careful as Matthew was, the twelve morphine tablets sliding into his hand sounded exactly like what it was — drug theft. A herd of buffalo storming through the living room would have been more subtle. Matthew felt exposed — caught red-handed — yet to his astonishment, the quiet held. Un-fucking-believable! Making casual, he walked back to the Green Room. In his excitement to stash the pills, he bumped the Slumber King and overturned the brimming cup of urine. He scarcely gave it a thought — hell, it would dry on its own practically without an odor. Well, maybe. Anyhow, this was no time to worry about a little spilled piss.

Matthew hurried to his mother's bedroom and peeked inside. When he saw her form under the covers, he went back to the kitchen. God! What a score! That fluffing-up procedure was amazing. He rubbed his hands together in delight. The perfect crime. He watched the Mr. Coffee machine sputter. Molasses in January. He had half a notion to unleash his expertise as a design engineer one last time and make a six-second Mr. Coffee, but the world that had treated him so badly didn't deserve such a prize.

Suddenly Matthew realized that he had *under*stolen. An opportunity like this came once in a blue moon. He slid across the room and shook out another twenty tablets. The container held 200 count. Twelve and twenty — that was thirty-two total — hell, round it out to forty. At forty, the fluff-up job looked suspicious. Reluctantly he returned four tablets into the pill bottle, replaced the lid, and went back to the coffee station. He wondered if he had gone too far. His moves were mechanical and the word *guilt* was written all over him. He needed to get back into the Green Room. His coffee cup was three-quarters full when he made the switchover to the pot. He quickly opened the fridge and poured some half-and-half into the cup and knocked down four of the morphine tablets. He *needed* morphine. His baby toe was throbbing like a bass drum. In a more humane society, pain would be treated in a less Calvinistic fashion. Jesus! He took the remaining pills back to his bedroom and hid them with the others. With his coffee he took two Xanax from his stash and swallowed them to accentuate the high that was about to come any time soon. He slugged the coffee down to dissolve the pills faster and then got on the Slumber King and assumed the position. It was like being at the opera or some gala affair awaiting the greatest production of pleasure life could deliver. Ensconced in the Slumber King, Matthew Billis, who had been so tormented by relentless depression, who had come to feel so bad that not even taking a shit felt good, and who was bereft of a single endorphin, waited for the buzz of a lifetime. It was a buzz

rettes to the floor and looked for more secrets. There were
several cloth-wrapped Hummel figurines — her treasures.
Crass stupid-ass junk really. As he was removing these from
his safe a recent prescription for 200-count morphine flut-
tered to the floor. A script for morphine! Lord, have mercy!
What a stellar find!

He took the cash, the pills, and the prescription back out
into the kitchen and set them on the table next to the mail
and the newspaper. Did she know that she was dying and
leave the safe open on purpose? With all of that blood on her
pillow, it was unlikely. She had simply died of natural causes.

Matthew's initial sense of objective detachment began to
deteriorate. He turned to the Rolodex and began to spin
through it looking for her doctor's number when it dawned
on him that she didn't need a doctor, not really. Not anymore. Well, who to call then? There wasn't much family left,
just cousins. Fuck them. He went back to the room and
studied his mother's body. A look of horror was affixed to
her face. She had seemed to diminish in size a good 20 percent. He pushed her mouth closed. Her limbs were still pliable. He wondered how long she had been dead. She had
somehow scrunched down low in the bed, and when he
pulled her forward, her mouth dropped open and a gush of
blood oozed out. Matthew quickly rushed out of the room
and went to the kitchen sink to wash the cold and slimy
blood from his hands. Suddenly he was into hand washing
in a big way. Lady "Matthew" Macbeth.

At last he opened the phone book and turned to the yellow pages looking for mortuaries. Did you just call them, or
did you inform the doctor first? If he informed the doctor,
he wasn't going to be able to cash that script for morphine.

It would be null and void. A waste of ambrosia. Man, she was still pliable! She must have somehow been hovering, clinging to life until only just recently. Matthew wasn't sure how long it took for rigor mortis to set in. He could drive to the drugstore now, cash in the script, and then make phone calls. Who was to know? He took another four-and-two combination and went back to the safe. He removed a pack of Luckies from the carton and sat in the kitchen, smoking cigarettes, drinking coffee as he thought things over. Matthew quit smoking when his mother first came down with cancer and now he wondered why. It was such a *pleasure* to smoke. It was pure enjoyment. That she was able to sneak cigarettes behind his back seemed amazing to him, but then, given his sleep habits, it wasn't surprising at all. But why did she sneak around about it? To fool herself! Yes, that was it! Denial. His analytical powers were most acute.

An inspired plan evolved. Matthew finished his coffee, snuffed out a cigarette, and retrieved his old Boy Scout sleeping bag from the spare closet. He unrolled it on the bed next to his mother. It had a musky smell. He reached under her arms and slid her body over onto the bag, careful not to let her head slump forward. Once he had her in the bag, he zipped it shut and then hefted her up, carried her out to the garage, and placed her corpse inside the freezer. Fit was not a problem as the freezer was only half full. He returned to the bedroom and got her Hummels. He placed these into the freezer with her in case she might need them in the Happy Hunting Grounds — she had plenty of frozen food, that was for sure. Heh heh.

One of the Hummels depicted a small boy with a beagle. Matthew had given it to her when he was eleven out of money he had saved mowing lawns. He remembered that the statue had cost thirty-five bucks. It had been a lot of money at the time, but he wanted her to have it. He wanted her to have something really nice. Jesus, what kind of shit was he pulling here? He didn't know, he was just playing things by ear. He went back into the kitchen and pulled some candles out of a drawer. He set them on the freezer and lighted them in her honor. The morphine was kicking in nicely now. Matthew said, "Look at it like this, babe: you aren't really dead until I thaw you out and call the doctor. In the meantime, as long as I can forge your signature, I've got all the job I need."

He thrust out his narrow chest and began to strut before the freezer, his movements suddenly fluid and rhythmic. Released from the morass of his neurotic fears, he was suddenly a kinetic art form as he popped his fingers and jived about in the garage. The Panasonic was airing a commercial in which a phalanx of ants was carrying off a bottle of Budweiser: "Do a little dance; make a little love; get down tonight! Get down tonight!"

Matthew was in a "get down" mood. He said, "'Get a job'? Who, me? Baby, you' talkin' to the kid! Get a job? Shee-it, man! Anyhow, why in God's name should we drag this through probate and take it up the ass from the government? Those fascist bastards! Why?"

Yes, why? Matthew retrieved a Diet Coke from the refrigerator in the garage. Back in the Green Room he shook out another four-and-two combo and slugged it down with Coke. Then hopped into the Slumber King and assumed the position. *Dateline Monday* was coming on and Matthew Billis felt absolutely, positively, right-on-the-money cap-*ee*-tal.

Tarantula

JOHN HAROLD HAMMERMEISTER arrived at W. E. B. Du Bois High School with grand ambitions. Harold loved to work, thrived on challenge, and could scarcely contain his excitement at the prospect of a new and difficult assignment.

Postings such as these were like the great wars: they provided one with opportunities for distinguishment. There was another thing, too — hard work took Harold's mind off the inner turmoil resulting from so many recent life changes. He had been racking up big numbers on the Hans Seyle Stress Scale. In less than two years he had weathered a divorce, suffered the death of both parents, and then, with the last of his inheritance, had come down from Canada — come down to Detroit to polish off the course work on a Ph.D. Now everything was done except for the thesis. It was just one last detail. A little trifling. Why, he would have it out of the way faster than you could say John Harold Hammermeister.

The principal who hired Hammermeister was scheduled to retire in a year, and Hammermeister, with his doctorate all but finished, had a "feeling" that the principal's job was his. All he needed was to whirl like a dervish for one year, a mere two hundred and twenty-six school days — dazzle them senseless — and the kingdom from on high would be his. And Harold was most definitely in contact with the kingdom. Before falling asleep each night Hammermeister tuned into the Universal Cosmic Broadcast. He was a psychic radioman who not only transmitted but received. He was connected, on the inside. It was beautiful, wonderful, mar-ve-lous!

Yeah, eyes closed at night, in red flannel pajamas, Hammermeister lay in the ancient Murphy bed of his studio apartment and *created* the future — and in that future he saw himself in the principal's office, in full command, in one year's time, a mere two hundred and twenty-six school days. The principal's office was just a little pit stop on the way over to district office proper, and he would most certainly ascend the ladder there. From the Murphy bed he created glorious visions of supreme success. He watched himself climb from the modest position of junior vice-principal all the way up to the summit of State Superintendent of Public Instruction! Why not try *that one* on for size? Heh heh.

The old Murphy bed was Harold's magic Persian carpet from which he could encompass the "big picture." He plotted his moves and savored future pleasures. Harold saw, smelled, felt, and practically *tasted* the smooth, dove gray leather seats of the burnished black Lincoln Town Car that would replace his ancient Ford. A car so quiet, the only thing he would ever hear was the ticking of the clock. In their gold-plated frames, the Lincoln's vanity plates would read: HAMMER!

In the mind-movie there was also a second wife, a newer and better model than the first. Beauty, brainpower, and refinement ("behind every great man . . ."). When she wasn't supporting him in his Machiavellian schemes, number two would be a well-rounded person in her own right. *Yeah, she gon' be so fine!* And the school district administration center would be Harold's seventh heaven of joy — secretaries in short skirts with a little piquant bantering among them by day. A little bit of hanky-panky, while nights and weekends involved a walled country estate with polo, fox hunting, and high society available at his pleasure. Yes, a *walled* estate! Wasn't that how the rich did the world over? They put up buffers and walls against the detritus of the everyday life. It was every man for himself in the swinish cesspool of the twentieth century. And why not be absolutely selfish? Was not beauty more pleasing to the eye than ugliness and squalor? To think of this new beginning, to think that it would all take off from a place like Du Bois High School — a veritable war zone, a sinkhole of black despair, a continuous scene of barbarous violence! Well, no problem, Harold would soon have it all squared away. They would have to do a double segment on *60 Minutes* to showcase Harold and the new reformation revolution in American schools. Du Bois would become the exemplar ghetto success story. Hope would replace despair. Yes, fairy tales could come true. Harold was going to turn things around on a dime. Only fair that he should reap the rewards.

The bestseller that his thesis would become would pro-

vide the means. Written in the snappy, popular vernacular, it
was a multifaceted jewel. Americans would read Harold's
terse, spellbinding prose with a curious admixture of horror
and astonishment. The *All-New Blackboard Jungle: An American
High School in 1999*. Probably make a movie, and playing the
role of the visionary reformer — the only actor capable of
playing real-life John Harold Hammermeister — may I have
the envelope please? — *ta da!* Ladies and gentlemen, the
only actor with sufficient authority and range to catch the
infinite subtleties — with the scope, the voice, intelligence,
maturity, the physical presence — ladies and gentlemen, I
present to you . . . yet another gifted Canadian, Mr. Donald
Sutherland. Was it Sir Donald? Well, it would be. The Queen
Mother could hop off her ass and beknight the man. The
dear fellow. It was high time. Just 'bout time, all right.

Boy oh boy, what the mind could behold, the mind could
make real. Hammermeister gave the kids a watered-down version of his visualization techniques whenever it was time to
light a fire under somebody's dead ass. Take pride! Pull yourself up by your bootstraps. It was always in one ear and out the
other; they didn't have a snowball's chance, but you had to
try. Professional ethics required one to take the idle stab.

Nobody but nobody knew anything about elbow grease
anymore. People were so friggin' lazy. Work like a German!
It was the golden key to riches and prosperity beyond imagining. Most American educators were shell-shocked, blown.
In the trench warfare of public schooling, one needed to
concentrate, work hard, confront problems and wrestle
them down. Engage the mind. Work! In the trenches,
friends, family, and personal recreation were inexcusable di-

versions. Inspid fuck-fiddle. You could pick up on that action later. Climb the ladder and then harvest the bounty . . . in the meantime, later, alligator.

IN HAMMERMEISTER'S OFFICE, on the left side of his desk in a small glass cage — the bottom covered with pea gravel, the top fixed with a warming lamp — Hammermeister kept a tarantula named Lulu. Hammermeister waited a few days before he brought the spider in. He wanted to get the lay of the land first. Lulu was a statement, and he wasn't totally sure how to "play" these Americans. A big-ass hairy spider could get to be *too much,* but then, with his pleasant, affable good looks, his Mr. Nice Guy demeanor, Hammermeister wanted to establish a darker aspect of himself — a presentation of danger. If it gets down to it, boys and girls, *if it comes down to it,* I'll fuck you up in a second! I'll mess up yo' face!

Did he really *say* that?

No, but he *conveyed* it just the same. He put out the vibe. When a recalcitrant student was sent to his office, Hammermeister liked to rock back in his executive's chair, tapping the edge of his desk with a number one Dixon Executive pencil, affecting a debonair Donald Sutherland style, and say, "You aren't getting through to me, my friend." Tap, tap, tap. "You aren't getting through." It got to even the baddest of the bad — the sneaky quiet malefactors, the toughest thugs, the sulkers, wrongdoers of various shapes and descriptions. Hang a leading question on the guilty soul and he spilled his guts. It never failed.

Hammermeister was the first administrator to show up in the morning and the last to leave at night. He attended the football games, the band, orchestra, and choir recitals —

plays. He even showed up at girls' B-squad volleyball games. He wanted everyone to know that he was at the school and of it, and that because of him and through the sheer force of his personality, the school was going to get better, improve, blaze into the heavens — and the plan was working. A man has to have a plan, and Harold had a righteous plan. Beautiful, wonderful, *mar-ve-lous!*

The students and discipline were his forte. He soon had them all under control — the wild-ass freshman girls, the dopers, the gang bangers; the whole spectrum of adolescent vermin. It didn't have to be "I'll fuck you up!" It hardly ever was . . . really. With Lulu on the desk he could focus totally.

The principal complimented him often about how well he handled the whole arena of discipline, but when Hammermeister asked for more responsibilities, Dr. White put him off.

"Not just yet. Why don't you settle in for a while, huh-huh-huh-Harold? Don't want to burn out, do you? Meltdown by May. That happens to the best of us, you know, even when things are guh-guh-guh-going well."

Christ, you could stand there for an hour to hear the motherfucker deliver one complete sentence.

"Seriously, Dr. White, I want to learn everything I can. I want to know this school inside and out. I'm part of the team, and I don't like sitting on the bench."

"Okay then. There is one little trouble spot that seems to duh-duh-duh-defy our coping skills: the cuh-cuh-cuh-custodians. They're yuh-yuh-yuh-yours."

Hammermeister quickly scheduled a meeting with all thirteen of the men. He had pizza brought in to foster conviviality, but instead of the friendly get-together he envi-

sioned, all thirteen janitors started in on him at once: the
year had never been off to a worse start! It was terrible!
There was a group of squirrely freshmen, and they were carrying food to all ends of the building — spilling pop on the
rugs, spitting chew, sunflower seeds, and peanut shells. A
particular bone of contention was a type of hot pink, new
wave chewing gum. This stuff didn't freeze when you applied aerosol-propelled gum hardener to it — freeze it so
you could smack it to pieces with a putty knife, pick up the
cold little broken shards, and throw them in the trash.

A red-faced custodian named Duffy harped on and on
about the gum hardener. "For one thing, it erodes the
ozone layer, and for another, it makes this fuckin' gum melt
and soak *deeper* into the fiber of the carpet. Opposite of the
very role for which it was intended, man. One piece of gum,
fuck! One kid, thirty-two teeth, give or take, and one wad of
gum equals twenty-five minutes of *my time,* which translates
into almost nine dollars of the district's money. One piece
of gum! I could *ignore* it, let the rug go to shit, but I take
pride. *I take pride!* For Chrissakes, why doesn't somebody tell
that jerkoff that fills up the vending machines to quit
putting chewing gum in — huh? Or at least use a normal
kind. I tried to talk to the man. I don't know what you have
to do with that guy. I can't get through to him. Mastication
of the South American chicle plant is against the law in Singapore, Harold, did you know that? I tell this guy that selling gum is against the law in Singapore! They got their shit
squared away over there. I tell this to Vend-o-face, an' he
ain't hearin' it. He's one of them passive-aggressive sons of
bitches who likes to drive fifty in the passing lane or who will
hang up an express line at the supermarket jacking around

with a checkbook, buying lottery tickets, and asking questions when others are in a fuckin' life-and-death hurry. Forgive my digression, but are you getting the picture? I never met anyone like him before; he's just an absolute asshole. You know the character, John Waite from *The Nigger of the Narcissis*? That's this guy. There's just no other way to describe this human piece of shit."

Hammermeister was so shocked by Duffy's stream of invective that his face went pale. In Canada, a man such as Duffy would be fired on the spot. What gross insolence! That Duffy had the nerve to speak to him in this fashion — obviously, there were different rules of engagement going on. Detroit, shit, what a very strange energy inhabited the city where such scenes were commonplace. Harold was almost certain he could smell alcohol on this man's breath. "John Waite?"

"Waite from *The Nigger of the Narcissis*. For God's sake, you're a college man, aren't you? Read the book. Don't teachers have to read in college?"

Another of the custodians chimed in. "Hey, the man is right. He knows what he's talking about. This vending guy is Johnny Waite! He should be banned from the fuckin' building."

Throughout this all, an enormous black man with a shaved head and silver nose- and earrings locked a hard stare on Hammermeister, like a heat-seeking missile. At last he said, "Hey! I'd like to get something off my chest. You called us all in here for a meeting, and nothing will change or get done as we all know. You have the secretary call me up to come to a fucking meeting at two-thirty in the afternoon when I work graveyard. Doesn't anybody have any consider-

ation? I need to come in and hear all of this Mickey Mouse
piss and moan. *The Nigger of the Narcissis*! Watch your mouth,
Duffy! I don't even want to hear you *thinkin'* 'nigger.' You
don't have the right, motherfucker! I'm the one's paid
dues." Roused to a fury, the large custodian wheeled on
Hammermeister and stuck a finger in his face. "How would
you like it if I called you up and told you you had to come to
work at three in the morning? *Three in the morning,* because
that's what this is for me, goddammit! Plus, I'm sick tonight.
Call me a sub. You done fucked up my biological clock! I
don't know when it will come back to normal, I'm still
fucked over from fucking daylight savings back in May or
whenever the fuck! Foolin' with Mother fucking Nature.
God! Great God! Goddammit, son of a bitch!" With that,
Centrick Cline kicked a metal folding chair out of his way
and stormed out of the room.

Mike, the head custodian, got up, ostentatiously glanced
at his watch, and said, "There's a volleyball setup in the gym.
Let's go. We're already two hours behind. Lord, we got to
boogie, folks, or we're going to be here *awl* night long."

Hammermeister watched the custodians file out of the
conference room. He looked down at the untouched pizzas,
sixty dollars' worth leaking warm grease onto the limp cardboard containers. He picked up a piece smothered with
sausage, pineapple, olives, and onions and ate it in four
bites. It was his first meal of the day.

All the screaming had caused Rider, the senior vice-
principal, to pop his head in the door and catch Hammermeister in a state of panic — catch him in a situation over
which he had no control. An abominable scene. Janitors . . .
Dr. White had been right. They defied the usual . . . well, hell,

they were out of control. He would call them in one by one. Isolate them. Break them down. Turn them into lap dogs.

They did have a point, however, the school did look like hell. The next afternoon Hammermeister got on the p.a. and told the students of W. E. B. Du Bois High School that while the year was off to a great start, food, candy, and pop were not permitted in the halls and classrooms. The following afternoon he repeated the message, shifting from the insouciant Donald Sutherland to the rather arch Donald. When Hammermeister continued to notice litter in the halls and classrooms, he ordered the pop and candy machines shut down for an unspecified period.

Hammermeister called the head custodian into his office and told him of this decision. "I want to help you guys out. We couldn't run this school without the custodians," he said with an ingratiating smile. "Anything you need in the way of supplies, or whatever, just let me know. And one other thing, the district has asked me to address the problem of sick-leave abuse. Du Bois is the worst school in the district in this regard."

No sooner were the words out of Hammermeister's mouth when Mike, the head custodian, proceeded to tell Hammermeister that his daughter had chicken pox and that he needed a sub for the rest of the week — moreover, Ralph, the day man, needed a sub for Monday because he was going in for some blood tests. And, oh, somebody else, too — he wasn't sure, well, yes, it was Ray. Ray had tickets for a rap concert and wanted to take a vacation day.

"So . . . Mike . . . at least talk to the guys. Can you do that much?"

"Yo," the head custodian piped as he turned and walked

away. For a head custodian, Hammermeister felt the man had a very bad attitude in regard to chain of command. *Well wait a minute, Mike. Come on back here, my friend. Perhaps that's too much to lay on you all at once. Maybe you ought to go home and rest. Take a year off for mental health. I'll catch your area for you and make sure all your checks are mailed . . . r'hat on time, bro. Izzat cool or what? I mean, I'm hip to all the problems you guys go through. I know your job . . . ain't no day at th' beach. I'm in full sympathy. Really. You don't think I got a heart? I gotta heart. I got a heart.*

A week after the pop and candy machines were shut off, the associated student body complained that they were losing the revenue from these machines and made it plain to Hammermeister that this revenue was the lifeblood that bought band uniforms, sports equipment, and other essentials. Hammermeister was shocked when he learned the figures. The students at Du Bois consumed enough fluid ounces of Coke, assorted beverages, and refreshments to half fill the swimming pool in a week. The Hammer didn't allow anything sweeter than fresh fruit back at the juvenile facility in Canada, and what a difference. There weren't any sugared-out junior gangsters like here, and the behavioral considerations, repercussions, etc. were extremely . . . interesting. Well, it would all be in the thesis. Soon the wide world would know.

In less than a week there was heavy pressure to turn the candy machines back on. Hammermeister lost his cool and exchanged heated words over the matter with senior vice-principal Rider. He came back later and made a cringing apology explaining that he wasn't used to making so many compromises, having come from a detentional facility where his word had been "law"; that he was grinding out his thesis and so on and when he reflected over the apol-

ogy, it occurred to him how weak and desperate he had
sounded — effete and obsequious. A wipe-out migraine
could do that to him, turn him white. The pop machines
went back on, and the school instantly became a pit.

Waiting for a pair of codeine #4s to kick in, Hammermeister dropped a succulent white grub into Lulu's cage
and watched the spider attack it with such speed and ferocity that Hammermeister jerked back in his leatherette executive chair. He thought, "What if I were that worm? Lulu
would show no mercy. And I wouldn't expect any."

The pace of the activities at Du Bois began to pick up.
Hammermeister was getting hit with building requests from
the science people — brainy types in Kmart jogging shoes,
who wore pen packs and watches with calculators on them
and who, generally speaking, displayed the whole range of
absentminded professor types of behavior. They were exas-
perating when you were trying to get from line "a" to line
"b" within a certain time frame and didn't want to screw
around with their spacey weirdness.

Worse than science were the special-education people,
they were the most eccentric bunch on the entire faculty.
Do-good, granola freaks in Birkenstock sandals, who came
in with problems of every description. Stories from left
field. All Harold could do was sympathize. He knew their
burnout rate was high, and he wasn't good when they came
in weeping, half crazy . . . they would shed hot, salty tears
over virtually anything! But there was no one to foist these
people off on, and he sat with a number one Dixon tap-
tapping. *I have never heard of a student openly masturbating in a
classroom. This is a mental health issue. Let me make some phone
calls.* When they left his office, he would mechanically open

his top drawer and pop two Extra-Strength Excedrins, a couple of Advils, and a deuce of Canadian 222s.

The people who taught social studies and history were coaches, mostly, and their minds were seldom on innovating the curriculum. They wanted to do everything by the numbers. One thing they could do — they could *read* the sports page.

The teachers in language arts complained that they had too many papers to grade. Harold hired part-time college English majors as assistants and fed as many student teachers into the language-arts program as he could. The math and business people, Hammermeister found dull. But dull could be good; it had its advantages. These people were undemanding and caused few problems. They were pure gravy in terms of his own job description. Ditto with the vocational-education types.

The group he cultivated most, although he had little interest in high school sports, was the coaches. The coaches who were P.E. teachers didn't count so much as those who taught academic subjects. P.E. teachers tended to be happy with the status quo. It was the latter bunch, the so-called academic teachers, who were ambitious, who would eventually give up the classroom and move into administration where there was more money.

Coaches had popularity not only with the students and the general public but with the administration. Winning teams meant high student morale and coaches were very important. With these imbeciles Harold laughed, drank, farted, and clowned. Whenever the conversation turned to the gridiron, all Hammermeister had to do was listen intently, carefully orchestrating his body language and throwing in a line like, "Geez, you really know your football, coach. I'm impressed. I never *saw* it that way before. That's absolutely brilliant. No wonder the students love you." He despised coaches, but collectively they had more juice than any other group in the building.

It was only with the women in the administrative office that Harold could let his hair down and be himself. He could tell they found him attractive, and before long, as a joke, he had everyone in the office saying "a-boot" in the Canadian style rather than "about." He wondered if they had Peter Jennings fantasies about him.

Sex was something for the next lifetime. It was tough learning the new job, but since he lived alone in a tiny apartment and required little sleep, Hammermeister was able to throw himself into his work, body and soul. He longed to get out of this rough-and-tumble high school and into the cozy air-conditioned district office building with the two-hour lunches, plush carpets, and countless refinements and amenities as soon as possible. He saw himself there. And sex was for then. He was a dervish, and he was whirling this year. Things were poppin'. There was suddenly so much to do. He had forgotten almost entirely about the janitors.

Then one day the activity director received a shipment of folding chairs for a district-wide choir recital slated for the gymnasium, and of the thirteen custodians in the school, only four were on hand after school to unload the chairs and get the gym whipped into shape. The activity director was highly agitated, and not realizing how little real clout the man actually had, Hammermeister became hysterical as well. When Harold saw the head custodian, he demanded to know where all of the other janitors were.

Mike was either in his fool-in-paradise mood — or "high." He stood before Harold and scratched his head for a moment. Well, three custodians were out sick and no subs were available. There were the two who worked graveyard: somebody or other had driven off to pick up a prescription, yet another had not acknowledged the "all call," and finally, still another, the very one who worked the gym area, did not report to work until five. Hammermeister listened to this, all the while his headache picking up steam and mutating into a kind of epileptoid craziness. Still, he managed to maintain his composure, and said, "I want that man in at two like all the swing-shift people, have you got that?"

Later that afternoon this very janitor, Duffy, walked into Hammermeister's office and caught him writing notes on his thesis. "Can't you knock?" Hammermeister asked. Duffy, who was red with anger, made a perfunctory apology. Hammermeister saw Lulu stir in her glass box. Duffy's eyes followed her movement.

"Shit, man, a bug! Weird! *Goddamm*it!"

"Its a spider, Mr. Duffy. Tarantula. Now what can I do for you?" Tap, tap, tap.

Duffy nervously stroked his mustache and short beard. He looked at the spider and then back at Hammermeister. "Mike told me you changed my hours."

"That's right, Duffy. Did he tell you why?" Tap, tap.

"He said something about unloading chairs for the concert. Only four guys were here or something."

"Yes, exactly. The next time this kind of thing happens there will be five, minimum." Tap.

Duffy took a deep breath and shook his neck to loosen up a bit. "Can I say something, Harold? I want to say this:

I've been here for ten years and this is the first time that any-thing like this has come up. It almost never happens. If I have to come in at two, there's nothing I can clean. The gym and the upper gym are in use, the locker rooms are in use — there's nothing I can do."

"I'm sure you'll think of something." Tap, tap, tap.

"Plus — after the game, like tonight. Tonight there's foot-ball. The team won't be out of the locker rooms until a quar-ter to eleven — everything will be muddy, a total mess, and I'm supposed to have gone home fifteen minutes previous —"

"On game nights come in at four. How's that?"

"Look . . . Harold. The reason I took that gym job was so I could baby-sit until my wife gets home from the auto plant. She gets home at four-thirty. If you change my hours, I'm going to have to hire a baby-sitter —"

Hammermeister rocked back in his chair, steepling his fingers. "I am familiar with your union contract, and I can change your hours to suit the needs of the school. Is that clear?"

"All right, we can play it that way. I tried nice, but we can take this motherfucker to the union, and we can sit in hear-ing rooms . . . *by the hour!* I know you got lots of homework. It's going to be fun. You can really make progress on that thesis of yours. Or maybe you can read a little Joseph Con-rad. It would do you good, Harold. Give you a little insight, Harold, into the ways of the world. I'm *filing*."

"You pay union dues, and I encourage you to use the union," Hammermeister said evenly. He swiveled his chair away in a little half twist and busied himself with a file folder, dismissing the custodian with a wave of the hand. He wasn't going to let the man scream or give him the satisfaction of making eye contact. Anger — for a lot of people, it was a hobby. They liked it. Why play their silly-ass game?

Duffy slammed the door so hard a draft of air lifted Hammermeister's thin, fluffy, light brown hair, which was combed forward to cover a receding hairline. He zipped open his drawer, popped two Excedrin, two Advil, swallowed a double glug of Pepto-Bismol, and then hunched over his desk and restyled his hair using a comb and hand mirror.

A few days later Hammermeister got a note from the district custodial coordinator stating that because of activities scheduling, Duffy's shift would revert back to the original 5:00 P.M. to 1:30 A.M. semi-graveyard shift. Hammermeister got on the phone and talked to the man, one Bob Graham, who told him Sean Duffy was one of the better custodians in the district and that he was not going to stand still for any aggravation. Furthermore, Graham characterized Duffy as one of the nicest, most easygoing people he knew. *Right! White was black, and black was white!* What *perfect* logic!

Whenever Harold needed time to "think," or to let his various headache medicines kick in, he would take a stroll over in the area of the gym and look at Duffy's work. It was hard to fault, but Hammermeister was quick to jot down "dings" with a retractable ballpoint — especially if he found them two or three days in a row. He would leave notes to Duffy. Pin them on the custodians' bulletin board for all of the classified staff to see. "To S. Duffy from H. Hammermeister: Black mark on benches, boys locker room. Why?"

When basketball season started, Hammermeister grabbed Duffy by the arm and pointed out a spilled Pepsi under the bleachers. It was the first thing you saw when you walked into the gym, and he told Duffy to go get a mop and clean it up.

It was an eyesore. "Hurry up, there, chop-chop!" Hammer-meister said, with heat in his voice.

Later that night, at halftime, when Duffy was giving the basketball court a quick sweep, the drill team came out, and Hammermeister made a theatrical throat-slashing gesture for Duffy to get off the court. Duffy waited at the opposite end of the gym, his face blazing scarlet with bilious fury, and after the drill team finished its routine, Hammermeister noted with satisfaction Duffy's embarrassment as he finished the job. Duffy was an aneurysm waiting to blow.

Well, there were the teachers, too, who were slackers — a good number of them. Hammermeister made note. They were easy to spot. They liked to show films or assign book reports and theme papers blocking out days at a time in the library. They followed the same curriculum year in and year out. Playing one clique off the other, Hammermeister ascertained who the lazy ones were and, if they were not coaches, he gave them heat, too.

Woodland, down in the portables, for instance. He dressed like some kind of Salvation Army bum. Beard right off a pack of Smith Brothers' Cough Drops. When Hammermeister caught Woodland smoking one day after school, he reminded the man that he was a master teacher and wondered out loud what his future goals were.

"I used to be gung ho and *all thangs,* but now I'm getting short. Have you got a problem with that, Hammermeister?"

"I'm not saying you need to wear a suit and tie. But you have to remember you are still on the job and you are a role model, Woodland. You are a senior teacher. Where's your self-respect, man? You want to be a good teacher, then work at it. You're *getting paid,* aren't you?"

As he walked down the ramp from Woodland's portable, he turned back and saw Woodland flip him the "bird." Jesus, look at them wrong and an American could get a hair up his ass and lose it. This Woodland had murder in his heart. There was less free-floating hostility at the prison back in Canada, which was tame by comparison. Hammermeister locked eyes with Woodland, but before violence was done, he abruptly turned and stalked back to the main building with his pulse pounding. He could feel the surge of it in his neck and temples. He already had a Tylenol #4 headache over that one, but you had to give them a little jab, to let them know who was running the show. He had given Woodland a jab, and the man had showed him as much disrespect as that custodian, Duffy — well, these people would be excised. Duffy sooner and Woodland later, when the time was right . . . in a bloodless Machiavellian style. For some short-term revenge, Harold managed to "lose" a work order Woodland had recently put in to have his air conditioner fixed. He balled it up and slam dunked it into his wastebasket. The next thing he did was write a note reminding himself to call Woodland into his office, on Harold's turf, where he could reverse any notions the teacher had about blowing him off. He would feign consideration, all the better to ultimately crush Woodland to dust. Hah!

W. E. B. Du Bois was far from an ideal school, and the more he got to know it and was dragged down by the inertia of it, the more Hammermeister was inclined to jab these slackers or to outright get in their faces. But he had to watch himself and keep it under control, at least for this first crucial year. He really belonged in the district office, and he would be there when he whipped this place into shape.

He had done well at the detention facility in Canada; he would do well here. Working in a low-morale school where so many of his colleagues were just going through the motions made Hammermeister shine like a red, white, and blue comet streaking through a night sky of blackest India ink — so, in a way, it was all to the good. *Blackboard Jungle 1999* was coming along, and in the meantime, the dervish continued to whirl.

Once the buses arrived and students started filing in, there was heavy action. Metal detectors going off. Fights picked up where they had left off the previous afternoon. Open drug transactions. Before you knew it, they were calling Hammermeister to put out one brushfire after another and another and another — all day long. Although he thrived on adrenaline, the pace of events at Du Bois was getting to be relentless. Harold was racking up some more big numbers on the Hans Seyle Stress Scale. Points that took you beyond the limits of human endurance! His stomach had become a volcano from all of the aspirin he was swallowing, and his tongue was black with bismuth from the cherry-flavored Pepto-Bismol tablets that he constantly chewed.

The high school was overcrowded, and after the first few weeks of timidity, the students mostly threw their good intentions (*"I be goin' to Princ'sun!"*) out the window. The joint became as bad as it had been advertised: *The Lord of the Flies.* The chaos at Du Bois made it seem far more dangerous to Harold than his well-regulated penal institution back in Canada, where Hammermeister had fond memories of courteous and compliant murderers, rapists, and stick-up artists. These American kids were savages. And those candy machines — all of that refined sugar was just adding fuel to the fire. It was in Harold's thesis, the magnum opus; you could read all about it there, or you could wait for the movie. Heh heh heh. Harold didn't know if he would have all that much say-so in the casting, but he needed to throw a glamorous woman into the picture — a kind of gal Friday. Something along the lines of a . . . Whitney Houston, say. Janet Jackson would be a stretch but . . . maybe Gloria Estefan. Or you could get a tough bird. Oprah Winfrey? He wondered if Whoopi was lined up with commitments.

SEAN DUFFY was giving the head custodian a hard time about Hammermeister, the custodians' new boss. Who *was* this asshole? Who did the motherfucker think he was? "Just because he's a vice-principal, does he think he's running the place? And Dr. White is letting him get away with it. That's what really riles me!" Duffy said. "White's going to retire, and he just doesn't give a shit anymore."

Mike knew that Duffy was hitting the juice pretty hard, but he could never quite catch him with liquor on his breath. Not that he really cared to — not as long as the man did his work. Was Duffy drinking vodka or something odorless? He always looked fairly fresh on Mondays, but as the week wore on, Duffy would get red-faced, with bloodshot eyes. Increasingly, he would launch long tirades against Hammermeister — tirades that went beyond normal fury. Tirades inspired by alcohol.

One night after the swing-shift custodians left and the school was all but vacant, Centrick Cline started complaining to Duffy about Hammermeister. Hammermeister didn't like his nose- and earrings, was a racist motherfucker —

"Hey, man, why didn't they hire Alec Baldwin for the job? This geek motherfucker said he comes by at three A.M. and he better not catch me in the weight room. I *clean* the weight room," Centrick Cline said, "an' I ain't 'posed to be in the weight room?"

Duffy's own latent anger flared. They stood together and pissed about Hammermeister for forty-five minutes. Then Duffy took a customary inspection of his area, making sure he had not left a beer can on a desk somewhere before turning out the lights. When this was done, it was close to one A.M. and Duffy slugged down two quick cans of Hamms, lit a Gitane cigarette, and furtively entered Hammermeister's office. He stood before the tarantula cage a moment and then lifted the lid. He took another puff on the Gitane and blew it on the spider.

The hairy spider shocked Duffy somewhat by setting itself down. But rather than confirming his worst fear by jumping, it froze. Duffy removed a long pencil from Hammermeister's desk and nervously positioned it over the spider's thorax. Closer and closer until suddenly Duffy thrust down at it, and the large body of the spider exploded like an egg, spurting yellow matter all over the room. When Duffy let go of the pencil the spider sprung straight up in the air and landed on his shoulder. He batted the spider down and scrambled out into the commons area, grabbed his coat, and fled the building.

Hammermeister came in Friday morning, and the first thing he noticed when he stepped into his office was that the lid of the tarantula cage was ajar. He hastily closed the door thinking that the spider had escaped, since he didn't want it to bolt out into the main office. Somehow he knew something like this was going to happen. He had a funny premonition.

Lulu lay dead on the seat of his executive chair, impaled with a number one Dixon. The Gitane butt was there, but Hammermeister was struck dumb with grief and all he noticed as he looked about the room was the gruesome egg-yolk splattered essence of Lulu on his seat, the walls, and the ceiling. When he finally composed himself, he stepped out of his office and told the secretaries that the spider had been stabbed (already he had a pretty good idea which students did it), and that it had crawled up to his chair to die. This peculiar detail had Hammermeister on the verge of tears. He wrung his hands to no purpose. His face fell as if he were the comic Stan Laurel confronted with some absurd calamity. Hammermeister's favorite secretary, Cynthia — the nicest-looking woman in the building — put both of her hands on his shoulders and said, "Are you okay, friend?" Hammermeister said that he was and woodenly made his way back into the office. Not fast enough for Rider to miss the tail end of the scene, however. Harold had a four-star migraine, but his gut lining was shredded from too much aspirin. He slammed down three Tylenol #4s and chased them with a Diet Coke. As he wiped the spider splatter from his chair with paper towels, the enormity of this personal loss caused his thighs to wobble. Harold gently lifted Lulu's corpse from the chair, neatly wrapped it in his handkerchief, and deposited the body in his top desk drawer. He sat at his desk with his head in his hands, wincing, waiting for the codeine to kick in, waiting possibly to just *blow*, perish, succumb to . . . internal spontaneous combustion! None of these things happened, and Hammermeister didn't get any worse. But he didn't get any better. He was alarmed to find that he stayed just the same for some time. At the foot of his chair he noticed a peculiar butt. It was a manufactured cigarette, but the tobacco in it appeared to be almost black. He picked it up and examined it. No doubt it belonged to the assassin. He shoved it into an envelope for evidence and placed it in his top desk drawer, locking it.

The secretaries were so moved by Hammermeister's "nervous breakdown" that on the weekend they went to a pet shop and bought a replacement spider for fifty-five dollars. They pasted a little note on the cage that said, "Hey there, big boy, Lulu's back in town!"

On the following Friday Lulu number two was found murdered in the same fashion as number one had been: impaled with a number one Dixon. In evidence was another cigarette butt. A vile-smelling thing filled with blackish tobacco. This one was not a Gitane, but it was unfiltered and it was foreign. Harold noticed such butts in an ashtray in Centrick Cline's janitor's closet. And what a place that was. There were militant anti-white slogans pasted on the wall, posters of Malcolm X and Huey Newton, and an accumulation of what seemed to be voodoo paraphernalia. Cline was not known to be a smoker. Yet most of the staff who smoked had keys to this closet and would sneak cigarettes there. Throughout the remainder of the day, Harold made hourly checks to see if any of the teachers had smoked such a cigarette during their prep periods. There were none to be found. But then there were none in the morning after the janitors' shift either.

Because of the pace and the pressing events of the

school, Hammermeister found himself playing catch-up. This alarmed him, since he was no procrastinator and was devoting every waking hour to his job. On a number of occasions the senior vice-principal came down hard on him, implying that his Ph.D. would have to wait until summer; there was a school to run. Hammermeister's objective "breath of fresh air" — the Canadian jet stream — was getting stale. Harold heard the talk and could only hope another burst of energy was available, and with it some new inspiration. When he was state superintendent of education, when the book was made into the movie and he was pulling in fifty-thousand-dollar speaking-engagement fees, Rider would still be on his fat, *Ahm a soul man, sweet potato pie* ass, forever mired deep in the middle of Detroit's blackboard jungle. In the meantime, not only was the staff all over him, but the students were becoming impossible to control. Harold was now somehow frightened by them — frightened terribly, and they could tell. Without Lulu next to him exuding encouragement, Harold grew scared and was overreacting. When he started nailing students with suspensions over petty grievances, Dr. White hit the ceiling.

White scheduled a personal one-on-one conference with Harold after school. He was far from courteous when he told Harold of the conference, and he did not stutter. The motherfucker was on the rag! Hammermeister staggered through the day, certain that he was about to be fired. But it wasn't that at all. White dumped a book challenge on Harold. At issue was John Steinbeck's *Cannery Row* — it had been called "filth" by an irate parent. White told Harold to handle it without saying exactly how. White just didn't want to get his hands dirty, that was all. There was a levy vote coming up and "how" had to mean: get the library to pull the book. Or did it?

After thinking the matter over, Harold went upstairs and spoke with the head librarian, who was horrified at the suggestion that the book be pulled. She vowed to "go to the wall." Hammermeister thoughtlessly warned her that librarians were a dime a dozen. It was the codeine talking. At least there were no witnesses.

That night Hammermeister left the building well after dark, and when he got to his car he discovered that all four tires were flat. Later, after a tow truck had hauled the car in, Hammermeister was informed that the tires were okay. The party that flattened them had simply removed the valve-core stems, then after the tires were deflated, poured Krazy Glue into the valves. The culprits didn't pull the valves and run, they were brazen enough to wait until the tires went flat and then carefully squirted glue into the valves. They even took the trouble to screw the valve caps back on. Professionals! The valves were of a type that wasn't available at that hour of the night. The car would be ready tomorrow afternoon.

Head down, hands in pocket, Hammermeister furiously strode the three miles to his apartment through a biting *Nanook of the North* sleet storm. Just as he cut through the back entrance, where the covered parking stalls were located, he heard the abrupt rustling of leather jackets. He barely turned his head when a large tawny palm engulfed his face like an eclipse of the sun. The mighty hand snapped Harold's head back and firmly cradled it between the abductor's solid chest and a rock-hard biceps muscle. As his face was getting squashed Hammermeister suddenly felt his

shins getting pounded with fierce woodpecker rapidity. The
tonk tonk tonk sounds were those of an aluminum baseball
bat. Hammermeister sagged halfway to the ground, but the
large hand held him firmly like he was some kind of rag doll,
and Hammermeister was not a small man. He stood over
6′2″, but with all of the recent stress, he was down twenty
pounds from his normal weight of two hundred and twelve.

The powerful hand that encased his face forced Harold's mouth to open in an "O" as a thick, wet, balled-up sock
was rammed inside, a smelly cloth was placed over his eyes,
and then, as Hammermeister heard the quick rip of duct
tape, the stinking rag was adhered to his face like a layer of
fast-drying cement.

There were two of them. The woodpecker with the bat
continued to expertly peck at his legs, knees, and elbows,
while the powerful strong-armed man spun him around,
cranked a solid punch into Hammermeister's solar plexus,
and then let him free-fall to the ground. For the next moment Hammermeister was kicked and pounded mercilessly.
He wondered if it was murder. The woodpecker was batting
him in the head now but not with massive, clobbering blows.
It felt like he was being poked with the knob end of the bat.
Hammermeister felt himself sinking into the black vortex of
hell, but then the shower of stars abruptly stopped, and in
the frigid night air he heard his assailants' cold, rasping
breaths tear through his brain like the sandpaper tongue of
a lion. It occurred to Hammermeister that the dictum "when
you lose your sight you become all eardrums" was profoundly
true. Hammermeister could distinctly hear the different ways
the two men breathed. If he lived to be a thousand, he would
never forget the way these men breathed.

The stronger man grabbed his wrists and pulled them behind his back. As a knee came down on his spine, Hammermeister heard the sound of duct tape being unreeled and torn again, and soon his hands were bound as tightly as if he were displayed in a pillory. Then, with a suddenness that was frightening, he felt himself being lifted like a suitcase and lugged away from the lighted parking stalls to a very dark place. Even though his eyes were masked, he had been able to see shadows — now nothing. All the while the hollow bat rapped away at him. Neither of the abductors said a word. Hammermeister attempted to scream through the sock, but it was a scream that just couldn't get off the ground.

The pain in his shoulders felt like a crucifixion. Harold emitted a high-pitched scream through his nose as he was hauled off into yet a deeper forest of blackness. After what seemed like an interminable voyage, he was dropped roughly to the pavement, where he wet his pants in abject terror, waiting for the mechanical action of some sort of firearm — the rotation of a revolver cylinder, perhaps.

Both of the unseen men were panting heavily. Before they shot him, they were waiting to catch their breath. After a moment he felt their rough hands pulling at his pants, ripping them down to his knees as they turned him over on his stomach. Harold let his legs kick out wildly, and this only made the men laugh.

Suddenly there was a jolting, searing-hot pain in his right ass cheek. Hammermeister could smell his own smoldering flesh. The whole focus of his being gravitated to the burn.

The other pains were gone, he was nothing but a single

right ass cheek. He writhed with the vigor of a freshly landed marlin. Then he felt himself lifted like a suitcase again. The two men heaved him up, and by the smell of things, Hammermeister realized he had been cast into the garbage Dumpster before he even landed. His body was greeted by cardboard boxes, nail-embedded two-by-fours, metal cans, offal — the slime, grit, and stink of coffee grinds and cat litter, rib and chicken bones, and cigarette butts.

There was a loud clang as the two men dropped down the metal door. There was the sound of the metal lid reverberating, followed by the squeak of sneakers peeling across the snowy pavement of the back drive, as the thugs made a New Balance getaway.

The pain of the burn was incredible. It gave Hammermeister superhuman strength. In just seconds he was able to wrest his hands free from the tape. In another few seconds he pulled the tape from his face and spit out the sock that was choking him. By the time he slipped out of his bindings and pushed up the lid of the Dumpster, the men were gone; the sleet had turned to snow, and a soft white blanket was laid about him like a kind of Currier and Ives/Edward Hopper Detroit. The Motor City.

Harold hastened to his room. After four tumblers of straight bourbon and a handful of Tylenol #4s, Hammermeister, still trembling, stood before his phone imagining what he would say to the police. When he finally called 911, a dispatcher answered with a disaffected tone and Hammermeister quickly replaced the phone in its cradle, afraid that his call would be traced and an aid car would be sent to his building.

He staggered into the bathroom and looked at the burn.

It was hideous, his buttock exuded a watery yellow fluid, yet the letters KKK were crudely apparent. They had somehow taken him to a prearranged spot where the hot iron was cooking. This sort of vicious calculation made him think of gangs. Of gang planning. Somebody really was playing hardball. Not kids. Not janitors. But who else except fucking kids and fucking janitors? Funny that they didn't steal his wallet or shoot him. Rip-off artists shaking down a random victim in a parking lot would go for the money. Kids and janitors had access to a high school metal shop where branding irons could be made.

Hammermeister went back to the phone to call an ambulance and was once again struck by indecision. It had been a warning. Maybe it would be best not to get the police involved. After all, how would he explain it to Dr. White?

One of the legs of his pants had been torn off completely. His legs were swollen with red and purple abrasions yet no bones were broken. He hurt all over, yet he really wasn't that hurt except for the searing pain on his buttock, which was an agony unlike anything he had ever known. Twenty minutes later, the burn seemed a thousand times more painful. Hammermeister took a warm shower and carefully soaped his wounds. It helped to take action. After he dried himself, he applied some antibiotic cream to his right butt cheek and placed a nonstick dressing on it. There was only one such dressing in his medicine cabinet that would fit it, a super jumbo — hell, in Detroit you would think that gun-trauma kits would be fast moving items at every drugstore. After Hammermeister put on a pair of clean Jockey shorts, he went back to the phone where he found himself again paralyzed with indecision. As the booze and dope kicked in,

Hammermeister felt a magical sense of relief. Suddenly he was packing his suitcase. He would drive back to Sondra in the morning. He missed her and the kids more than anything. God, he had been a dick. Sometimes it took a real shocker to bring you back to your senses. Well, this night had been an epiphany. The booze and the codeine were so good, so nice, he was thinking straight for the first time in years. He had a proper sense of perspective again.

In the morning Hammermeister abruptly came to in a world of pain. The burn felt more like a chemical burn, like a deep burn — like a *real deep* burn. He couldn't look at it. Instead he immediately dosed himself with vodka and codeine, and then, when he realized that his car was in the shop, he wondered about his plan for claiming the vehicle and driving back home after all. You could not drive when you could not sit down. Canada — shit, the bridge had been burned. He really hated his wife, and while he loved his kids in a way, it was one of those deals like "out of sight, out of mind." There was no going back.

Nipping from the pint of vodka, Hammermeister laced up a pair of heavy weatherproof brogues and walked to work, stopping at McDonald's for two Egg McMuffins and a large coffee to go. He was going to the school where he would confront Duffy and Cline. He wouldn't even have to ask a question, all he would have to do is listen to them breathe.

It was a zoo day. The place was a zoo. First period the head of the English department — tough, smart, and formidable — came into his office and told him there was no way in hell her department was going to see John Steinbeck banished from the school. Hammermeister told her it was a matter between himself and the librarians, and she closed the door, took three powerful strides over to his desk, where he stood looking through his memos. "Now you just wait here, buster!" In casting this role, Harold was suddenly thinking in terms of Bette Midler or Cher on a tirade.

Boy! Twenty-five Hans Seyle stress points for that one. Hammermeister had tried to appeal to her sense of reason. "We've got a levy coming, we don't need this right now. What will you say if I tell you we can't buy new language-arts books this fall?" His voice was hollow. His legs, the shins especially, began to hurt more than the burn on his ass. He gulped down more codeine with the last of his cold coffee. Why in the hell had he come back to this hellhole? To nail Centrick Cline and Sean Duffy, that's why — and from the stack of morning memos he could see that both of them had already called in sick. His secretary gave him their numbers, and he called them both at home. Neither of the malefactors answered their phones. Off somewhere together, drunk, sniggering in iniquitous delight.

Later that morning he was forced to phone the parent who had raised the hullabaloo about *Cannery Row*. She was a real kook. What the fuck! Yet Hammermeister deferred to her, sympathized and told her off the record that he was in full agreement with her. It was necessary to placate this woman. Dr. White had insisted upon it. Hadn't he?

Events quickly came to a head when the issue was thrown in at the tail end of the monthly board of directors meeting the next evening. The librarians throughout the district were on hand, as were librarians from nearby school districts. The word spread fast. "Oh God," Hammermeister thought, "a cause célèbre." He had to go home and crash before the meeting, and then, heavily medicated, he over-slept and showed up looking like Howard Beale coming in to deliver the news in that old movie *Network*. Harold's buzz cut was sticky with tape, he needed a shave — he looked like a madman. But he was high and didn't care. He had not prepared for the debate; he had decided to just "wing it." Sometimes it paid to be spontaneous and genuine. You were walking on thin ice, but sometimes it did work.

The W. E. B. Du Bois High School librarian was dressed like a model of propriety. Armed with a thick packet of note cards, which she hardly ever seemed to look at, she gave a convincing pro–First Amendment presentation. This was followed by an eloquent statement by the head of the English department. Then Hammermeister suddenly found himself on his feet making counterarguments, all weak and vapid. The beneficial effects of the nap were short-lived. He was strung out from too much booze and Tylenol #4, and as he scanned the room looking for a sympathetic face, the fact that there seemed to be none inflamed him with hollow fury. This was a setup. The board members, the superinten-dent, and his own principal looked at him expectantly. The formality of the room was hard, as were the faces of the peo-ple sitting in the gallery. A press photographer snapped photos of Hammermeister, and as he did so, a feeling of de-personalization overcame the Canadian. Exhausted by the previous evening, the present onslaught was too much for him. He found himself saying, over and over again, that he was about to receive a doctorate in education, as if that were germane to the situation at hand. He said something about how a society that was too liberal became soft and festered with decay. Harold said something about the rightness of trying to change society for the better turning to "wrong-ness" when everyone focused on gender, sexual entitle-ment, and the color of skin. Whatever happened to genuine achievement leading to entitlement? You couldn't play cen-ter for the Tigers just because you were white. No! You had to be the best center fielder in Detroit. So what was the problem? What did sex or color have to do with genuine achievement? Why did society have to allocate prizes and create heroes out of sex perverts and deluded, talentless know-nothings, be they black, white, or brown? Why did they have to hand the keys to power over to fools? The right-minded liberal inclination to make the "all men are created equal" utopia had led to ruin. Utopia-building, good in the-ory, simply did not work anymore. It only led to ruin, decay, and dispersion. It was time to resort back to the police state. Life Duffy had said — Singapore!

Somewhere in the back of his brain he realized it was the codeine talking — a medicinal "misadventure" — yet Ham-mermeister could not stop himself. He told the audience that America was going down the sewer as it coddled weak-lings and slackers. He began to talk of racial polarization and the subway shooters, until finally the superintendent, aghast at Hammermeister's presentation from the first, shot him a withering look and cut him off. "That will do, Mr. Hammermeister. Thank you for your views."

In the morning, Dr. White was sitting in Hammermeis-ter's chair reading through Hammermeister's thesis when Harold came in. He looked up at the Canadian and said, "We'll pay your salary through the year, but don't ask for any job recommendations. You aren't gonna want my recom-mendation. I'm sorry for you, huh-huh-huh-Harold. There are people of cuh-cuh-cuh-color out there who can dance circles around your qualifications. It's my fault for letting you buh-buh-buh-bullshit me during the interview. I wanted to hire a white man. I wanted some diversity. I wanted you to succeed, but you're a buh-buh-buh-bad person!"

"I didn't bullshit you. I can do this job. I can *do* this job!" Hammermeister began to spill his guts about the janitors, his beating and abduction. Dr. White drew his head back in alarm.

"You don't believe me, do you?" Hammermeister shouted. He pulled down his pants and showed the man the burn on his ass and the bruises on his legs. "It looks like Kaposki's or whatever they call it." Hammermeister began to spin his theory that the custodians — Duffy and Cline, the weight lifter — had beaten him, gang bangers had stabbed his spiders . . . and so on.

"That's the most preposterous thing I've ever heard. For one thing, those spiders were ridiculous, and for another, Duffy has been with us for ten years and I've never heard a single buh-buh-buh-bad word —"

"Bullshit! He's an alcoholic! He's a drunk! Everybody knows it. Where have you been?"

"He hasn't taken a sick day in the whole ten years," the principal said incredulously. "The buh-buh-buh-best attendance record in the district, sh-sh-sh-short of my own."

"Alcoholics are *like* that. With their low self-esteem, they overcompensate at work. Have you ever read *The Nigger of the Narcissus*, Sidney? Do you know the character, Waite? That piss-and-moan, do-nothing crybaby! Well, *that's* who Duffy is. *Duffy is Johnny Waite!* And if you haven't read the book — judging by that vacant look on your face, I dare say you haven't — then by God you should!"

"Harold. I don't know what happened to your legs or how you got that burn, but the alcohol fumes in here are bad enough to knock a person down. I think you should check yourself into . . . a facility! The district has a progressive policy —"

"Duffy and that burrhead in the gym, Cline — that's what you call a bad nigger."

"That's it! I've heard enough — you've got fifteen minutes before I call the police!" Dr. White said, standing up. "Puh-puh-puh-pack your stuff and get out."

"Fine," Hammermeister said. "Fifteen minutes. That's just fine. 'The custodians are a little trouble spot,' remember? 'They seem to defy our coping skills,' remember? Shit, why did I have to be born white! It's a curse!"

The principal walked out of the room, shutting the door behind him.

Hammermeister began slamming his personal supplies into a box. There wasn't much. He picked up *Blackboard Jungle 1999* and began to read. There was the truth. The American public would be shocked if they came to these schools and observed. Something very dangerous was going on inside. Well, the public did come. They were invited to come with open arms, but only to well-orchestrated events with canned speeches, lies, bullshit inspiration. If America really knew what was going on, it would be shocked. If they could see the school, day in and day out. The quality of education was an abomination!

Harold began to dictate into his personal recorder. "The

school-board system: you've got a superintendent. What is his job? Why, he goes to a meeting now and then. He gets a haircut. Plays golf. Around levy time he sweet-talks some newspaper people. The taxpayers would be better off if they let the district secretary run things! When I came into this field I thought that by hard work and determination I could make a difference, but I have been swallowed up in chaos and futility. The American public has been greatly deceived! It is not only your hard-earned tax dollars that I am concerned about, it is our youth and the future of this once great nation! We need parental involvement. You can't send them to us for seven hours and expect us to undo. They're going loco. We need more metal detectors in the school. We need drug testing. We need a crime-prevention program. There should even be AIDS testing and quarantine like they've got over in Cuba. Are we going to let the rotten apples spoil the whole barrel? Goddammit, democracy just isn't cutting it anymore. Someone has to step in and get the fucking trains running on time again or it's closing time in the gardens of the West!"

Two uniformed police officers in squeaky leather jackets stepped warily into Hammermeister's office. Harold looked at his watch. Fifteen minutes? "It hasn't been fifteen minutes."

"It's time to go," one of the police officers said.

Hammermeister looked at the box. He threw his thesis in it. He attempted to place Lulu's glass cage in the box but it was too large. He set it back on the desk. He would have to carry the cage under one arm, and the box with the thesis, the Dixon pencils, coffee mug, Pepto-Bismol, aspirin, Tylenol #4s, Advil, his spare sports coat and neckties, etc., under the other arm. Except that now he was so spaced from the codeine and round-the-clock vodka drinking that he knew he would never manage it.

"Let's go," the officer said.

Hammermeister stuffed his pockets with the codeine #4s, then on impulse flipped the thesis into the wastebasket, dumping the remainder of the box in after it — the pencils, coffee cup, neckties, spare sports jacket, everything. He was dizzy with rage. He had a crazy impulse to dash over to the office safe and grab the nine-millimeter they recently pulled off a drug peddler and fire off a few rounds. If Sean Duffy and Centrick Cline were not there, he'd just shoot . . . whomever. Get Rider and White first. Instead, he flung the cardboard box aside and placed Lulu's empty cage on top of his wastebasket. He raised a pebble-leather, oxblood brogue over the cage and then stepped down several times, crunching the glass.

The police officers braced for action, but then Hammermeister sagged. The only picture that came to his mind now were those of the flattened tires of his Ford. Gone was the movie, the new and better wife, the Lincoln, polo, and country clubbing. His shoulders slumped and he turned to them defeated. "I'm ready," Harold said with a melodramatic flourish, presenting his hands for cuffing. "Read me my Miranda and let's clear out of this place."

The police officers, one short, one tall, exchanged a significant look. The short one said, "No need for the handcuffs, sir. They just want you off the grounds. It's a routine eighty-six, that's all. They just want you to leave."

Hammermeister seemed disappointed that he was not under arrest. He felt cheated but let the police officers lead

him through the party of "concerned" but not entirely un-
sympathetic office secretaries. They led him out into the
throng of students who had heard the sound of smashed
glass and had gathered to witness what they intuitively knew
was a very strange and very bad scene. Several of the students wondered out loud as to what was going on. One of
these, a student who had once been mesmerized by Hammermeister's power of positive thinking spiel, and who had
a certain affection for the former junior vice-principal,
asked, "Wha'chew got, man?"

Hammermeister looked over his shoulder and cried,
"Murder one."

And with that he was led out to the parking lot to a squad
car, driven to the bus stop, and dumped off. He had never
taken a bus in America, didn't know how, didn't know when
one was coming, and when he could no longer stand the
cold, he gulped down a couple more codeine tablets with a
slug of vodka and surveyed the landscape before him. Hammermeister realized he was the only Caucasian in the neighborhood, and he began to feel conspicuous. A couple of
thugs, also brown bagging, joined him at the bus shelter. One
carried a ghetto blaster. Clarence "Frogman" Henry was
singing, "I'm a lonely frog, I ain't got no home." Hammermeister watched as the man inserted a rock in a crack pipe
and took a hit off of it before passing it to his companion.

Moving from the shelter of the Plexiglas bus stop, Hammermeister dropped his head down against yet another
Nanook of the North sleet storm. A mere pedestrian in the heart
of the Motor City, new citizen John Harold Hammermeister
caught the shoeleather express back to his apartment.

Mouses

RODENTS INFILTRATED my place at the first hard frost of the fall. I had a minor premonition that this would happen, and then, lo, it happened. For a couple of days it was in the back of my mind, in the twilight area where minor worries flourish — no big alarm bell rang, because most of the stuff you worry about never comes to pass. But then came the evidence, the irrefutable fact that not only did said perpetrators (previously unknown to me) claw and chew through a box of Wheat Thins, they defecated at the scene of the crime, leaving sizable pellets behind. Apparently "Don't shit where you eat" isn't in the rodent codebook. Hygiene is not a big concern with them. At first, I was in a state of denial. My place is sealed as tight as a drum. How could they get in? Also, I was thinking, I don't need this now. I really *do not* need this. I was facing problems at work. There were rumors of a cutback at the plant. In spite of my seniority — I've been an en-

gineer for ten years — I knew I was high on the shit list. I'm
a convenient target. Why? Because I'm very short in stature.
Five feet nothing. And I have a slight spinal deformity — a
hump. No matter what goes wrong at that hellhole, I get
blamed. "Anson, the midget, did it." A computer goes
down, blueprints get lost, milk sours in the lunchroom refrigerator: "The midget did it!"

So at first I buried my head in the sand. I had woken up
late that day, no morning coffee, and my feet had barely hit
the floor when I saw the chewed-to-shit Wheat Thins box.
What a sight! It looked as if a wolverine had gone through
it. There I was, standing in my pajamas in a state of complete disbelief. This was no time to conduct a full-scale pest
investigation. I was late for work.

That night in bed, when fears are greatly magnified, not
only was I worried about my suck-ass job, I began to think
that the intruder might be a big black rat with an appetite
for human flesh. Jurassic. The Wheat Thins box looked like
it had been blasted by a shotgun and, as I said, the waste pellets were mighty big. For all I knew there could be a whole
pack of vermin running around my place bearing disease
and pestilence. Off a ship from Africa or something. Can
you get rabies from *proximity*? That's what I was thinking.
About 3 A.M. a miasma of moldy rodential air came wafting
into my bedroom. I hadn't noticed *that* before. Somewhere,
unseen, these vermin were stirring about, revved up into a
state of high activity, giving off odoriferous secretions.

The next morning I was up early to see what dirty work
had occurred during the night. I entered the kitchen with a
heavy brogan shoe in my hand, and it was just as I thought:

they had been at it again. Bolder than ever! I had thrown out the contaminated food, and closed the cupboard tight, but — hey! — no problem: the culprits had gone to the breadbox! It's lid was ajar, a good inch and a half. Had I closed it? You'd think you'd remember a pertinent detail like that, especially if you're in a batten-down-the-hatches frame of mind. And what if I *had* closed the breadbox? This rodent must be very strong. This rodent might very well be a rat — a rat that bench-pressed No. 3 vegetable cans and probably played tackle for the local ratball team. Black Bart, the Norway power rat. Fangola from Borneo.

On no sleep, work that morning was an ongoing hell. I had to sneak out to my car at lunch and catch a nap, but I woke up three hours later not in the least refreshed: it wasn't a nap, it was a damn coma. The boss called me in: "Yeah yeah, ying ying, ya ya, where in the *hell* have you been?" Put the fear of God in me. I stayed late working on the annual report, which made no sense to me anymore. I was just sitting there, "pretending," which is a lot harder than actually working. You could chop logs all day, stack thirty cords of wood, and not get as tired. When the boss bagged out, I waited five minutes and then left. My back was killing me. The hump veers toward my left shoulder. It was all hot and knotted up like an angry fist. Just complete agony.

I stopped at the supermarket for some Advil and asked a stocker where the mousetraps were. Evidently, there'd been a run on rodent traps. "Cold weather," he said.

I said, "You haven't been selling *rat* traps?"

"Rat traps, yeah, sold a few," he said, pointing them out.

They were huge rectangular slabs of pinewood with monstrous springs and rectangular clap bars made of heavygauge metal. Big enough to snag a Shetland pony.

"Whoa, man!" I said. "I hope I don't need one of those."

"Where do you live?" he asked me, and I told him the neighborhood and he said no doubt my problem was mice. Rats don't frequent upscale places, he said. They go for the shitholes where people leave garbage around. He couldn't guarantee it but he was ninety percent sure. Then he left me alone in the aisle to inspect the merchandise. I chided myself for being melodramatic. No rats, just some mice. And others were having the same problem. I was reassured. I was fortunate to be able to get any traps at all. There were only five left and I bought all five.

I thought of using poison, going for complete and certain eradication, but I wanted to see the corpses. Your mouse poisoner is like a bomber pilot flying miles above a war zone — the bloodless battle. That's cool, but sometimes you hear of poisoned mice dying in parts of the house that are inaccessible to the homeowner and giving off a horrible smell. People start yanking off drywall panels to get to the smelly things, knocking down chimneys, tearing up the foundation.

Vacor, for instance, a rodenticide that looks like cornmeal, destroys the beta cells of the pancreas, causing instant diabetes, followed by chest pain, impaired intellect, coma, and finally death. A diabetic mouse with severe hyperglycemia will develop an incredible thirst and head outside to look for water — you don't have to tear your house apart tracking down odors. Strychnine is another possibility. An overdose of strychnine destroys the nerves and causes convulsions. The sick rodent cannot bear noise or bright light. It dies a prolonged, agonizing death of utter torment. That kind of mouse wouldn't opt for the hustle and bustle of the outdoors. That's a hide-in-the-drywall mouse.

All in all, the trap is more humane. But I was so angry at the inconvenience I had been through — disturbed sleep, fright, the loss of snack foods — that the thought of a mouse writhing in pain out in a field somewhere did not bother my conscience in the slightest. The opposite was the case. It gave me satisfaction. Die, suckah!

I SET THREE of the traps in the kitchen using peanut butter as bait. I put another in the bedroom and one behind the living-room couch. That night, moments after I turned off the lights, I heard one of the kitchen traps go off. *Wap!* Man, I almost hit the ceiling. I wasn't sure if I heard a shriek or not. It all happened so fast. In the blink of an eye, an execution.

I'm embarrassed to admit that I was a little afraid to confront the consequences. But what could I do? I picked up my heavy shoe and went out. The victim was a gray mouse with broad, powerful shoulders, prickly chin whiskers, red beady eyes, and a short stumpy tail. Its mouth was open, exposing a crimson tongue and sharp yellow teeth. Ahggh! The trap had snapped its neck. I picked up the trap and quickly tossed it in the garbage. How that mouse had so totally destroyed the Wheat Thins was beyond me, but such are the mysteries of life. There, I'm thinking. Done! Half an hour later I was sawing logs.

In the morning I got up and went to the kitchen to make coffee and I saw another mouse, this one still alive, with one paw caught in a trap. It was trying to drag-ass out of there. I got my work gloves out of the garage and picked up the trap, the mouse hanging down from it, wriggling. I put the mouse in a coffee can, and then — I don't know what made me do it, maybe because Christmas was coming — I punched some holes in it for air. The mouse's foot was smashed, but otherwise it was OK. I set the can in the garage and went off to work.

I was tired again, with moderate-to-severe hunch pains. Except for short-lived bursts of activity when my boss passed by with a scowl on his repugnant face, all I could do was sit at my desk and "pretend" all day. Even though I'd got some sleep, I was thrashed, body and soul.

When I got home I threw some wood shavings into an old aquarium and put the mouse in there. If it was in pain, I couldn't tell. I gave it a little dish of water and some corn-flakes. The thing was this: I couldn't stand having an invisible invader prowling around in my house at will, but with the animal caged and me in full control, I could tolerate it. I mean the mouse was just trying to get by like the rest of us. I named him Al.

After a few days, Al's foot turned black and fell off. He wouldn't eat for a while. I think he had a fever. A close call with death. I put out some whole-wheat bread with peanut butter on it. He loved that. He was going to weather the crisis. He started to gain weight. I found a hamster wheel at a garage sale and the guy just gave it to me to get rid of it.

That's when Al began his rehab therapy. Without his foot, he got by hobbling, but his whole left shoulder was weak. On the wheel, he struggled and became disoriented.

To encourage him, I put his favorite treat, a Hershey's chocolate square, in a little box in front of the wheel. Stick and carrot. Pretty soon Al was running his ass and lost all the weight from his peanut-butter days of convalescence. With treats to motivate him, he'd put in five hours a night on the wheel. One night, just as I was getting him his Hershey's square, he hopped into my palm and let me hand-feed him. It was a momentous transition. Suddenly this little wild animal was on the road to domestication. He trusted me. I felt like I was in tune with the universe. But not for long.

THE NEXT DAY at work, the boss stuck his ugly face inches from my own. "You're terminated, Anson. Clean out your desk! You have one hour."

The heartless bastard. I'd known it was coming, but I was devastated just the same. He couldn't wait until after Christmas. I immediately drove to the unemployment office. Filled out the forms. Stood around and waited. Geez, what a seedy stink-ass joint.

If you're an engineer, a job in these times is the hardest thing in the world to find. There are thousands of engineers.

I put together a résumé and scanned the want ads. There was nothing. One of the no-jobs at the unemployment office told me that nobody hires during the Christmas season, so just chill out.

At night I watched TV. It was me and Al, with him crawling up my arm and on top of my head and whatnot. Once in a while out slipped a mouse pellet but what are you going to do? Al is my friend, so it was no biggie. I wondered if he missed his life in the wild. I wondered if he was bored. If I let him go in the spring, with no foot, what would happen?

One night after a futile and discouraging day of handing out résumés, I popped over to the pet shop and bought a companion for Al. A pet mouse cost a dollar and eighty-nine cents. I got a female and named her Angela. I put her in with Al and they sniffed each other out for a bit, but when I turned my back they started fighting. Angela was kicking ass. She bit the piss out of Al and he was left bleeding all over, especially from his stub. I broke up the fight, stuck her in the coffee can, and put her in the dark garage for punishment. Then I put hydrogen peroxide on Al's wounds. If it wasn't for the incredible cardiovascular reserve he'd built up running the wheel, I think she would have killed him.

I took to hand-feeding Al again — I had to — and he eventually came around. He seemed to like the mouse chow I got him. I figure that animals have body wisdom and will eat the right thing if you provide it for them. Pretty soon Al was on the wheel again, and we were watching TV together at night, and everything was just hunky. He padded around on my scalp with his three little paws, up and down my arm, with no fear at all. It was like we'd been pals in some previous lifetime. Bosom buddies.

I fashioned a divider panel for the aquarium and took Angela out of the punishment can. But I was still hating her. I gave her nothing but peanut butter. I denied her access to the exercise wheel. And in a couple of weeks she was a disgusting tub of lard. Meanwhile, Al, on his good diet, exercise regime, and nightly entertainment, was the very picture of health. Angela was practically eating her body weight in peanut butter every day. She ballooned up. I started weighing her on a postal scale, and one time she bit me. She didn't break the skin, but after the infraction it was three more days in the punishment can.

BY NOW I had been to every fucking engineering firm in the city. Nobody was hiring. If you're a senior engineer, forget it. They hire a guy out of college, pay him a substandard salary, and get him to do the work of ten people. I reformulated my résumé and started looking for a job as a technician.

Angela was still eating peanut butter by the tablespoon. One day I came home and she was lying on her back with four feet in the air, stiff. Heart attack. In just six weeks' time. I enjoy peanut butter myself. I had been carrying peanut-butter sandwiches in my briefcase as I canvassed the city looking for work. I switched to lowfat turkey. It costs a fortune and, hungerwise, it doesn't satisfy, but I got to thinking of all the stuff I had eaten in my life, the whole pile of it. In peanut butter alone, there would be a warehouse. Cigarettes? Truck trailers full. After what I'd seen happen to Angela in six weeks, I felt lucky to be alive. I squared my diet away.

I got some Just for Men and colored my hair jet-black. I began to figure that my age was another handicap. But then one of the no-jobs at unemployment asked me if I'd lost my mind. "Anson, you look like Bela Lugosi!" Another said, "Man, that's a dye job you can spot a mile away." Some skaters on the street asked me if I was the singer Roy Orbison. Maybe they said this because I was wearing a pair of shades, or maybe they were just dicking with me. I said, "No, man, I'm Junior fuckin' Walker."

When I got home and checked myself out in the mirror, I saw that the no-jobs were right about my hair. It was too dark and it made my skin look pale. It was almost green. I looked like an undertaker. Plus, I'd lost weight, and my clothes were too big. Overnight, I had metamorphosed from a Stage One no-job to a Stage Three. Up all night with pain, I finally dropped off and didn't get up till four in the afternoon. Too late to go out. I didn't shave. I was thinking, What's the point of looking? They don't want to hire you. Capitalism sucks. The big companies just want to get rich. I got to hating everybody.

I DROVE OVER to the pet store and bought two dozen mice and a separate wire cage for each. You read stuff in medical reports about how a certain drug or vitamin did something in some study but it will be five years before the general public can get it. Or you read that something has produced miraculous results in chickens but they haven't tried it on humans yet. I'm the kind that figures, hell, if it works on a chicken it's going to work on everybody. I mean, if some guy spots mold on bread and turns it into penicillin, why not me? If I can't get a job, maybe I'll just go out and win the Nobel Prize.

I put the mice on a variety of diets and subjected them to various stresses. I kept a control group and fed its members the same mouse chow I fed Al. Other mice — eating a diet similar to my own, drinking a proportionate amount of coffee, and keeping the same hours — were dead in five weeks. Challenge, a momentary adaptation to stress, then exhaustion and death. I accepted the results with equanimity. I knew what was in the cards for me; once again I had evidence. Maybe I was lucky to have been canned. What I needed now was a plan: I wasn't going to be a victim anymore.

At 3 A.M. I took off my white lab coat, washed my hands, and called up my ex-boss. *Brrringgg! Ding-a-ling! Brrringgg!* When he answered, I hung up! Ah, ha, ha, shit! I then had a snack and about twenty minutes later — just when he'd fallen back to sleep — I called again. Ha, ha, ha, fuck! I pictured him lying there seething.

I put another batch of mice on a regime mimicking my old schedule, but I fortified their diets with vitamins. They died in just *under* five weeks, confirming something I always suspected: vitamins, especially the kind that have a strong smell, not only make you feel bad but can hasten your demise! The result held even for the mice that had the antioxidants cocktail: flavonoids, soy, red-wine extract, beta carotene, etc.

To some mice I gave huge amounts of coffee. Coffee mice became very aggressive and would often bite me. For each attempted bite, it was no coffee and three days in a punishment can. It skewed the validity of the experiments, but I already suspected the ultimate outcome. They say coffee is pretty much harmless, but after studying a coffee mouse's brains at autopsy I calculated otherwise. Shrunken thymus glands, a swelling in the cranial cavity, and a shriveling of the adrenal glands. They could run the most complicated labyrinths I constructed, but they were burning it at both ends.

ONE NIGHT I called my ex-boss and he fucking *made* me. He said he got Caller I.D. and knew it was me on the line. He threatened to turn me in to the police. I didn't say boo, man, I just hung up. I worried until dawn. I could hear my heart thumping in my chest. Was what I'd done a jailable offense? So much for the job recommendation.

And then, lo, one of my hundreds of résumés bore fruit! I got a call from a large electronics firm, went in, and took some grueling tests involving math, calculus, even physics. I was interrogated by a panel of hard-ass guys with starched white shirts and stern faces. At the conclusion, they said I was one of fifteen people being considered. Two hundred applicants had already been rejected. They told me that employees were subject to random drug tests. They said they would do a background check. Then they'd call me.

THE HARDIEST of my mice turned out to be the swimmers and walkers. The walkers were put on exercise wheels equipped with speed governors and forced to march at a nine-mph pace eight hours a day. Along the bottoms of their cages were metal grids wired to give them an electric shock if they decided to hop off the wheel and shirk their duty. A few rebelled, but the rebellion was dealt with easily: I merely dialed up the electricity. This made me realize the folly of my so-called punishment cans. A nice dark spot in a quiet room was not "punishment." True punishment, such as that reserved for recidivist biters, now took place in a proper punishment room with hot bright lights and severe jolts of electricity. A yoga mouse that I happened to take a dislike to, a little Hare Krishna crybaby who couldn't handle the nine-mph pace, died after thirty-four hours of continuous exercise. The shock burns on its feet, tail, and stomach were secondary to cardiac arrest. Hey! I'm sorry, but it's survival of the fittest. My tests demonstrated that a reasonable amount of hard physical labor each day produced health and contentment. Bodies are made for work, not idleness.

MAN, WHAT ELSE could go wrong? I was standing on a corner, minding my own business, and this no-job I knew, a Stage Three, came along and offered to buy me dinner at a Greek restaurant. I said sure, thinking some windfall had come his way. We did a fair amount of drinking and then had this big meal, several courses, with rounds of ouzo for the house. Then he got nervous for some reason. When he reached the register, some drastic thought passed through his brain like a dark cloud. He said to me, "Have you got any money?" I told him I had about sixty cents, and he stood there for a moment. He looked up, down, over his shoulder. Suddenly he yelled "Run!" and bolted. I was standing flat-footed. A couple of waiters took off after him. So did the cook, with a fifteen-inch blade. What a shocker! Too late, I ran the other way, and the older waiters started after me. Six long blocks they chased me. The no-job got away. Me, I was arrested. The police handcuffed me, shoved me into a patrol car, and whipped me off to the precinct station with their lights flashing. I spent the weekend in jail and finally arranged bond on Monday morning. To cap things off, when I got home I found Al in his aquarium with his three feet in the air, stone dead. I won't lie to you. It was very upsetting. I burst into tears. The lady living above me heard my raking sobs and knocked on the door to see if I was OK.

HANNIBAL WAS a well-exercised gladiator mouse. He had a piebald coat, white and tan. I fed him a diet of meat, vegetables, and grain. I gave him testosterone injections from ground-up mouse testicles. He got little boils at the injection sites, but he also became supermuscular. Hannibal won the first annual Gladiator Mouse Championship, killing in succession two swimmers, two walkers, a coffee mouse, and the remaining population of yoga mice — seventeen victims in all. I just kept throwing them in, one after another, getting more and more excited by the ferociousness of the battle. I felt like Caligula. Oh, man! It was too much.

Hannibal's capacity for work and his resistance to the usual stressors, including the punishment sessions, exceeded that of any of my previous specimens. His entire torso was pure muscle. The discipline he showed on the wheel, in the maze, in the pool, or defending his life in the gladiator pit, his appetite for work, and his willingness to meet any challenge made him my most interesting success. I knew I was on to something huge if only there was some way to dampen his murderous impulses, his relentless aggression, and his compulsive sexuality. To be able to harness all that drive and latent productivity. What a challenge!

I was able to farm more testosterone, and I injected it into female mice. The results were dramatic — similar to those which had occurred with Hannibal. But the female supermice, with a natural supply of estrogen, were more tractable. I was at a crossroads in my research. Was this the answer? A female named Cynthia defeated Hannibal in a tooth-and-nail gladiator bout. Yet she stopped short of killing the former champion. I removed his battered body from the little arena and administered adrenaline to his wounds, and then Hannibal bit me on the quick of my fingernail. Yeowza! What happened next was a blur. I slammed Hannibal against the wall like Randy Johnson hurling a ninety-eight-mph fastball. He bounced off and started scrambling around on the floor. I gave chase and stomped him to death in my stocking feet. What an ingrate! And after all I'd done for him.

A few weeks later I was at the university veterinary school, checking out some books on mouse anatomy, when it seemed to me that people were purposefully avoiding me. It went beyond the normal thing you get from being little. Was my fly open? Did I have something in my nose? As I walked up to the checkout desk, I smelled B.O. I put two and two together and realized that the B.O. was coming from me. I tested my breath by licking the back of my wrist and smelling it. It was awful. How far had I sunk? I had a brief panic attack outside and quickly made for home. After I'd had a long bath, the episode passed off.

With the help of the textbooks, I started harvesting other mouse hormones, even though the organ systems were often so tiny I felt I was performing microsurgery. It was also frustrating. The boils Cynthia developed from growth-hormone injections turned into large hard lumps that eventually proved fatal: upon autopsy, I discovered that these were tumors. Cynthia's liver nourished tumors as well. One by one, all my female supermice developed the same symptoms. Another dead end.

I never got the call from the firm that interviewed me. A month had passed, so, taking the bull by the horns, I called the firm and said that I had enjoyed our meeting and would be grateful for a job. I knew it was too late, and it made me angry. Just because I'm five feet tall! I hinted at the possibility of a discrimination suit. A vice-president got on the line and told me that my size had nothing to do with it. They were impressed by my qualifications. I had the job in the bag, but my former boss had given me a poor recommendation: he said I made harassing phone calls at three in the morning. The man said I could have even skated on that charge, but he'd noticed an item in the police blotter involving an incident at a Greek restaurant. I was so shaken by this disclosure that I said it must have been someone else with the same name as mine. A transparent lie. Despondent, I went out and bought two six-packs of beer. The next day I couldn't get out of bed. Nor on the following. I got a violent, three-day hangover and vowed never to drink again.

Court. Oh, God! The very thought of it. I went over to the restaurant and offered full restitution. Nothing doing, they said. I tried to explain what had happened but they made furious Greek gestures at me — God knows what they meant. They said, "See you in court, haffa pint! Broke-a-back. Shorty pants!"

Well, wait a minute, I said. It was the other guy's fault. I gave them the whole story. They said, Tell us who the other guy is and we'll drop the charge. Actually, I don't know the guy. I mean I "know" him, but he told so many lies I don't know if up is down with him. At one point he told me he was an actor and had been engaged to Catherine

Deneuve. He was a smoothie, and handsome — I half believed him.

I threw myself on the mercy of the court and got reamed with a two-hundred-and-fifty-dollar fine, court costs, six months probation, and a hundred hours of community service. Plus, now I've got a record. Also, I got hit for a hundred and fourteen in unpaid traffic tickets.

After court I lost interest in the mice and fell into a deep, Stage Five no-job depression. The Nobel Prize? Screw it. I went to a clinic and got a prescription for antidepressants and anti-anxiety drugs. On them, all I wanted to do was sleep. Twenty hours? No problem. It was a pleasant escape. After years of insomnia, I was in heaven.

But the medicine made me fat. Bloat weight. I gained back all that I'd lost. Pretty soon I couldn't get into the clothes that had once been hanging on me. I got a huge gut, a pair of thighs like twin water heaters, and a fat ass that stuck out like a clown's. I'd never thought that I could sink this low. I resorted to wearing sweatpants.

I started setting my alarm clock for late-afternoon appointments and even then I missed about half of them. I wondered how I would ever reassimilate myself into the mainstream of American life. I felt so low and so bad I didn't want to talk to anybody. The landlord came by: people were complaining about a smell. I didn't want him to see my mouse lab. The way things were going it would have been a federal bust — Dr. Mengele Nabbed At Last! I told the landlord I was taking care of a pair of hamsters for a friend, don't worry, I'll deal with the smell. He said, "Man, Anson, you gained weight." Well, no shit, Sherlock!

I cleaned out the mouse cages, replacing the soiled sawdust with fresh cedar shavings. Then it occurred to me to put the mice on this antidepressant that was kicking my ass so bad. Whenever I tried to get off it, I got this full-body pulsar buzz, and everything began to vibrate until I took another pill. I calibrated doses and started medicating the mice. Within three hours all of them were out. Dead? I couldn't tell. But it turned out no, they weren't dead — they were in comas. I wondered if that's what I looked like at night. One slept for two days and didn't change positions: frozen in one posture. I put another on the punishment wheel, and it was oblivious to the shocks. Blue sparks were popping off its paws and it ignored them.

I mentioned earlier that most of the bad stuff you worry about never comes to pass. But sometimes, I was now discovering, it does. You fall into a kind of Bermuda Triangle of hard-ass reality. How long was this going to go on? I asked myself. I finally managed to get off the drugs by taking smaller and smaller doses. And slowly the bloat weight came off. I phoned for an interview for a technician's job at a factory less than a mile from my building, and I was hired that very day. I couldn't believe it. The job was a piece of cake, too. I went in and read the paper and drank coffee for an hour before anyone got ambitious. There were numerous breaks and good camaraderie all the way around. Even so, it was hard to get through a day. I didn't have the stamina. Coming back from Stage Five was tough business. In the annals of no-jobdom, it's rare. Almost unheard of. I had pulled off a big one.

Pretty soon some of the design engineers were hanging out with me, asking my advice on projects and so on. One thing led to another, and I was promoted to senior engineer and making a third more than I got at the last place. It was easy duty, this job. I got into the work and — zing! — the time just flew. I never had a job I *liked* before. I didn't think such a thing existed.

THE MICE, as they died off, I buried in little toilet-paper tubes. They have a life expectancy of three years. I didn't replace them. Ashes to ashes, dust to dust. What I did was pretty unconscionable. Absolute power, as they say. I'm not proud of my behavior. I had been living without checks and balances. The crap I pulled makes me think of what the space invaders will do to us if they conquer the world. Make slaves of us, eat us, flay us alive and torture us, do every kind of sinister thing in the book. There's a dark side to intelligent beings, an irrational craving for war, personal defilement, and reckless destruction, even if we know better. So if aliens are out there and they do come down I don't expect good things. Aliens aren't out there flying around on errands of mercy or benevolence. To them, we're just so much protein. We're calories. When the space invaders take over, it's the end of the human era. Before that happens, I want to get in a few good times — travel to Ireland, learn how to dance, take tuba lessons, who knows. Happiness is like the gold in the Yukon mines, found only now and then, as it were, by the caprices of chance. It comes rarely in chunks or boulders but most often in the tiniest of grains. I'm a free-floater now, happy to take what little comes my way. A grain here, a grain there. What more can you ask for?

A Midnight Clear

FOR DAYS Mrs. Gordon beseeched her stepson, Freddy, to drive her up to the state hospital in Granite Falls. Every Christmas she put together a fruit basket for her third cousin Eustace. His principal relatives had carried out the annual deliveries over the years, but winter had struck early in northern Illinois, and struck with a vengeance, dumping one record snowstorm after another. The storms were followed by fierce winds and two weeks of bitter cold. Christmas spirit notwithstanding, no one in the Gordon family wanted to venture outside, especially for a fruit basket mission to the mental hospital. So Mrs. Gordon worked on Freddy, who had been bragging recently about the virtues of his Swedish Saab, a car undaunted even by polar climes.

"If this car is as good as you say, twenty miles on a four-lane highway will be a cruise. Are you the right man for the job? Am I talking to the right fella?"

At last Freddy said, "The car is an ace. I'll do it."

Mrs. Gordon had never been to a state mental hospital. For her it conjured up images of gothic horror. In a small way, this was part of the visit's appeal. Also, reports of Eustace's recent stroke made his future seem pretty iffy. One more blood clot and he could be out. Mrs. Gordon knew she could not live with herself if she did not make a last-minute appeal for this poor soul's heavenly salvation. Because Freddy was a doctor, she figured he would know what to do if things got out of hand. As an emergency room physician, he wrangled with crazed drug addicts, autistics, and demon-inspired assault-prone schizophrenics on a daily basis.

Freddy showed up at four in the afternoon, three hours late. Although he was dressed in a jacket and tie, he did not look presentable. The hair on the back of his head had rooster-tailed and he needed a shave. His eyes looked like two balls of fire. In spite of being late, Freddy demanded caffeine. Mrs. Gordon wanted to kill him. Instead she convinced him to clean up while she made a pot of Starbucks. Freddy was blowing his nose when she barged into the bathroom with a plastic traveler's cup of coffee. "Let's get this show on the road," she said.

The sun sat low in the winter sky and they weren't even out of the driveway yet. Freddy complained that the coffee was too hot and got out of the car to break off a hunk of snow to cool it down. By now Mrs. Gordon was having second thoughts. She had spent most of the morning putting on makeup and getting dressed. Then she'd paced about the house like a madwoman, exhausting herself thinking of the barbarous scenes that might transpire at the hospital.

Freddy started the car and flipped on the soundtrack from the film *Crumb*. Concentrating on his coffee, he drove the Saab through the west side of town and then caught the highway to Granite Falls. *Crumb*'s syncopated ragtime rhythms were like theme music, by turns festive, exuberant, and depressing. Except for roadwork vehicles and the intrepid Saab, very few cars were out. The road was ghostly.

Highway 31 ran parallel to the Fox River and when the Saab wasn't chugging through heavy snow, it faced winding curves slick with ice. Freddy braked for a van, the car spun, and Mrs. Gordon slapped her hand against the dash. Freddy smiled. "You don't trust my driving skills."

"The road conditions are utterly *harrowing*, and you're driving one-handed. I got up at nine, I've been drinking coffee all day and I'm a nervous wreck," she said. "Absolutely shot."

Freddy laughed. "You said I look bad? You look worse. Haggard. A bag lady."

"I'm hagged," Mrs. Gordon said, letting out a sigh. She studied the old estates lining the river. Such scenes normally gave her pleasure, but now all she could think of was the upkeep and the heating bills. The owners would have to be millionaires, literally, with money to burn. She turned to Freddy and said, "What if someone attacks us? Crazy people have the strength of thirty. They're like Samson. Even the little ones."

"That's why they lock them up," Freddy said. "Given enough time the mentally ill — an M.I. — will pull some crazy-ass shit. Most are tame, but murder and mayhem have a way of unfolding in their presence. We *could* be killed at the hands of some violent monster. More likely I'll roll the car and we'll drown in the river. I'm not Mario Andretti. I can't believe I agreed to do this in such shit weather, with a hangover yet."

"You're driving like a maniac!" Mrs. Gordon said. "I need . . . Dramamine or something. One more wild curve and I'll die. I can't take any more."

Freddy raised his voice over the music. "I can't take it either. I'm just trying to get this whole thing over with and get my ass back home and into bed. This was all your big idea. Eustace won't even remember us. He's not there, never was."

Mrs. Gordon bristled. "He's got an immortal soul," she said, "and this is Christmas."

Freddy shook his head with finality. "He won't be judged. He's defective."

"His dad took him to *whores!*" Mrs. Gordon said. "That's sin of the worst sort."

"What did you say?" Freddy cranked down the stereo. "He took him to a whorehouse? I thought they were big Christians."

Mrs. Gordon corrected her posture. Looking straight ahead she said, "When he came of age, Eustace sort of got out of control. His doctor had the name of some woman. It wasn't a whorehouse."

Freddy scratched the stubble on his neck. "Geez. I never figured that Eustace got laid. Just that he fell ninety-five feet off the water tower. Somehow I never imagined anything sexual happened with him."

"Once a week," Mrs. Gordon said, "something sexual happened."

Freddy turned off the stereo. "I have to fight to hear you. What did this woman look like?"

"She must have been a bird," Mrs. Gordon said. "To be able to put up with that. But, then, it was probably over quick —"

"And it calmed him? It did the trick?"

"As far as I know. But you just can't say he won't be judged."

The Saab hit a straightaway by the Campana factory and Freddy turned to his stepmother. "Eustace is an imbecile! You want to bring him to your house and take care of him in the true Christian spirit? Change diapers and stuff? No! I didn't think so. You think a fruit basket is going to help? The glue factory. That's where we're going. I'm not a Nazi. I'm just sayin'."

The Saab's radar detector began to blink as they approached the city limits of Granite Falls. The state hospital was situated on the east side of the highway, across from the river. It consisted of twenty-two Victorian-era buildings, only half of which were still operational. The hospital had been built on spacious grounds at a time when land and labor were cheap. It sat amid a grove of oak, elm, and maple trees, their branches laden with dripping daggers of clear ice. Snow swirled in drifts over a deeper layer of packed snow, white, untrampled, except for animal tracks. Mrs. Gordon clapped on a pair of sunglasses and studied the frigid landscape. A formidable wrought-iron fence, interspersed with brick pillars, surrounded the grounds. There was no chain-link or razor wire, but the fence was tall and artistically deceptive. It was there for security. Freddy wheeled through the main gate and parked in the visitors' lot. "Here we are at last, my dear, the bughouse. The snake pit. Vermin and reptiles abounding."

Mrs. Gordon's throat was dry. "I don't know if I can go through with it."

"Well, you simply must, dear heart. And let me say that this is yet another fine mess you've gotten us into!" Freddy grabbed the fruit basket from Mrs. Gordon's lap. "One more." As he opened the door, a bitter crosswind hit him like a slap in the face. He pulled up the collar on his overcoat and cursed himself for not wearing a hat. Mrs. Gordon put her head down against the wind and followed, vainly attempting to preserve her hairdo.

"Slow down," she said. "I'm wearing heels. I can't keep up with you."

"Flash frozen," Freddy said. "Antarctica. It's like liquid nitrogen."

A patient in a stocking cap and a Navy peacoat stopped Freddy to cadge a cigarette. Freddy shook off his gloves and pulled a pack of Kools from his pocket. He gave them to the man and said, "Keep them, buddy. I quit as of now. My New Year's resolution."

At this, a very short man wearing an overcoat and a dark homburg came around from the side of a beige Electra. His mustache was white with frost yet he seemed oblivious to the cold. The Buick had a flat and the two men were attempting to replace it with a mini spare. Now that he had been engaged, Freddy felt compelled to help them. He pulled on his gloves and replaced the lug nuts on the wheel. The man in the peacoat tightened them with the lug wrench while Mrs. Gordon held her ears and winced.

"Va-boom!" the short fellow said. His voice was deep and powerful. "Done. Ah-ho-yeah!" But as he let the jack down and the full weight of the car came to bear, the mini spare went flat. "Oh, brother!" he said. "What's this country coming to? Why can't they give you a real tire for a spare? I *knew* this was going to happen. I'm calling a tow truck, Norman. This is intolerable!"

Freddy asked where Ward Six was located and the short man pointed at the hospital clock tower. "The gray building behind the clock tower," he said. "Jarrad Hall. There's a plaque on the door. If you get to the water tower, you've gone too far. Those two chimneys from the power plant beyond . . . see there? It's the last outpost of civilization. Chinese Turkistan, Outer Mongolia, man. You will never make it back alive."

Freddy nodded his head at the two men. "Gotcha! Good day, gentlemen."

"Come on," Mrs. Gordon said as she plodded on ahead. "If we stand here another minute, I'll die."

"The guy is right, those little tires are ridiculous. I mean, who thought of that? It's not exactly what you call a grand inspiration."

"They were thinking in terms of space saving," Mrs. Gordon said. "Cargo space. If you want to transport dope, a dead body or something, there's more room."

"Yes, of course, but what stupid, fucking goddamn assholes they are just the same. The empire is in terminal decline."

"You have the foulest mouth of anyone alive," Mrs. Gordon said.

Freddy looked at her sharply. "I traverse hell on a daily basis. I'm known for my poignant effusions. To imagine that any human escapade could turn out well seems unthinkable to me, but this trip, Iona? Oh, do forgive me! You know I have a perception of things very few can endure. I will abstain from burrowing any further into my fourth dimension of despair except to say that this very planet has gangrene."

"The earth has gangrene," she said. "It's not paradise. Not by a long shot."

The pair followed the walkway around the clock tower and reached a gray building with locked doors. Freddy bolted ahead until he came upon the water tower. He turned around and ran back to his stepmother. "We're lost. I don't know what to do. I haven't even got a plan." He pulled off his coat and put it over his head like a blanket. They stood together shivering for a moment until a maintenance worker driving a snowplow stopped and gave them a lift back. He pulled a key ring from his belt, unlocked the door, and let them inside.

The lobby was dark and empty, but it was warm. Freddy kicked off his loafers and began to rub his feet in a savage fashion. "Son of a bitch, it's cold!"

Mrs. Gordon blew on her hands and rubbed her face. "Oh God!" she said. "That was absolute hell!"

"Changing that tire. Shit! Goddamn motherfucker! Why was I born?"

"You were born because your dad screwed a bimbo," Mrs. Gordon said. "And now that you're here, you just have to make the best of it, like all the rest. Don't think of the philosophical implications."

Mrs. Gordon sat on a narrow bench next to Freddy and had begun to rub her own feet when a voice rattled over the intercom. "Please step forward and state your business."

Freddy spotted a small TV camera just above the inter-com speaker. He moved before it and said, "Dr. Frederick Blaine here to see Eustace Elliot Eckstrom."

Freddy heard some giggling in the background. The same voice pitched an octave lower said, "Eckstrom, Eustace, joost von moment. Es he yah patient, doc-taw?"

"He's my relative!"

Mrs. Gordon clutched her body under her coat. "I'm frozen down to the core level," she said. "How do penguins take it?"

"I don't know. They have antifreeze in their blood. Maybe they hate their lives." Freddy peered through the metal mesh gate that bisected the lobby. "I'm not kidding, if I could push a button and never have been born, I'd push. The deal is this: We are in hell. It's just that they call it earth. If they just called it hell, it would make more sense."

"People could take it better if the right information were put out," Mrs. Gordon said. "I agree with that. Calling it earth is propaganda. Chinese Communist bullshit."

The intercom crackled. "Dot's Ward Six, duke-tor. I wan' you an' the little lady to prozeed down zee 'all to elevator C and take her to d' t'oid floor. How's zat sound to y'all?"

"That's peachy, sir," Freddy said. "That's dandy! We're coming. We're on our way. So look out."

A buzzer sounded and the iron gate slid open. Assaulted by a variety of indefinable but powerful odors, they followed the buffed terrazzo hall to elevator C.

The entrance to Ward Six was an oversize steel door painted with shiny white enamel but covered with greasy handprints, dried blood, snot, scuff marks, and indenta-tions that made it look like a guardrail at the Indy 500.

Freddy pointed them out. "Look at that! The Incredible Hulk. After his TV series bombed, they sent him here."

"He's in there with green skin and a bad temper," Mrs. Gordon said. "We were fools to come."

Freddy smiled. "Think *hell* and it will all approximate fun."

Mrs. Gordon checked her lipstick in a cosmetic mirror, "H-E double hockey sticks!"

Freddy rang the buzzer, then cupped his hands to peer through the thick yellow Plexiglas window of the door. A lanky orderly in a white uniform was seated at the charge desk reading a paperback copy of *The Sea Wolf,* by Jack London. He had a short black beard and long hair, and his reading glasses were attached around his neck by a lanyard. Freddy watched him take off his glasses, set the book down, and remove a large brass key from his belt. The man wore a name tag that read STEPHENS. He opened the door and said, "Evening visiting hours are over at five-thirty."

Freddy flashed his hospital identification and Stephens waved the couple inside. Stephens went back to his desk and returned to his book. Freddy asked where Cousin Eustace could be located and, without looking up, Stephens adjusted his glasses and pointed to the back of the ward.

A group of patients watching TV turned toward the door to see what was going on. They did not look nearly as crazy as Mrs. Gordon had imagined. In fact, they looked pretty normal. In a moment they turned back to the television, where Christopher Walken was doing a song-and-dance routine with elves and a snowman. Suddenly the biggest woman Mrs. Gordon had ever seen got up from a large chair and began to bear down on her.

Orderly Stephens jumped up from the desk, pointing a finger at the woman. In an even tone he said, "Stop it right there, Marla! I'm in no mood for fucking bullshit today. So just cool your jets!" Stephens sat down and bent back the spine of his paperback, waiting for Marla to comply.

Mrs. Gordon smiled nervously, hiding behind Stephens and Freddy. Not only was Marla tall, everything about her was large. She had enormous shoulders, huge hands, and big legs. She had coarse facial features. Her teeth were large, but they were regular. Her hair was black and cut at shoulder length. She wore a plain black dress that looked homemade, a pearl choker, and black penny loafers. She waited behind a grizzly, middle-aged man in a blue-striped cotton robe and pajamas who was smoking a cigarette and playing a game of solitaire. When Stephens had beaten the spine of his book into submission, he made a flicking motion with his hand, as if he were shooing a fly. "Eckstrom's way back thataway."

That ward was hot, and the air heavy and stale. Freddy unbuttoned his coat and loosened his tie, looking around. He had never been to Granite Falls before, but he had been in more than a few psychiatric facilities. For a state hospital, Granite Falls was not a bad place. The dayroom was L-shaped, with a high ceiling, a blond-stained oak floor, and four large alcoves of leaded glass windows that were obscured by thick mesh screens. It was a capacious room, and though there was much evidence of hard wear, it retained a kind of bygone elegance. Apart from a set of old mahogany dining tables, the furniture in Ward Six was a hodgepodge of Salvation Army couches and lounge chairs. In the center of the room, next to the television, was a nine-foot Christmas tree that was festooned with tiny blinking lights, tinsel, and at least a dozen paper angels. Pine wreaths, brightened with glossy red holly berries and more homemade angels, hung from the mesh window security screens.

As the pair continued to linger, Stephens beat his book cover against the edge of his desk and said, "Go on, get out of here. I'm sick of looking at you."

Freddy smiled, put on his I'm-in-hell-it-doesn't-matter voice and said, "Thank you for your patience and consideration, Mr. Stephens."

As Freddy pulled Mrs. Gordon away from the charge desk, a man wearing a crucifix and a black cloak sidled up to the visitors. He had thick curly red hair, bushy red eyebrows, and a face full of freckles. His pale green eyes were ringed with gold flecks that made Freddy wonder if he suffered from Wilson's disease, a syndrome that is marked by the inability to metabolize copper. The man said, "Good afternoon. Mr. Eckstrom is in the back attending to matters of the highest importance. I'm Charlie White. Allow me to present my dear friend, Marla Hollingsbury."

"You look like Jacqueline Onassis," Marla said. She had a deep voice and a theatrical manner. "Are you her?" She reached out and took Mrs. Gordon's hand.

"Well, people tell me that," Mrs. Gordon said. "I think it's because of the way I do my hair. I mean, I don't try to cultivate the look." She tried to withdraw her hand but Marla continued to pump it vigorously.

Freddy was getting a kick out of this. He smiled at the man in black. "If your name is Charles White, how come you wear all black? You wearin' a whole lotta black."

"I'm a man of Dostoyevskian complexity," Mr. White said.

"I thought maybe you were like Zorro or something," Freddy said.

Marla continued to pump Mrs. Gordon's hand with such vigor that Iona inadvertently stepped out of her left shoe. "Charlie has seizures," Marla said.

"That's true," White said. "But otherwise I'm in perfect health."

"Take it easy, Marla, you're hurting me," Mrs. Gordon said. "Let go of my hand!"

Marla began to laugh hysterically. "I'm really nervous."

Charles White grabbed Marla's wrist, which seemed as thick as a railroad tie, and loosened her grip. "Marla's excited. She doesn't meet many celebrities in this place."

"But I'm not a celebrity. My name is Iona Gordon."

"We know that you aren't the former first lady," Charlie told her. "She's been dead for some time now! Three years, seven months, four days, and twenty-one hours, sixteen minutes."

Marla continued to giggle. "Charles and I are Jackie's Granite Falls fan club. I'm sorry, Iona. You're such a lovely woman. You do look like her."

Mrs. Gordon was appalled at Marla's tongue. It was black and seemed to be a yard long. Freddy picked up his stepmother's shoe and began to usher her away. She stopped to slip it on. The back of the ward was dark and they moved in that direction with trepidation.

"What's with her tongue?" Mrs. Gordon whispered.

"Pepto-Bismol. The bismuth does that," Freddy said. "Stomach upsets. Either that or she's a chow dog."

Cousin Eustace was on his knees at the back of the day-room, carefully laying a bead of ketchup along the oak baseboard. "Hey-ya," Freddy said. "What's going on, bro?"

Eustace Eckstrom was in his middle fifties, but he looked much older. He had gone entirely bald since Freddy had last seen him. The left side of his face was sagging. His mouth was set askew. His right eyelid twitched. Eustace wore a pair of loose khaki pants, shower shoes, and a dingy cotton singlet. He had the sort of beard that made him look badly in need of a shave, even after a shave. This effect was accentuated by his skin's deathly pallor. Eustace's shoulders were slumped and his countenance was downcast. He took in the presence of his cousins and said, "Those motherfuckers are at it again — pumping gas in here."

"Oh yeah?" Freddy said.

"Yeah!" Eustace said. "I can hear them talking when I take my urine. I can't see them. Just hear tinkle voices."

"In your piss?" Freddy said.

"Yeah, my urine."

"That can happen," Freddy said with a mischievous smile. "I wouldn't worry about it. Hey, look who came here to see you."

Cousin Eustace worked the ketchup container like a caulking gun, edging the nozzle along the baseboard. "It's Aunt Iona," Cousin Eustace said. "I already saw her. She sends me the same thing every year and I never eat it. Trying to poison me and collect on insurance, that's all."

"You could do with some vitamin C, Eu," Freddy said.

"Soda crackers. That's all I eat. Saltines."

Mrs. Gordon said, "You're working awfully hard, Eustace. Would you like to have a little visit with us? Go out for a ride, maybe? I'll get you a present you really want. What do you say?"

Eustace got up and laid a bead of ketchup along the base of a window. "Smell the gas?"

Freddy shook his head and said, "Brother, it smells like you got a load in your pants."

"There's a war in heaven," Cousin Eustace said. "That's what the piss voices say. I'm on the punishment brigade. You better just leave me alone from now on."

Freddy wriggled a finger in his ear and said, "Aunt Iona brought some really boring family pictures she thought you might want to see."

"I'm busy here," Eustace said.

"OK," Freddy said. "I'd like to ask you a question. What's this I hear about you having sex on weekends back in the days of your youth?"

Eustace's features brightened. "Did you talk to Vera?"

"Is that her name? What did she look like?" Freddy said.

"Vera Simpson?" Mrs. Gordon said. "Ho boy! I remember her."

"She sent me a Christmas card, Aunt Iona. From Oklahoma. Drive me there! OK?"

"To Oklahoma?" Mrs. Gordon said. "I don't know. That's pretty far."

Cousin Eustace thought this over for a moment and a dark look came over his face. He said, "You offered me a present and then you chink out! Go fuck!"

Mrs. Gordon followed Freddy back to Stephen's desk. It was obvious that everyone in the ward had listened to their conversation. Iona Gordon felt so conspicuous she hardly knew how to walk.

Eustace called after them. "I'm not a woman, Fred. I have an Adam's apple."

A patient in a knit hat looked up from the TV and cried out, "That's right! And you are one snoring-ass mother-fucker. Know what else, asshole? Romeo and Juliet? If they don't commit suicide, they get sick of each other. Put them in a hotel room for six weeks! Six dick-fucking weeks and they'll be singing a whole different tune."

Stephens looked up from his book and yelled, "Can it, Edwall!"

At the charge desk Stephens told Freddy he would need an OK from a staff physician to review Cousin Eustace's records. "Today that would be Dr. Bangladesh," the orderly said, picking up the phone. "I'll page him. He might still be around."

Freddy looked at the patients watching television. Others were sleeping on couches, even on the floor. Various isolatos sat or stood, preoccupied with their thoughts and seemingly oblivious to their environment.

Charles White twisted the crucifix hanging from his neck. He said, "We are held in lower regard than barnyard animals. This is a warehouse for the damned."

"I've been told there's a war raging in heaven," Freddy said.

Charlie fluffed his curly fringe of red hair and Freddy saw large yellow flecks of dandruff spring into the air. "More than war, it's a reckoning," White said. "From your flippant tone I can tell you aren't picking up on this. I'm here. I'm on the inside. Michael and his angels fought against the dragon; and the dragon fought, and his angels, and prevailed not. And the great dragon was cast out, that old serpent called the devil, and Satan, which deceiveth the whole world. He was cast out into the earth, and his angels were cast out with him."

"So that's what's wrong with the world?" Freddy said. The tumbler on the steel door's lock rattled and the short man Freddy had encountered in the parking lot walked in. His black mustache had thawed and, while it was thick, joining his lip to his hawklike nose, it was no wider than a postage stamp. He wore a pair of half-frame glasses that were steamed from the weather. Freddy watched as he reached up and hung his homburg and overcoat on a wall hook in the meds station. Although his face was ruddy, he did not seem to have suffered especially from the cold. If anything, he seemed invigorated. He slipped on a white lab coat and clipped a beeper to his belt. When he spotted Freddy through the office window, his eyes twinkled and he walked back into the ward. "Va-boom!" he said. "Ay-ho-yeah! So we meet again. I'm Oscar Bangladesh. How can I help you?"

"I'm Freddy Blaine from the city hospital. And this is my stepmother, Iona Gordon, wife of the late Dr. William Blaine. I wondered if I could take a look at Mr. Eckstrom's records. He's a relative. My cousin."

Dr. Bangladesh escorted the visitors back into the office and dropped the venetian blinds over the window. Freddy, who was 6'1", towered over the psychiatrist. "New shoes?" Freddy said. "Two-tones. Very snazzy."

The doctor wore a pair of white-and-brown Bostonian shoes with smooth toe caps. "Hah! Correct. Christmas present," Dr. Bangladesh said. "Special order from Massachusetts. It's expensive as hell being a little person."

"I never considered that," Mrs. Gordon said. "But it must be true. All the stuff in your house must be different. Your furniture, I mean."

"So true. I live in a gingerbread house," Dr. Bangladesh said. "It requires constant attention."

From the ward Charlie White called, "It gets green mold on it. Or he gets hungry and eats it."

"Isn't that amazing?" Dr. Bangladesh whispered. "The most incredible sense of hearing I've ever encountered. And he can calculate numbers like a wizard. Baseball stats are his thing."

"I am a genius," Charles said. "You are a house eater."

"Yes, Charles, periodically I become ravenous and devour an entire house. Of course! In fact, I could eat a skyscraper right now! The Empire State Building — an appetizer. Hah! Va-Boom!"

Mrs. Gordon realized she was staring at the little man. Apart from his new shoes, Dr. Bangladesh wore a brown three-piece gabardine suit that was beginning to shine with age and a dirty yellow tie festooned with miniature golfers driving off from tees. He stood before Freddy and Mrs. Gordon with a square hand tucked into his vest, Napoleon style.

Freddy said, "Eustace doesn't look so hot. There's motor impairment on the whole left side of his body, slurred speech, his eye —"

Dr. Bangladesh smoothed his bushy eyebrows, then steepled his blunt fingers and took on an air of doctorly concern. "Yes, Mr. Eckstrom. A stroke, but there was all the previous physical impairment from a fall he suffered. He hasn't done well here. Twelve years now and nothing but trouble. Few have sufficient ego strength to withstand the rigors of long-term confinement. Have a seat, both of you, please."

"No, thanks. I'm going back out there," Mrs. Gordon said. "I can't breathe." She brushed past Freddy and stepped out into the ward.

Dr. Bangladesh snapped on a floor fan. "Does it really *smell* in here? People say it does. I've been here so long, I can't tell anymore." He pulled a manila-backed chart from a battered gray filing cabinet, glancing at it before passing it to Freddy. "Mr. Eckstrom suffered a series of small strokes, was sent to the city hospital, and when he stabilized, he was returned to the ward. He's been on heparin and there's been bruising. We didn't know he had family. Is there anyone who might —"

"Take him in? I don't think so," Freddy said. "Not possible."

Dr. Bangladesh's hand clung to the top drawer of the filing cabinet. He hung his head and looked down at the floor. "Well, I'm afraid he can't last much longer."

Freddy poked his head out into the ward and took a look at the back of the room. Eustace was again on his knees with the ketchup container. "He told me someone is pumping gas into the ward."

"Someone *is* pumping gas in here," Charles White said from a dining table chair. Freddy watched him scratch his fringe of red hair.

Dr. Bangladesh stepped into the ward, hiking up his slacks. He placed his hands on his hips, large hips for such a small man. "I've already explained this to you, Charles. Our ventilation system is old. It's inadequate."

"Bullcrap! They've been making buildings for thousands of years." White slammed his fist on the table. "We've got windows! Why can't we open those windows? There's gas in this suckhole."

Dr. Bangladesh looked at the floor and shook his head wearily. "And what sort of gas would that be, Mr. White?"

A woman who was sitting alone in a dark corner crying wiped tears from her eyes with the sleeves of her pajamas and sat up defiantly. She had a British accent. "It's vaguely . . . buttholish. We could do with some fresh air, Doctor. Everyone is turning yellow."

From the back of the ward a faraway voice cried, "This motherfucker smells like a ripe ass."

A thin man in his seventies pulled off his plaid snap-billed cap and slapped it against his thigh. "Smells like cat pee," he said.

Stephens clapped his hands and pointed a finger at the old man. "Hen Pierce, you calm down, mister! I'll have you in an isolation cell so fast you won't know what hit you."

"Are you talking to me?" Pierce said. "What I said was mild. People are throwing the F word around again."

Charles White turned to Freddy. "Zyklon B, Dr. Blaine. You're in it with him. They must have sent you over here from Germany with a new supply."

Freddy said, "You're a fraud, Mr. White. All I'm hearing from you is clichéd nuthouse ideation. I think they should give you a bottle of Dilantin and discharge you. Get a job! Hack it out there in the real world."

Dr. Bangladesh pulled a roll of wintergreen Life Savers from his pocket and peeled off the foil top. He put four of the candies in his mouth. "Think of it like this, Charles. If the staff were pumping gas in, would we not also be asphyxiating ourselves?"

"Selective infusions. You're never here for them, Oscar," Charles White said. "Once in a blue moon you pass through the joint and that's it. All you do is play golf."

"Don't attack me. Your argument just doesn't hold up and you know it. Who plays golf when it's twenty below?" Dr. Bangladesh removed his half frames and wiped them with his sleeve. There were beads of perspiration on his forehead. He looked at Freddy. "It's hot in here, I'll give him that."

Charles White said, "Two things: hot and no oxygen."

"Bring it up in group on Tuesday. In the meantime, kindly subdue yourself! I'm tired too."

"You are tired," Charles said. "Very tired, Oscar. Not good at all."

Stephens set *The Sea Wolf* on the charge desk. "Knock it off, Charlie, or I'll come over there! Those isolation cells are ready, willing, and able. I'm counting to three!"

Mr. White turned away and plopped down in a chair before the TV set. He draped his arms along the sides of the chair and sulked. Freddy watched him for a moment. His head and right hand twitched every few seconds. Suddenly he got up and changed channels. Another patient snapped out of a hypnotic daze to protest, and the two started arguing. They could barely be heard over the high volume of the TV.

Dr. Bangladesh waved Freddy back into the office and shut the door. He lowered his voice and said, "Being in the presence of a manic personality is exhausting for me. They suck up all the energy in the room and leave you drained.

Every time I walk in the door, there he is, ready to assail me with the most unimaginable kind of stupid crap you could ever think of. A forty-five-minute rap over nothing."

Freddy studied the doctor's face. "He's right, though. You don't look very well. Your left pupil is a pinpoint and the right is dilated."

Dr. Bangladesh took a step back, alarmed. "Really? What does that mean, medically? I'm not a doctor, I'm a psychiatrist. Is that some cardinal signal?"

"Probably it means nothing," Freddy said. "Just tired, that's all."

"No, there's more," Dr. Bangladesh said. "I feel sicker than a dog. Everything is swirly. An attack of hypoglycemia?" Dr. Bangladesh braced himself against the wall. "Damn! I feel actively sick. I'm dizzy as shit. You don't think I might have an aneurysm or something, do you?"

"Get something to eat," Freddy said. "You haven't got an aneurysm. You're tired."

Dr. Bangladesh held his head in his hands. "I have a very rapid metabolism. I need to eat. Feel free to sit in here. You will be more comfortable. Excuse me, I have to go eat a little bite and lie down for a minute in the staff lounge."

The doctor's two-tone shoes squeaked as he walked across the oak floor. Freddy watched him reach up to open the heavy steel door and then disappear. As the door slammed shut, Freddy shook his head. Either the job was getting to the man or he had never been quite right in the first place. He closed the door of the office, sat down, and began to page through the Eustace Eckstrom chart. What was there was much as he had expected. Eustace had dangerously high blood pressure readings, but there were no recorded vascular studies or MRIs. He was being treated with beta-blockers and diuretics that were adequate but not exactly state of the art. He was receiving stupendous doses of the blood thinner heparin, also Haldol for auditory hallucinations, and large doses of a standard antidepressant drug — a tricyclic that was too much, really, for a person with a tricky circulatory system and funny heart rhythms. On top of that, they were giving Eustace valproate for seizures. Cousin Eustace had a stated IQ of 82. Freddy flopped his tie over his shoulder as a nurse with small breasts, a pitted face, and a low-slung ass came into the office. "Are you Dr. Blaine?"

Freddy set the chart down and said, "Yes. What's wrong?"

"It's Dr. Bangladesh. Please, come with me," she said. "He's out."

Freddy and the nurse ran down two flights of stairs to the staff lounge, a small room with a table and chairs, a refrigerator, microwave oven, and a coffeepot. Dr. Bangladesh was lying on a Naugahyde couch, bathed in sweat. One of his new shoes was lying on the floor.

"What's going on here?" Freddy said.

"I don't know," the nurse said. "He was all right one minute and then he just started acting like he was . . . out of it. I couldn't make any sense out of him. He said something about being gassed."

Freddy laughed. "Gassed, huh?"

"Yes. He was sweating furiously and then he passed out."

Freddy unbuttoned the little man's jacket, vest, and shirt. "Any known health problems? Heart disease? Diabetes?"

The nurse thought for a moment. "He guzzles water and goes to the bathroom constantly."

"Where's the house physician?" Freddy said as he removed the doctor's lab coat, jacket, and tie. "I don't even work here."

The nurse lowered voice and said, "The house doctor, Zarkov? We don't want him. He's a bungler."

Freddy took the nurse's stethoscope and began to listen to Oscar's heart. "Meningitis in this place?"

"No," the nurse said.

"Get me a glucose meter and a glucagon kit," Freddy said. He expertly moved the stethoscope about the doctor's chest and then began to poke his abdomen.

When the nurse returned, Freddy said, "I can hear a squeak in his lungs. His pulse is 170. His organs feel normal. Run a check on his sugar. Have they got tuberculosis?"

"No." The nurse pricked the doctor's finger with a spring-loaded lancet. She cocked the device and did it again, looking up at them in frustration. "I can't get any blood," she said. "His hands are freezing."

Freddy took the lancet from her, recocked it and popped Dr. Bangladesh in the earlobe. He squeezed a drop of blood onto the test strip. "Never fails," Freddy said. "Ready? Here we go: countdown!" The glucose meter flashed 45, and second by second the numbers began to run backward as pulses of red light flashed through the test strip. "How does one acquire a name like Oscar Bangladesh?" Freddy said.

"It's not his real name," the nurse said. "His parents are very high up in India, I think. Maharajas or something. Did he lay that 500-watt smile on you?"

"Yeah. 'Va-boom! Ah-ho-yeah!'"

The nurse laughed. "His parents were pissed that he didn't marry a traditional woman. What they don't know is that he's gay. At least that's the rumor. It must be true — he listens to Broadway show tunes. And here's the clincher — he has three Burmese cats!"

"Three? That cinches it. He's a flamer."

The glucose meter beeped and the nurse handed it to Freddy. "He's down to twenty-eight."

"That's pretty low. Saw a guy walk in with a seven once, and he was . . . walking! Look." He held up one of Dr. Bangladesh's tiny hands. "The tips of these three fingers look like pin cushions. That's why you couldn't get any blood — he's got calluses from self-testing. And look here," he said, pulling up the doctor's shirt. "See these bruises all over his abdomen? Injection sites. He's a diabetic, over-weight." Freddy removed the syringe from the emergency kit and squirted the diluting solution into the bottle of powdered glucagon. He shook it for a second, drew the mixed solution back into the syringe, and injected it into the doctor's thigh. "What's the date on the package?"

The nurse picked up the box and peered. "It's fifteen months old. It expired three months ago."

Freddy said, "It should work fine. Essentially there's a thousand times more, or so, than he needs, and he's a little guy."

The nurse said, "You really are a pretty cool customer, Doctor. Where do you practice?"

"At City. Trauma surgery. In the eye of the storm. Only then am I calm. I cannot say why that is so."

The nurse preened her hair. "Would you like to go out for a drink sometime?"

"I'm pretty busy," Freddy said. "I work. It's about all I do. But thanks just the same."

"You aren't gay are you?"

"I don't have any Burmese cats," Freddy said. He lifted up Oscar's bare foot, pointing at his little toe. "This little piggy has bunionettes," he said.

The nurse laughed. "You mean he's too small to get actual bunions?"

"Bunionettes, a.k.a. tailor's bunions, commonly occur with bunions. He's going to end up with a hammertoe."

The nurse laughed. "A hammertoe!"

"Check out the proximal interphalangeal joint on his middle toe. It's swollen. He's got a corn on it. It's a hammertoe, fucking waiting to happen."

"It's just bent a little," the nurse said.

"The hammertoe is the converse of the mallet toe, but his metatarsal phalangeal joint is contracted as well. Let me revise my opinion. I predict a claw toe, which is the superwhompo-jumbo combo — hammer and mallet. Bad shoes don't cause claw toes." He kicked the brown shoe on the floor. "No one knows really what does. It can be something systemic like diabetes. Probably just that. When I eyed his foot in the beginning, I was thinking in terms of Charcot's joint. A breakdown of the ligaments and tendons — joint dislocation. This is a very strange foot, nurse."

"Nancy. My name is Nancy. What's yours?"

"Frederick. See here, he has no hair on his foot or toes. He's got shit for peripheral circulation. The nails are thick with fungus. Fissures, dry skin. Ought to try some Sporanox for those nails. It works. The metatarsal head of the big toe is pushed medially and the phalanx is pointing toward the second toe, see?"

"Yes. So what?"

"It's no big deal," Freddy said, "in the cosmic sense. But take an interest in medicine. It's your job. Don't you like it? Aren't you fascinated by it?"

"I hate this place. And I'm beginning to hate you."

The color returned to Dr. Bangladesh's face and he opened his eyes. Freddy said, "Welcome back to the very strange world of rock and roll, Doctor."

Dr. Bangladesh looked at him without comprehension. "Where am I? What happened? It felt like I was drowning. Some horrible Godzilla-like reptilian monster was strangling me."

Freddy said, "You just had an insulin reaction, my friend."

"That's not possible!" Dr. Bangladesh sat up. "I vehemently deny that scabrous accusation. I have an extremely rapid metabolism. I eat nine thousand calories a day. I vaguely have hypoglycemia. I'm overworked. Hell, they work me like a goddamn hound. Where are my glasses?"

The nurse picked up his glasses from the floor and handed them to him. As soon as he put them on he looked at Freddy. "The work of forty Sabine slaves and seventeen horses and never so much as a thank you!"

"It's not against the law to be a diabetic," Freddy said.

"I'm not!" Dr. Bangladesh said.

"Hey, brother, I'm just sayin', you know." Freddy reached over and picked up the doctor's shoe. A lace was broken.

Dr. Bangladesh snatched the shoe from Freddy's hand. "I demand confidentiality on this, from both of you."

Freddy said, "You had a severe insulin reaction. I just want to make sure you know what you are doing. Get a second opinion. You're just feeling rowdy from the incident.

I'm not going to say fucking shit to anyone, but I'm right and you've been told."

The little doctor snarled. "Swear."

Freddy held his palm up and backed out of the room. "I don't know nothin'."

Freddy took the stairs back to Ward Six. In a moment the nurse, Nancy, caught up with him and pressed a card with her number on it into his hand. Her cheeks were flushed. She said, "Call me."

Freddy pocketed the card and said, "See that Dr. Bangladesh gets something to eat. Tell him if he doesn't educate himself about diabetes, he's a goner."

The nurse stood before Freddy with her hands on her hips. She said, "You won't call, will you? Well, you can just go to hell!"

Freddy buzzed back into the ward and waited for Stephens to open the office. As he was returning Cousin Eustace's file, he spotted a medical bag lying open on the floor. Inside it was a glucose meter and two portable insulin syringe cases. Also two bottles of Dexedrine. He wondered why Dr. Bangladesh would be taking speed. Probably for kicks. He closed the bag and stepped back out into the ward.

His stepmother was in the middle of the dayroom working Marla's hair over with a brush and a can of hair spray. An array of cosmetics had been laid out on a table. She shifted her weight back on one heel and studied Marla's face. After examining Dr. Bangladesh, Freddy found it hard to factor a giantess into his consciousness. Marla was huge. Mrs. Gordon was saying, "Your hair is very dark. I think we could go with some more rouge."

"We have recreation in the gym," Marla said. "The men let me play basketball with them. They always choose me. I'm good at softball too. You know, I was watching a rerun of *Cheers* the other day and the bartender, Sam — the one who was supposed to be a baseball player — came out from behind the bar and was walking around, bending over and stuff, and I was shocked to see how skinny his legs were. Toothpicks. I don't think it's realistic for the audience to believe that he used to be a professional ballplayer with those thin legs. From the top up, maybe. But not after you get a load of those legs. I used to enjoy the program until I made that observation. I can't get into it anymore. Sam should lift leg weights or something. That guy Woody has a pretty nice body, but too many of the characters on that show are bald. Count 'em. Count baldies next time you check it out. Plus, nobody can be as stupid as Woody. With a chick he would never get to first base."

"I think they're both cute," Mrs. Gordon said.

Marla said, "Frasier is a cue ball. Sam has cotton candy for hair, blow-drier hair. The post office guy is another baldy and he makes me depressed. The fat guy has hair but he's so fat! And it's that wiry kind of hair. Imagine a ton of that all over your pillows or in your bathroom sink. Ecchh! It springs! I can clog dance. I mean . . . I'm learning how."

Freddy plopped down in a chair next to Marla and said, "What's going on here, some kind of total makeover?" Without waiting for an answer he said, "Christ! I'm having a nicotine fit and I gave away my cigarettes."

Marla said, "Mr. Stephens smokes. Bum a coffin nail offa him."

"He's gone," Freddy said. "Where in fuck, I don't know."

Mrs. Gordon gave Freddy a reproving look. "Stop swearing so much. We're just having a little girl fun. Calm down and check this out. You're going to like it."

She placed her sunglasses on Marla's face. "Perfect, no?" She handed Marla a little hand mirror so she could see herself.

Marla said, "I want a man with a head full of hair, not some cue ball."

Mrs. Gordon snorted.

"Some damn cue ball with a hatchet face," Marla said. "It wrecks the entertainment value of the show, which sometimes has good lines."

Mrs. Gordon shuddered with laughter. Marla pounded her fist against her knee, threw back her head and roared.

"Christ, have you two been smoking a joint, or what?" Freddy said.

"We took a hit off a doobie, so what?" Mrs. Gordon said. "Don't be such a tightass."

"What, can you smoke dope here?"

"Not officially," Marla said.

There was a clamor in the hallway. In a moment the steel door swung open as Charlie White and Stephens struggled to push three aluminum food carts into the ward. Freddy gave them a hand setting up the carts as patients began to line up, selecting trays and utensils.

Once the carts were in place, Charlie White slipped on an apron. "Christmas dinner, folks! And not a bad one for a change. Hot turkey and dressing, the vegetable medley, spice cake with raisins. Mira, turn off the TV! You, Hen P., quit that grab-assing. There's plenty for everyone. And you two, over there laughing. Cut it out. I mean it."

Marla mimicked a scene from *Cheers*. "'Can I get you another beer, Norm?' 'Yeah, sure, sticklaig. 'Cause those ain't legs, them are laigs.'"

Before Charlie White began to ladle out food, he cleared his throat. "Dear Lord, thanks for the food, leftovers though they may be, and the roof over our heads. Thanks for the crappy weather since it canceled the VA Christmas entertainment. That was a blessing. Amen."

Marla and Mrs. Gordon joined the line, picking up serving trays while Freddy helped Stephens pull a case of milk out of the refrigerator and set it next to the serving table. When Stephens gave Freddy a cigarette and a light, Freddy said, "The devil has left the premises!"

Charlie White said, "He's gone. Through the power of dynamic prayer, I can make the sick well. Hemophiliacs, I can cure by the dozen. Or when inclined, I lay a spell on you."

"You better be careful there, Mr. White," Mrs. Gordon said, her eyebrows raised. "They call him Shootin' Bill."

Charlie looked at Freddy. "Who? Him?"

"That's right," Freddy said, taking a big drag on the cigarette. "I'm Shootin' Bill. And I'll shoot ya."

Charlie's face dissolved into a warm smile. "Oh yeah?"

"Take heed. I'm deadly," Freddy said. "So look out!"

"Or you'll be in big trouble, Charlie White," Marla said.

"It's true, I'm a malefactor," Freddy said. "Check it out. The Christmas program got canceled, but two mysterious strangers arrive on the scene. Angels? Possibly. Watch this." Freddy moved away from the serving cart and went to the tables, performing a magic trick he often used to great effect with the children in the hospital ER. "The disappearing hankie. Where did it go? Why, nobody knows."

"What else can you do?" Hen Pierce said. "Is that it?"

Freddy picked up four saltshakers and began to juggle, mugging to the audience. The slower patients responded with peals of laughter. "I can't always make the sick well, and I cannot turn water into wine," he said, enlarging the arc of the spinning saltshakers. He would pretend to let one fall, only to kick it back into the configuration with the side of his shoe. The patients waited for him to drop one, but Freddy was adept and well practiced. He edged over to a table and fed two pepper shakers into the arc. His cigarette was pursed in the middle of his mouth and he squinted his eyes against the smoke. "What I can do — I can patty-patty-bop-bop-wop-bop-a-shoo-bop."

Mrs. Gordon said, "You're getting salt all over everything."

Hen Pierce said, "He reminds me of that ice-skater, what's-his-face."

"Brian Boitano," Marla said.

"No," Hen Pierce said. "Scott or Kent or somebody. A fairy."

"Already told ya. They call me Shootin' Bill," Freddy said. "If I had my six-gun I would demonstrate my deadeye aim, but firearms are prohibited in this ward." He caught the saltshakers, set them on the table, and dusted himself off.

"Shootin' bull is more like it," Hen Pierce said.

The steel door banged open and Dr. Bangladesh stepped into the ward. His eyes sparkled and his entire condition seemed much improved. "I'm as hungry as a bear," he said. His shoes squeaked as he walked over to the food carts.

Marla set down her food tray, fluffed out her dress, and

said, "I'm really feeling happy today. I will dance for you. Guys? C'mon!" Marla stepped away from the table and began to dance and sing, "Have a holly jolly Christmas, it's the best time of the year. . . ." She danced like a marionette on strings. Her massive shoulders became liquid and she let her dangling elbows and wrists jackknife akimbo. Her shoe leather slapped against the hard oak floor.

Charlie White said, "All right then, enjoy yourself. Just remember, it all comes to nothing. Our trials and tribulations on this earth are lamentable."

"So does everything come to nothing," Dr. Bangladesh said, taking a bite of turkey. "Please, Charles, no more of your negativity. I've been through absolute hell today —"

"And you think I haven't?" Charlie White said. He handed Eustace a carton of milk and a green plastic bowl filled with cellophane packets of saltine crackers. "OK, Doc, though I've been grazed by every form of failure in the world, I'm not just your plain ordinary loser, and I resent the way you imply that I am."

Dr. Bangladesh set down his fork and picked up a carton of milk. "Have you been taking your meds, Charles?"

"Don't you give me your evil eye, Oscar, the one you learned in Gypsy camps in Afghanistan. I've been taking my meds — taking my meds, taking my meds! There! I've told you three times: Yes!"

"The man takes his meds," Freddy said.

"For God's sake, Charlie, chill!" Stephens said.

Dr. Bangladesh looked over the top of his half frames. "We all like the highs, but the lows aren't so good, Charles. I'm going to have to review your chart. I really hope you don't start in with your multiple personality shenanigans. I will not tolerate it!"

An orderly from another ward buzzed to be let in. He said, "I've been looking all over for you, Dr. Bangladesh. There's a guy on his way in a tow truck. Who's on the damn phones, anyhow? I've called up here a million times."

"I'm serving dinner," Stephens said. "Marla, knock off with the dancing and sit down."

"Triple A? Is on its way?" Dr. Bangladesh said, walking rapidly to the window. "Send him up when he gets here. The Wienermobile has a flat." He raised up on his tiptoes and looked through the mesh wire. "I can't see anything. You can never get a cab to come out here, and I don't want to be stranded all night." Dr. Bangladesh removed an Allen wrench from his key ring, unlocked the protective mesh guard, and cupped his hands on the steamy window. "I can't see anything! When in the hell is the last time anyone cleaned these windows?"

"Never," Charlie White said. "Since never."

The psychiatrist wiped his small hands on his white lab coat. "Yech! Nicotine," he said. "It's terrible. A rotten dirty mess. Somebody get me some window cleaner. Stephens! Call down for some window cleaner and some terry cloth towels. For crying out loud."

Stephens walked over to the call desk and picked up the phone. Dr. Bangladesh returned to his meal. Without bothering to sit down, he began shoving turkey and dressing into his mouth. He looked over at Freddy and said, "I make no apologies, I like to eat. What the hell. I won the pie-eating contest at the Fourth of July picnic. No one can outeat me.

Ate a huckleberry pie, a raisin pie, apple, cherry, pumpkin, peach, apricot, blueberry. These were good pies. The secret to a good pie is the crust. And the secret to the crust is lard. When I was done, my little belly stuck out like a bowling ball. Mr. Stephens, what sort of scrumptious goodies do we have for dessert?"

"The spice cake," Charles White said. "Or chocolate-flavored tapioca."

"Give me three of each and call an ambulance," Dr. Bangladesh said. "Hah!"

"You can't get Freddy to eat anything," Mrs. Gordon said. "He's skinny beyond belief."

Dr. Bangladesh took off his half frames, wiping the lenses on his coat. "You are anorexic, Dr. Blaine."

"I got sick in Africa," Freddy said.

"Whereabouts? I spent seven years in Zaire," Dr. Bangladesh said. "Before the virus."

"I was there," Freddy said, "after the virus."

A staff custodian came into the ward with an armful of towels and three spray bottles. Dr. Bangladesh said, "Bring that stuff over here. I want to show you something. Come here. This ward is a mess. Look at the lights, for instance. Half the bulbs need to be replaced."

The custodian looked up at the ceiling. "Hey! This isn't my area. I don't even work in this building. I just brought up this stuff. They told me you wanted it. I'm supposed to be on my lunch break."

Dr. Bangladesh took a towel and a bottle of window cleaner and went over to the first alcove. He said, "Some people, professional cleaners, use squeegees and a bucket of ammonia water. Some use vinegar. That's fine if you're on a skyscraper one hundred stories high, where every moment is a peril. Ah! What adventure! Well, for small jobs like this, nothing beats a commercial product like Windex or Glass Plus and a good absorbent towel." He squirted some glass cleaner on a section of the window, stopped to fine-tune the spray nozzle, and began rubbing the window with a towel. "Start from the top and work down. I'm too short actually and there's no ladder. Fie!"

Marla got up and went over to the doctor. He handed her a spray bottle and a towel. "You fold the towel in quarters, Marla, spray the glass, and work from the top down."

"I know what to do," Marla said. With her long arms, she was able to cover the entire top of the window in a few swaths. When she was through she looked at the towel. "It's filthy."

"Turn the towel to a clean surface and hit it again," the doctor said.

"This is the most rotten dirty window I've ever seen in my life," Marla said.

After the second try, Dr. Bangladesh handed her a clean towel. "Hit it again. Repeat the whole process."

Marla sprayed the window, and when she began to wipe it down the glass squeaked. "Hear that?" Dr. Bangladesh tucked his right hand in his vest and bounced on his toes. "It's squeaking. You're finally getting it clean. Ho-yeah!"

Marla said, "I need another towel. I haven't got it all off yet."

The patients at dinner fell silent and listened to the squeaking of the glass.

Charlie said, "He's never here. We never see him, and now he comes in like this just to show off, bossing everyone around."

"Look! Guys!" Marla said. "You can see the river. You can see the city lights. Cars going by. Cool!"

Cousin Eustace moved next to Marla and took in the view. He said, "Cars pass by the window."

"The nighttime is the right time to clean a window, any window," Dr. Bangladesh said. "The sun's glare will fool you. The nighttime is the right time! Heh-heh." Dr. Bangladesh polished a section of the glass and then handed Cousin Eustace a towel. "Wipe down the mesh with this wet one. I don't think these windows have been cleaned in fifty years."

"I want to do another one," Marla said. "At last we can see."

Dr. Bangladesh unlocked the wire mesh guards on the next set of windows, and Marla immediately set to work.

A few patients got up from their tables and came over to look out the window. "Whoa!" Hen Pierce said. "There's ice-cycles on them trees. *Staglatites!*"

"Stalactites," Charles White said. "Those are *stalactites!*"

"There are so many of them," Pierce said.

At this, everyone got up and went to the windows.

"Don't just stand there gawking, all you lazybones," Dr. Bangladesh said. "Pick up a towel and get to work. I'll open the rest of the screens."

"This is great," Marla said.

"It's fun," Cousin Eustace said. "I like it. Goddammit! Look at that! A shooting star! Right through the trees."

"I saw it," Marla said.

"Where?" Hen Pierce said.

"God! Look! There goes another one!" Marla said.

"Shit, yes," Hen said. "It lasted too."

Dr. Bangladesh said, "It was no hallucination." He handed Marla another towel. "Who did your hair, girl? You look, like, great."

"She looks terrific," Charlie said. "I've been saying that all along."

Mrs. Gordon removed her blazer and draped it on the back of her chair. "What are you doing?" Freddy said.

"I'm going to pitch in too," she said.

Freddy said, "Wait until tomorrow: the three-day pot hangover."

Mrs. Gordon said, "It's like Tom Sawyer whitewashing a fence. That thing. It's infectious."

"Little Oscar isn't doing diddle," Charles said. "All he's doing is just handing out towels."

"Charlie!" Stephens said. "Quit your fucking goddamn bitching all the time!"

Mrs. Gordon began to clean the windowsills. "I wish I had windows like this," she said. "They have to be worth a fortune."

"I'd jump," Charlie said. "But it's not high enough for suicide."

"Make a note, Stephens," Dr. Bangladesh said. "Mr. White has been tonguing his meds. That's why he's so grumpy. Heh-heh. Come on, get with it, Charlie. We are all having a good time over here. It's very simple, you know. Human beings need to have purpose, we need meaning. It always comes down to just exactly that."

Charlie laughed. "You're the man who said it all comes to nothing, that you went through hell today."

"That was before I ate. All my troubles are gone. I feel great. Ah-ho-yeah! It's a beautiful night. The windows are clean. We've got a clear view. The majestic oaks and maples are covered with a profusion of genuine ice-crystal stalactites. It's a wonderful life. It's just going to get better and better and better, on and on, forever and forever. Come on, take a look, Mr. White. On a midnight clear, you can see forever."

"You're the one who needs lithium," White said. "What's with all this big-time cheer?"

"I feel good, man!" Dr. Bangladesh said. "Hey, Dr. Blaine eat your cake — it will make you feel better."

"You say it with such conviction." Freddy looked at the cake before him. It looked dry and nasty.

"Trust me," Dr. Bangladesh said.

"He's right, Freddy," Iona said. "You have to eat. I don't know what you think you're doing."

Cousin Eustace said, "Go on, Fred. Eat something."

Freddy bent forward and took a whiff of the cake. It had been hard to single out any one particular odor since he walked into the hospital. All the odors seemed to meld. "A scrumptious goody," he said.

"Eat the goddamn thing before I stuff it down your throat," Stephens said.

Cousin Eustace snagged a piece of the cake with his thumb and shoved it in his mouth. "Look!"

"Now, I'm really not going to eat it," Freddy said.

"Eustace ate cake," Charlie said. "He actually ate something new. Hurrah!"

Cousin Eustace said, "The war in heaven is over."

Stephens popped over to the table and set a fresh piece of cake before Freddy.

Marla said, "It's happy cake."

Freddy said, "I hate cake."

Cousin Eustace brought the fruit basket up from the back of the ward and peeled away the cellophane gift wrapping. Freddy selected a red apple and took a bite.

"Yeah." Cousin Eustace rubbed his hands together with enthusiasm. "Charlie told the old devil to get lost."

"Good going, Charlie. I knew you had it in you," Dr. Bangladesh said. "Tra-la-la! It came upon a midnight clear."

"It's about time I got a little credit," Charlie said petulantly. He reached into the fruit basket and selected a Bartlett pear. "Come on, everybody. There's fresh fruit."

The patients took fruit from the basket but then gravitated back to the windows, dragging their chairs with them so they could sit and look outside. Only the first alcove had been done properly. The second had been abandoned and dirty towels lay all about the floor. Hen Pierce bit into a peeled orange and had to jump back from the spray. "I hope there's more shooting stars. I like them long-lasting dudes."

Outside, headlights from the cars passing the state hospital reflected off the crystal daggers of ice hanging from the trees, causing them to shimmer. The night air was clear and the star show profuse. A hush fell over the patients of Ward Six until Charles White broke the silence. "It's a magnificent sight. A good omen portending the remission of evil. It's Christmas."

Freddy said, "The Christmas spirit has been eluding me this year."

Dr. Bangladesh said, "One of those stars belongs to you alone, Doctor."

Freddy shrugged. "If one of those stars belongs to me," he said, "I presume it to be a dim and unlucky one. A celestial dud. I will cling to it nonetheless and nevermore will I complain."

"Look! Another one," Oscar shouted. "A real shooter. Va-boom!"

Hen Pierce nudged closer to the windows, licking orange juice from his fingers. "Those are the biggest, the best, and the most. Never in all my life have I seen such beautiful staglamites."

Daddy's Girl

PA LIKED Tootie the best. We were three girls, and then Hubert died at six weeks of whooping cough. Pa always wanted a boy, and when Tootie came along, number four, she was as close as you could get. Tomboy. Followed Pa everywhere. Out in the garage all the time with the mechanics was Tootie. Tootie could fix cars. She knew how they worked, and when something went wrong with one she could diagnose its troubles. All I knew of cars was to get in and go. When I was fifteen, I said to Pa, "Pa, when you going to give me a car?" There was an old Ford in the lot and he said, "You can have that Ford, Junk," and he tossed me the keys. He always called me Junk, which is not to say he didn't love his kids, but he didn't like women, and this is one way it slipped through, by calling me that name. Pa was good to me and although he was what you would call a ladies' man, he really hated women. He treated Ma awful. He would go with floozies and buy them diamond pendants and then tell Ma about it and make her nuts to the point where she would almost faint. He would get her so riled, me and my sisters would have to put a cold rag on Ma's head at the back of the store in the kitchen where no customers could see. She would go back in the kitchen and nearly faint because of the way he would throw it in her face.

Anyhow, Pa gave me the keys to an old Ford that was parked under the oak tree back behind the car shop. It was a convertible, and me and Barbara Carpenter drove it down Lake Street past the stockyards, glad to stir up a little breeze, it was such a hot day. Of course, I didn't know how to drive and we smashed into a fire hydrant in Montgomery. No one was hurt, but we had to walk home along the side of Lake Street, which was so hot that day the tar was melting and the heat of the pavement burned through our saddle shoes. The dog days of August. I told Pa what happened and he didn't get mad or anything, he just told one of mechanics who had some spare time to take me out in a new Chevrolet and learn me how to drive — that's what he sold, Chevrolets — and when I learned how to drive, I had a new car. Pa was good that way. Whey my sister Ida wanted to play tennis, he had the tennis courts built and Ida got fancy tennis clothes, but after a few weeks she got tired of it. I think Pa just built them to show off, because at the time all of the rich people were putting up tennis courts. Pa had them build two courts and put a big fence around them so no one would have to run down tennis balls. They still have morning glories growing on the fence. If my arthritis isn't too bad I like to go and look at them and smell the lilacs when they bloom.

Tootie could play tennis and beat anyone in the whole south end of town. Grown men she could beat, but when she played Pa she would let him win even though Pa was pretty bad at tennis apart from the fact that he was a big and strong man.

Pa had this punching bag in the basement and he liked to punch on it and show off, and all the kids in the neighborhood got pretty good at it. Because he liked kids and knew how to fool with them, all the kids in the neighborhood thought Pa was swell. I could punch the bag like all the kids, but Tootie could actually box and would box with Pa. She could beat up any of the boys, even the ones that were quite a bit older. This went on until she was about thirteen and she got her period, which was normal but really threw Tootie for a loop.

You know, Pa could play the fiddle and dance and call square dances. Everybody liked Pa. The mayor and big shots in town, the poor people — just about everybody liked Pa. He had Ma pack lunches for us in a straw basket so he could take us kids out on summer picnics, usually to the gravel pit for swimming. In the fall he liked to take us out birdwatching and got binoculars for everyone and would point out the birds. There was all kinds of different ones in those days. The best present he ever gave to Tootie was a book on tropical birds, and she used to tell Pa she was going off into the jungle someday to see birds like this. Ma never went along on the picnics — she always worked the store — but she was glad for us to go.

ALL OF US GIRLS were pretty, but Tootie was the best. She looked like a movie star. She looked like Rita Hayworth. All the boys was after her. She cut her hair short and dressed like a boy, but her beauty came through; you just couldn't hold back that kind of beauty. Pa was drinking bad by then, losing money, giving it to women, ruining his business, taking money from Ma. She kept her store money in Dutch Master cigar boxes or White Owl boxes, and he would get to drinking and just take it from her until she got to hiding it. One time he pulled out a .32 pistol and stuck it in her neck up in the bedroom because she wouldn't give him any money. She was pregnant with Moonie at the time and nearly lost her. Pa called Ma filthy names and kicked her down the steps. It was terrible, but in those days things like that was common, Pa being drunk — scenes like that you used to hear about regular and think nothing of it. That's just how life was in those days.

When Pa pulled out his .32 that was the only time he ever laid a hand on Ma, but he had done worse things. All of us girls had to run the store while Ma laid there in bed worried about Pa and went into labor. No sooner did Ma give premature birth to Moonie, the fifth girl, than Pa came home sick to death. They brought him home because he had gone blind drinking bad moonshine booze. It was Prohibition times and he ruined his liver. I remember the doctor said there was nothing they could do. Pa screamed something horrendous and vomited blood all over the bedroom for five days before he died. We girls had to take care of him. Ma was busy with Moonie and wouldn't have anything to do with him, and he laid there and died in the same bed where his youngest daughter had just been born.

Really I was the main one who had to take care of Pa and look after Moonie and run the store to boot. I was the oldest and stuck with all of the responsibility.

Sometime after the funeral a lawyer man came and told

Ma that they were going to take the property away because of all the debts Pa had left. Ma got another lawyer and told him that if she could keep the store she would pay him back all the money Pa owed, which was $63,000. In those days that was like millions. But Ma worked the store day and night and paid back the money.

Of all the girls, Ma didn't show any favoritism except maybe for Moonie. When Moonie was little, she had curls and looked like Shirley Temple. All of the customers in the store would come in and rave about her and make a fuss. It wasn't Ma so much as it was the customers. Moonie seemed even prettier than Tootie because she liked being feminine and liked clothes and dressing up, but whenever Tootie halfway tried to look like a woman, she was gorgeous. She had the most beautiful shiny red hair like you see on those Irish. Beautiful smoochy lips, a pretty face — there's no denying. She just couldn't hide it.

When Tootie was about sixteen, the boys got after her something awful. She wouldn't go out with them. She would play baseball and basketball with them and horse around with them because she was still this awful tomboy, but she wouldn't "fool" with them. Tootie got sick headaches like Ma — they had that in common — and we would have to go up in her room and put ice packs on her head. It didn't seem like Tootie to get sick, because she was so tough — because she was such a toughie and could go without sleep and work like a man — but when she got headaches she saw lights dancing in her brain and talked to angels. Sometimes she talked to Jesus. All of these headaches came after her first menstruation.

Everything Tootie did had to be just so. She did good in

school because of this. She was the valedictorian of the high-school class. She went off to college and studied to be a doctor. One time she came home for Christmas and told me the men in college was after her and she didn't want any fool man. This is because she was her daddy's girl and no man in the world could be like her Pa for her. Pa was far from perfect but he was Tootie's pal, and whenever you told her how Pa kicked Ma down the stairs and pulled out his .32, Tootie would walk away or she would defend Pa. Once she hit Ida in the face over a quarrel about Pa and broke her nose. Tootie could hit like a man. It was a curse that she was so beautiful, and at medical school she got fat to cover it up. She went into a fat period. Tootie was the first woman doctor in all of town. Ma helped — it was the German way to get education and better yourself in life. Tootie won scholarships and went to the University of Chicago, which is where all of them intellectuals went. She inherited Ma's spunk and wasn't afraid of nothing.

MA SENT ME to secretary school, but I was running with Chunky then and quit after three months. Ida married Harry and he was good to her, although he liked to run with women and cheat. Harry got rich and moved them to De Kalb, and we didn't see that much of them after that. Moonie married Tom when she was eighteen; then after the war he left her for some floozy and she had a nervous breakdown and we had to look after her and the baby until she got over it and married Wilson.

Mary Lou, the second oldest and the one most like Tootie, got married to Monk and moved to Oswego. Ma ran the store on her own except there were always grandkids to

take the clinkers out of the furnace and shovel coal, stock
the shelves, and do all of the heavy work, and we girls was
never far away. Moonie never did much to help in the store.
She was the opposite of Tootie. She was crazy for men.
Happy-go-lucky whenever one came around.

I can remember the way Ma used to stand behind the
counter in the store and talk to customers. She had a way of
standing, her legs one in front of the other but spread wide.
She always wore a cotton dress with an apron, and when she
would talk to customers she would always say, "Ain't that
swell?" No matter what they were telling her it was always
"Ain't that swell?" She had a big belly and little stick legs.
She was left-handed too. Ma was pretty when she was young,
but when she got older she lost her looks. She looks like
George Washington in the last picture I have of her, and her
little stick legs look like Babe Ruth's.

Chunky and I lived in the house across from the store.
Chunky was a weakling and never kept a steady job. He was
sickly. He was always seeing Tootie about some ailment, and
she made him feel better. If she couldn't kid him out of his
troubles she gave him some pills. What they were was sugar
pills. We all had to laugh because we knew, but Chunky was
in the dark and said those pills made him feel like a new
man. Tootie liked Chunky and would listen to him after he
got religion. Tootie was interested in religion since the time
she got her headaches and saw the dancing lights of heaven
and talked to the angels. One day she came home and told
Ma she had joined the Catholic Church. We were Lutherans, German Lutherans, and Ma just about died. I remember there was a big fight about it in the store. And while the
fight was going on there was a terrible thunderstorm with

lightning. Lightning hit the walnut tree, which sat just out-side the window near the cash register. Scared me enough to kill me. It sounded like the world coming to an end, with a smell like I never knew.

When Ma was a kid living out on the prairie, one of thir-teen kids, she was sitting by a Franklin stove when lightning struck through the stovepipe and knocked her out. That's why she had lightning rods on the store — three of them. There was one on the gas station. Three on the garage. Two on the little house. One on Weasie's shack. One on the back house. Two on the barn, but none on that blame walnut tree. Boom! It sounded like the world cracked in half.

Ma always got upset during a thunderstorm; she would get to shaking, and she was doing this during the fight with Tootie. I remember the electric went out and I was lighting candles in the store when she and Tootie got into the fight about the Catholic Church. Ma was almost as upset as the time Pa pulled the pistol on her. The storm and the fight all at once. Ma's cat was so scared it started tearing around the walls until it was running on the ceiling through the power of centrifugal force. Nobody believes me, but that cat was running on the ceiling, completely upside down, or so it seemed to me. Maybe I was wrong.

It began to hail the size of grapefruits. They always say when it hails that it was the size of golf balls or grapefruits, although if you were to see it, you would see that it hailed the size of BB's. But I was there, and it hailed the size of grapefruits! Smashed up the roof on Mrs. Idoc's house. Tootie left in her doctor's Buick, which got dented on top from all that hail, and I had to help Ma upstairs and put ice packs on her head.

A week later we got a letter from Tootie — she had gone and joined the Catholic Church and they made her a nun. About a year after that we got a letter from her from Africa. All these beautiful stamps on an envelope that looked like wax paper. Tootie was a doctor in a leper colony. She said she was happy serving the Lord.

Because of Chunky, I left the Lutheran Church and became a Baptist. Chunky was a street-corner preacher. He worked odd jobs when he could. Then he died of heart trouble at thirty-one. The last thing he said to me was, "I told you I was sick, Junk. But now I'm going to a better place."

After Ma died, blind with diabetes, and the money was split up, Tootie wrote a letter to Ma's lawyer and said she wanted all of her money to go to the mission to buy medicine for all of them lepers. Mary Lou tricked the lawyer — she was smart and had a head for figures. Of all of the girls, Mary Lou was closest to Tootie and wrote to her in Africa every month telling her about her life with Monk and raising Pug and Barney and so on. It was a happy life. Mary Lou didn't have to work because Monk made good with his welding and so on and eventually became the plant manager at the Durabuilt. So Mary Lou wrote her happy news and told her what everyone in the family was doing, not mentioning the bad things that happen in all families. Mary Lou tricked that lawyer and held money back for Tootie, and it was a good thing.

WHEN MOONIE called to tell me Mary Lou had cancer, she just said, "Mary Lou called me and said 'The doctor told me I've got cancer in my breast.'" Just as plain as that. Moonie said that Mary Lou didn't seem that worried about it. She said she'd had a lump for two years and tried to make it go away by practicing Christian Science. When Monk found out about it he took her to the doctor and they took off the breast. Monk was pretty upset. He could count on Mary Lou. Mary Lou and the kids were all he lived for. They took off the breast and Mary Lou went home. She used to tell me, "I haven't got cancer anymore. I can just tell." But it went to her lungs. They had to put her in the hospital on oxygen, but she finally suffocated. I hope I don't die that way, and with diabetes I probably won't. Diabetes gives you a heart attack; Chunky said it feels like a truck driving on your chest. Real bad pain, but it's over in ten or fifteen minutes. Ain't that swell, the way we have to live and die and suffer on this earth?

It was a relief to see Mary Lou's suffering end, but still, after the death, Monk was left with a hole in his life. He didn't want another woman, although Pug and Barney tried to tell him that it would be a good idea. Then his dog died and Monk went through a drinking spell. Nobody wanted to be around him. That's how the family is about drinking — down on it. Ma drilled that into us pretty good.

Then Tootie comes home from Africa in her nun clothes. She isn't pretty no more, she's almost fifty years old. Her face is pinched and white, though you'd think it would have been tan — as black as the ace. It's a hard life over there in Africa, with bad food and constant work, she says. "The futility of it all," she says. "Such . . . futility." She talked like the world was coming to an end, and that wasn't like Tootie, even with her headaches. Futility, I had to look the word up in a dictionary. It means hopeless.

The Catholic Church gave Tootie a leave, and so she gets

Monk straight off the booze and puts me on insulin shots. She didn't come home for Ma's funeral or for Ida's funeral after Ida died of kidney failure, but aside from Pa, Mary Lou was her closest friend and she flew home on a jet plane.

I asked her if she seen all of those birds in the jungle, and she said she did. I said, "Tootie, you look bad. What happened to you?" She said a big mamba snake, nine feet long, went crazy and bit five Africans and some goats. Tootie cut off its tail with a hoe, but that only made it mad and it chased after her and bit her too, over there on the Dark Continent. Her life and health was bad ever since. Still she gave me hell because of what I eat, and I told her that if the Lord wanted to take me, I was ready go. I would go up to heaven and see Chunky again and Wilbur, my second husband. Since Tootie was a nun, I asked her who I was supposed to be married to — Chunky, my first man, or Wilbur? Tootie told me she didn't believe in God. I said, "Tootie, you are a nun, and when you was little and had your headaches, the angels talked to you and Jesus talked to you," and she just laughed a bitter laugh. She told me that being a nun was no different than if she had stayed in Aurora and lived a normal life with a man. She said there wasn't nothing to it and for sure there was no God. It was all just make-believe. But Tootie took Monk to the AA. She had a power over people and could make them well without giving them shots or medicine, she believed in herself so. Every day for ninety days she drove Monk to the AA, sometimes two and three times a day. In this she was a hypocrite, because she didn't have any more belief in God, but she could still lay it out pretty good, and for Monk this was the cure, not the AA. She even got him to quit smoking.

One night Tootie came by in her car and caught me eating fried pork rinds and peanut brittle. It made me guilty but I told her, "Tootie, you can talk to me until you're blue in the face; I ain't going to change. I'm too old for it. A person has to eat."

She gave me hell upside and down and then drove me down to Oswego to check on Monk. After Mary Lou died, he'd kept everything in the house the same — we walked in through the back porch as always, and Monk was fixing himself something to eat in the microwave. It was like old times. He was glad to see us and he had a lot he had to get out. This was before his son Barney died and he gave up hope altogether. We went and sat in the living room, and Monk looked at Tootie and she looked at him, and I saw real love between the two of them. The love of two friends. Monk had the emphysema and it was hard for him to talk. He said, "All that welding in bad conditions with no ventilation, three packs of Chesterfields a day. Coming up in the depression, it was hard. I had this old Oldsmobile — I was just a kid and it was my first car. It had a split windshield and the left side was broken out and, I don't know, it must have been January. I remember I went over to my girlfriend's house in that car and drank Coke and we played the player piano — 'It's a Long Way to Tipperary,' 'Happy Days Are Here Again,' 'The Dark Town Strutters' Ball' — when it started to blow real hard and I realized how late it was and I had to get home. I had to be to work the next day. The dagblam Oldsmobile overheated. We didn't have antifreeze in those days but ran alcohol through the radiator, and the closer I got to town, the hotter the car got and the slower it was going until I finally made it downtown and stopped at the

Strand. A Chinaman there gave me some water for my radiator. I practically had to beg for it, since it was midnight and they were closing. No gloves. Twelve below. Lightweight coat. No hat. By the time I got to the store the car was overheating again, and it kept going slower and slower until I had to downshift into first gear as I drove out Jericho Road toward my mother's house. Finally the old car lugged to a stop and smoke started pouring out of the engine. I flipped up the hood and fire was coming out of the carburetor, so I ran over to the side of the road, scooping up frozen snow with my bare hands alongside a barbed-wire fence — can you imagine that? — trying to put it out. But that didn't work, so I beat the flames with my jacket, and that caught on fire, and by the time the fire went out I was crying because I knew the engine was ruined and I just wanted to die. I was out there on Jericho Road by Blackberry Creek and I saw a light go on in Bobby O'Neil's house and saw a face come up to the window and wipe away the steam. Bobby made a cup with his hands to look out — I can see his face now with that stupid look of his; he was half crazy — but then the light went out, and I was too ashamed to go knock on the door and ask for help, so I got in the car and huddled down, and before long I was in and out of sleep and realized that if I didn't get up and do something I was going to freeze to death. Tootie, the wind was blowing so hard I had to walk home backwards! I thought the wind was going to cut me in half. Three miles of this. Frostbite ears, frostbite feet. My mother soaked them in cool water and put me to bed covered with wool blankets, and I just passed out, didn't get to work on time, and was fired. There I was. The girlfriend two-timed me a day later, my car was shot, and no job. People

don't know how hard it was in those days." This is what
Monk said. Tootie and I got nuts the way he was telling the
story, and we was laughing so hard we practically wet our
pants. I hadn't got nuts and laughed like that since Ida was
alive. Ida could be fun and get you nuts — make you have a
good time.

This guy I saw on the *Donahue* show said if you laugh all
the time you can heal yourself from fatal diseases and that
some guy healed himself by watching the Three Stooges
and the Marx Brothers. Well, I guess I'll just have to die, because I could never laugh over something so stupid as that.
Really, Monk knew what he was doing and made the story
funny to make us laugh like that — he was always a kidder.
But after Barney died right after the dog and Mary Lou,
Monk caved in. All that good stuff he learned at the AA
about the higher power, which helped Monk quit drinking
and smoking, the higher power Monk chose to call God —
it all quit working. Monk was no dummy. He could see
Tootie was just practicing the Hippocratic oath with no real
feeling. Although she tried to cover it up, Tootie went into
a depression, too. She didn't feel right at home and she
didn't want to go back to Africa. She put up a front, but
Monk could see through it. No matter what Tootie did for
him or what Pug did for him, he just sort of dried up inside.
Pug was with him when he died. Pug was with Barney when
he died and with Mary Lou. Three in five years. Pug said
Monk was rational right up to the end. He didn't say nothing about Jesus taking him to heaven. What he said was,
"Ain't this a bitch?" After he said that, Pug said he rolled
over and died. Maybe Pug saw it wrong. Maybe Monk closed
his eyes and prayed for his own salvation, for the forgiveness

of his sins. Late at night when I can't sleep, I think of Monk up in heaven with Barney and Mary Lou and the whole family short of Pa, who died cursing God.

MY DOCTOR gave me an operation because my lower eyelids were growing up and going into my eye. The pain was horrible. Tootie did the operation over, to get all of the eyelid roots out, but they still sprout up and stick me in the eye and I have to tape my eye open, put drops in it, and take aspirin. Sometimes the pain is so bad I just have to lie on my bed and hold a picture of Jesus to my heart and pray for Him to come and take me, or pray for Him to save Tootie's soul. She has done good things for the world, but only through the grace of Jesus are we saved. Our righteous acts are as filthy rags. Everybody knows that one.

Tootie quit the Catholic Church and used the money Mary Lou held back to start her own doctor practice. Dermatology. In the daytime she cures pimples on teenagers and at night she goes out with men and lives the fast life. Her looks are gone. She dresses wrong. She doesn't know how to act right after all of those years in Africa. She comes on too independent. Maybe being around those lepers and those African drum dances put Satan in her life. Satan made her forget how Jesus sent an angel to save her from an elephant stampede and another time from getting shot by those rebels in Angola, or how He saved her from her snakebite. Satan is the prince of this world and his powers are strong. He prowls the earth like a hungry lion looking for souls to devour. He knows his days are short, and he's trying to make hay and catch every sinner in his net of evil. I never thought he could get Tootie, though.

Or maybe Tootie's troubles was because of Pa. Tootie was her daddy's girl, and that can be too much of a good thing. I do believe that a Catholic can go to heaven, but not unless they accept the grace and salvation the Lord offers us. It's so easy. It's so simple. Tootie don't think its rational, and it isn't rational. Lions playing with lambs and eating straw sounds ridiculous, I guess, especially if you've been to Africa and seen how they do and have been bit by a nine-foot mamba snake . . . who am I to judge? It's not rational; it's what you call a paradox. You have to believe like a little child. Believe it because it's impossible. There's no need for holy water or praying to a lot of saints when you can talk to Jesus direct. When I think I can't take it no more, I hold my picture of Jesus against my breast and pray for Tootie and my family and for all of the lost souls in the world. I say, "Jesus, I cry my bleeding heart out every day for you; come down to earth and forgive them all, *for they know not what they do.* Come down and give us a thousand years of peace like you said you would and throw Satan down in the pit where he can't get at us no more." When I do this the grown-up in me dies and I'm like a little child and can see the world fresh again. *Born again.* Sometimes I don't really believe in no life after death, but I do believe that Jesus has saved me. Other times I believe it all — tigers eating straw, the water turned to wine, the Red Sea parting, the Tower of Babel, and a thousand years of peace on earth with our Lord and Savior, Jesus Christ.

I am ninety-two years old and I had to get this in before I go.

My Heroic
Mythic Journey

FELL IN LOVE. Bleach-bottle blond with a cheating heart. I couldn't help it. You can't regulate things like that. I couldn't get enough of her. I just loved being around her. She was always interesting to me. She could get up in the morning with a cigarette in her face and a ratty bathrobe, and to me, she looked great. I was always hot for her. I could do it with her and a half hour later, do it again, wait a half hour and do it again, and so on. Peggy.

Good-sized woman. By that I mean tall. Almost as big as me. Nice legs. Good muscle tone. Green eyes. A cute nose, although right away you could see it was once broken. Somehow the fact that it was once broke made it cute, you know. Beautiful white teeth in spite of smoking. Peggy was not a girl that reeked of cigarettes. She had some way of seeing to that. She was a good dresser. Classy dresser. Ivy League kind of dresser. The only picture I got of her she's wearing a tartan skirt and penny loafers, crisp cotton blouse with a ribbon tie and a blue blazer, and she's laughing with her head tossed back with the sun glistening on those beautiful white teeth, a healthy pink tongue, full beautiful smoochy lips, the bloom of youth, and the way the sun picks up the highlights of that creamy white-blond hair — she looks so luscious I want to take a bite out of her.

Man! Thinking about her! I'm the one who took the picture, and she's looking at me like I'm the valiant prince rode in and slayed the dragon, and we're about to go off and live happy ever after. How can you fake a look like that? Maybe she meant it at the time. Who knows? Five days later she unloaded four shots from a .38-caliber revolver into my thoracic cavity, hit me in the knee and creased my ear with the sixth shot. Then the bitch dumped the empty cartridges onto the white plush carpet and calmly started to reload the gun.

You want to know what it feels like to get a shot with a .38? Have four guys spread-eagle you against a brick wall and let five-time pro-bowler Ricky Waters do a fifteen-yard sprint and spear you in the chest with his Seattle Seahawks' football helmet.

I got her around the ankles, knocked her down, got the gun away, and called for an ambulance. A team of surgeons took out my spleen, half of my stomach, and a lobe of my left lung in fourteen hours of surgery. They said I was lucky to be alive. Still got a bullet sitting near my spine. I carry it with me like a love letter.

I hovered near death for three weeks after the major surgery and then began to recover. After this, they operated on my knee. Took off the knee cap. Scraped out a bunch of gristle. I can handle a lot of pain, but I maxed out — set the record for the most morphine given to a hospital patient at Valley General over that knee.

You want to know where she is now, my Ivy League princess? She's hog-fat, married to this manic-depressive in Sacramento, California. She quit her whoring ways. Loves the guy. That creamy platinum hair now looks like common straw and the sun in the Sacramento Valley has played hell on her skin, as has that chain-smoking.

I don't know who — Carl Jung? — says when you fall in love, what you're doing is looking for your other half — the anima. Now the anima can be a femme fatale or she can be some goddess like the Venus de Milo. It's whatever turns you on. When I was fighting, I had plenty of dough, girls, the whole world was mine. I had the whole world, and you know something — it wasn't nothing.

I went back to boxing after a hitch as a Vietnam marine; I got out and got a job at the post office with my VA points, got to juicing — two hundred fifteen pounds, fired, then whatever jobs I could pick up, fired, broke, living off my old man. He tells me, "What's the matter with you, haven't you got any self-respect? You're going to cry the blues because you spent thirteen months in a war zone? End up in the penitentiary?"

He packed me off to detox where I read the biography of John L. Sullivan, America's first great sporting hero. Before he had really made his name, John L. Sullivan went on a three-month drunk and almost died — a priest comes in and reads him his last rites, but, of course, John L. Sullivan has an incredible constitution. He recovers, and broke at the age of twenty-nine, and on crutches, he signs articles to fight Jake Kilrain. Almost immediately after he goes into training he starts hitting the juice again, so his friends tie him up and take him to the farm of William Muldoon, the heavyweight wrestling champion, a man who knew more about physical culture than any man in his era. He knows Sullivan is an alcoholic so he weans him off the liquor, puts him to work as a farmhand. Soon, he has him training. Sullivan sneaks off and gets drunk one night — sixty-six gins in a sitting, but Muldoon becomes even more of a hard-ass after that. He tells Sullivan what it would mean if he lost his title. He lays that part out good. Soon the flab melts, and Sullivan no longer cares about alcohol. What he really wants, what he looks forward to more than anything is the moment he can crawl under the covers at night and let his head hit the pillow. Sullivan drops from two hundred forty pounds down to two hundred nine. He was a tremendous athlete who could run a hundred yards in ten seconds. He scored a great victory over Kilrain in the last bare-knuckled heavyweight championship fight of all time, a seventy-five-round fight that lasted two hours and sixteen minutes under a brutal, blazing Fourth of July Mississippi sun. It is said that the sound of Sullivan's fists beating against Kilrain's ribs could be heard at seventy-five yards. The fight ended when a doctor warned Kilrain's handlers — "If you keep sending him out there, he'll die."

I came out of detox. Got a job pushing a broom. I had a hangover that lasted six months. Sullivan's story had inspired me, and I did what I could to get back my health. I was still very young. By and by, I went back to the fight gym. I never thought of taking a pro fight but I was fighting well and settled in at one hundred forty-seven pounds. As a pro, I lost a couple of two-hundred-dollar, four-round "crowd chasers," and in the process, I realized I was in no kind of shape at all.

I trained harder. I liked to train. For me, it was a holy experience. The structure of a fighter's day involves two daily workout sessions, the morning run and the afternoon workout. I was a little old to start fighting pro, but I had had a lot of amateur experience, and I thought I could give to boxing everything, and in this was my salvation. There was no time for anything else. There was no time to cry the blues about Vietnam and what I saw and what I did over there. You can pound away a lot of anger and a lot of hatred on a heavy bag or a sparring partner and go home with a heart full of bliss — at least for a time.

Before you know it, I'm down to one thirty-two in spite of the fact that I ate three pounds of steak a day. My metabolism had revved into high. I couldn't eat enough. My trainer went to the stockyards at night and got me a quart of hot beef blood to drink, to keep up my strength, but still I lost weight.

I win a few fights, get pumped up, train even harder, and the next thing I'm down to one twenty-six — featherweight. I am six feet one and one-half inches tall.

I've got long arms, and I've got big hands. Big hands are important in fighting. The reason is because big hands weigh more than small hands. If a man hits you with a small hand, no matter that he's big and strong, the physics of the punch translates like this: he's pounding a nail with a small hammer. The little hand is the finishing hammer and the big hand is the sledge. So, in this, I was blessed.

Most featherweights are only five feet five inches tall at most. I didn't have a whole lot of punches, but I didn't need

a whole lot of punches. I towered over the average featherweight like Goliath.

When I mugged them with the left, when I had them
staggered, then I came over with the right hand and that
was about it. I felt sorry for them. I mean, it didn't even
seem fair. Twenty-seven straight knockouts, and I went down
to Melbourne, Australia, to fight Devin ("The Tasmanian
Hurricane") MacKenzie who held the unified featherweight
title and was often mentioned as one of the best fighters
pound for pound in all of professional boxing.

Devin said a lot of bad things about me. He said I was a
freak. He said I was soft to the body. He said I was too old.
He said I never fought anybody. Devin said he had a plan for
me and he quoted Friedrich Nietzsche in the Melbourne
papers: "To have a purpose for which one will do almost
anything *except betray a friend*, — that is the final patent of
nobility, the last formula of the superman."

I knocked Devin MacKenzie out in the first round and
became the unified featherweight champion of the world.

I liked being the featherweight champion of the world,
even if I wasn't a household name. Like being the tenth-best
chess player in the world; chess freaks probably know who
the guy is, but not your man on the street. Still, I made good
money. I made more than most small fighters because I
knocked men out in dramatic fashion. It was hard work, but
it was better than weighing two fifteen and peddling the
U.S. mail. It was better than factory jobs in Aurora, Illinois,
or planting trees near Centralia, Washington, or picking or-
anges in Milpidas, California.

The best part, the part I really liked was that I had found
a kind of purity in my asceticism. I could read the Sermon

on the Mount or the *Upanishads* or the *Rig-Veda* in those days of heaven of championship fight camp and *I knew!* I was in the world but not of it. Sounds like a cliché, but it's true. Paradise is there if you can find the right magic and slip in, it's yours.

PEGGY WAS a lower vibration. She was the Fall. It was capitulation to Satan. I couldn't make one twenty-six anymore. Not with her. All I wanted to do was party — cigars, cocaine, champagne, junk food, and fucking. It was mostly the fucking. I was so ashamed of myself.

I blew a one-hundred-thousand-dollar payday and had to forfeit the title because I didn't make weight. Three days in a steam bath. Wake up in the night *crying* because of the thirst. Who was that rich man in the Bible begging for a drop of water down there in Hell? Just one drop. The voice comes back, "I'm sorry, my man."

Well, like I said, I had had the whole world and it wasn't nothing, but I *had been* in Paradise until she came into my life with her lower vibrations.

Temptation. Hexagram 44.

I lost fights. The money went. I fell into the classic pattern: ghetto kid — hungry fighter, you give him a little glitter and tinsel, and that's all she wrote. I blew every dime. The thing that makes you champion of the world, it makes you extravagant with money, excessive in your habits.

I wasn't too bad of a lightweight, but I lost my holy nimbus and the string of knockouts. They don't want to come in and see you take a decision win. I wouldn't pay the price anymore. I wouldn't train. I got bigger. As a welterweight, I had no reach advantage nor the power I had as a featherweight. I had no stamina. It was pathetic. I suffered a half-dozen ignominious knockouts, and before long the magic of my name was threadbare. Bitch left me.

I ended up as a punch press operator at the Vendo Company in Aurora, Illinois. I chopped off half of my dynamite left hand for an insurance settlement. Got a quarter of a million. Peggy hears about the money. She comes back. It was no good the second time.

You think I could have had the sense to put a little nut away, but no. Like I said, people who have that kind of sense don't usually succeed at the Sweet Science.

I DON'T KNOW how I lived through the shooting. The doctors were amazed. With only a part of a stomach, I couldn't hold my weight. I looked like Auschwitz. Dachau. I looked like a junkyard dog.

An old friend from the fight days, he owns a construction company, he carried me after I was shot. He said, "Drink beer. Your stomach can absorb that."

He was right. I'm up to one ninety-five. Ironworker. Aurora, Illinois. Ironworkers, the ironworker mentality — it's rough. It's a lower vibration. All this beer drinking and fighting, cigarette smoking and lewdness . . . sex with ugly women.

The thing that worries me is that some *Boxing Illustrated* writer is going to do an article about me when I'm dead — you know, he ended up like Beau Jack shining shoes or he ended up like the Battling Siki shot dead in Hell's Kitchen. Kid Chocolate. Leon Spinks.

"He was an animal: he didn't know nothing. He didn't know better." And that's what my fans will think. I can't stand the idea of that sort of humiliation. I would like them to know that I went on a heroic mythic journey, slayed the Tasmanian Hurricane, and won the golden fairy princess. The writers at *Boxing Illustrated* won't put that part in.

He didn't know nothing. He didn't know better.

I knew better. I knew myself. I experienced clarity. It's just that it's gone now, and it's not going to come back.

"Lazarus, hey man, how about just one little drop of water, baby? Man, it's horrible down here."

I Love You,
Sophie Western

FRANKIE DELL tried to get a fix on the bathroom mirror. He was jangled and wired still from an acid trip on Saturday night and had a wicked case of double vision. The surface of his arms and legs tingled and deep down in these extremities he felt his very bones buzz. All shook up. Yeah, shook up, and with his electric bones, Frankie was moving around the bathroom only partly sure of what he was doing, partly sure of what was going down. Barely had a clue. Getting ready for school? So it would seem.

Fifteen seconds after Frankie dropped the acid, he knew he had made a grave error. Now, he was drawing blanks. He couldn't remember diddly. He would never know the whole truth. Funny he wasn't back in the nuthouse. Funny, he was in his own bathroom. Like, funny-ha. He opened a medicine vial, shook out two lithium tablets, and dry-swallowed the pills. There was a pimple in the crease of Frankie's nostril. He took a drag on his Marlboro and studied it. Of all the damn things. It was a hot one, too. It looked dangerous. He felt like callin' the old lady in and have her take a look at it. Call a dermatologist or sumthin'.

Looking at the zit, Frankie frowned, making his hooded black eyes look cruel. Bushy eyebrows, snake-dead eyes. From the front-and-center mugshot view and from the profile, it was such a bad look he was scared of his own fuckin' self.

"Frankie, I'm late. I gotta go," his mother said through the door. "Don't forget to take your lithium. You were up prowling all night. If you start another cycle, I'm gonna lay down an' die, Frankie. Lay down an' die."

THE MONDAY MORNING homeroom scene was dismal, but Darlene D'Arcel was there, and that was unusual for a Monday. Her neck was full of hickies and Darlene seemed proud of them. In spite of all the skin flicks Frankie knew by heart, sex was still a mystery. God, he wanted some of that fine stuff and Darlene D'Arcel knew it. She could read him.

Hey, Frankie, whatcha doin'? Checkin' out my hickies, ain't you? Caught ya, ha ha. You wan' some nookie, doncha? Ha ha. Eatcha heart out, kid.

Darlene spread her legs and flashed a little white thigh meat before she gathered up her books and twitched her hot little ass out into the hall . . . *ssst ssst boom.* Patent leather Mary Janes, lace-fringed anklets, slender legs, and nice, firm breasts. Humongo! Frankie flashed his cool look as he slung his books under his arm and moved out behind her.

Darlene D'Arcel couldn't have been sixteen, but Frankie regarded her as a grown woman. She had those kind of

moves. He knew she went out with some real bad testosterone motherfucker who drove a jet black 'vette, with the
rear license plate framed in blue neon. It went without saying that she was putting out.

Following Darlene through the hall, he was so entranced
that Jesse Stillman hit him like a freight train. It happened
way too fast. Stillman got right up in his face, his horny finger thumping Frankie in the chest, a deep basso voice. "I'll
see you after school!"

Shit! Frankie came down from the pink panty cloud real
fast. Man, why did he have to run off his mouth so much behind Stillman's back? He doubted that Stillman knew
Frankie had flattened his tires. He hadn't told anyone that.
He hadn't told Altman on LSD night. Or had he? God!

Second period math, and Mr. Harding called Frankie to
the board to do a geometry problem. Frankie glowed red as
he fumbled with the chalk, knowing he couldn't solve the
problem if he had a year. And Harding didn't let him off as
usual.

"I can't do it," Frankie said, his body shifting from pose
to pose. He couldn't do the problem but at least he could
show a little attitude. So hip. So cool. So tough. Such a bad
motherfucker! Then he thought of the pimple. He wondered if it was popping through the blotch of Clearasil. He
crinkled his nose and a little white Clearasil dust settled on
his lips. Christ, if he was standing there with a Rudolph-the-
red-nosed pimple he was a double fucking fool. He said, "Ya
know, Mr. Harding. I don' get it, man."

Frankie gave a short, chesty laugh. Embarrassment up-
the-ass.

"Obviously you don't get it, Mr. Dell," Harding said with

an air of shrill amusement. "Perhaps tomorrow you can re-deem yourself a bit by expounding on Heisenberg's uncer-tainty principle."

"On what?"

"Heisenberg, sir. Go to the library and check it out or you're going to fail, my little friend."

Half the class tittered, but a girl in the second row didn't. She gave him a conspiratorial wink. She was on his side. Or was she? There was definitely eye contact, but he was so damn paranoid and hungover he didn't know how to inter-pret the look. He had never even spoken to her before. Was it a look of compassion, or did it contain a hint of mockery and disdain? The more he thought about it the more para-noid he got. Ever since he got out of bed his whole life had become a ludicrous cartoon. Frankie went to his third pe-riod hall monitor station feeling weak all over. He was shot. Goddammit! Couldn't someone call an ambulance? Jesus Christ!

Once the halls cleared Frankie walked into the boys' toi-let and torched a Marlboro. The smoke calmed him a little and after he flushed the butt he stepped up to a urinal. With visions of Darlene D'Arcel's glossy thigh meat and her pink panties dancing through his brain, he just had to com-mit an act of self-abuse. It was tension reduction, pure and simple. Get it over with and try to reestablish contact with reality. He was so strung out, he didn't know if that was pos-sible.

As soon as he had his pleasure, the door to the boys' rest-room bounced open. Frankie quickly stuffed his dissolving erection back into his blue jeans. He tried to compose him-self and casually stepped away from the urinal as though he had just taken an everyday piss. To an astute observer the truth would be obvious. Fortunately it was only the janitor, a fat guy with a Brylcreem pompadour.

"You feel okay?"

"Yeah, why?"

"You're all red there, short man."

"Naw, I'm all right. It's hot is all." He had a blinding headache and everything started to spin.

"You been smokin' in here?"

Frankie staggered out of the restroom, walked back to his locker, and stuffed his math book inside, giving the book a quick, mean little smash, bending it a little. *There! Serves ya right, ya boring piece of shit.* He withdrew his English book and moved over to Altman's locker. Altman was in the habit of setting his lock one digit from "open." Frankie exchanged his mother's dry baloney sandwiches with Altman's, whose mother made fresh-delicious lunches. It was just a little payback for Altman's scamming that rat poison windowpane as a thirty-dollar hit of ecstasy. Ravenous, Frankie stood before the locker and devoured Altman's lunch. It revived him somewhat but it still felt like he had been laid out by something really heavy.

During lunch, Altman, an acne-ridden, six-foot, one-hundred-and-thirty-pounder with hunched shoulders examined his sandwich with disgust.

"Lookit that thing — no butter, no lettuce, no nothing. Nine-day-old bread. It's fuckin' dry."

"It looks like she made it with her foot," Prescott said.

"Don' she usually make good ones?" Frank asked noncommittally.

"She's been pullin' this shit all month and I keep forgetting to asta 'bout it when I get home." Altman stuck the sandwich back in the bag and crushed it while Frankie struggled to restrain a guffaw. Altman said, "What's so funny, fuck face?"

Frankie slapped his thigh and laughed out loud. "That's one ugly fuckin' sandwich. Eat your carrot."

Altman withdrew a dirty carrot from the crumpled bag and looked it over. "Fuck. It ain't even peeled; it's still got topsoil on it." He rapped the vegetable on the table and it made a hard knocking sound.

Frankie laughed. "That ain't no carrot; that's fuckin' hardwood. A fuckin' beaver couldn't put a dent into that motherfucker. Whadja get for dessert? A turd? Ah ha ha ha, hargh!"

Prescott recoiled. "What's with you, man? Are you off your rocker? Shut up."

Altman said, "He's off his lithium again."

Prescott smirked and offered Altman a package of Ho Ho's from his own lunch. He turned to Frankie and said, "Do *The Shining* for us, man."

Frankie was glad to oblige and quickly slipped into character. "'It is so fucking typical of you to create a problem like this when I finally have a chance to accomplish something, when I'm finally into my work. I could really write my own ticket if I went back to Boulder now. Sweep out driveways. Work in a car wash? Would that appeal to you, Wendy?'

"'Oh, Jack, I —'

"'I have let you fuck up my life this far, but I am not going to let you fuck this up!'"

Altman and Prescott began to squirm. "Geez, calm down. God." Prescott said. "You better take your pills. You're going to end up in the nuthouse again."

"It's just a fuckin' scene from a fuckin' movie."

"You're talkin' loud, dudeski," Prescott said. "I mean loud."

"Fuck you! I'm talkin' normal."

Prescott got up from the table and said, "You're talking loud. It's embarrassing. I ain't hanging with you no more. You're a fucking loser, man."

FRANKIE'S English class was studying *Great Expectations*. Frankie had read it and liked it. While he was terrible at math, he was a speed reader with something close to a photographic memory. When he was in the nuthouse, in spite of the Haldol and lithium, Frankie could burn through thick books, a couple a day — they were like excursions to different worlds. Options, new possibilities for his own life occurred to him when he read good books. But back at home, in spite of his resolves he quickly fell into the old, bad habits as if he were in the very grip of the devil.

After class Frankie remembered Stillman's threat and managed to collect his jacket and notebooks and take them to P.E. so he wouldn't get caught at his locker after school. He made a clean getaway after P.E. and went to Booker's Pool Hall to kill the couple of hours before work.

After a dozen games of eight ball, he stopped in at the Red & Black Spot for french fries and a Coke and then walked down the hill to his job at the movie theater.

Wesley Lame Duck sat in his orthopedic chair in the projection booth. He was examining a set of stamps with a magnifying glass and comparing them to those in one of his countless stamp manuals. Frankie slipped into his uniform before the projectionist even knew he was there. Wesley was a clubfoot with back trouble. His left leg was a full six inches shorter than his right and he wore a prosthetic Frankenstein boot on this foot. Wesley was a pedophile who got so excited cruising the shopping malls, he often walked until the foot bled. And by the looks of things, Wesley had had a very good afternoon. He had the foot exposed. The skin on it was raw and weeping fluid. Rather than feel pity for Wesley, the sight of his foot enraged Frankie. The dillfuck way he was studying the stamp manual made Frankie want to strangle him. Wesley heard Frankie zip up the fly on his uniform, fire up a cigarette, and clap the lid of his Zippo shut. He looked over his shoulder and said, "Well! How was the big weekend, Frankieboy? Did you get laid?"

"Yeah. I got laid. Sure. I always do. But my weekend sucked just the same."

"How so, sport? Are you all right? You don't look very well."

"I'm all right. How was your weekend?"

"Marvelous," Wesley said. "I finally got a much-needed infusion of 'Captain Berg's Stamp Hour' on the shortwave."

"Oh yeah? What's that motherfucker up to?"

"He was talking about the Pony Express. The riders didn't actually ride ponies, you know, they rode the fastest most powerful horses available. America, just before the Civil War. They used big horses but hired wiry little studs like you for twenty-five dollars a month. Seventy-five miles per shift. There were one hundred and fifty relay stations along the two-thousand-mile route from St. Joseph, Missouri, to

San Francisco. Each of these valiant young men carried a rifle and two Colt .44s. If they couldn't outrun a desperado or a whole gang of them who laid in wait to bushwhack these butch young studs, the riders would have to shoot it out with them. Believe me, it wasn't any cakewalk, Mary! Swapping horses on the fly. What a life! They forged raging rivers, galloped over mountain passes, through hostile Indian territory — barren deserts, narrow gorges. For twenty-five dollars a month, these courageous young bucks risked life and limb to deliver the U.S. mail. Think of the buns they must of had. Anyhow, the whole trip took eight days, whereas shipping mail around the Horn took three weeks. President Lincoln's first Inaugural Address was carried by young men such as yourself: tough, fearless, and utterly butch and studly. Kit Carson was a Pony Express rider. Buffalo Bill. People think stamps cost a lot today, but let me tell you: it cost five dollars a half ounce to send something in a Pony Express pouch and even then it was a losing proposition."

"Five bucks a half ounce," Frankie said. "You could buy acreage — the fuckin' Ponderosa — for that kind of bread."

Wesley rocked back and clasped his hands behind his neck. "If you think in terms of real dollars, in those days, why I'm sure you could," he said. "The entire Louisiana Purchase went for something under nine million. Princess Di spent that much on her wardrobe."

IT WAS "Old Oscar Week" at the Tivoli and there were only twenty-eight people at the seven o'clock showing of *Alfie.* Some kind of 1960s shit. Frankie gave the restrooms a preliminary cleaning and then went out into the lobby to jaw with Donna Wilcox, the popcorn girl. He loved the refreshment stand where the boxed candies were neatly arranged under the immaculately clean plate glass of the dark oak display counter. The Tivoli sold the everyday cheap junk that you could get at any theater, but also hard-to-get stuff the bohemian types liked: Holloway Suckers, Slo Poke's Walnetto's, Necco Wafers, and Juji Fruits. The centerpiece of the refreshment oasis was a vintage corn popper inside a glass display case bordered with narrow strips of green, blue, and yellow stained glass. There was a "Fresh Popcorn" sign hand-painted in bright red with a yellow border on the front of the hopper and just beneath it was a cardboard placard painted by Wesley, the projectionist. "Our popcorn, the finest available in the world, is organically grown in Amana, Iowa exclusively for the Tivoli Theater. Choose between our iodine-free, coarse sea salt, harvested from the crystal shores of northern Morocco, or from the familiar Morton's Salt in the classic 'When it rains, it pours!' salt boxes. Farm fresh hot creamery butter is available upon request."

This was all a lie. The storeroom was stacked with sacks of generic salt and shiny aluminum tubs of thick white coconut oil and rancid margarine. Earl, the Tivoli's manager, approved of the deception and jacked up the price of a family bucket from three bucks to five after Wesley produced the sign.

Like Frankie, Donna Wilcox wore a uniform reminiscent of bygone times. She looked like a candy-striper at a hospital. As she sliced a wedge of congealed coconut oil and dumped it into the corn popper, she smiled at Frankie and said, "So what's it like inside a nuthouse, Frankie? Or is this the nuthouse, this life we have here?"

"Nuthouses are boring," Frankie said. "Give me a box of Juji's."

Donna reached under the counter and Frankie saw a little cleavage. Donna's cotton uniform showed her figure off to good advantage. She had pretty skin, full lips; at certain angles she almost looked okay. Donna handed Frankie a box of candy. "They'll rot your teeth, but here," she said pushing a box of candy over the glass case. "You don' look like a nutcase. You look like a normal guy. A cute guy."

Frankie began to launch Juji's up toward the ceiling and catch them in his mouth. He got to feeling cocky. Then he winced and raised his hand to his jaw. He flipped the box back on the corner. "Jesus! These are too hard, man. They been aged too long. Gimme a box of Black Crows."

He got another peek at Donna's cleavage and caught a faint whiff of Jungle Gardenia. Frankie ripped open the box of Black Crows and began catching them with his mouth. He flipped one up for Donna and she caught it. He popped a few more up and they made a game of vying for them. Frankie arched a long one up near the ceiling and after he caught it, he and Donna fell together. She planted her mouth on his and kissed him deeply, pressing her soft bosom against his chest. Frankie's cheeks got hot and he sprung an instant boner. Donna kissed him again and then suddenly pushed away. "Oh shit," she said, "here comes Earl."

Donna quickly dumped another chunk of grease into the corn popper and Frankie swept around the concession stand. By then it was time to take tickets for the second show, *Tom Jones*. There was the usual bunch of bohemian types, people with whom he felt an odd kinship. Earl relieved him at the ticket stand and as soon as Frankie completed cleaning the bathrooms, he got lost in the upper balcony. He turned to leave and there she was, triple-life-sized and Panavisioned up on the silver screen, the beatific vision of his life, Susanna York in the role of Sophie Western. With one look Frankie knew his life had been changed irrevocably. Sophie Western, angel, the antithesis of everything he had known. She was radiance, a melodic birdsong on a soft summer morning. She was life.

What a great world, how unlike his own, and, oh, Jesus, God, if ever there was a more beautiful woman than Sophie Western — well, there just couldn't be. Frankie walked home in a trance. What was that poem they had done in English?

> *Whenas in silks my Julia goes*
> *Then, then (methinks) how sweetly flows*
> *That . . .*

Liquid something. Sophie was like that poem. Refined. And that's what Frankie would aspire to. Culture and refinement. He had imagined there was time, that he could reform at his leisure, but that time never seemed to come along. It was like, wake up, motherfucker — the time is now! The movie was the signal he had been waiting for. He needed to change and he knew he could do it. A photographic memory was a gift, a terrible thing to waste. He needed to put it to good use.

After work, Frankie followed the tracks past school and on home. He would apply himself, learn something, find himself. Forget the old bullshit, it was definitely time to show or to go.

Frankie had a bowl of cereal and just after midnight, he went to bed with Fielding's novel. By dawn he was penciling out a book report at the kitchen table when his mother crawled out of bed and staggered into the kitchen for coffee. Frankie had plugged in the pot and had everything ready for her. He had not taken his lithium, but for homework that was allowed. He felt great.

This was certainly a better way to begin the day than coming down from an acid trip. He was afraid his mother would start nagging at him for staying up all night but she saw him so absorbed with his homework, she did little more than chirp a CW tune as she started breakfast. Frankie finished the paper, redotting the i's with a final flourish, and then began to eat. He complimented his mother's greasy eggs and ate her oatmeal in spite of the fact that she had run out of milk. "It's no problem, Mom. I should have gotten it myself. I should be helping you around the house more."

Frankie thought of Sophie on the way to school. Sweet Sophie. Things were going to be different now, there were resolutions. He tossed a pack of Marlboros into the bushes along with his Zippo. Smoking was over. So was jacking off. It was nothing but sordidness and negativity. It's over, God, I quit! What else? What else? It would all come to him. He whistled as he walked. It was a merry tune from the movie. He was taking the long route to school. He paused to smell a lilac bush. The odor was so glorious it made his eyes water. The breeze shimmering through the scented bush sounded like a freight train — but this was not an acid flashback — this was how it really was.

Suddenly Frankie found himself walking next to the girl

from geometry class, Suzie Trowbridge. He was saying witty, clever, wonderful things, things he didn't know he was capable of saying.

Her eyes were like Sophie's, and her hair, too. She was laughing with him and he seemed to get funnier as he went along. His rap was inspired and it just came rolling out with no forethought. He was telling her how he was going to be a great actor someday, after he won the middleweight title. Hell, he might even play second base for the Mets in between fights. He could do it, too. Susan appeared to be convinced of it. The way it was all coming out was inspired. Frankie couldn't wait for her to ask the next question, so boss were his answers. Yeah!

When he asked her to the Saturday night school dance and she said, "Yes," he had to turn his face away. He felt like hiding it in his jacket and dashing away from her but she took his hand, the hand-of-a-thousand-jerk-jobs-that-would-never-jerk-again. Numb with ecstasy, Frankie recited the capper:

> *"Whenas in silks my 'Susan' goes*
> *Then, then (methinks) how sweetly flows*
> *That liquefaction of her clothes.*
>
> *Next, when I cast mine eyes and see*
> *That brave vibration each way free;*
> *O how that glittering taketh me!"*

She kissed him on the side of the mouth as they rounded the corner and neared school. "Christ, you know Shakespeare by heart," she said.

"That's Robert Herrick, not Shakespeare."

"You gotta monster zit by your nose," she said.

Frankie's face blazed red. He was suddenly so embarrassed that he found it almost impossible to move, to put one foot in front of the other. Yet they walked together silently for a moment and then it seemed that Susan had picked up the pace as if to get away from him. He had to hustle to keep up with her. As they turned the corner near the Red & Black Spot, Frankie spotted Stillman and a bunch of the school wrestlers. Suzie waved at Stillman and Frankie waved, too, a limp passive wave, hoping Stillman would wave back. Instead, Stillman threw his Mets cap on the ground and charged.

Frankie was paralyzed with fear and disconcerted by an already large, forming crowd. Only at the last second was he able to move. Sidestepping Stillman's rush, Frankie cuffed him hard on the ear with a right, then turned, planted his feet, and pumped a double jab in Stillman's face, coming over the top with a right hand. The speed and placement of Frankie's punches stopped Stillman cold and caused his eyes to glaze over with a milky white film. The right connected to Stillman's chin like a heat-seeking missile, and the jabs busted Stillman's lip. Frankie kicked Stillman in the balls, doubling him over, and then kneed him in the face. Frankie lashed an elbow out with such ferocity that he lost his balance and fell to the ground. He quickly scrambled back to his feet and stood in front of Stillman hardly able to breathe. There was just enough time to pick up a rock, inflict a disabling blow, and win, but as the tenor of the crowd shifted into Frankie's favor, he was undone by it.

He stood there like a wooden Indian frozen with indecision, as a strong and familiar born-to-lose vibe pulsed through his soul. And then it was too late.

The glaze cleared from Stillman's eyes and he felt his bloody lip, laughing. "Hey there, friends and citizens, we got us a live one he-yuh," Stillman said. An excited crowd huddled around the two fighters. Stillman bashed Frankie in the face with one short punch, breaking his nose. A small geyser of blood spurted on Stillman's jacket, and he began to bash Frankie's face until his hands hurt.

Susan Trowbridge tossed a forelock of hair away from her eyes. "Leave him alone, Jess, you big asshole, you're sixty pounds bigger than him; he's just a kid."

"Fuck you," Stillman said. "How could you be seen with a fool like this? How could you possibly walk with this snakey motherfucker?"

"I needed help with my English."

"You want help with yer English? See me," Stillman said leaning back, easing off.

The blood from Frankie's nose was running down his throat, choking him. Stillman turned to him and elbowed the broken nose one final time.

"That'll teach you to let the air out of my tires, goddammit."

The crowd began to chant, "Pants him! Pants him!" Frankie went crazy trying to get away, but Stillman still got fresh hold on him. Then in one quick jerk, he pulled Frankie's pants off and then the size 28 Jockey Classic Briefs. Wriggling free, Frankie cupped his genitals with both hands and tried to bull his way through the crowd. As he did, he saw a big grin on Susan Trowbridge's face. He saw her blond hair spilling down on the front of her navy blue car coat. It was the most beautiful hair. The next thing she was shaking her head back, flipping her hair back over her shoulders like the slut that she was.

Frankie punched through the circle and ran until everyone was out of sight. He ran all the way home naked from the waist down.

The old lady had left for work, thank God for that. Frankie took a long shower and bawled. Jesus Christ, Susan had laughed right along with the rest of them! After he dried off, Frankie snagged a handful of the old lady's Darvon and headed for the pool hall.

That night at work, high on Darvon and a quart of Bud, Frankie burst into the projectionist's booth and confessed the whole scene to Wesley Lame Duck. He had to tell someone.

In rambling, slurred speech, Frankie told him all about falling in love with Sophie Western, about the poem and the lilac bush and the sound of the freight train. Frankie told him how much he loved Susan Trowbridge and Wesley said, "Stop it right there," and gave him a lecture about how that sick-in-love, kicked-in-the-stomach feeling would max out in three days and totally peter out in two weeks. It was all brain chemicals.

Alfie had the right idea, he said. Hadn't he seen *Alfie* last night?

No? "Then you watched the wrong fuckin' movie, Jim."

Wesley told Frankie that he should save some money for the downstroke on a Mustang, get a ragtop in midnight blue. The adolescent female wasn't looking for the real person inside — all that mattered to them were clothes, hot cars, and so on. Also, you had to radiate confidence and self-esteem. "Show them some shit, pachuco. Hey, man!"

Wesley was in an uncommonly vulgar mood. It was as if some new demonic personality had emerged. He suggested that Frankie could quit school and get a full-time job in a factory and keep his night gig at the Tivoli. "Are you listening to me, Frankie, or are you completely fucked up on pills? I must say this crybaby routine is a definite turnoff for me."

Then Wesley suggested the car would be there all the quicker if Frankie went down on him. He started stroking Frankie's thigh. "It's plain and simple. No big deal at all," Wesley said, peeling off a pair of crisp fifties — "A hundred bucks, Ace, deal?" And Frankie, half ready to puke, stared blankly into space. Everything was just sort of spinning around; but one thing led to another and pretty soon he found himself with his face in Wesley's lap, staring at a fish of a dick.

The part of him that was outside of himself watched curiously as he took Wesley's cock and stuck it in his mouth. It didn't actually have a taste to it although there was a smell. He worked the organ up and down to get it over with and forgotten as soon as possible. Wesley was soon choreographing a fairly sophisticated blow job. It was a paradox, Wesley said, giving a guy a gobble job so you can score some pussy, but life was like that.

Wesley closed his eyes, let his head loll back, and began to grind his soft, wide hips as Frankie mechanically worked his mouth up and down.

The screen flashed brightly and the thwack/crackle of the old movie snapped Frankie back into awareness. He could hear his precious Sophia on the sound system and started to look up to her but Wesley yanked his head down hard. "You can forget that shit, Susannah York has got to be pushin' sixty by now."

Bleary-eyed, like a man climbing out of a well, Frankie raised up to Sophia. But Wesley slapped Frankie across the face and pulled his head back down. "You took the money and now I'm going to fuck your face, Mister!"

He grabbed Frankie's hair with one hand and the front of Frankie's uniform with the other as he bucked up. His semi-erect penis slid in and out of Frankie's mouth, stabbing him in and about the face.

Wesley continued to bark instructions until the very last, when his pecker engorged fully, his head fell back, and he came in the back of the young man's mouth. As he pulled out, Wesley slapped Frankie so hard it snapped him sober. "Cop the load, dammit! Or you're not getting paid."

Frankie looked up at Wesley with sheep eyes and he swallowed.

You Cheated,
You Lied

Jonas Vitias's neurology clinic was located in an old neocolonial-style bank building across from Aurora's Leland Hotel. The bank building sat on the Western fork of the Fox River, which split around the central downtown, isolating it into a geographical island. There were two nine-foot dams on the northern sides of the river, and four major sandstone bridges to facilitate traffic across this pathetic vessel of water. Muddy with farm runoff, the Fox could put out a considerable stench in the summertime. The smell could be forbidding and it didn't help if you looked for contributing factors. As often as not there were large carp beached along the shores gasping for oxygen — suicidal whales in miniature and no rescue teams from Greenpeace. Nada.

Sprung from a Lake in northern Illinois, the Fox traversed through a belt of heavily industrialized cities — after Elgin, Joliet, Geneva, and Batavia, it carried with it some very heavy metal action from the iron and aluminum foundries poised alongside the river, in addition to the pesticide runoffs, sewer effusions, and other ecological crimes. The vessel of concentrated poison wound down a valley dressed with handsome oak, elm, and maple trees to Aurora, not exactly the most "toddlin' town" but the ersatz pearl of the Fox River Valley nonetheless. This short nasty river was named after a tribe of Indians of which little was memorable except for the speed with which they folded after their first confrontation with the paleface.

The old Leland Hotel, at twenty-nine stories, offered the best view of the river and the city of Aurora. During the Roaring Twenties, Al Capone would sometimes drive down in a black limousine to hold forth in the Sky Club, a glass-domed nightclub at the top of the skyscraper, which was at that time, the tallest building in the state of Illinois outside of Chicago. Quiet, devoid of G-men, and with easy proximity to Chicago, Aurora was convenient for Chi-town gangsters. In the depression years, John Dillinger and his gang once buried a body on the south end of town after a downstate gun battle with police. My uncle Alex told me of the twenty-dollar tips Dillinger gave him after he gassed up the bandit's fast Fords. Alex ran a service station behind my grandmother's store, where the criminal sometimes sat on the back porch swing drinking root beer. "He liked Hire's Root Beer. He wouldn't touch anything stronger," Alex used to say. "Even when he had his fingerprints burned off with acid, he 'just took it' — no ether, chloroform, no nothing. You see, Will'am, this man did not want to get caught. He may have been a criminal but he was smart; he had guts, and the heat on him at this time was simply ferocious. He was a hero to every wop and

dumbfuck German farmer on the south end. Your grandmother used to cook for him in the back of the store."

I knew that Dillinger once holed up in an old Victorian
mansion on Aurora's East Side. The house was complete
with an underground tunnel that led to a church on the opposite side of the street. It had been built for an Anglican
priest who was so senile he couldn't be trusted to cross the
street. That he was trusted with the souls of his parishioners
was another matter.

"If only he had stayed there," Alex would lament. "If *only*
he had laid low, he could have been greater than Jesse
James. I wasn't the only person on the south end that
grieved when they gunned him down. No sir."

Capone, on the other hand, was not a hider — he had
too much hubris for that, and for many years, when he was
riding so high, he had no need to hide. Big Al came to Aurora to coordinate vital crime business. He built a house for
his brother there, and some say he also had girls. Well, no
doubt. Standing atop the Sky Club, looking down at the
muddy brown river as it squiggled through the town like a
sick slug, could hardly have been a thrill, however. As it got
older, the Leland Hotel looked as if it might fall with the
next brisk wind. People were afraid to go inside. I made the
trip only once, just to see what Big Al saw.

While the downtown of Aurora was in decay even in my
youth, it remained a hub of secondary activity where the
seedier second tier of goods and services were still available.
Dr. Vitias had a river view from his consulting room, and
when patients complained of the stench, Dr. Vitias said that
while it was lesser known, in point of fact the Fox River was
actually much cleaner than India's holy river, the Ganges. In

this second-tier part of town, Vitias was a third-tier sort of
doctor. No matter how long the consultation, his fee was always the same: $15. I came to see him for temporal lobe
epilepsy. I could have afforded a better doctor, but all of the
amateur fighters from the gym used Vitias. Not only was he
cheap. He would write a script for pain pills on almost any
pretext.

To get to the inner sanctum of the consulting room a patient first had to endure the waiting room. There was no
river view there, not even a window, but the room had it's
own distinctive character. It was a large, dark mahogany-
paneled room with a tall ceiling, with straight well-made
oaken chairs, frosted-glass valances, standing ashtrays, and
the general ambience of a film noir. In the cooler months a
ceiling-mounted heater roared pure dragonfire every thirty
minutes and then would suddenly kick out with a loud and
unsettling clunk. For the regulars, like myself, it became a
good way of marking time. Antarctic glaciers moved faster
than Dr. V. Most of the patients knew this and most came
prepared to wait. They brought knitting needles, books,
magazines, and crossword puzzles. They brought meals.
They chain-smoked cigarettes and filled the sand trap ashtrays with crushed butts. They did all of these things and
sometimes they also fell to pieces right before my eyes. Most
of them were desperate souls, hopeless and broken. Neurological maladies often brought forth a dimension of fear
and incomprehension lacking in more straightforward diseases. This added element of strangeness very often turned
patient's lives into a living hell of pain, dysfunction, and
absolute despair. Too often the waiting room was a Sartrean
hell, and I think I sometimes became floridly psychotic

there myself. I dreaded the place. That was until a new character entered the mix, a beautiful young woman named Molly Bloom.

It was on a cold Saturday in January. I was reading passages to Norman Jones about philosopher Arthur Schopenhauer's pal, Karl Witte, the boy wonder who entered the university at Göttingen at the age of ten. Mr. Jones, a black man of seventy suffering from Parkinson's, kept nodding off until I blurted out some new astonishing precocious ability displayed by the preteen academian. On the other side of the room, smelling of heavy-duty pigshit, sat "Ham" Hamsun, a Swedish farmer with an uncanny resemblance to "Babe" Ruth. Ham, who was holding it together with the thinnest of emotional glues, looked over and said, "It's the same thing with you, every week, Will'am. You sit there on your dead ass with a thick book. Who cares about some goddamn kid that lived a hundred years ago?"

"Yeah, Will'am, Jesus," said a bearded junkie who came in to refill a script for pain pills. "Put a cork in it."

I said, "Why, Andrew Wayne Miller, what's the matter there, cupcake? Tired of waiting? You need to turn that frown upside down."

"Fuck it," he said as he grabbed his coat and straight-armed the frosted-glass door. It was just then that Molly Bloom stepped into the room like radiance, sunshine, and stardust. Flashing a beautiful smile, she paused theatrically. "Well, hello. Cold enough for ya? Hee hee. My name is Molly Bloom."

She slipped out of a black cashmere overcoat and turned to hang it on the old-fashioned clothing rack. I closed my book to take her in. Molly was a blond with a strikingly beautiful face. She was moderately tall, about 5'7", with a medium frame. She had long legs and a narrow waist. Her breasts were firm and well formed, straining behind a white linen blouse. She appeared to be about twenty years old. After she removed her gloves and hat, she turned back to the room, planted her feet, and with a playful glint in her eyes, tugged at her scarf, pulling it back and forth behind her neck in a brief and subtle parody of a striptease artist. She certainly had my attention. Her only detectable flaw was a wandering left eye. This little defect only made her seem all the more real to me and caused her beauty to crush my heart. Suddenly the hole in my life — the great empty abyss — had been filled.

Hamsun seemed oblivious to her act, and to her beauty, but he was always glad for a new ear into which he could deposit his troubles. "I got up at four-thirty this morning. I had to go outside and set the heaters for the pigs. Figured to find them dead. It was cold, brother! Dark. Cold! Well, what do I find? The pigs was okay but my cat was frozen stiff. I couldn't believe it. What in the hell? I'm walking out there thinking, 'Is that Herbert?' And suddenly, by God, I realize that it is! It is! Herbert is dead. No warning, no nothing. Just dead. Stiffer than a board."

"That's terrible," Molly said. "What did you do?"

Hamsun leaned back in his chair and examined a hangnail. "I was in a hurry to come here so I stuck him in a pizza box and threw him in the trunk of my Ford. But, hell! I could have drove to Florida and buried him the way things are going here." He looked at Molly and said, "What time is your appointment, little lady?"

"Three," she said. She crossed her legs at the ankles and

pointed her knees in Ham's direction. "Tell me, what are you going to do with that cat?"

"Bury him, come a thaw," Ham said yawning. "Boy! How long do you wait? I'm glad I had some eats. Over at Harner's Bakery. Quite a bunch of rowdies at that place, and you can't top the food. It sure beats sitting here." Ham extended his fingers and examined them for more trouble. His exposed skin was covered with psoriasis.

Molly smiled at him and said, "You've heard this a thousand times before, no doubt, but you *really* look like Babe Ruth, mister."

"My claim to fame," Ham said morbidly. "I look like the Babe. Can't play ball worth a damn, never could. How could I? I grew up in Sweden."

"The man gets up earlier than anyone else in the county," I said.

Hamsun shot me a look and said, "What time did *you* get up, Will'am?"

"Noon," I said. "Just after actually. Every day I get up later than noon I consider a victory. I chart it out. A silver star for noon. A gold for two P.M. and sometimes I even go platinum."

"What time is 'platinum'?" Molly Bloom asked as she held the edge of her black skirt and recrossed her legs at the knee.

"After four," I said.

"That's just ridiculous," Hamsun said. "Layabouts like you should be shot. It's no wonder you're always depressed." He caught Molly's eye and said, "How about you, little missy? What time did your feet hit the floor?"

Molly stretched her arms and suppressed a yawn. "About

eight. I'm a frigging insomniac. I've got insomnia of Russ-
ian dimensions."

I laughed at this. Ham moved forward in his chair and
extended his left leg full straight and massaged his knee.
"Eight, huh? I got my morning chores done by eight! The
outside heaters going for those damn pigs, burning up electricity like there's no tomorrow. It's expensive. Eight! Hell, I
am up and *moving*. I'm ready for pie by eight! Tell me, lady,
are you some kind of beatnik with those black stockings?"

"Not especially," Molly said with a bright smile. "I wasn't
aiming for a fashion statement when I put these on. I was
going for warmth." Molly drew her slender legs up in the
chair and hugged her knees to her breast.

"*Molly!*" Ham said with a glint of mischief in his eyes. "I
like that name." He popped out of his chair and flattened
out the palms of his large square hands like he was about to
pull some sort of Marcel Marčeau mime action. He was
either deflecting shrapnel or peeking out of a window; I
wasn't sure. He forced his voice into a high-pitched squawk
and sang, "'Good *Golly*, Miss *Molly! Sure like to ball.*'"

Norman Jones jerked back like he was shot.

Ham sat down and said, "What does that *actually* mean?
Ball?"

Molly said, "It means, she sure likes to fuck."

It was the farmer's turn to be shocked. His red face,
parched with psoriasis, flushed crimsom. He pushed himself back deeply into his chair and said, "How can they
broadcast a song like that on the radio?" The muscles
around the farmer's eyes began to twitch. He removed his
ball cap and furiously scratched the top of his scalp, sending
a shower of yellow flakes to the floor. "Are we supposed to

keep running out and dumping nickels into the parking meter?"

"He runs late. You should know that," I said. "Park in the public lot and you can avoid the hassle."

Hamsun replaced his ball cap, sat back in his chair, and let out a weary sigh. "Carbon monoxide is not an easy way to go, I don't care what they tell you. Next time I'm using a gun."

Norman voiced a guttural reply to the farmer's statement. Molly smiled at Norman and said, "I beg your pardon?"

Norman raised his hands and just waved her off. It was too much effort to enunciate for a newcomer. In a three-piece suit, shabby though it was, Mr. Jones had the look of some minor distinction. When he grunted again, Molly Bloom looked to me for a translation. I said, "He wants to know what kind of gun Ham's got."

Hamsun slapped the side of his overalls with his ball cap. He was on his feet and began pacing back and forth in the room. He returned to his seat and began to twirl the bill of the cap through his thick red fingers again. The farmer said, "A .22 caliber bolt-action rifle."

Norm raised his voice and spoke out in plain English. "Go bigger," he said. This was followed by another utterance.

"What?" the farmer said.

"Do the *job up right;* get yourself a .12-gauge," Norman said.

"Oh yeah?" the farmer said. "I thought I did do the job up right. How was I to know she'd find me?"

"Maybe you were meant to live," Molly said. "Did you

ever think of that? Maybe there's an angel looking out for you?"

"It was my ex-wife — the devil's worst battleax. She came by wanting her back alimony!" Hamsun stood up again and started searching through his pockets. "Since then they've got me on a kidney machine three times a week. I walk away from that contraption and my whole brain feels like it's filled with cotton. Mouth tastes like tin foil. Half the time I can't even remember my old dog's name. I've just about had it, all the way around." He took a wooden match from his flannel shirt pocket and began to clean his ear.

Molly picked up a magazine, Norman Jones began to doze, and I returned to Karl Witte, the boy wonder. The farmer abhorred silence and said, "You spend half your time wishing you were never born and the other half scared you're going to die." He consulted his pocket watch and noted the time with a dour look of exasperation. "All I came in for is a damn B-twelve shot and to check the blood pressure. How long does a person have to wait? It don't take no longer than a couple of seconds. My time is valuable too, you know. I just don't know where doctors get off making you wait."

"That's so sad," Molly said. "I'm sorry for you. And for your cat."

The farmer bristled. "Sad. Why? Feel sad for yourself."

"I'm just sad that you don't want to go on living," Molly said. "Life can be wonderful —"

"Oh, spare me the horseshit?" the farmer said. "Save your feeling sorry for someone who really needs it. I made my bed, and I guess I can lie in it."

"*I* can be sorry for your pain, sorry that you would ever

feel like killing yourself. There must be something you want to do — take a trip? Have you ever been off the farm?"

"The war. I served in the South Pacific. Marine Corps. Had me a regular wahine in Honolulu, too. Yes, I did."

"Maybe she's still waiting for you," Molly said.

"Little grass shack," Norman said.

"Oh, Ham, you *want* to go back to that little grass shack, don't you?" Molly said with a pealing laugh. "In 'Key-al-la-ka-hoo, Hawaii.'"

The farmer laughed. "Now that is a good one, Missy. It could be Hawaii, too. This room is hot!"

Humming, Molly began to hula around the room. "You know the tune, doncha?" she said as she slithered over to Ham and pulled at the farmer's shirtsleeves. "C'mon now: 'I can hear the old guitar a playin' on the beach at How Now Now; I can hear the old Hawaiian's sayin' Ko-mo-mai-no-kah-oo-ee-e-kah-ha-lee-wall-la-ka-how.'"

Molly could dance and sing like a professional luau entertainer. Her hands expertly undulated the hand language of the hula as she raised them over her head and let her fingers fall like feathers from heaven. She clearly had control of her hips and belly. Ham got up and danced along with her as Molly flashed her eyes and sang, "I want to go back where the hooma hooma nooka nooka apu apa goes swimming by."

There was a shuffling of chairs, and shadows of movement behind the frosted window of Dr. Vitias's consulting room. The door opened and Charlie Leimbach, a plastering contractor with ALS, limped out into the waiting room. Norman Jones struggled to his feet. I thought he was anticipating his appointment and started for the consulting room, but he had a frolic of his own in mind. Norman crunched forward in the signature Parkinson's stance. A wedge of a smile cracked his frozen mask of a face and he butt-bumped with Molly, singing, "Nooka nooka, hooma hooma."

Flapping his elbows Norman did a little footwork on the floor, singing, "Hambone, hambone, where you been?" He patted his breast, his elbows, thighs, then bent forward and made a scissors motion with his knees. He was able to straighten up to the three-quarters posture but no higher. He pointed his left toe and sang, "Around the world and back again," as he did an about-face and then reversed himself, getting stuck in a Parkinson's freeze. Dr. Vitias had to help him back to his seat. All of us were deeply impressed. I had not seen that much dexterity from Norman in two years.

Molly took Dr. Vitias by the hand and said, "Hey there, Doctor — 'hooma hooma nooka nooka' —"

"'Apu apa goes swimming by —'" Ham said. "Hah!"

Dr. Vitias finally folded his arms and said, "What's going on out here? Did you guys just come from a bar?"

"No," Ham said, "But we're about ready to head for one."

We all laughed at this. Molly picked up her sweater and sat down again. She said, "See. There are laughs out there. When there aren't, you have to make them happen."

"A philosopher," Mr. Leimbach said. He turned to me next. "Hi, Will'am, are you still boxing, young man?"

"He better not be," Dr. Vitias said. "You aren't boxing again, are you, William? There will be hell to pay if you are."

"I don't mean to embarrass you but I saw your name in the police blotter again," Mr. Leimbach said.

"I got eighty-sixed from the Irish Club," I said. "It wasn't anything special, and it wasn't my fault either."

Mr. Leimbach said, "Of course not. Give my boy David a call."

David Leimbach worked in the prosecutor's office and had thrown out cases against me for disturbing the peace and for driving under the influence. "I appreciate that, Mr. Leimbach. I wanted to ask but was ashamed to do it after you've done so many favors for me already," I said.

The contractor's entire right arm hung uselessly to his side, and when he moved, I saw that he was dragging his right foot. As he pulled his jacket from the coatrack with his left hand, Dr. Vitias moved forward to help him. Only a few months before Leimbach was still carrying heavy pallets of plaster with that arm. Now he rocked back slightly off balance. He was wearing a new chrome-plated brace on his right foot. "You okay, Mr. Leimbach?" I said.

"I'm fine. I'm into a whole new thing, William. You betcha I'm okay. I'm back in the church and I'm right with God. In some ways, I've never been better."

Leimbach used his left hand to put on his fleece-lined plaid hunter's cap. With the entire room staring at him, Mr. Leimbach limped to the door. When he got there, he turned and straightened, clicking his heels together as he snapped off a goofy, left-handed military salute. He had lost a great deal of weight and his coat was swimming on him; his hat was askew. He looked old, like the last photograph ever taken of Dwight D. Eisenhower, yet he was a man scarcely fifty years old. In the softest of voices, he said, "I'm dying. God bless you all." With that he turned and limped out the door. For a second everyone in the waiting room fell silent and listened as they heard the metal brace thumping down the hall.

"There's nothing to be done," Dr. Vitias said. "It's a tragedy."

"That poor dear man," Molly said. "And such nice manners." She wiped a tear from her eyes with the sleeve of her blouse.

"Good manners are the WD-40 of polite society," I said.

"Well spoken, William. You are truly the philosopher," Dr. Vitias said. "Now what was the Hawaiian celebration all about? It's wintertime, no?"

"Not in here it ain't," Hamsun said, pointing up at the forced air heater. "It's like Tahiti in here. You could start a banana plantation."

Dr. Vitias looked at Ham sympathetically, "You're used to being outdoors," he said. "I'm sorry for running so late today. Forgive me." Since the doctor did not employ a nurse or a receptionist, he turned to escort Norman Jones inside the consulting room. Norman was locked up and no longer the merry performer of "Hambone." He looked as if he was in pain. But he waved the doctor off and said, "Let that man get his vitamin shot; I can wait."

Dr. Vitias escorted the farmer inside. The frosted-glass door swung shut. I was growing restless and had visions of Ham recounting tales of dialysis treatments, begging for suicide pills, and maybe concluding his visit with extensive and far-flung views on the latest episode of *Gunsmoke*. Ham was known for marathon sessions.

"You must like the entertainment today, Norman," I said. "Usually you can't get out of here fast enough."

"No," Norman said. "Christian charity. He'll bust if he stays a minute longer."

I returned to my book as the overhead heater kicked in

again. In a few moments, Norman's head fell to his chest and he began to snore. When I next looked up, I caught Molly staring at me. Her sweater was down and her breasts bulged against the tightly drawn white linen. She had her legs crossed at the knee and was swinging her foot and playing peekaboo through steepled fingers. Her nails were painted red and bitten down. Whenever I looked over, she quickly covered her eyes with her fingers and then opened them again, like venetian blinds.

She was the palest of blonds but I couldn't tell if she bleached her hair or not. Despite my best intentions my focus kept returning to her breasts. To avoid leering, and by the sheerest act of will, I looked back at her face, which was nearly as compelling, as was her hair, which was shoulder length, expensively cut, and adorned with tortoise shell barrettes. Her clothes were simple but elegant. She wore fashionable Italian shoes. She let off with the peekaboo and forced her face into an angry grimace, mimicking the farmer. "You could start a banana plantation!"

"It's true," I said.

"Watcha reading?" Molly said in a jocular fashion. Her voice was husky. I set my book aside and watched her shake a Lucky Strike from the pocket of her cardigan sweater. She lit it with a man-sized Zippo.

"Schopenhauer, a biography," I said.

"It must be funny," she said. "You keep smiling as you read. So much mirth on that face — that cute-guy face of yours. It's endearing."

"Schopenhauer's observations are funny to me because they are so dead on the money. The smiles are little convulsions of relief."

"Uh huh," Molly continued to swing her foot. "Tell me, Will'am, have you got a big cock?"

"God! What a thing to say!"

Molly barked a formidable laugh. She stubbed her cigarette out and stuck a piece of Juicy Fruit in her mouth letting the wrapper and aluminum foil casually float to the floor. "Cigarettes — I smoke 'em for the vitamin C, but I don't dig the aftertaste," Molly said, offering me a piece of gum. She arched her neck exposing her throat as she primped with her hair, all the while smiling. "Now let me get this straight, Will'am, what you're saying is that Schopenhauer is not for certain people who, say — just might feel virtuous simply because they get up early in the morning, when the birds are still chirping a melodious tune, and these 'certain people' then go out and have breakfast in a sort of Calvinistic cocksure fashion? The thought that these people are giving themselves 'platinum' stars for early wake-up calls riles you, doesn't it? Makes your blood boil." She squeezed her fists in mock anger and bared her teeth. "And these 'certain people' act so sanctimoniously and judgmental about every other goddamn thing they can think of. Well, you just hate them because you know it is *they* who rule the world. You could just take a knife out and stab each and every one of them — but they exist in legions, no? Rrrrrr! Gruff! Is that it, tough guy?"

"Pretty much on the right track with that remark," I said. "Tell me, Molly, have you yourself read the works of this greatest thinker mankind has ever known?"

"No," she said, bored at the very idea. "I'm not very big on costume dramas. How big is your cock, really?"

"Who paid you to come in here and do this to me?" I said.

She assumed a coquettish Lolita-like pose, working the chewing gum overtime. "Nobody did, pretty baby. I just wanna know, that's all."

"My dick is my personal business," I said.

Molly shucked another piece of gum and folded it into her mouth. "Can I touch you for good luck?"

"Don't be so forward," I said. "And don't you dare touch me. Don't even think about it."

Her eyes flashed playfully, "What a commanding presence you have. And you are handsome — you have to know that. Girls just naturally want to touch you, I can understand that."

I picked up my book again and said, "Okay, I think that's about enough. This is getting ridiculous and I'm starting to feel really embarrassed. Plus, I've exhausted my vocabulary of fifty-cent words. I'm done."

She pitched forward and barked another disturbing laugh, "Hah!"

Norman suddenly jerked awake. His mouth dropped open and a string of saliva rolled from the corner of his mouth. Both of Norman's hands, black and withered, were trembling violently. With his thumbs and forefingers he made the classic Parkinson's pill-rolling maneuver. Molly reached in her purse for a Kleenex and stepped over to the old man. As she wiped away the drool, I realized that she was taller than I first imagined. Her legs, my benchmark test of true and enduring screwability, were perfectly long and slender. Before she sat down I withdrew behind the book, and when I next looked up she was playing peekaboo again. I said, "Maybe you just did come from a bar? Most likely you did."

She laughed again, but more in the melodiously angelic persona. I was suddenly caught up in her carefree frolic again.

Norman Jones looked at us and said, "Hey, what's happening?"

I said, "Nothing, man, we're just acting like a couple of silly fools. Incidentally, Norman, allow me to present Molly Bloom."

"My daddy was an English professor," she said. "Until he gassed himself. It all had to do with *Finnegans Wake*. It's this book that drives people crazy. It should be banned, if you want to know the truth."

I said, "Norman used to be a professional musician, Molly, and he taught at a university as well. In fact, as a youngster, Norman once heard the great Buddy Bolden play."

"Who is Buddy Bolden?" Molly said.

"You know 'hooma hooma nooka' and you don't know Buddy Bolden?" Norman said. His rheumy eyes began to tear. "I was jes' a kid, you see, in raggedy pants, the only ones I owned, but I seen him, man! And I heard him play. And I jes' had to do the same," Norman said. "When Buddy put it out, wham! You could see actual colors come out of his horn. Yes sir, Buddy Bolden was my man."

Molly said, "How come you can sometimes speak so clearly, Norman? And other times you mumble."

"Maybe because you got him interested," I said.

Norman stomped his cane on the oak floor. He said, "A-men!"

Molly perked up at this. "So Buddy Bolden could blast pure primary colors from the mouth of his trumpet? That must have been something. I'd like to hear that."

"Too late," Norman said.

I said, "Buddy Bolden ended up in a mental hospital in the Deep South, and after many years in residence, he died there. I don't think he ever picked up his horn the entire time."

"Genius bona fide," Norman said, rubbing his stomach. "Never will be another like him."

He settled back in his chair and began to drowse again. Molly pulled a tube of dark red lipstick from her purse and applied a fresh layer to her lips. She caught me watching and said, "You wanna try it out?"

"Huh?"

"You want to 'try it out'? Press your lips to mine?"

"Kiss you?"

"You aren't a fag, are you?" she said.

"No," I said.

"Okay," she said. "You just don't want a kiss. What happens when you do rev up?"

"I talk," I said. "I give sermons. I go on tirades. When no one listens, I talk to fire hydrants," I said, "and then I go home thinking everything I've ever said and done in my life was either cruel and mean, or meaningless and ridiculous, total foolishness, without a sliver of truth, with no love or dignity expressed, ever at all, and I want to start talking again to explain it and reframe it — it goes on endlessly. I think it's an Oedipal hang-up at the oral stage. A beer bottle in my mouth, a cigarette —"

Molly said, "How about oral sex? Are you into that?"

"That I am," I said.

Molly sneered, shucking the jacket on a third piece of Juicy Fruit. "That's what I figured. Thanks for the confirmation. You're not a Schopenhauerite, Will'am, you have no self-control; you're a Nietzchean, an anarchist. What do you do for a living?"

"I'm an A-operator on the Noodles Almondine line at General Mills," I said. "Sometimes I work cornflakes. How about yourself?"

"Me?" she said. "Nothing, really. I just got out of the nuthouse again." Her expression grew dark at the thought. She said, "It was so boring in there." She unrolled the sleeve on her right arm and showed me the fresh suicide scars on the inside of her forearm. "Souvenirs from my fifth attempt."

Molly lit another Lucky. "You know, it's goddamn cold out. What say we go to Hawaii, Will'am? Get a little grass shack, do the whole number?"

MOLLY BLOOM moved in with me that very night. I was still living in the small home I had grown up in. My mother left it to me at her death. It was a small place. I had forgotten just how small it was until Molly came to stay.

She wasn't there long. A few days later, I came home from the Noodles Almondine line. My next-door neighbor collared me and said the police picked Molly up as she walked naked along the freeway in search of a cigarette machine. I had to excuse myself when the phone rang. It was Molly's mother, Muriel. She hardly seemed distressed about the recent incident but did say that while most of Molly's enthusiasms were short-lived and inevitably earmarked for failure, Molly had expressed the notion that she had fallen deeply in love with me. "You're the one, William. I've never seen her like this before. William 'this' and William 'that' —

she's gaga. You're the one person who can turn her around and make her happy. I'm convinced."

Only later did it occur to me that Muriel had rattled that speech off like she was reciting passages from a well-rehearsed script. When I finally got to the hospital, which was located clear on the North Side of Chicago, I ran into a petulant ward nurse. Molly was sedated, she said, but that was good news; the restraints were off and she was sleeping at last.

"Restraints?" I said.

Eventually the ward resident came to the reception area and looked me over with undue suspicion, like I was a bug in a specimen jar. At last he said, "So, you're the one."

"What is that supposed to mean?" I said.

"I'll tell you what it means; I'll spell it out for you. I've got a seriously depressed, highly disturbed female patient in my ward and you are encouraging her to read Schopenhauer. Buddy, have you lost your fucking mind? What in the hell were you thinking?"

I DID NOT get in to see Molly that evening. Nor the next. I was back and forth to the North Shore in my Austin Healy many nights without getting in. Finally, Muriel summoned me to the estate in Wayne, Illinois, where I met her husband, Harry, the plastic surgeon, and Muriel's mother, Olga. The doctor excused himself and went to his study to make a phone call. When he returned he told me I was on the list of approved visitors. He apologized for all of the bother. "Molly is okay," he said, handing me a stiff gin and tonic. "Off the lithium is all, and how many nights without sleep? Well, you would know, William?"

"She didn't say anything about taking lithium," I said.

"Well, there you have it," Muriel said. "She's perfectly fine when she's on her medications."

"Why is she seeing Dr. Vitias then?" I said.

"Oh that," Muriel said dismissively. "Migraine headaches. Once in a blue moon she gets a headache."

"Migraines are akin to epilepsy in a loose sense," the doctor said, "or so I've been told. You do have seizures, right? Yet you drive. How is that?"

"I can tell I'm going to have a fit in advance," I said. "Dr. Vitias would never call the Motor Vehicle Department," I said. "He wouldn't do that. He's my friend."

The doctor eyed me warily. He was a cold fish and seemed incapable of deep feeling. What I hated most about him was the look of Hart, Shapner and Marx. Muriel was a little softer, a little more Brooks Brothers. They struck me as vain and shallow. Muriel said, "Do you have literary ambitions, William?"

"Hardly," I said. "I'm saving for college. I go off and on, whenever I get enough dough —"

"With a view to do what?" the plastic surgeon said.

"I've been taking courses in psychology, sociology."

"It must be a challenge," he said. "If things work out with you and my stepdaughter, Muriel and I would support you if you have some viable plan to establish a solid lifestyle."

"It sounds like he wants to be a social worker, Harry. That's what I'm hearing from this kid," Muriel said.

"No. I'm more ambitious than that," I said. "And science comes easily to me. I'm going to be a doctor."

"Really," Harry said.

"Since this thing has happened to me — the epilepsy," I said, "I've had a burning desire to do something important with my life."

It was a hollow delivery but I had just uttered the magic words. A week after Molly's release from the hospital, Harry took us both to the Polo Club, where there was an indoor arena. Molly was an accomplished rider, as was Harry. I was given a mare with a reputation for being easy to ride. Amid the polo set, I felt so conspicuous that I could hardly function. I was thrown twice trying to get the hang of the game. Sympathetic players told me that the horse could sense my lack of confidence. In a pair of Harry's jodhpurs, with no saddle horn to grasp for safety, I tried to convey to the horse beneath me that I was in charge. The absurdity of the game and of my outfit made me giddy. Finally, as a number of horses converged, all the while trying to concentrate on the game, I was unable to post with the mare, and I bounced up and down in the saddle like a hapless, lowborn stooge from Aurora and ripped off a series of farts. The players were shocked and astonished, Harry most of all. They were even more mortified when my composure collapsed entirely and I began to guffaw like a helpless idiot.

On the ride back to the house not a word issued from the front seat. In the backseat, Molly run her hand up and down my leg, teasing an erection. That one was achieved at all had everything to do with hormones. I couldn't believe she would do this in front of Muriel and Harry. After the long fart, I was especially uncomfortable in their presence. I was also uncomfortable with their lives. I wanted to be away from them all at once and forever. I realized that Molly was playing me against them. To Harry and Muriel's credit, I wasn't officially banned from the home, only given a kind of short shrift.

Molly found the farting incident charming. One evening I re-enacted the fart ride and got Molly laughing so uncontrollably she pissed on the hard tile floor — louder and harder than the proverbial cow pissing on a flat rock. It was just at this moment that Harry, Muriel, and another couple stepped in from the garage dressed in formal wear. As Harry passed by he said, "And we had such high hopes for you, William. Alas."

A few days later, Molly got drunk, and in the snow and ice, ran my Austin Healy into a telephone pole. She blew a .03 on the Breathalyzer. I had to take a cab to the police station to bail her out. She was unhurt. The Healy was totaled and I had let the insurance policy lapse thinking we would be in Hawaii by then. Molly and I got into a screaming and pissing match back at my apartment. I started slamming down rum and coke. Edgar Alan Will'am.

IT WAS some days later before I regained my right mind. I remember struggling to consciousness like a man crawling out of a well. I was lying on a plastic-encased mattress. I was not hung over but I was feeling very strange. I had never "escaped" a hangover. I knew I should have had one then, but I didn't. That was my first thought and the whole ground of my being. Then I spotted the green glow of an "exit" light and saw a dimly lit hallway. In the bed next to me a man who looked vaguely like George Washington was snoring. I looked around and saw an empty bed on the other side of George. I got up and made my way to the hall. To the right

I spotted a nurse charting medical reports. I padded down the hall. She looked up and smiled. "Well now, Mr. Doe, what can I do for you?"

"Where am I?" I said.

"You can't tell me?" she said. She wore a white rayon slack suit and a nurse's cap with a bright red and gold R.N. badge pinned to it. She was young, fresh, and attractive.

"The nuthouse," I said. "Which one?"

"Providence," she said.

"How long have I been here?"

"Three days, Mr. Doe. Are you hungry? I see on your chart that you haven't eaten since admission."

"I'm famished," I said.

The nurse put her pen down and led me to a little kitchenette. I watched her slap together a roast beef sandwich. She sliced an apple and placed orange slices on the plate. I watched her pour a glass of milk. She seemed so calm and pleasant. I dug into the food while the nurse filled me in regarding my circumstances.

It turned out that I was on the lockup ward. Providence was a private hospital. I had been discovered in a phone booth wearing a T-shirt — in January. It wasn't until I had a grand mal seizure that they put two and two together. Early the next morning I placed a call to Molly. Muriel answered the phone and she was furious. "I'm angry, exasperated, and fed up with you, William!" She ripped into me for letting her daughter get drunk and drive my car, which she called "a stupid toy."

"I was at work when that happened," I said.

"Well, where are you now?" she said. "Molly is back in the North Shore Hospital. She thinks you ran out on her. You will never know what you have put me through this week, never, if you live to be a thousand! Get to her immediately."

"I can't . . . do that," I said. "I'm in lockup myself with epilepsy."

I gave Muriel the number of the pay phone on the ward and then I was swept up in a herd with the rest of the patients and ushered to the dining room.

I took a seat next to a slender young woman named Joanne. Both of her arms were black and blue. Joanne told me she was undergoing insulin shock therapy. I watched her dump a pile of sugar over her cornflakes and devour them. She had eggs, bacon, and a stack of pancakes drowned in syrup. She put double packets of grape jelly on single slices of toast. I was almost as hungry. We looked up at one another and chuckled like naughty kids. Back in the ward, Joanne noticed I had no socks and gave me a pair of hers. Then, when I said good morning to the patient who looked like George Washington, Joanne slapped me across the face.

"Jesus!" I said.

"That's for *ignoring* me all this time," she said.

"Goddamn!" I said. My face stung. My ear was even ringing. Joanne struck with the power of a man. "Christ!"

The general admissions lockup wards are the most interesting places in a psych unit. This is where all the action takes place. As I readjusted to the seizure meds, I began to feel normal again.

Molly thought it was a scream when I told her that I was in a lockdown ward as well. I told her that Dr. Vitias was going to release me as soon as I stabilized.

Molly complained that she had been having regular headaches. Behind-the-left-eye migraines. Marty Feldman

Specials. "I was having one when I smashed the car. I was trying to get to the emergency room for a shot, Will'am. It's
the only thing that will make it go away," she said. The mere
mention of my smashed car was enough to give me a
headache, and in spite of my afflictions, headaches had
never been a problem. As I was talking to Molly, Joanne
came along and began to question me about the call. I told
her I was talking to family. "So you *don't* have a girlfriend.
I'm your girlfriend, right?"

"Baby, it's you," I said. This seemed to placate Joanne
and she walked away taking a position by the TV lounge
where she could keep an eye on me. As Molly began a long
rant about her headaches, I could only think of my wrecked
car. I felt like hanging up the phone and never seeing her
again. I was sick of all the bullshit, but could only say, "Yes,
uh huh." Finally another patient demanded to make an
emergency call. Molly overheard him and was off the line in
seconds. I drifted back to the ward television and sat holding hands with Joanne as we watched soap operas, enjoying
a pleasant Thorazine buzz. That night Joanne slipped into
my room, removed her robe, and climbed into bed with me
and fucked my brains out. She was easily the best piece of
ass I experienced in my short history as a fornicator. Insane
women were generally good in bed.

But then there were problems. Even as I fucked her, I
knew there was a price to be extracted. It came in the form
of a teenage nymphomaniac on the ward named Karla.
Karla somehow attended school in the mornings, but she
was too restless to do homework, and I passed some of the
dead time on the ward reading to her or helping her write
social studies reports. Karla was a chubby, irascible creature,

but Joanne watched every move between us. I soon found myself relating to this young girl as if I were a zombie, to be sure Joanne didn't get crazy on me. Joanne was in the hospital for stabbing her husband.

A young man named Aaron was admitted to the ward to have his narcolepsy regulated. Aaron tried to tutor Karla as well, but would fall asleep at the turn of a hat. When he wasn't sleeping, Aaron ate one Eskimo Pie after another yet never gained an ounce. All about the ward I spotted Eskimo Pie wrappers, often at the sites of Aaron's narcolepsy attacks. Aaron said it was impossible for him to gain weight because of all the Dexedrine he took. His metabolism was redlining, yet he could sleep in spite of all the speed he was taking.

A middle-aged man who drank a bottle of Drāno took the empty bed adjacent to George Washington. He was a draftsman who cracked up when he was given a promotion. I listened to his tiresome stories until I could recite them myself. The only reason I put up with it was to prevent him for ratting me out about my nightly sexual escapades with Joanne. I couldn't wait to get out of the hospital. Double shifts on the Noodles Almondine line, in the end, were a far better way to live.

A team of student nurses doing rounds in psych was assigned to the ward. When I was cleared to take escorted visits, I roamed an abandoned hall with a student nurse named Elizabeth. Beth had a romantic notion about me because I had scored well on an IQ test. My MMPI results were so interesting to her that she was planning to write a paper on them. What this meant, I never knew. Beth was convinced that I was a genius — another Karl Witte. We exchanged stolen kisses during these handholding strolls. She told me she saw the movie she wanted to become a psych nurse after seeing, *David and Lisa,* twenty-four times. In fact, she did look a little bit like Janet Margolin, the fragile waif who starred in that film. Beth told me to stay away from Joanne. "You know, she stabbed her husband clean through the chest. She almost severed his head from his body," she said.

"What?" I said.

"Schizophrenia," she said. "Voices telling her to do things. When she stabbed him, he looked at her and said, 'Now look what you've done.' Isn't that incredible? And here's the funny part. With his head nearly off his body, he was still alive. He lived for nine hours. Joanne was in the city jail when he died and she saw his ghost come to her cell the moment he died. That's how she ended up here."

"Is she going to court?" I said.

"She's incompetent to stand trial," Beth said. "She's going to skate."

"Joanne suffers greatly as it is," I said. "Punishment enough."

Elizabeth considered this to be a thoughtful and judicious remark. She took my hand and said, "I don't know about you, but I'm getting it bad. I think Cupid shot me with the big arrow."

I dicked her in a storeroom. She just lay there and let it happen, and I regretted it almost from the word go. Joanne had set a new standard but I could no longer stand either one of these women. I wanted out in the worst way, and Vitias stalled. I knew if I didn't wait for a discharge, it would be hell going back to work where they would demand a doctor's sanction to return.

Late one afternoon I spotted Joanne in the visitor's area

with three beautiful children and what I took to be her parents. Until that moment it was exciting for me to have sex with a murderess. Seeing the children and the grieving parents, however, had an unsettling effect on me. The next day, I got a pass to go to the lab for some blood work. I spotted a locker with clothes that were about my size and exchanged them for my robe and pajamas. I walked out of the hospital and hitched a ride back to my house.

I bought an old Buick from a guy I knew at work. It cost fifty dollars and ran beautifully. Molly got out on a ward pass from the North Shore Hospital and we rushed to the backseat of the Buick for urgent sex. Molly wasn't earth-shattering sex like Joanne, but she was beautiful; she didn't kill people. When she wasn't preoccupied with herself, Molly pretended to recognize me for the genius that I took myself to be. I figured it was just her sociopath skill at play, but she was very good when she wanted to be. I cleaned out my bank account and bought two one-way tickets to Honolulu. That was a Saturday. We were air bound Monday afternoon. By then I guess we had fucked maybe ninety-five times including a couple stand-up jobs in the airplane restrooms. I was fucked out, but Molly had only just begun to warm to it.

We found an apartment in an area of Waikiki known then as "The Jungle." It was a "cheap rent" district popular among the surfers and university students who liked proximity to the beach. This place was just a few blocks back from Kalahaua Avenue, the main drag running along Waikiki. Molly and I did the usual touristy things. I kept bugging Molly to phone her mother merely as an act of human decency. She kept putting it off, but when she finally did call, Muriel was relieved. Molly gave her a song and dance about making an application to the University of Hawaii. Education and self-improvement were big on Muriel's agenda. Molly had three older sisters at Yale, Harvard, and Vassar. She wired Molly two thousand dollars, and Molly started blowing money on clothes. I bought a used Honda Nighthawk, and one afternoon Molly and I rode over to the university, which sat in the lower part of the Manoa Valley. We made inquiries about admissions. A friendly South American woman we met told us that the university did not charge out-of-state tuition. She invited us to lunch at the International Center where you could get a very good meal for less than two bucks. The woman, whose name was Eliani, was a physician from the southern part of Brazil. After lunch we went to the admissions office where we were given the run-around, but a few days later in Waikiki we ran into Eliani again. She was an attractive woman except for a shriveled leg, a consequence of childhood polio. She introduced us to one of her companions, a young woman named Tanya who was, of all things, the former Miss Hawaii. Soon Molly and I became regulars at the International Center. Eliani and Tanya introduced us to their distinguished circle of friends, and before long, Molly and I were privileged to attend parties at Tanya's beachfront home on Diamondhead Road. I was suddenly meeting people not only from Brazil but all of South America as well as Europe, Africa, and Asia. It was an improvement over the mental hospital bunch and the factory workers from West Chicago. One evening, wearing a borrowed sports coat, I attended a ballet with Molly, and at the party Tanya's father held after, I found myself shooting the bull with Rudolph Nureyev. The party crowd included Honolulu's high society, but there were a number of young people present and the mood was fairly informal. Tanya escorted "Rudy" and me out of the party and took us down a winding staircase to the beach. I found myself walking along the beach with a ballet dancer and Tanya's two dachshunds. Nureyev told me that he had been sick recently and missed three days of practice. "It was two weeks of hard work before I could perform again," he said, glancing at his watch. "Always the body I am taking care for," he said. "Always." I looked at him and nodded in the meaningful way I had seen my new ensemble of sophisticated friends do. Once while I was training for a national boxing tournament, a dancer was brought to the gym to teach us balance. I told Nureyev this, and he wanted to see what I could do. My cheeks flamed. "Nothing," I said. "I don't remember it. I've got epilepsy."

"Oh," he said. "That's too bad."

"But the dancer. None of us could catch her. She got in the ring and nobody could get near her," I said.

Shortly after we returned to the party, I saw Molly in a circle talking with Dame Margot Fonteyn. Tanya sidled up to me and gave me a wink. "Rudy likes you."

"Hey, c'mon, I'm not like that," I said.

Molly came over and recognized my embarrassment. "I was just teasing your boyfriend," Tanya said.

"I've never done anything — I'm totally straight. Geez, Tanya."

"Oh, go ahead and let the girl in you out," Molly said. "It might do you some good."

Tanya laughed and said, "I'm sure I saw sparks fly between them, didn't you, Molly?"

Molly said, "I'll fuck him if you won't, Will'am."

"He isn't fucking anybody," I said. "He wants to get back to the hotel and go to bed."

Molly smiled and said, "Relax, baby, we're just teasing you."

Tanya winked at me. "Anyone want a refill?" she said. "What are you drinking, there, Will'am, a gin *gimlet?*"

"I guess I'm just a fag waiting to happen," I said. Tanya headed for the bar. Molly told me that Margot Fonteyn had a husband like our friend Mr. Leimbach. "He's dying of Lou Gehrig's disease," she said. "The whole world is a neurology ward, I reckon. Huh, sport?"

Molly produced six tabs of some windowpane a fellow in a white linen suit had just given her. It turned out that this somebody was Tanya's brother, Brady. He lived in a pad across from us on Gardenia Lane with a bunch of surfers. "Why would he live in that shithole," I said, "when he could stay here?"

"The old man is a judge. Brady likes to surf and smoke dope. Figure," Molly said.

"And he just laid this dope on you for nothing?" I said. "He's hot for you."

"Don't go jealous on me, Will'am. You know my heart belongs to Daddy," she said, running her hand along the lapel of my borrowed jacket, which I later learned also happened to belong to Brady.

When Tanya came back with fresh drinks, we each dropped a tab of windowpane. A half hour later I was high and the three of us were dancing to the Shangri-las' "You Cheated, You Lied." It was a song that seemed to last five years. More people seemed to come. Soon the dance floor was packed.

One of Tanya's dachshunds came over and barfed on the floor. It was a fat sausage of a dog with a gray muzzle and patches of dried skin. Tanya scooped it up, telling us that the animal suffered from diabetes. Molly and I followed her into the kitchen where we watched her draw some insulin into a syringe. "Is all Mama's fault," Tanya said, talking baby talk to the dog. "She forgot to give Zimmy his shot."

"Dachshunds do get diabetes," Molly said. "More than any other purebreed."

"What about the other one?" I said.

Tanya looked up at me. She was wearing a semiformal outfit and was stunning this night. "Go round him up, will you?" she said. Zimmy's eyes were cloudy and his head was lolling about.

Molly gave me a little shove. She said, "Go, Will'am, I can't stand to see animals suffer."

Tanya nodded at me. "This just happens sometimes," she said. "Don't worry. It will be all right."

After the dogs had their shots, I helped Tanya carry them to the back of the house. Zimmy was heavy for such a small dog. Tanya was wearing heels, and trailing behind her, I couldn't help notice what lovely posture she had and how nice her ass looked. How beautiful her legs were. She was wearing a scent that blended nicely with Hawaii's lush fecundity. "Too much excitement. But they'll be fine," she said.

"I can't believe you are doing all of this complicated stuff. Aren't you stoned?"

"Yeah," she said. "So?"

"Well, I'm ripped. I can hardly walk," I said.

"You are acting completely normal. I don't know what's going on inside your brain, but you look fine." She bent down and released a dog much younger and thinner than Zimmy. Tanya was wearing silk stockings, and as I glanced at her exquisite knees and her well-toned thighs, I was sure that she must know I was leering. She straightened up and ran her hand over her dress. "Molly is really causing quite a stir tonight," Tanya said.

"Rudy didn't seem too interested in her," I said.

"His eyes were *else*where," Tanya said.

"Hey! I'm not kidding, he didn't *hit* on me. I bored the shit of him. He made me for a dickhead. And I don't *care*. You, of all people, must know what it's like to be hit on, Miss Hawaii."

"Oh! I'm over the hill. Your Molly's quite the doll. She so fresh and lovely."

"Too beautiful," I said. "Everywhere you go, guys are lookin'. She flirts with anything in pants."

"She just likes feeling sexy, Will'am. Don't you?"

"Feel sexy, me?"

"Why not? You're attractive enough. The two of you make an adorable couple."

"I never thought of it like that," I said. I was aware of predatory behavior in recent weeks, yet always felt myself to be something of a sexual prude. The acid was kicking in to another level. Tanya reached out and stroked my cheek. It seemed like a friendly gesture and no more. I returned it in kind. Tanya held my look with her dark eyes and suddenly I knew that I wanted her and had no compunctions. She shut the bedroom door. Before long we were stretched out on a bed with our clothes off. "What if Molly walks in," Tanya said with a teasing voice.

"I'll tell her that I'm too busy to talk right now — come

back later, baby, I'm busy!" I said as I buried my face into Tanya's belly. Something about her question hung in the air. I looked up and said, "Why?"

Tanya smiled at me and said, "Eliani and I are lovers."

"God!" I said with a start. "Really?"

"Yeah. Just thought I'd warn you."

I didn't want to talk; I wanted to fuck. I pressed my tongue against her.

"Ohhh," she said. Tanya continued to moan and get very wet. I was tripping so hard I hardly knew what I was doing. Tanya's thighs began to twitch as her muscles started to contract. I had been running through the alphabet over her clitoris, standard stuff, but she was wild for it. I backed off whenever the contractions came with predictable regularity. I didn't want her to come until every inch of her cunt, thighs, and ass was committed to my memory in triplicate. I thought she was going to tear my hair out by the roots before she came. It hurt, but I felt truly appreciated.

Tanya closed her thighs as I moved to mount her. I pushed her legs apart but she grimaced as I entered her, in spite of the fact that she was so wet. In a moment we found the correct position, and when I felt her long narrow fingers caressing my back, I knew that she wasn't that much of a dedicated lesbian at all. Meanwhile, I had to do algebra problems in my head to keep from coming too soon. Before long she was digging her nails into my back as she got off for a second time. It was only then that I permitted myself the entire pleasure of fucking. Barely had I done so when Tanya quit flaying my back and I could feel her begin to dry up. I was glad for the friction and finally came. A fragrant cool breeze blew in off the Pacific Ocean. Tanya said, "Hold me in your arms. I just want to be held. It's mostly all I ever want."

Tanya was almost as tall as I was but she was light and her body was cool. It felt great to hold her. I was stoned to the hilt, but I knew that we had been gone long enough to make anyone who was paying attention take notice. Yet I couldn't initiate any return to the world. Tanya's long ivory limbs and her smooth, cool skin were heaven. Necking with her made time stop for me. Tanya was nine kinds of gorgeous, and I wasn't going to leave until they dragged me away. I knew that something eventually would happen that would end the experience. If someone didn't burst into the room with a shotgun, the sun would rise — something would put an end to it. It was inevitable. Yet the acid had kick to it. We were both feeling invigorated. Tanya said, "Can you do everything you just did to me all over again?"

I could feel her cool skin turning to flame and felt wetness running between her legs again. "Do what you did all over again and I'll write you a check for any amount."

She climbed on top and in just seconds got off. After this she gave me head, and while I came full-blown scenes from my early life flashed before my eyes. I decided to forget worrying about Molly when Tanya jumped up and frantically began pulling her clothes on. I started to do the same and she pointed me to the shower. "No, no! You can't go out there smelling like a French whore. Go take a shower. I'll see you out front."

When I returned to the party, I saw neither Molly nor Tanya. I struck up a conversation with a Chinese superior court judge who told me how he had thrown the book at three haoles that afternoon. They were university students, who had recently robbed a Brink's truck. "Boys your age, educated. Now their whole lives are ruined. Twenty-five years in Oahu Prison. Forgive me, I shouldn't talk shop," the judge said, "but I find the ballet to be a terrible bore."

"I hated it, too," I said. "Every minute. Except for some of the jumps. The hang time."

"Yes, but otherwise stupid nonsense," the judge said. "I'd rather be home canning pineapples than go through that again. The wife, you know. She used to be a dancer. What do you do, young man?"

I felt like telling the judge that I worked the Noodles Almondine line at the GM plant in West Chicago but he supplied an answer. "Student, no?"

I nodded. The judge said, "One of the beautiful young people. Enjoy your youth and beauty, sir. Appreciate it. It's been so long since a woman looked at me in that *certain way*, you know? I don't know what I would do if one did anymore. Die! I think I would die. Impotence. Prostate troubles. Going to pot all over. So much time I spend just being old, my friend. Toenails are harder to cut. What hair that is left must be colored, not to mention growing out of your ears, nose, on the back — a whole world of shit. What did you say your name was?"

"William," I said. I was glad to see Tanya, Eliani, and Molly walk in from the beach. Molly was wearing a big smile. "We were just looking for you. Tanya said you were swimming, and so you were," Molly said, looking at my wet hair.

"Yeah," I said. "I got as far as the Fiji Islands, did a flip turn, and came back. After sitting on my ass for three acts, I needed some exercise. Did you miss me?"

The judge laughed at this. Eliani introduced him to

Molly. I had the feeling he was going to be a hard guy to shake, but I was thanking my lucky stars that I had pulled off my betrayal so effortlessly and with so little remorse. As Molly took my hands, I saw unalloyed love. "My god, you're so beautiful," I said. "You're a dream."

"So are you, baby. You're the best thing that's ever happened to me."

"Nice sentiments," the judge piped up. Tanya yawned and except for the judge, the rest of the circle caught the infection. It was late.

Eliani dropped us off in Waikiki. Our apartment was light on furnishings. Our bed consisted of some mattresses on the floor. Most all of the apartments in "the Jungle" were squalid, but the air was fresh with the floral scent of jasmine and gardenia. Royal palms and colorful tropical flowers were in abundance. As soon as we stepped in the apartment, Molly was pulling my clothes off. I was fucked out and beginning to experience the downside of the acid trip. My muscles ached and felt tight. I didn't think of the scratches on my back until my shirt was off, but with only the low light of the bathroom on, they seemed to escape Molly's notice.

My tongue felt like an item that had been tenderized by a meat cleaver. Molly drew it into her mouth as if she meant to consume it. Whereas Tanya's form was sleek and her breasts small, I was suddenly confronted with Molly's ample bosom. Under the influence of the acid, Molly began to come as I nibbled her nipples with my teeth. She undid her skirt and I noticed that she wasn't wearing underwear, something she was fastidious about. She sidled backward, presenting her womb to me. I didn't know if my tongue was up to it. She opened her legs and pulled me to her. I looked up at her; my neck was very tired from spending so much time holding conversations in this posture. "Lick me," she said, "taste it."

She pulled my face into her so that it was almost impossible to breathe. Blessedly, she was soon finished. She rolled over, panting for air. She said, "You fucked her, didn't you?"

"What?"

"You fucked Tanya."

"What in the hell are you talking about?" I said.

"Okay, you *didn't* fuck her."

"Right. I *didn't* fuck her. You're on some kind of acid paranoia trip," I said. "How many tabs did you drop?"

"I lost count," Molly said. "Eighty!"

I didn't want to fight. Molly dug an elbow into my ribs and said, "Well?"

I said, "Well *what*?"

"Are we going to *do* it, or aren't we? You can't just leave me like this, Will'am. Don't make me beg for it."

"But you already *came*," I said. "What the fuck are you *talking* about? You accuse me of shit and you turn away. And your pussy is tasting rank."

"I'll take a shower if you want me to," she said in a sudden move to be compliant. She was resting on her elbows and her breasts, even under the waning power of acid, had never looked better. "Okay, but let's do it dog style," I said.

Molly quickly turned over and leaned forward. She reached for my dick and guided it inside her. As I entered her, I was certain that the backs of her thighs were glazed with either cunt secretions or another man's come. I didn't know whether to feel betrayed, or if the scorecard had merely been evened. Whatever it was, I hardened like a rocket and Molly suddenly became the hottest piece of ass in the universe. She had done something new, something unfamiliar, and now I was her most devoted slave. I found myself hoping I would knock her up and thus, however feebly, own a part of her forever. I was fucking her so frantically that I kept slipping out and she was forced to reach back and reinsert me. In the end, I had her rammed up against the wall where she could steady herself, and we came like animals.

The harsh glaring sun burst through the louvered window screens. I had never come with such velocity or pleasure — I knew that much, but I was also convinced that I had just crossed a very dark line. Exhausted to the bone, I was hoping that if Molly had also been fucking that night, it had been with Eliani and not some other man.

She was dressed in a fresh royal blue muumuu with a white floral pattern splashed over it. The muumuu showed off her breasts and neck to their best advantage. She was tanning nicely and it set off her hair, which she wore up, tight against her head. Her bone structure was perfect. Even her ears were perfect; they were close to her head and adorned with silver earrings. I looked at my watch. It was only ten in the morning. "Aren't you shot?" I said.

"I've been up since eight," she said. "I'm hungry. Let's go out."

Molly and I had breakfast at the Royal Hawaiian, where there was a buffet. I went for the scrambled eggs and unlimited amounts of papaya and guava. Molly drank cups of coffee and smoked Luckies. "I thought you said you were hungry," I said. I saw *Three Faces of Eve* coming around the bend, bearing down on me in a big hurry.

"I'm getting too fat," Molly said. "I changed my mind."

"You have to eat *something,* dear heart," I said. "And you're not even slightly fat," I added. "You're the most divine creature on the planet."

"Compared to Tanya, I'm a whale," Molly said, blowing smoke across the table. "How was it, Will'am? Can ex–Miss Hawaii *suck* a cock or can't she?"

"I hate to point it out, but you weren't exactly lonesome last night. I didn't take you for a dyke though."

"I'm not a dyke," Molly said. "I may be a submissive masochistic nymphomaniac, but I'm not a dyke."

"Okay, so then who did *you* fuck?"

"No one."

"Bullshit! Who was it?"

"I don't even know, Will'am. What's the difference?"

I got up and threw my napkin on the table. "You fucking bitch!"

The diners at the surrounding tables spun their heads in our direction. "I can't even —"

"You can't believe the implications, right? Well, grow up, Will'am!"

I stalked out of the dining room. As I passed the cashier, I turned and pointed to Molly. "Give her the bill." I saw Molly's shoulders tremble. She was crying. I was furious. I wanted to kill her but I wanted to comfort her. I wanted her dead and I wanted her resurrected. I went back to the table and said, "Who was it? Was it that fucker Brady?"

"No, Will'am. He's too fey. Never in a million years."

"Well, who in the fuck was it, then? He was all over you last night. If not him, who? Goddammit, how could you possibly do something like that? No shower, no nothing."

Molly winced and held her face in her hands. "Will'am, my head. Please. I've got the worst headache in the world and no pills."

I said, "Eat something. It's no wonder. Eat."

"I can't. I'm deathly sick," she said. "Don't leave me. Please! Will'am. Don't leave!"

I sat down again and crossed my arms. A waiter came by with a pot of coffee. "Is everything all right?" he said.

"Yes," I said. "Can you get the lady some aspirin?" I said.

"Sure," the waiter said.

Molly raised her head and said, "Make that Bromo Selzer if you've got it." As soon as the waiter left, she laid her head back on the table and began to weep. The other patrons shot me angry looks. I reached for her cigarettes, shook one from the pack, and lit it.

An elderly woman came by and placed her hand on Molly's back. "Are you all right, dear?"

"No," Molly said.

"How can I help you, dear? My name's Cora. What's yours?"

"She suffers from migraines," I said. "The waiter is getting her something."

Cora took Molly's hand. "Do you want me to call a doctor, honey?"

Molly raised her head. Her hair had come undone and strands of it were wet with her tears. Her eyes were red. She was trouble, she was crazy, but I couldn't stop looking at her cleavage. I said, "I'll call Eliani. She's a doctor. She'll know what to do."

Eliani didn't answer her phone until the fifteenth ring. She was still in bed. I apologized for waking her up but when I explained about Molly's migraine, she said she would be at the hotel in ten minutes. She helped Molly to the restroom where she gave her a Demerol shot. The color came back to Molly's face by the time we reached the apartment. Whatever had been said in the restroom caused Eliani to revise her opinion of me. I was wearing a T-shirt and a pair of shorts. I needed a shave and my hair was so dry from the swimming that I could tame it down only with pomade. In short, I looked far worse than Molly — I looked more like Molly's tormentor. Molly gathered some things and told me she was going to spend the night with the Brazilian lesbian.

"I want to keep my eye on her," Eliani said. "These headaches are no joke," she said. I watched them drive off and went back into the apartment, convinced that Molly had just dumped me for a woman. I barely managed to fall asleep when I heard someone rapping on the door.

It was Brady. He introduced himself to me all friendly like, and asked me if I surfed. He was a slightly built, lithe young man, with a dark complexion. He wasn't Molly's type. I knew this immediately.

"That was some pretty wild acid you gave Molly last night," I said.

"Yeah. The boys and I found a nice connection. You want to try it some more?" he said. "Hit the beach? I've got an extra surf board."

Brady took me next door and introduced me to his bros. One of them was a part-Samoan dude known as Five-O. Five-O looked as if he belonged in the sumo ring, not on a surfboard. Yet I later learned that he was one of the better surfers on the island. He used a big board and liked to ride the big waves at Sunset Beach on the opposite side of the island. So did they all, but their truck wasn't running and the surfers had been passing the days on the tame but regular waves of Waikiki. Brady was a graduate of Punahoe and had good manners. He used them to make pocket money as a beach hustler. Five-O also picked up some money giving surfing lessons. He knew his business. I was riding six-foot waves with a fair amount of competence before the afternoon was over. I was on my second round of windowpane.

Back at the surfer's place, Five-O demonstrated his passion for poi, a tuberous root concoction tasting like library paste. The sight of the dungy gray mess sickened me. Fortunately, Five-O had another specialty that involved adding cooked hamburger and onions to cans of Chef Boyardee spaghetti. It wasn't half bad. I got drunk with the surfers that night, and when I went back to my apartment, Molly had still not come home. Without her presence to enliven things, the place was small and depressing — absolutely and completely awful. It was a shack, all right, only it wasn't grass. It was a Shit Shack. I went to bed in complete despair.

In the morning, Molly, Eliani, and a former lieutenant from the Ethiopian Army named Phalle came bursting into the place. They were all in high spirits. I was wretchedly undone by two consecutive acid trips and was unable to get Molly alone for a moment. It seemed that whatever sexual infidelities had occurred, as far as she was concerned, they were forgotten. Neither of us could keep our hands off one another. Eliani drove us to the Chinese district in her new Chevy Impala. Along the way she told us that she came from a very large family in southern Brazil where her father owned a coffee plantation. Her oldest brother was running it now. Her father had Huntington's chorea, yet another neurological masterpiece of horror. When I told her of my dislike for poi, she laughed and countered by saying that when Molly and I came to Brazil, she was going to serve us boa.

"You mean as in snake," I said.

"Yes," Eliani said, laughing. "It's a delicacy. You will see, Will'am. Very good. You won't be able to get enough."

Chinatown was the most original and interesting part of Honolulu. The Chinese had been the first immigrants brought to Hawaii to work in the cane fields. Ultimately, it was the Chinese who became the richest and most influential members of the community. Eliani explained that the Japanese were the next wave of immigrants. Most of them had settled in the Manoa Valley behind the university. They were also quite well-to-do. Although Hawaii was called the great melting pot, where people of various races lived together harmoniously, the racial lines were nonetheless emphatically drawn. And if I had seen enough looks that made me feel like a living turd as a haole, it was worse for the Koreans and the Filipinos, and so much more so for the blacks, such as my latest new companion, Phalle. As we walked through the street stalls, I felt myself to be in a foreign country. The main point of the visit was to acquaint Phalle with the area. He had been afraid to come alone. Eliani pointed out a club where cockfights were held on Friday nights. Phalle was eager to see this blood sport. Molly and I walked arm in arm listening to Eliani's running commentary. After lunch, we drove to the Pali lookout. A windy cliff overlooking the ocean that was the site of a battle among the warring Hawaiian tribes. There King Kamehameha defeated his enemies by driving them off the cliff. Yet the wind was so strong that we were able to flatten our bodies and levitate. Eliani told us on the ride back to Honolulu that cars were often overturned at this site.

As soon as we got back to the apartment, Molly and I made tender love with one another. We were on our best behavior, and the sex, which composed the bulk of our relationship, was only so-so. Unlike Tanya, who was so cool and easy to hold, Molly seemed to have a fast metabolism and generated considerable body heat. Lying close to her was like being in a furnace — not so bad in the cold climes of northern Illinois, but another matter in the tropics. Now that she was mine again, I wasn't so sure I wanted her. As lovely as her breasts were, I began to envision them in later years. And the whole business of her mental health gave me great pause for thought. She had stopped taking her lithium entirely. When I quizzed her about this, she said it wasn't necessary. Hawaii was a land of sunshine and fresh air. She didn't *need* lithium.

She slept less and less. She became ever more restless and talkative. One evening at a party with the International House set, she became upset at Tanya's unexpected appearance and started pounding down the liquor until she was blind drunk. I had to carry her out to Eliani's car. By the time we got back to the apartment, Molly had wet herself in the backseat of the car. She had a colossal hangover coupled with a headache. "Another Marty Feldman," she said. "Call Eliani and tell her I need a shot."

I told her that I thought it would be best if we didn't push our luck with Eliani at the moment. Instead, I ran to the store and got her a large bottle of Bromo Selzer and

a pint of brandy. Every hour she took a sip of the brandy
to ease the hangover. Finally, she drank the whole thing
straight. When she fell asleep at last, I made an escape
and joined the boys at the beach, glad to be away from her.
The Shit Shack was like an ICU ward when Molly had a
headache. And this latest one seemed to age her a good
twenty years.

Yet when I returned it had passed off and she was looking better than ever. I walked into the apartment with my
surfboard and she said, "So you've been to the beach, huh?"

"Yes, but I kept coming back to check on you through
the whole vigil," I said.

"You mean in between the times you were fucking Tanya.
Well good for you, Will'am. Go on and go. Have a good
time, you beach-party-bingo motherfucker. See if I care."

She seized on this until the whole business about Tanya
began to consume her. Night after night we would fight
over it, only to make up and fuck until dawn. A succession
of orgasms would return her to sanity for a few hours, but it
was with relief that I got up at the first crack of light,
grabbed my board, and stole away for the beach. I was committing myself to nights of total sexual abandon, going far
and above the call of duty to please Molly, but no amount of
fucking was ever enough. "Is your pussy made out of steel?"
I would say. "Does it have to have a dick in it constantly?" I
would have traded any amount of time in the Noodles Almondine line for some respite at this point.

The whole prospect of adulthood was now beginning to
seem like a series of ongoing horrors — work, marriage,
parenthood, and then old age, where a "diagnosis" was followed rapidly by the prolonged agonal affliction, and

then — out! Dead. Molly gave me no argument on this but even as she lamented the futility of life on this planet, she would demand more sex, the very thing that perpetuated the whole goddamn business in the first place. "It's been a half hour, Will'am. I'm bored. Let's do it," she would say. "Christ, I'm horny out of my mind! Screw me in the ass, I don't care. Beat me! Fuck the living shit out of me! Just fucking do *something!*"

AT THE END of the month, a bunch of sailors who rented a large apartment at the end of Gardenia Lane came back from three months of sea duty and the sailors commenced to party. There were roughly twenty of them in all and they used the place for weekend liberty. Although Waikiki Beach was a tourist mecca in 1967, single women were at a premium. It was almost impossible for a Caucasian to date a local.

Five-O vaguely promised to fix me up at the box factory where he worked the graveyard shift. It was a job that sounded like hell on earth.

Meanwhile, to the sailors at the end of Gardenia Lane, the first glimpse of Molly was a pure vision of heaven. Their presence seemed to raise her spirits as well.

One morning shortly after the sailors' arrival, the surfers rushed into the Shit Shack to say the waves were breaking at fifteen feet over at Sunset Beach. Five-O's truck was up and running and they were stoked to go. I piled my board in their pickup, and we drove to the other side of the island. The waves were bodacious. Paddling out was taking your life in your hands, and the wipeouts were merciless, but catching a good wave was the best thing — the most incredible adrena-

line high on par with the best moments I can ever recall.
Here I was surfing, not taking my own medication, which I
had run out of. I was in danger of having a fit in the water
and drowning, but such was the invincibility of youth that it
just didn't seem possible that I would ever die. Anyhow, I had
developed a theory that if I stayed mildly drunk on beer, it
would suppress brainstorms much the same as did conventional anticonvulsants. As a surfer I was a novice really, wan-
ton in my recklessness. Catching that perfect wave was the
ultimate, all that mattered. I wanted to do this forever. We
surfed until the tide went out and it became utterly dark.
On the way back to Waikiki, we stopped at a joint for Hula
Burgers — hamburgers with a sweet orange pickle sauce
plastered on them. They were ubiquitous, but unlike poi,
something you could learn to like. I had four that night. By
the time we got back to Waikiki, I was dead tired. I carried my
board back to the apartment and showered to get the smell
of brine out of my hair and off my body. Molly was not in evidence, but down at the end of Gardenia Lane in the sailors'
apartment, I could hear Sam and Dave rocking out, "Hold
on, I'm Coming." The sailors were having a full-fledged Saturday night. As tired as I was, sleep was impossible.

I got dressed and migrated down to the sailors' place.
When I looked inside I saw Molly dancing — not with just
some "guy," not with one of the boy-men sailors, but with a
fully grown man. I was told that this guy's name was Amos.
He was from Hollywood and in the movies; he made a lot of
dough. In fact, Amos was famous. He looked to be about
thirty-five years old and, oh boy! the sailors were saying, did
he ever have some righteous cocaine. "Brother, this shit is *so
fine*." When the music reverted to slow dancing, Molly fell

into Amos's muscle beach arms, and in shock and disbelief I watched as the pair started dry-humping to the music. Well, she was coked up. What else was new?

As with most of life's affairs, the outcome of this adventure didn't look too promising to me; a very bad scene was about to unfold — a scene with no possibility of a happy outcome. I tried out feeling angry, but Amos looked like a musclehead who grew up eating steroids in a Venice Beach gym. He was a formidable and fully grown mature man. And here he was giving these sailors free dope and dancing with my girl. She was at a high pitch of mania, with cocaine amplifying her insanity to a whole new level. The handwriting was on the wall. I should have known. I picked up a six-pack of beer from an ice tub and went back to the mattresses in the Shit Shack. No need to let it get me down all that much. But, shit; fuck it, goddamn everything and everybody just the same! The fucking bitch! Ready to write her off forever just that afternoon, I was her love slave again.

In the apartment, I slumped down against the wall. The trade winds were blowing in from the ocean. The heat of the day, which had been considerable, was gone. Now I was almost chilly in the apartment. Due to the influx of wind, a heavy odor of gardenias for which our Shit Street in this Shit City was famous permeated the miserable Shit Shack hell-hole with a funereal smell. Not only was I starved (Hula Burgers notwithstanding), and freezing; I felt outrageously betrayed. I was at once and for all the worst fool as well as the most tormented soul that ever experienced existence. I chugged down three fast beers and smoked a cigarette and actually began to shiver. We had no blankets, only sheets. I flipped on the lights and saw a hundred cockroaches scram-

ble for cover. Only a hundred, I thought, the chill was even
impeding their action. I scrounged through my suitcase for a
sweatshirt, found one, and slipped it on, but it helped almost
not at all. The chill seemed more systemic to my body rather
than having to do with the temperature in the apartment. I
smoked the last Marlboro in the pack and had another beer.
There was a five-dollar bill in my wallet — my last five in the
world. I thought about going to the nearest market for more
smokes, but I was so depressed over the entire folly of hook-
ing up with Molly that I couldn't move. Without her spend-
thrift habits, I would have been able to surf and goof for the
better part of a year. Seeing her in a stranger's arms was un-
bearable, but I wanted her more than I did the day I first laid
eyes upon her. I lay back on the mattresses and tried to put it
all out of my mind. Falling in love, I decided, was the most
dangerous thing in the world a reasonable person could do.
Shit! On top of everything else, I was fucking freezing to
death. I curled up in the fetal position in an attempt to get
warm, thinking I'd take India and an arranged marriage any
day of the week. She can be ugly, God, she can be fat — I
don't care; I'll take her. Heartbreak is for the birds.

I was sick to the depths of my soul. I heard mocking
laughter from the sailors' apartment. I wondered if I could
still fight. I would run them down, each and every one of
them; I would isolate them and beat them within an inch of
their lives.

The door to the Shit Shack had a lock on it but the lock
was useless since you could reach through a hole in the
window screen and flip it open with a twist of the fingers.
Now I heard this familiar sound. A few seconds later, Molly
was kicking off her Weejun loafers and crawling into bed

next to me. She placed her hand on my back expectantly but a moment later I felt it slide away. I commenced to spend an entire season in hell trying to fathom the meaning the touch had conveyed, if any. Was it the touch of hope — of repentance? Or was she just making sure I knew where she had been? I was Job at the pinnacle of doubt, and what was worse, I was a Job who had no moral lesson to offer the rest of humanity. I was the Job of insignificance and purposeless suffering. Job in the lower case.

I had no idea how late it was. Molly soon rolled over, turning her face away from me. In seconds, she was dead asleep. The knife of betrayal had done its work. The wound in my heart was mortal. How could deadly poison come in such a pretty package?

Another half hour of ruminations gave way to the greatest of life's blessings — sleep. Just as I escaped into slumber, I was startled by a voice of suppressed urgency and alarm. Amos was saying, "Please, baby, you've got to; it's hurtin' real bad. What's the big deal all of a sudden? Said you'd suck me off; that you wanted to. All I'm asking for here is a hand job. I can't take the pain of it anymore."

Suddenly Molly was pressing her toes against my legs. "Will'am! Wake up. Get him the fuck out of here."

I heard Amos saying, "Come on, Molly. Shit! I'll give you forty bucks. I know you need the bread. Just a little hand action; I'm getting impatient."

I rolled over and looked up to see Amos hovering above me. His cock was out of his jeans and bobbing in the air like a pole. Molly stood opposite him, making no attempt to cover her breasts. Her nipples were hard. Was that just because? Or was that because she was turned on? She was having trouble breathing. It appeared she was seriously thinking it over — that she was excited. Amos had his hand on his cock and reached out for her. "Hey!" I said. "What the *fuck* is this?" As I started to pull myself up, Amos squatted down and in one deft move smashed his elbow across the bridge of my nose. A stunning, blinding pain laid me straight out on the mattress. My whole body went limp as hot sticky blood rushed out of my nose.

Molly went for Amos's eyes. He shoved her back, but then she came forward slapping at him. "You mother*fucker,* get the hell out of here!" I watched as he backed off, putting up his arms to protect himself. My nose was gushing. I got up on my haunches and managed to throw a body block at his blind side, knocking him to the floor. I bounced to my feet and kicked him in the side of the head with the ball of my foot a couple of times and then laid heels into his kidney. He struggled to get up, but I could see he wasn't going to make it. My face was a mask of blood. I reached for the sheet to staunch the bleeding as I contemplated where to kick him next. Molly stepped between the two of us like an impartial referee. He got in a position approximating a push-up. From there, she helped Amos to his feet. Mr. Drunkmouth said, "Oh man, hey! I'm sorry! I mean it, man. I was just trying to ding you a little. I broke your fucken nose. Holy fucken shit. Jesus!"

"Out," Molly screamed. "Get out!"

Amos dropped two twenties on the bed. "Here's for, you know, stuff — bandages," he said. "I'm drunk. I didn't mean anything. I'll leave you good folks be."

Molly wadded up the money and threw it after him. Amos caught it adroitly enough, pocketed it, and backed out of the room as I pitched forward into the bathroom. I had swallowed enough blood to be sick. Blood came up in the first wave. Hula Burgers in the second. When I was done, I looked in the mirror. The nose was a mess, broken in two places. I cleaned off my face with our one towel and tried stuffing toilet paper in my nostrils. I had to hold my head back to staunch the flow of blood. Molly crowded me out of the narrow bathroom so she, too, could take a turn at being sick. It was the perfect way to cap off an evening in the Shit Shack.

Blood still leaked through the toilet-paper nostril plugs but there was no more paper on the roll. I returned to the mattresses. Blood backflushed into my throat. When Molly came back, she said, "You sure are *some boxer,* Will'am. That was the sorriest display of self-defense I've seen in my entire life."

"Go fuck yourself," I said. "Here you are dry-fucking this guy at the party and then you get mad because he wants to screw you. What kind of psycho whore are you?"

"Don't you accuse me!" she roared. "I can't believe what a stupid asshole you are, Will'am. I can't believe I was ever dumb enough to fall in love with you or ever let you talk me into coming here to sit around counting cockroaches while you get sunburns on a piece of Plexiglas in the goddamn fucking ocean."

"I'm sorry I interrupted your brilliant career as a mental patient, Molly. But that's what love gone wrong can do, derail you from your true destiny — committing suicide."

Molly was up off the mattresses and into her Weejuns. One moment it seemed like reconciliation was near, judging by past squabbles — now she was out the door. I could hear the hard leather soles slapping on the walk outside on Gardenia Lane. After the requisite number of footfalls, I heard the sound of the sailors' apartment door open and slam shut. Into Amos's loving arms? It was too absurd to fathom. I had to race back to the toilet to make a deposit of Hula Burger and black bile. I was momentarily past caring about Molly, one way or another.

In the morning Brady, Five-O, and four of the Hawaiians burst into my apartment. Five-O had another nickname; people sometimes called him One-Punch. He checked me out and said, "Hey, bruddah, fisticuffs last night? Shit, man, why didn't you come get me? Who did this to you? Broke your nose. Shit. Fuckin' haole assholes."

"I know I got a real deep suntan, Five-O, but it shouldn't pass your notice that I'm a haole, too," I said. "He did sucker punch me though."

"Who was it?" Brady said.

"Amos. The movie actor."

"That Erik Estrada–lookin' motherfucker?" Five-O said.

"Yeah."

Brady laughed. "He isn't any actor, dude, he's a carpenter who sometimes works as a set-builder, part time. Actor — that's bullshit! The closest he gets to acting is dealing coke to bit players."

"Let's go! Point him out to me," Five-O said. "All you gotta do, bruddah, is point the cocksucker out. I kill him!" Five-O's actions were at odds with his words. His feet were planted on the floor as he flicked his Zippo and pulled a deep toke from his hash pipe. A red coal within glowed like a miniature nuclear reactor as the pipe rasped and gurgled. Five-O handed it to me and said, "Take a hit offa diss one, bro."

I took a toke. Within seconds everything in my field of vision turned into various shades of white. Color per se was gone. Even objects consisting primarily of chlorophyll — the luxuriant profusion of tropical plants that grew unhindered along the whole of Gardenia Lane — were now white. I liked this new look and took a more ambitious hit from Five-O's hash pipe. The world of white seemed even richer in distinctiveness than that of the fuller spectrum of colors. As I exhaled, I said, "Thanks for asking, but let's forget this guy. I'm going to chalk the whole motherfucker off. I'm done with her. She gone, he's gone, she, he, et cetera. Good! Better I learned sooner than later. I'm down to my last five and ready for the box factory."

"Start you out first t'ing Monday," Five-O said. " 'Cause you're a righteous cat; you put on some moves today. Sunset Beach, that was some heavy surf and you wuz out there, cuz. Bonzai pipeline and Will'am be goin' wild."

Brady marveled at my gutless resolution concerning Molly and said, "I told you the dude's a fucking philosopher. She walks and he's totally cool about it. Fucking Mr. Spock. No emotion. A stone-cool motherfucker."

"Well, Will'am may be cool, but I ain't. This shit with them fuckin' sailors has gone too far," Five-O said. "I will find the mothuh and put some hurt on him, the fuckin' haole cocksuckin' faggot," Five-O said.

It seemed impossible to me that Five-O could find rage behind all the hash he was smoking. I took another toke as it came around. The palm trees were whiter than all the patent leather in Cleveland, Ohio — even the coconuts were white. I asked Brady if he had any codeine left from his recent wisdom tooth extractions. He nodded yeah and ran across the lane to get it as I listened to Five-O vow to hunt Amos to the farthest ends of the earth. Amos, who was less than three doors down. The Hawaiians had a lot of hash, and Five-O wanted to smoke it. He would be dead of lung cancer before making good his threat, but I didn't care. Brady came back with a vial of pills, a sixer of Primo, and a half pack of Pall Malls. I thanked the guys for the supplies and the moral support and watched them head back to their place. I retired to the mattresses. It seemed awfully important to get horizontal.

The codeine and beer took the edge off my painful nose, which clumsily cantilevered from my face with all the weight of the Baja peninsula. I drank another beer and realized that sleep was now a definite possibility. I was beginning to feel pretty mellow until I heard the sailors' screen door slam and the distinctive sound of Molly's Weejuns pounding across the pavement. She stepped inside, picked up her suitcase, and resolutely threw it open. I thought my entire sense of sexuality was in permanent cold storage but yet again I fell victim to the sight of her slender shoulders and her heaving breasts. She looked at me and said, "Are you all right? I just talked to my mother. I'm going back to Illinois to resume my career as a mental patient, Will'am. No offense intended, but this whole thing just isn't working out. Cockroaches and shit; it gets old pretty fast. As bad as Harry and Muriel get, we still have a maid, air conditioning, and clean sheets."

Molly started throwing dirty laundry into the suitcase. I propped myself up against the wall and watched her blow a wisp of hair from her eyes. She said, "You aren't going to ask me to stay, kick the shit out of me because of that guy — nothing? Okay, fine! Fuck you!"

I took a pull off a bottle of warm Primo beer. "You got a ticket home?"

"Yeah, I do," she said. "Which brings up a delicate point. My mother knows better than to send me money. The ticket is waiting for me at the airport. I have to present myself and I haven't got cab fare. Have you? Or should I go back and give Amos his hand job?"

"Get Eliani to drive you," I said.

"I am no longer a welcome member of their polite society," Molly said.

"You must have a really rotten hangover," I said, trying to stay cool. "How are you going to be able to handle the plane ride?"

"Actually I don't have a hangover," she said. "I just did some coke. I feel pretty good. Pretty goddamn fine, if you want to know. This is no time to be petty, Will'am. I'm going to miss you. Are you going to miss me?"

"No," I lied.

She shrugged and transformed back into the other person — she hid behind the hurt and bitter shell and became unlovable again. "Fair enough. So look, do you want to fuck one last time? I still love you." She locked her pupils onto mine and struck a sexy pose. "I want you to have me right now. I want you now, Will'am," she said. It was cocaine talk. I knew it but I couldn't resist her. She unbuttoned her loose seersucker blouse and presented her breasts to me. She grabbed my dick and squeezed it, whispering, "Take me, baby." Cocaine talk, nothing more than that. It's an overrated drug, no better than a triple espresso, but it can make you say anything.

I buried my face in her breasts and kissed her nipples the way she liked it. I pulled her to the mattresses and tugged off her shorts and panties. She hastened to pull me

to her, and as she spread her legs I spotted fresh beads of se-
men in her short thatch of pubic hair. I drew back like I was
shot. My breath came in heaves and I turned away.

"I know," she said. "I'm sorry. Just fuck me anyhow."

"No! Shit, no! No fucking way!" I got up raging. I had a
throbbing erection that seemed utterly ridiculous to me in
this new context. It was like a useless stage prop. I had to
take a second look at it; it had never been so white before.

Molly was up after me. She pulled at my arm, "You want
to," she said. "I know you do. Puh-leeze, Will'am. A goodbye
screw, baby?"

I stepped into my shorts and tried to get control of my
breath. "What time does your plane leave?" I said.

"Jesus, Will'am, you really *are* useless," she said. She
wiped her cunt dry with her soiled panties, then she wrung
them in a ball and flung them at my head. She moved to
slap me, but I caught her wrist and twisted her to the floor.
Her eyes glared with hatred. "You fucker!"

The tussle caused my nose to bleed. I let go of her arm
and went into the bathroom. By the time I returned, Molly
was sitting on her suitcase as if nothing at all had happened.
Her knees were crossed and she was swinging her foot, with
the back of her loafer half dangling to the floor. She said,
"My flight leaves at three-thirty. What time is it?"

I glanced at my watch. "You've barely got the time to
make it," I said.

"Uh, I told you. I haven't got any money."

When I didn't respond, she shrugged her shoulders and
got up. "I'm sorry I hit you. I wouldn't have bothered if I
didn't care. I just said those horrible things to turn you on,
I hope you know that."

She was Little Red Riding Hood, lost in the woods. "Well good-bye," she said meekly. "I guess I can hitchhike or something."

I watched her heft the suitcase over to the door. Finally she set it down and said, "I don't need this shit; I'm just going to leave it. Fuck it!"

"Oh Christ," I said as I stepped forward and grabbed the suitcase. It was made of burnished calf leather and looked like it was worth a lot of money. No matter what she did, I couldn't stay mad at her. I said, "We'll have to get out to the Kalahaua to hail a cab. There's not a lot of time."

"Right, Will'am. You're so right. Time is ever fleeting. Why, it seems like just yesterday that I spotted you in Dr. V.'s office and let you steal my precious little heart right out from under me," she said. "That was a bygone time of romance and heartbreak, nothing to waste time lamenting over anymore. This is it. Adios, see you later. No good-bye screw, no nothing. Life goes on. Well, someday you can read about yourself in my prize-winning novel. You will be the guy who plays the shithook of all time. Richard III, Iago, and characters of their ilk will seem like Florence Nightingale compared to you — vile demon! Goddamn you!"

"You're nuts," I said as I moved down the lane. "You need Thorazine or shock treatments or something." She followed after me, taking little-girl skips. As we passed the weekend party palace, I could see a snigger on the faces of the sailors, who lay inside burning off hangovers of their own. Prominent among them was not-so-famous Amos, who hardly looked hungover at all. He was the picture of "cocaine" health. Sixty bulging bloodshot eyes were upon

Molly and her fabulous tits. I felt like taking a flamethrower and torching the entire place.

I was sweating when we reached Kalahaua Avenue. I tried to flag a cab headed in the direction of the airport but we were crowded too far back on the sidewalk and passing groups of tourists obscured our view of the street. Molly said, "How are you going to make out? You're broke? Tell me you'll be all right, even if it's a lie."

"Five-O got me a job at the box factory starting next week. Night work. Watch the papers, you'll probably read about me soon. William O. Smith: surfer by day, boxmaker by night. Full-time seeker of truth. Fornicator no more. A haole on the narrow road to righteousness."

"Screws nevermore? Oh Will'am, you'll be screwing Miss Hawaii before my plane achieves fucking liftoff." Her voice contained a vestige of the original Molly charm.

I moved into the street and managed to stop a cab. A Samoan driver with a bad attitude pulled over. I slung Molly's heavy suitcase into the trunk. I pulled my wallet out and handed the driver my last five. Before I knew it, Molly stepped forward and was giving me her good-bye kiss, a semilingering kiss, neither here nor there. Yet I was quick enough to respond with the newly white pole, and her hand found it. Passing tourists stopped to stare at the kiss — or simply to stare at Molly; no matter what I was truly feeling, or what was truly best for either of us, she had showstopping looks. When the kiss broke off, she held eye contact with me for a moment and then hopped into the back of the cab. She rolled down the window as if to say something but there were tears in her eyes and she turned away. Honking his horn, the driver swung back into traffic and shot down to the first red light, which from my then perspective was perceived as a variation of white.

I was going to give her the distance to the Royal Hawaiian Hotel — if she jumped out of the cab and ran back into my arms, I might have despised myself forever, but I would have welcomed her back and would have stuck with her. I watched the cab inch along in traffic. I was still into white monovision, although it no longer seemed quite so groovy. Even the famously pink Royal Hawaiian was white. It took the cab at least five minutes to get there. There was no look back. Still, I waited. When the cab finally disappeared from my sight, I felt utterly bereft and alone in a desolate universe. I felt like Mary Mallon, the Irish immigrant who came to America at the turn of the century. I read about Mary Mallon on a long afternoon in Dr. Vitias's waiting room.

More than any other wave of immigrants, the Irish most decidedly found that not only were America's streets unpaved of gold, for them conditions were actually worse than in the homeland they had so eagerly fled. Mary Mallon found work as a cook in New York City and worked seven days a week from daylight till dark for pennies. She was a big strapping woman who took pride in her humble occupation, but no matter how hard she worked, like the rest of the Irish she was reviled. Out of necessity, she moved from job to job. Funny thing — people that ate her food had a way of getting sick. In droves they got sick. One of them even died. Through the stealth of a public health official, "Typhoid Mary" was tracked down, seized, and placed in an isolated cottage on North Brother Island, near the Bronx. North Brother Island was the site of the Riverside Hospital, a tuberculosis sanitarium. A newspaper writer, who came to view Typhoid Mary's cottage, reported that even the TB patients were afraid to go near the place. A terrified courier delivered meals to a slot in her door three times a day and also collected a stool sample. After two years of this, after petitioning the Supreme Court, Mary Mallon was set free conditional upon a promise never to work as a cook or food handler again. Mary kept her word for two years, but times were tough, one thing led to another, and then she began cooking again. She was good at it and she liked the job. Soon twenty-five people were felled by typhoid fever in a single stroke. Two of these died. Typhoid Mary was returned to the grim cottage on North Brother Island. Since she was merely a carrier of the disease, poorly educated, and uninformed, Mary felt blameless. When the hospital doctors wanted to remove her gallbladder, the organ that harbors the typhoid bacillus, Mary thought it was just one of their tricks so they could gas her and say she died during surgery. In all, she was responsible for three deaths — you would have thought it was a million. I can appreciate how alone and rejected she felt in that cottage on North Brother Island, but from the pictures I've seen of it, it looked like a much happier place than the Shit Shack. She spent the rest of her life there, more than another twenty years.

How long I stood on Kalahaua Avenue watching the last traces of Molly Bloom disappear, I don't know. I remember getting soaked in a quick shower and then drying out when the sun came back. Still fucked up on hash, I remember seeing white rainbows as the rain clouds moved back into the Manoa Valley and as the sun chased after them. The bands of the rainbows were white both in terms of shade and texture, from flat white to glossy enamel, from sandpaper to shiny white leather — they hurt my eyes and yet I felt compelled to study them until I felt nearly blinded. Their significance was promised to be revealed to me and then I found I could look no longer. It was like seeing the reputed face of God — lethal.

I headed back to the Shit Shack. As I passed the sailors' apartment, I was cognizant of some serious cocaine vibes. I could see Amos perched on a stool with a wide and defiant grin on his face. That's cool, I told myself. Let them crow. But then there was one little facetious, torqued-up snigger too many. I turned around and went back. As I stalked in the door, the servicemen straightened up and braced for action. The grin on Amos's face diminished not in the least. I had seen featherweight boxers take out two-hundred-plus-pound body builders in my time but I was too heartsick to fight. I realized that at bottom, I came in just to get my ass stomped. Yet before Amos could even put up his hands, Five-O burst into the apartment and flew across the room like a contestant in a fat man race. But what a very very fast fat man. He cut through the heavy air like he had been spray painted with Teflon. His big right hand spun past my face in a blur. The blow had a downward cant to it, and Amos was off the stool as if he'd been struck by a freight train. The force of the blow was sufficient to split the chair beneath him, and as bad as the punch was, the fall was worse. Amos was unconscious when his head hit the hard tile floor, and it bounced like a bowling ball. I saw teeth spill across the floor like so many Chiclets. His face became a mask of blood in an instant. For a moment I thought he was dead. We all did. Finally his chest heaved as he began to gasp for air. The breath had been knocked out of him —

pretty close to almost permanently, I'd say. Everyone in the room had collectively held his own breath waiting for Amos. For whatever reason, I was glad that he was still alive. I'm not so sure Five-O cared either way.

"There," he said declaratively, as he dusted his big hands, "nose for a nose. Snort some cocaine now, mother-fucker. Like to see you try."

I followed Five-O back to the surfers' apartment. I had a whole new appreciation of him. He was the Polynesian war god, Pele. No wonder they also called him One-Punch. Back at the surfers' apartment the two of us smoked some more hash — smoked so much my color vision came back. Five-O suggested we grab our surfboards and head over to Waikiki. As we passed the sailors' apartment, he banged his hand on the screened lanai and said, "And if any of you other hoale cocksuckers wanna get it on, just step right outside now." Their apartment was as quiet as a church. They had Amos lying on a couch with towels propped behind his neck while he held an ice bag to his face. With my surfboard balanced on my head, I followed Five-O down Kalahaua Avenue. A heavy cobalt blue sea tossed wild, white-crested breakers into the coral reef of Waikiki, where the surf was tamed into evenly formed six-foot waves. Brady was standing under the banyan tree on Kalahaua with his sister, Tanya, and a pair of her girlfriends.

Tanya bestowed her sympathy on me while Five-O told Brady about taking out Famous Amos with one shot. Brady looked to me for confirmation — "He crumbled the guy," I said. "Squashed him. I never saw anything like it. I mean, this guy wasn't some lightweight. Teeth were flying and everything, man. He hit him with the big Kahuna."

Five-O tucked his hands under his armpits and looked up and down the beach. "I'm going to paddle out. Are you guys coming or what?"

Brady said, "Talking to these gracious ladies is all. Be with you in five, Big Dude."

Tanya flashed me the ultrawhite smile of expensive porcelain crowns. I wondered if life put out a few *seeming* beauties like Molly and Tanya as rare decoy birds. These decoys were merely there as a gross deception, and in truth, in a world where the willing was never still, and where one gratified desire led only to ten or ten hundred more, a permanent sense of happiness clearly was an impossibility. Still, in terms of general endearment and overall sweetness, Tanya was my decoy bird of the moment. Two hits of windowpane and a night of sneaky/guilty sex had provided me with a perverse thrill, but had it been love? I suddenly realized that a vain and self-obsessed person such as myself was incapable of mature love. Still, she must have found me good to look at, since her body language was giving go-ahead signals.

"Yeah! Five-O kicked ass big time," I said.

Brady cried after Five-O, "Go, Kahuna!"

It was the sort of accolade Five-O would remember for a long while. I wondered if true love awaited him someday, somewhere on some Polynesian back street of Honolulu. His surfing skills got him laid on occasion. And I found that lots of girls admired him for his size and power. Actually, he was knocking down more tail than most. He was a loyal friend and he was utterly dependable. Unemployment was high in Honolulu but he managed to get me a job at the box factory.

It was much worse work than I expected. Charles Dickens would have been appalled by the place. Still, it was a job. I dragged my mattress over to the surfers' place to save on rent, but I didn't have the upfront money to see a doctor and get more epilepsy medicines. In some naïve sense, I thought myself cured by the sunshine, beer, and clean ocean air blowing in over Waikiki. It was just wishful thinking, but I was beginning to like Hawaii. I took the Superhawk over to the university to check on the status of my application. The clerk told me they were still awaiting transcripts from Illinois. I figured to have enough money to enter school in the fall. I quit drinking and smoking. The box factory was bad enough without going in hungover. I began dating Tanya, but we weren't able to recapture the sexual magic of our first night together. I began to realize that apart from having been Miss Hawaii, she was now merely the spoiled daughter of a wealthy judge. Although she tried to overcome it, I think my being a haole troubled her. We were far from inseparable, and after a while I began to see that she wasn't all that smart either. Still, it was a thrill to go out with her in public and watch the heads turn. That doesn't qualify as love, however. I continued to enjoy the surf and looked forward to enrolling at the university.

Then one Sunday morning we piled in Five-O's truck and drove over to Sunset Beach. The surf was outstanding. I remember catching about six nice waves, and the next thing I knew I was looking around without being able to see anyone — the surf was dangerously high, and I began to feel very queer. The smell of burning rubber assailed me. Next a sense of fear and impending doom overwhelmed me. The ocean beneath me presented monsters like some kind of horrible nightmare out of some Carlos Castenada peyote hallucination. Through sheer luck the fit didn't happen until I was back in the shallow water, close to the shore. The surfers claim I was blue when they pulled me in. Someone gave me mouth-to-mouth. It was all pretty vague — pretty hazy. I remember spending some time in a regular hospital ward, weighed down in the aftermath of a fit, a fugue state, and heavy medications. My memories didn't pick up any consistency again until I was back in Illinois. Dr. Vitias listened to the story in amazement. Over and over again, he said, "You could have drowned!"

"It didn't seem like it," I said. "I mean, when you are paying attention, you usually don't seize. It doesn't happen. I've had most of my fits just before I fall asleep —"

"How many weeks without medication, William? Tell me! You don't even look penitent. When are you going to wake up to the reality of your condition?"

I let my head sink. I knew he was right, but I still felt that I was entitled to a real life, whatever that was.

Dr. Vitias pulled bottles of medication from a metal locker. Pharmaceutical samples. He set them on the table. "Phenobarbital. Valium. Elavil. All on the house," he said. "And I hear your car is ruined. What about your job? They called me and asked if you were capable of returning to work. I had to stall them to save your job. It hasn't been easy here — escaped from mental hospital, whereabouts unknown."

"I know," I said. "But I can go back to work if you write me a note. They will probably call you to verify, but we have a good union; they pretty much have to take me back."

"You can't keep doing this," Vitias said. "You are making

me old before my time, William. You could have drowned.
My God, look at your skin, you will probably get melanoma."

I said, "I owe two thousand in hospital bills."

"You escaped further perils. Count your lucky stars. I
know you are young, but you can't let your dick do all of
your thinking for you."

"That's over," I insisted. "I'm reformed. I've been reading my Schopenhauer and I am trying to become more
moderate in my habits."

"It sounds more like you've been reading Alan Watts.
You're not going to run off and join the Moonies on me,
are you?"

"No, I'm not, Doctor. Well, I don't know, maybe I am.
Look, I better get going; the waiting room is jammed. I
don't feel so good. I think I'll go home and hide in my basement for a couple of days."

"When you're in the middle of the big shit storm with
the shit really flying, what do you do, William?"

"I dunno," I said. "Put on rose-colored glasses? Die?"

"You go on. You ride it out. You have a lot of hidden
strength in you, William. You are a brave young man. Tell
me this: What holds you up when God lets go of you?"

Agog with psychic exhaustion, I said, "I don't know."

Vitias said, "A person can't control how he feels, but he
can control what he does. Do right and your life will work
out for you. You must take positive steps to overcome this
business. No more backsliding. I will be here to help, you
can always come to me."

Riding out a depression was only marginally better than
bucking one tooth-and-nail — that could exhaust you totally — but we had had this conversation before. If Vitias

had offered to sell me a Chevette with 280,000 miles on it, at this point I would have gladly paid him a quarter of a million dollars just to get out of the office. As I rose to get up, he said, "Do you want a B-twelve shot? It will make you feel better. A little pick-me-up?"

I consented to the shot and as I stepped back into the waiting room I was shocked to see Molly Bloom sitting on a wooden chair next to a couple of back pain junkies. She was reading a copy of *Cosmopolitan*. Our eyes met more or less simultaneously. The first instant of delight was followed by a moment of hesitation. I said, "You got your eye fixed."

"Yeah," she said. "What do you think? You like?" She twisted her head from side to side and batted her eyes. She had a short haircut and was dressed casually in a pair of corduroy pants and a sweater. She was wearing a pair of glasses but looked darling in them. "Pretty good, no?"

"I liked your eye the old way. You're going conventional on me."

"My God, Will'am, I can't believe you!" she said. "I'm totally at a loss for words. Say you're glad to see me? I've been a good little Girl Scout. Six months on the lithium. Minimal headaches, and check this out — I got a *job*."

"A job! You have to be kidding!"

She laughed and said, "It's nothing to brag about. I work in Harry's office, all right? After the Hawaii caper, Muriel has been a pisser. It's like maximum security out there. Jesus, Will'am! How come you never wrote, you *fucker*, you? I should be cross with you."

"I didn't get a lot of mail from you, dear heart. None that I can recall."

"You should see all the letters I wrote to you and *didn't*

send," Molly said. "I was afraid. I thought you hated me. Why are you looking at me like that?"

"I'm just standing here like an asshole. Am I going to get a hug or not?"

"Oh Christ," she said. "Do you really want one from me?"

"Of course I do, Molly. Fork one over, buttercup."

I took Molly in my arms. All the physical and chemical vibes suggested love. I said, "It feels so good holding you, baby! I didn't expect to see you here."

"Why not? I'm one of the regulars. A permanent customer."

"What's the old gang been up to?"

Molly beamed. "From our first date — the farmer, Mr. Hamsun, remember him? He's okay and everything. He buried his cat — his frozen cat in the pizza box. He did all of that. But get *this,* he wrote to his old girlfriend in Hawaii. I helped him with the letter, sitting right here in this room. And check this out, she wrote him back, she remembered him, lah-dee-dah. Can you believe that? She lives on the Big Island now and he's planning on going over there to see her."

"She's not living in a Shit Shack on the Big Island, is she?"

"It's a regular house house, you fucker. I saw a picture. So how are the boys, anyhow? Whatever brought you back? I thought you were hard-core box factory? What happened?"

I shrugged, "Epilepsy," I said. "The same old scenario —"

Molly stepped forward and interrupted me with a kiss. I went with the kiss. I was liking it. One of the junkies sitting behind Molly said, "Why don't you two go and get a room or something, huh?"

This comment was ignored.

Molly said, "What else? Let me think. Your friend, Mr. Leimbach — he's in the hospital. Not good. Norman went over to say hi, but it was depressing, he said. Mr. Leimbach can move his eyelids and that's about it. He's a cheerful guy though, and Mr. Jones is the same as ever."

The junkie flashed me a dirty look but I had to laugh. "Brother, you need to turn that frown *upside* down," I said. He shook his head like I was a fool. I had almost forgot that this was Aurora, Illinois, where eye contact often resulted in murders. I turned back to Molly and said,"Look, did you just get here? How long do you have to wait?"

She paused to think this over and her whole train of enthusiasm began to derail. She chewed on her lower lip and said, "I just barely walked in the door. I've got a ways to go, I think. You don't have to wait for me."

"Remember that Buick of mine? The one and only time I ever got a deal on anything," I said. "When I got back, it turned over on the first start. Can you believe it?"

"Oh God, and to think of how I wrecked your sports car —"

"Oh shit, don't mention that car; I could still strangle you for that! On the other hand, it's so good to see you, Molly, Jesus."

"Like, ditto, I'm so completely happy," she said. "But maybe we should proceed with caution here. Things absolutely did not work the first time. What makes you think we're going to somehow have things turn out perfectly the second time? Neither one of us is an emotional rock of Gibraltar."

"Just a friendly dinner. That's all I'm suggesting."

"Oh Will'am, I don't think it would be a good idea. I mean, I'm feeling that old chemistry. We sort of had a problem in that regard if I remember correctly."

"Get a room and get laid," the junkie said.

"Hey, like, really say something rude," Molly said to the man. She pulled me to the other side of the old familiar room.

"I think the gentleman has a good point," I said. "We should sleep together and clear the air."

Molly wagged her finger at me. "Will'am, you know I can't resist you."

"Well, I'm going to wait it out," I said. "I'm not leaving until you do."

"There aren't even any chairs left," she said.

"When the next patient goes inside, then there will be two chair vacancies."

"Unless someone else comes in before someone leaves," Molly said.

"That's been known to happen," I said. "I never thought of that."

Molly struck a playful pose. She turned away and then looked back at me saying, "Hey, Estragon, 'We always find something, eh, Didi, to give us the impression that we exist?'"

I picked up on this reference and said, "I've got my eyes out for Godot. That doesn't mean he's coming, baby."

We stood together in the waiting room, talking this line of shit for some time. We were trying to figure out what was the best thing to do. There she was standing before me and suddenly I was a Molly addict all over again.

She said, "A really cool guy, wise beyond his years, fella

named Will'am, once told me that falling in love is absolutely the most dangerous thing two sensible people can do," Molly said.

"William! I know that stupid asshole. He's a moron! Don't pay any heed to him. He's a buffoon," I said. "Each and every case is highly variable."

"You will never really forgive me for sleeping around?" she said.

"William also slept around."

Molly shook her head in admonishment. "Really, Will'am, you and I, we're too much like oil and water."

"Mollykins, really! We need to work on that low self-esteem. Great golden moments of joy and happiness await us. I was the most depressed person on this planet as I walked out of that office, and then I laid eyes on you, and now I am reborn."

"Will'am," she said.

"I am positively transformed! Clarity has pierced through the blackest darkness and I now see love all about me. Milk and honey flowing freely. Molly Bloom is in this world and that makes it a heaven beyond description. My spirit has been restored in the fullest measure. Oh babe, you're a vision of purest delight."

She withdrew her hands from mine and turned away from me. I thought she was turning to leave the office, to escape me forever, but she just stepped back and removed her glasses to take me in better. I flexed my fingers before my face like venetian blinds, playing peekaboo. "My eyes will burn holes through you if you don't stop looking so angelic."

"Will-i-am," she said twisting my name into a song. "You are also a sight for sore eyes, as they say."

"Molly, Molly, Molly," I said. "Good golly, how I loye thee."

She let loose with a short chortle. "That's so sweet, Will'am," she said. She looked away and then turned back with her own fingers poised for peekaboo. The two of us, Molly and William, hanging out, doing stupid shit like this for the rest of that Saturday afternoon in Dr. Vitias's waiting room. If ever a romance had less than a snowball's chance in hell, it was ours. I knew that. But then there we stood, more in love with one another than any two people that I've ever heard about, and brother, let me tell you — I'm talking since the dawn of mankind.